Books by Brenda S. Anderson

COMING HOME SERIES

*Pieces of Granite*
*Chain of Mercy*
*Memory Box Secrets*
*Hungry for Home*

Coming Home Series, book 2

# memory box SECRETS

A NOVEL

BRENDA S. ANDERSON

VIVANT
Press

VIVANT PRESS

ISBN-13: 978-0-9862147-2-1

Scriptures taken from the Holy Bible, New International Version®, NIV®. Copyright © 1973, 1978, 1984, 2011 by Biblica, Inc.™ Used by permission of Zondervan. All rights reserved worldwide. www.zondervan.com The "NIV" and "New International Version" are trademarks registered in the United States Patent and Trademark Office by Biblica, Inc.™

Cover Design by Think-Cap Design Studios

Printed in the United States of America

First Edition: April 2015
15   16   17   18   19   20   21       7   6   5   4   3   2   1

To:

*Gary and Sandy*
*Thank you for demonstrating*
*the beauty of adoption.*

*"So in Christ Jesus you are all
children of God through faith ..."*

**Galatians 3:26**

## PROLOGUE

*Eighteen Years Ago*

W e're moving." The chill in her mother's voice shivered through Sheila's phone line.

"I ... I don't understand." Why would her parents give up their beloved Minneapolis home? A home they loved more than they loved their own daughter. Waiting for her mother's response, Sheila leaned back in her desk chair and stared out her dorm window. Jack Frost's artwork framed an outside world layered in snow and ice. Snow and ice. Just like her mother. The long distance connection somehow sharpened the bite. One would think that February temperatures in Madison, Wisconsin couldn't sink any lower. Whoever thought that, didn't know her mother.

She should be used to it by now.

"What's there to understand?" Sharp as an icicle, her mother's voice pierced the silence. "With you in college, your father and I can finally retire."

Reining back a tear, Sheila tore her gaze from the window and focused on the notebook on her desk. Music Theory. Love for music was the one thing she had in common with her parents. Trying to loosen the tightness in her throat before responding, she doodled whimsical shapes across an open staff. Yet, tension traveled from her throat to her shoulders. It wasn't her fault she'd been born and kept them from an early retirement. As it was, she'd graduated from high school early—started college a semester early. They should be happy.

"When?" Sheila finally answered, keeping her tone even, hoping to match her mother's frigidity, needing to mask her fear.

"The end of the week."

She bolted upright and dropped her pen. It clattered off the desk onto her floor. The end of the week and they were only telling her now? She hugged herself, fending off the shakes. "I can't help. I've got a major project due next week. I need this weekend to work."

"We don't need your help."

She squeezed her eyes shut and held back a whimper. They never needed her. They hadn't wanted her to begin with. She drew in a breath, steadying her nerves. Her mother couldn't know she was scared. "Where are you going?" Her voice came out flat and indifferent. Exactly the way she wanted it to come across.

"Arizona. We'll forward our address."

Sheila held back a laugh. She doubted she'd get the address. Did that even matter?

"Our neighbor, Estelle Barrows, said she'll store your belongings for you."

Her belongings? Anything of importance, she already had at school. Whatever she'd left behind could stay there. She had no use for more bad memories.

She sat up tall in her chair and suppressed her emotions. "Tell Estelle thank you." Sheila should be thankful that her parents were moving. Finally, she'd gain full independence from them. If she were lucky, she'd never have to hear her mother's nippy voice again.

Yes, this was definitely good news. Her shoulders relaxed and a smile even tugged on her lips. Good riddance to them. "Tell *Daddy* goodbye." Sheila hung up before her mother could respond, and chuckled as she pictured her mother's face turning red at the despised name.

Daddy. A name Sheila promised herself to never speak again.

# CHAPTER *one*

*May*
*Minneapolis, Minnesota*

What kind of fool would turn down a seven-figure contract? With a Fortune 500 Company? In Manhattan? Richard Brooks leaned back in his chair and studied ACM Technologies' offer on his secretary's computer monitor. With a groan he shook his head, closed the e-mail attachment, and glared at the ceiling. And he'd thought nothing could spoil the day.

"Problem hon?"

Richard startled and glanced toward the door, a grin overtaking his frown. If choosing his wife and family over New York meant he was a fool, then he was one ecstatic fool. He wouldn't let ACM's attempt to worm back into his life ruin the day. He crossed his arms over his chest, taking in the vision standing in the doorway. He could gaze into Sheila's maple-syrup eyes for a lifetime and not get bored. He nodded toward the computer. "Looks like I'm a wanted man."

"Really now?" She stepped into the room and the door closed behind her with a faint whoosh.

"Afraid so." He pushed away from the desk and walked around it, not taking his eyes off his wife of two months. Tonight was going to be one memorable celebration.

She tugged on his tie, straightening it. "You want to talk about it?"

"And spoil our evening? I won't give ACM the satisfaction."

"Ahh. Now I see." She splayed her hands over his suit jacket. "I have a little news to share too."

Excitement stirred in his gut. Was he going to be a father? "You know already?"

"Not that. I promised I wouldn't look without you, and I meant it."

He rested against his assistant's desk. "What is it?"

Sheila walked to the waiting area, her acorn-colored hair bouncing on bare shoulders, and picked up the Minneapolis newspaper off a table. "They want to interview me for a point/counterpoint piece, seeing as I now speak for the opposing viewpoint."

"You didn't say you'd do it, did you?" They'd rip her to shreds. The paper's editorial team didn't even attempt to hide their bias against the pro-life community.

"Someone has to."

He took the newspaper from her and slapped it on his assistant's desk. Shaking his head, he ran a hand over his chin. As much as he hated the thought of Sheila being skewered in the media, he knew of no one better to speak out than his wife. "I'll be right beside you." Adding his own perspective. It was time someone stood for the fathers who'd lost children. Might as well be him.

"I knew you would." She cuffed baby-soft hands over his cheeks and kissed him.

Maybe they had time for a pre-celebration. Richard wrapped his arms around her and felt for the zipper on her cobalt sheath dress. Kissing her shoulder, he nudged at the slender strap that led to a V-neck.

Sheila pushed away then straightened the lapels of his

14

Armani jacket. "You're getting ahead of yourself, aren't you?"

The woman knew exactly how to tie his body into knots, and her dimpled smile told him she enjoyed it way too much. "But—"

She patted his cheek. "Later, dear." Her dimples deepened as she dug into her purse and pulled out a toothpaste-sized box. "I don't want to wait any longer."

He stared at the box and nodded, but then he reached behind her neck, pulled her to him, and brushed his lips over hers. "Don't be too long."

"Ten minutes tops." She sashayed from the room. Humming. Her hair swaying to the beat.

Later tonight, they'd both be humming. Regardless of what the early pregnancy test showed. If the results were negative, they'd have to keep trying.

He hummed his own off-key tune as he walked from the reception room into his office. He'd shoved his desk against the wall making room for a two-person table set beside a wall-sized window. Minneapolis' skyscrapers were all backlit by May's dusky sky. A perfect location to view the Twins post-game fireworks.

A fantastic sight, even though this view couldn't compare to his Manhattan office view. Nothing compared to that.

Yet, there were many similarities between the two cities. Like his New York City view, even at this time of night, lights glowed from building windows, many highlighting the workaholic spouse-parent-friend who placed career above relationships. Like he once had done.

If he returned to Manhattan, it would be easy to fall into that trap again. One more reason to refuse the tempting job offer. Perspective changed so many things.

He stepped away from the window and double checked the table setting. A white brocade tablecloth disguised a round card table. He'd topped it with the china, silver, and crystal goblets he'd brought from home. A crystal vase, half filled with water, sat in the middle of the table and awaited Sheila's touch.

Sheila. Reason number one to ignore ACM's e-mail. She deserved to know what a loving family was, like the family he'd grown up in, one that modeled his company's motto: Faith and Family First. He intended to give Sheila that family, and a return to New York would undoubtedly tear at the family fabric.

Tonight, he might learn of reason number two to remain in Minnesota. God could grant him no greater wish.

Richard grinned as he pulled a book of matches from his pants pocket to light the tapers framing the vase. He shut off the office lights, and the candles' shimmering glow veiled the office setting, creating a romantic ambience. Not that he and Sheila required mood enhancements, but tonight was going to be a night for the memory books. He prayed so anyway.

He smoothed his silk tie, the one Sheila chose to match her dress for the night. It was evenly knotted with the dimple centered perfectly beneath the knot. He buttoned his jacket over the tie. Sheila had insisted he wear the Armani. Its tailored fit did look good on him. He'd better look good. He'd paid an atrocious amount for the suit he now only wore twice a year at the most. Once upon a time, he'd needed it more often, but that was before ...

Before everything had changed. Before his closet had become a neglected treasure chest relegated to holding idle investments. Had it all been a waste?

Blowing out a breath, he bowed his head. Why did that job offer come in today of all days? He couldn't face Sheila with this roller coaster mindset. Not tonight when his lifelong desire to become a father might finally be realized. He glanced at his Rolex. Five minutes had passed. Still time for a quick conversation.

He opened his center desk drawer and pulled out a pocket book of Psalms. No other book provided snapshots of the heart like this one did. He could have written Psalm 107 himself. He sat in his desk chair and cradled the book in his hands, letting it fall open. Without looking down, he knew what it opened to. In the candlelit office, he couldn't see the words, but that didn't matter. He knew them all by heart. Holding the dog-eared book gave him the physical connection he needed to ground his heart where it belonged, keeping faith and family as his number one priority. He prayed the Psalmist's words would erase Manhattan's siren call.

*DO MIRRORS SPEAK THE truth?* Sheila studied her reflection in the office building restroom. This silky cobalt dress was Richard's favorite. He liked her in anything blue, but cobalt was the shade that left him speechless. The dress's alluring cut, with half inch straps flowing into a V-neck and back, and sloping just low enough to hint and tease, always heightened his response. The fabric clung to her shape, a shape she was still proud to show off.

A figure and face that eerily resembled her mother's.

Sheila fingered the plastic stick in her hand but didn't look. If this test were positive, how much longer would her figure last? Would Richard still find her body sensuous? How would a child affect their lifestyle?

Would she parent like the woman Sheila saw in her reflection? Sheila shivered.

Breathing deeply, she tapped the stick in her palm, then moved away from the memory. She and Richard would look at the results together, hopefully celebrate together. If the test was negative, they'd both be disappointed. But she doubted it was. She clutched the proof in her hand as she left the restroom and walked across the hallway to Richard's office. She couldn't wait to see how he'd turned his workplace into a romantic setting.

She passed through the dimly-lit reception area, the only light coming from the cityscape outside the windows, and paused at Richard's door. Nothing would make Richard happier than becoming a father.

She pushed open his door and stood beneath its frame. Oh, the man could steal her breath. He walked toward her carrying a flower, his black suit flowing naturally with his strong physique. And that smile, which tilted more to the right, always made her heart flutter. Simply magnificent. She was a blessed woman.

"Breathtaking." He breathed in her ear as he skirted his arms around her back.

She kissed him, letting her mouth communicate her love for him, telling him he could expect more later, regardless of the test results. She pulled away from the kiss, but he clung to her, again not appreciating the "later" part.

"I hope you can back that up." He released his tight hold and handed her the orange rose.

She brought it to her nose and breathed in its subtle perfume. "How can you doubt?"

With a roll of his eyes, he placed his hand on her back and guided her toward the table. She settled the rose in the vase, completing the romantic setting. A gentle laugh whispered from her throat. He'd done it. Turned his office into a private romantic getaway. The fireworks they'd watch later, though, wouldn't compare to the fireworks she and Richard would make together. Her husband could write a book on romance.

He pulled out her chair—a padded folding chair he'd disguised with a brocade covering that matched the tablecloth. She sat, and he glided the chair in.

"Our food should be here any minute." Richard sat across from her and rested his chin on folded hands.

"And that would be ...?"

He smiled.

A surprise, of course. Chicken breast Charlemagne with sautéed vegetables would satisfy her cravings. Hopefully he'd picked up on her not-so-subtle hints earlier in the day. "Can't you give me—"

Something tapped the outer office door, and Richard pushed

away from the table. "I'll be right back and then we'll see ..." His gaze flitted to the test she clutched in her hand, then rose to meet her eyes. "You didn't peek, did you?"

"Would I do that?" She could be as evasive as he.

Squinting, he held up his pointer finger. "Wait."

Oh, she would wait, but it was difficult. Even now she was tempted to check if there was a plus or minus sign, but they'd agreed to look together.

He returned carrying two paper sacks and wearing a mischievous smile.

Her jaw dropped, and she wrinkled her nose. "McDonald's?"

The mischievous smile became a grin. "Not just McDonald's, but kids' meals. Thought it would fit the evening."

She slumped in her chair. He'd succeeded in spoiling the perfect evening.

"I got you chicken, like you wanted." He reached into a bag.

Rubbery, tasteless, overcooked chicken. What was he thinking?

He pulled a clear plastic container from the McDonald's bag.

Blinking, she waved fingers in front of her eyes. "You sneak!" He set the covered dish filled with chicken breast Charlemagne on the table. Emotional over chicken. She had to be pregnant.

Still grinning, he plied off the plastic top.

"I'll take it from here." Her stomach rumbled. More evidence of pregnancy.

He sat opposite her, reached across the table, took her hands, and offered a prayer of gratitude. Then he pulled two paper-wrapped burgers and two sides of fries from a bag, followed by two toys encased in plastic. A grown man wearing Armani, eating McDonald's, on china dinnerware of all things. This had to be a first.

"See?" He picked up one of the toys. "Hot Wheels. Our baby's first toy."

"And if our baby's a girl?"

"She can't play with cars?"

"Touché. And if I'm not pregnant?" She would accept no more diversions.

"Let's find out." He came around the table, stood behind her, and cuffed trembling hands over her bare shoulders. Perhaps she should make him wait a moment longer.

"You sure you're ready?" She bit into her chicken and rolled her eyes in pleasure.

"Absolutely."

She chewed slowly then wiped her mouth with her napkin. "Positive?"

"Just turn the thing, already."

"I guess you're ready." She raised the test from her lap and turned it over.

The truth was clear.

# CHAPTER *two*

## *Rural Minnesota*

Almost done?" Lauren heard her dad's voice, followed by footsteps on the unfinished basement stairs as dawn's sunlight streamed through the narrow window above her.

Lauren pulled a pair of jean shorts from the dryer and folded them on top of the washer. "Just a couple more things." Then they could celebrate. Birthdays were always cause for a celebration. They'd learned firsthand that one more year of life wasn't to be taken for granted.

Her dad laid a hand on her shoulder.

"Happy Birthday, Dad." She dropped clean socks into a basket and turned into his hug.

"You remembered."

She snickered. "Could be that sticky note you left on the bathroom mirror."

"You saw that, huh?"

"Funny." She shrugged out of his arms and pulled a white undershirt from the dryer. After shaking out the wrinkles, she laid the shirt on the top of the washing machine and began folding it. Her dad chuckled behind her.

"You know, I never bothered folding those shirts."

"Yeah, I know." As a matter of fact, he'd trained her to roll it into a ball and stuff it in his drawer. What was the purpose of neatly folded underclothes, especially with his machining job? She'd learned differently. "Come here." She tugged her dad's arm. "Let me show you how." Now it was her job to train him. When she left for college in another year, who would take care of him? He needed to learn how to be on his own. If she'd had any purpose growing up, it had been holding her father together. Now it was in teaching him to let her go.

He dragged a shirt from the basket.

"If you can operate those big machines, you can fold a shirt." She demonstrated, and he copied her motions. Still, his ended up looking like a wrinkled blob.

With a laugh, he picked up the shirt, unrolling it. "I think I need a few more lessons."

She laughed along. Lately, he'd been laughing a lot more. Smiling more, too. Even singing again. That men's group he'd recently been invited to join seemed to be doing wonders for him. Maybe he was finally realizing he had more to live for than her.

"I could go to your school and take Home Ec."

"It's FACS, Dad." He could never get that right. In seventh grade, her Family and Consumer Science class taught more than how to cook and sew. It had trained her on how to run a household. She felt proud knowing she'd applied those skills well over the last several years.

"You've got the whole next year to teach me all those things I should've been teaching you." The smile drifted from his voice as he attempted another fold.

"You've taught me all I need to know. Faith and family." The important things. He'd done the best he could, being a single parent running his own business. School had filled in on those areas her mother normally would have taught, except for the birds and the bees. She couldn't imagine having that chat with her father, and her mother had died long before the talk was necessary. No, learning that lesson in school was fine with her. But was it even necessary at all? As if a boy would ever show an interest in her.

She took the shirt from her dad and redid it. Maybe once she left home, he'd finally decide to date again. She hoped he would. He didn't deserve to be all alone. Of course, she'd be alone too, but she'd known little else.

Her dad wrapped an arm around her shoulders as she refolded his shirt. "I need to head out to the shop and—"

"But it's Saturday, we were going to ..." She bit into her lip, stopping her complaint. Her dad didn't need the pressure of her disappointment. They could make the two-hour trip to Lake Itasca any day, but seeing where the Mississippi River was born always meant more on their birthdays.

"Tomorrow."

Tomorrow would be fine. It had to be. What choice did she have?

He kissed her forehead. "I got this last minute order in from Quality Steel and they accepted my high quote. I couldn't turn them down."

"Then let me help." She loved running the CNC machine and watching it shape and grind holes in steel.

"Not today, hon. You work too hard. Why don't you take the day off? Go into town? Call a friend?"

"Sure." She forced a smile. "I'll do that."

"Atta girl." He gave her shoulders a squeeze. "When we're done, I'll take you out for supper. Treat my special girl." He tapped her chin. "You know you're special, don't you?"

Yeah, she knew. At least to him ... and maybe to God.

He squeezed his eyes shut and rubbed his temple.

"Are you okay?"

He shook his head. "Just a little headache again. I'll be fine."

"Make sure you take some aspirin for that."

"Yes, Mom." He winked and walked away. His work shoes

clomped on the wooden stairs as she placed the folded clothes into a plastic laundry basket. She carried the basket up the stairs and shut the door to the empty basement. Funny how its emptiness seemed to cling to her.

*Call a friend*, he'd said. How could she tell him she didn't have any? How could she tell him the only attention she ever received was when someone picked on her? Her dad didn't need that added stress. Probably make his headache even worse.

Instead, she'd give him a great birthday. If he was going to be working all day, she could bake a cake and clean the house. Maybe see if his friend, Marcus Brooks, wanted to come over for the evening and watch baseball. She'd even grill them hot dogs and make popcorn. Yep, that's exactly what she'd do.

She left the laundry basket in her bedroom and called Marcus. He loved the idea of spending the evening with her dad and promised to arrive before supper. After completing the call, she baked a spice cake and layered it with penuche frosting, setting some of the frosting aside for him to snack on. Then it was time to tackle the house cleaning of their two-bedroom, one-bath home. Not that the two of them were terribly dirty. In two short hours the entire home was cleaned, dusted, and vacuumed, and she'd even finished the laundry.

Standing by the kitchen sink, she glanced out the window at the pole barn where he'd built his shop. She could bring him a sandwich, but then she'd have to explain why she was still hanging around home. He'd pull something from his shop fridge anyway.

It wasn't noon yet, her chores were completed, and her father would likely be in the shop till supper. That left her with plenty of time for a long bike ride. She rode to the county park and followed the paved paths to a lake. There she sat, book in hand, and lost herself in a story.

Four-plus hours later, she biked home. She stopped by the shop and listened at the door. The machine was still running, and her dad didn't like being interrupted except for an emergency. So she went to the house, popped in a movie, and got comfortable on the living room couch. Its floral cushions were still firm even after ten years. Her mom would be pleased.

A yawn grew from inside her and she rubbed sleep from her eyes. Apparently, all that sun and exercise had worn her out. With the movie playing in the background, she stretched out on the sofa and covered herself with a blanket her mother had crocheted before Lauren was born, a blanket now held together by thinning threads. Lauren didn't dare wash it anymore.

She closed her eyes and dreamed of her mother.

"Lauren." A male voice broke through her dream.

She blinked her eyes open and wiped them dry before sitting up.

"Lauren." The voice called again. Her kitchen door slammed and footsteps pounded across the linoleum floor.

"In here." She threw off the blanket and stood as Marcus hurried into the living room. He stopped when he saw her and looked down, but not before she noticed his red-rimmed, glassy eyes. His Adam's apple bobbed as he stuffed hands into his jean pockets.

Her chin quivered and she bit into her lip. She tried to say "What's wrong?" but sound refused to exit her throat.

He sighed, crossed the carpeted floor, and wrapped trembling arms around her. "It's your dad." His voice quivered.

No, no, no. She heaved in a breath and pushed away. "What?" The words grated from her throat.

"Sweetheart." He reached out and took her hand, tears trailing down his cheeks. "He's ... he's ..."

"He's hurt?" She broke away from Marcus and aimed for the outside door.

Marcus caught her and drew her to his chest. "No, honey, I'm so sorry. Your father's dead."

CHAPTER *three*

*June*
*Brooks Family Farm*

Sheila grasped Richard's hand and silently prayed she'd be able to keep her emotions in check. Sunday picnic dinner at Richard's parents' farm was the perfect time and location for making their news public. God had even blessed them with a cloudless, low-humidity afternoon.

Richard squeezed back and nodded.

She tapped a spoon against her plastic cup, but the family's continuous banter drowned out the sound. She cleared her throat, but that also went unheard. Well, she'd have to resort to option number three. She stuck two fingers into her mouth and blew out a shrill whistle.

All heads jerked toward her, and Richard's family was finally silent. She took in a breath and connected gazes with this family who'd accepted her as their own, who loved her in a way she hadn't dreamed existed. "We have an announcement to make." An announcement that could melt Sheila into an emotional puddle.

Smiles erupted on many of the faces, but would those smiles remain? With that kind of lead-in, they'd likely be anticipating a baby announcement, so she exchanged a somber glance with Richard and nodded for him to take over. It was time to add a little drama and diversion. His idea, not hers. She'd rather blurt out their news. As it was, she found it difficult keeping her mouth shut.

Richard let out a sigh and slumped in his chair. Hmm, he was a better actor than she anticipated.

"What is it, son?" Richard's dad leaned toward them.

Richard folded his hands on the table, his face impassive. "There's no easy way to say this, so I'll come right out and tell you."

Frowns replaced everyone's smiles, and Sheila shot Richard an anxious glance. Maybe they should skip this charade and tell the truth. But he gave his head a slight shake. When this was over, she was going to point the finger directly at him. No way was she going to accept the blame for this deception.

He cleared his throat and put his arm around Sheila's shoulders. "Sheila and I will soon be taking new positions." All chewing stopped. Grilled burgers and hot dogs dropped to paper plates. And all was silent save for the songs of nature playing around them.

"What, are you nuts?" Richard's younger brother shook his head. Sheila coughed to cover up a laugh. Marcus was easily riled, so this reaction was exactly what they expected from him.

"Maybe." Richard shrugged.

"Maybe? How about absolutely." Marcus pushed back from the table and crossed his arms. "Of all the idiot—"

"Marcus." Richard's mom shot her son a warning glance and nodded to the kids' end of the table.

"Right." He clenched his jaw shut.

Richard covered his mouth, faking a choke, but Sheila saw that gleam in his eye. Her husband loved to stir up trouble, and he was having too much fun with this.

Whereas she'd burst if they kept stalling, so she looked directly at Marcus. "We've prayed about it and know this is the direction God wants us to go in. We've no doubt."

Richard's mom nodded to Richard and Sheila. "Who are we to question God's leading? You'll have our complete support."

"We knew you'd support us." Sheila wiped away a rogue tear. How could she be laughing one second, then weeping the next? She whispered a quick *thank you* to God for gifting her with this family, for a mother- and father-in-law who loved her like their own child and demonstrated what it really meant to be parents.

Richard's younger sister shifted her newborn to her shoulder, and he responded with a juicy burp. Chuckles lessened the tension surrounding the family, but didn't eliminate it.

"That's my nephew." Richard reached over and patted the baby's behind.

His sister Debbie huffed, but couldn't disguise her smirk. "Maybe I should be glad you're moving away so—"

"Whoa, whoa back up one second." Richard raised his hands palms outward. "Who said anything about moving?" His mouth eased up into the smile Sheila adored.

She couldn't help but smile too.

"You're not going back to New York?" Richard's dad scratched his head. "What's going on?"

"We're staying right here." Sheila gestured toward the family. "Nothing could make me move. Nothing." And there were those nasty tears again. How was she going to make it through the next months?

"Whew." Debbie drew a hand across her forehead. "I was worried I was losing my best friend."

Sheila felt the same way. Not only was she an adopted member of this family, but she'd found a best friend in Debbie.

"I'm still confused." Marcus' wife picked up a tray of bars and passed them around the table. Apparently, their appetites had returned. But then, this family was always hungry for Janet's baking. "Ricky, you're always bragging about your business—"

"Bragging?" Richard stabbed a fist to his heart.

"Bragging, gloating, boasting ..."

"Janet, you used to be my favorite sister-in-law." He pointed to the plate of desserts. "By the way, pass me a peanut butter bar."

Janet grabbed the plate and held it inches from Richard's reach. "Uh-uh. Time to fess up. If your business is doing so well, why the change?"

Richard shrugged. "It's true, my business is going well. Very well, actually. But this is a new joint venture with Sheila."

"What kind of venture?" Marcus took a couple of peanut butter bars off the tray and passed it in the opposite direction from Richard.

He moaned. "Come on, pass the bars."

"Sorry." Marcus set the plate in front of his teenage sons. With their insatiable appetites, there wouldn't be any bars left for Richard. Served him right.

"Well ..." Sheila kicked at Richard's leg. He winced but stayed quiet. It was time to get this over with. "It's a brand new challenge for both of us. We're eager to begin but—"

"We're scared poopless." Richard grinned.

Marcus' teen boys howled with laughter. Sheila groaned. Her husband was an oversized child.

"When do you start?" Debbie's husband folded hands on the wooden table.

"Technically, we've already begun, but the real work starts in about seven months." Richard gave Sheila a side-armed hugged.

"Mo-om." Debbie's daughter stood on her bench seat and jumped off. "This is boring, can I go?"

"You say, 'May I be excused, please'?"

The seven-year-old rolled her eyes. "May I be 'scused, please?"

Debbie waved her hand. "Go ahead."

That brought a mass exodus from all the kids, but the eldest. At seventeen, Marcus' son considered himself too grown up to play with the others.

"Come on, Nathan. You'll pass the bars to your favorite uncle, won't you?" Richard patted his stomach. "I'm starving!"

Nathan grinned and pulled the tray close to his chest. "Get your own plate."

"You guys are killing me here."

"Yeah, and you deserve it, too." Debbie wagged a finger at Richard. "What's up?"

Sheila whispered to Richard. "No more stalling."

A grin slid to his face as Richard pulled his wallet from his back pocket. "One second." He flipped open the wallet and took out a bunch of newly-printed business cards. "This should explain it."

He handed the pile to his dad, who chuckled, took a card, and then passed the pile on to Richard's mom. She gasped and handed the cards to Janet who fluttered hands in front of her face.

Marcus took a card and then laughed. "You got me. Good one."

"I can't take this anymore." Debbie reached across the table and grabbed the business card from Marcus. "Richard and Sheila Brooks, President and Vice-President of the ..." Her wide-eyed gaze rose to Richard. "What? Mom and Dad Corporation?"

Sheila nodded and her smile broke free, as did the tears. So much for reining in her emotions today.

"Oh my gosh, congratulations!" In her excitement, Debbie patted another burp from her son.

Sheila wiped away tears as the family surrounded her and Richard, offering hugs and congratulations.

"Congrats." Marcus slapped Richard on the back. "This is exactly the news I needed today."

"We know." Richard stood and drew his brother into a hug.

Sheila knew it had been a tough week for Marcus, culminating with the funeral yesterday at which he was a pallbearer. And tomorrow, he and Janet had more news to break

31

to their kids. The initial purpose of this family picnic had been to lend support to Marcus, so it was very good to hear him laugh.

Sheila rubbed a hand over her yet-flat stomach as she and Richard fielded questions: Slugger, as Richard nicknamed their baby, was due mid-January, around Richard's birthday. No, they didn't know the sex yet, nor did they want to find out. She wasn't feeling sick. Just tired and over-emotional.

"The important question is—" Debbie rested her chin on folded hands "—when do you want the baby shower? Before Christmas or—"

"No shower." Absolutely not. She'd endured one for their wedding only months ago. They couldn't force her to have another one. No way.

"Sorry, Sheila, we had to have one; now it's your turn." Janet offered a coy grin.

"But we don't need anything."

"This isn't just for you, dear." Richard's mom put her hand on Sheila's. "It's for family and friends to celebrate with you and Ricky."

"We'll have a couple's shower then." If she had to suffer through one, Richard would too.

"Uh-uh." Richard kissed her cheek, and she sent him a scathing glare. "We Brooks men don't do showers."

Sheila's gaze pleaded to Janet and Debbie, who shook their heads. She raised her hands in surrender as an idea popped into her head. "Fine, then. Throw the shower with all the silly games, but we donate everything to Vivant, for women and men who go through unplanned pregnancies."

Silence surrounded her, and she held her breath, hoping. "Please?"

Richard kissed her cheek. "Perfect."

"Janet? Debbie?" Biting her lower lip, she looked to Richard's mom.

"Sounds like we're planning a donation shower." Richard's

mom clasped her hands together.

Yes!

"Ricky, where would you like this?" The booming voice of Richard's dad came from behind Sheila, and she turned.

He lugged a large wooden trunk about the size of a cradle. The name "Ricky", in block letters, was etched into the front, and a border of tools was carved around the perimeter.

Richard hurried to his dad and relieved him of the load. He set the box in front of Sheila and grinned. "My old toy box. Marc, Debs, and I each received one, engraved by our grandpa, Mom's dad."

"My, he was talented." Sheila rubbed her fingers over the intricate carvings.

"It's my gift for the first baby in each family." Richard's mom motioned to the trunk. "Take a peek."

Sheila unlatched the hinged cover and raised it. One look inside, and her breath left her. Baby pictures. Books. Cassettes. A baby blanket, and more mementos of Richard's childhood. None of which she had. Tears threatened, burning her eyes, but she couldn't release them. Not now, anyway. Slowly, she closed the lid and focused on her lap to hide her distress. "I think it would be more special if Richard and I went through the box in private."

She'd cry later, so they wouldn't see her wounded heart.

## CHAPTER *four*

Nathan Brooks took his place at the dining table and drummed his fingers on his thighs as he watched his parents whispering in the kitchen. His younger siblings, Joshua and Jaclyn, were already seated and waiting patiently. Of course. Those two brats were always obedient.

Family meetings were rare and never good. The last time they'd had one, he'd learned Uncle Ricky was in jail. He shivered thinking about it. This couldn't be worse than that.

Could it?

His parents finally joined them at the table, bringing a pitcher of milk and a plate of homemade fudge and seven layer bars. All his favorites. Bribery. That's what this was. Proof that this meeting was bad news. No matter what, he wouldn't be bought. Still, he filled his napkin with bars and fudge.

"What's up?" Nathan stuffed a piece of fudge into his mouth.

His dad smiled at his mom. "Your mother and I have an announcement to make." She grinned back. Maybe this wasn't going to be so bad after all. "Our family will soon be increasing by one."

Bad? No. This was worse. Wrinkling his nose, he slumped in his chair then peered up at his mother. "You're pregnant," he muttered.

She giggled. "No, Nathan. I'm not pregnant."

*Whew*. Breath rushed from his lungs. "Thank goodness." But

then what? "I don't get it."

His dad took his mother's hand. "It's about Brent Bauman."

The guy his dad found dead? What did that have to do with their family?

Dad cleared his throat. "Ten years ago, when Brent's wife passed away, he approached me and your mother about being legal guardians for his daughter Lauren should anything happen to him. Your mom and I gladly accepted the responsibility."

Nathan blinked. "What? That was ten years ago."

"You're right." Dad looked directly at Nathan. "But Brent's wishes never changed, and it makes sense. Lauren'll be graduating with you next spring. She needs some stability, familiarity. She'll be staying with us until she leaves for college and, hopefully, she'll still consider us family after that."

"So, I'm getting an older sister, then?" Naturally, Joshua took the news like it was an everyday announcement. Nathan rolled his eyes. His twelve-year-old brother could be such a suck-up.

Mom chose a bar from the tray. "We're to welcome her as part of the family."

Borin' Lauren, his sister? Wonderful. This couldn't get any worse.

"Jaclyn, do you know who Lauren is?" Mom asked his four-year-old sister.

"Miss Lauren from Sunday school?"

"Yep." Mom nodded and Jaclyn's face lit up.

"Miss Lauren's gonna be my sister?"

"She sure is." Mom smiled.

"Yippee!"

*Yeah, yippee.* Scowling, Nathan crossed his arms over his chest.

"Can she sleep with me and my nanimals?"

Mom gave Dad a wary glance then focused on Nathan. "That's something we need to discuss yet."

His gut tumbled like a cement mixer. What they wanted was

obvious—for Joshua to move into Nathan's room. His parent's eyes said as much. "You've got to be kidding. There's no way I'm rooming with that brat." Nathan jutted his finger toward his little brother.

"You think I want to room with you?"

At least they agreed on that much. "Come on, it's my last year at home. You can't do this to me. It's not fair."

"You're absolutely right." His dad threw a half-eaten bar down on the table. "It's not fair." His dad's voice took on that stern tone that told Nathan he'd gone too far. "It's not fair that this poor girl lost her mom when she was seven years old. It's not fair that she's now lost her father. It's important that we not only make her feel welcome, but that we allow her to bring as much of her home with her as possible. It'll make things tight for the next year, but we can handle it. She'll be spending a few more nights with out-of-town relatives, before moving in here. Tomorrow, Josh will move in to your room."

Nathan laid his head on the table and moaned.

"Your mother will paint Lauren's new room this week and then, next Saturday, the family's all coming to help Lauren pack and move."

Silence smothered the room. Nathan's life was ruined. How would he explain to his buddies that Borin' Lauren was living in his house? The teasing would never end.

"Josh and Jaclyn, you may be excused, preferably outside. Josh, keep an eye on her." Without looking up, Nathan felt his dad's riveted gaze.

"No prob." Josh lifted Jaclyn from her chair then planted her on the floor. "Come on kiddo. Let's go swing."

What a kiss-up. And to think Nathan would have to room with him. There had to be another way.

The screen door slammed shut, and his dad pulled his chair closer to the table. "Nate, we realize this will be hardest on you. Your mom and I don't like asking this of you, but it is necessary."

"Why? Can't you build another room?" His dad was a contractor. Adding a room would be easy for him, wouldn't it?

"For one year? Makes no sense, Nate. We all have to make a few sacrifices. We'll survive. You'll survive."

Barely. Nathan kept his head down as he grabbed a bar. "I know."

"And we're also concerned with bringing a young lady into our house, especially one your age. You need to think of Lauren as a sister," his mom said.

Seriously? Nathan coughed, spewing seven-layer bar over the table. His mom hurried to grab a dish rag.

The thought of him being interested in Lauren gave him the shimmies. That would absolutely *not* be an issue. "You think me and Lauren ..." He bit into the bar again and shivered.

Mom wiped the table in front of him. "You're a young man, and she's a pretty young lady—"

Nathan choked and fudge sprayed across the newly-wiped table. "I'm sorry, Mom, but that won't even be a thought. Lauren's a ... you know, she's ..." Dang, why hadn't he kept his trap shut?

"She's what, Nathan?"

Uh-oh. There was his dad's tone again.

Nathan squeezed his hands on his thighs. His clairvoyant parents would see through a lie. They always did. "She's ... she's a geek, okay? She's not someone I would hang out with, and I'm trying to figure out what I'm gonna tell the guys."

"I'll forget you said that." His dad pushed back in his chair, stood, and plodded to the cupboard. He pulled out a ceramic cup and poured in some freshly brewed coffee. "Want some?" He asked Mom, but not Nathan. She shook her head.

He returned to the table and glared at Nathan. What he'd give to be able to slide under the table and disappear. This was the treatment he got for telling the truth. He raided the treat plate and awaited his punishment.

Dad took a long drink then wiped his mouth with the back of his hand, all while glaring at Nathan. "I thought we raised you to be kind, respectful to everyone."

*I'm not a bully.* Nathan stuffed a bar into his mouth but tasted little of it.

"Well?" His dad's knuckles whitened as he clung to his cup.

"I am respectful." Really, he was. "I'm just not her friend, okay? I've never made fun of her like other kids. I wouldn't do that."

His dad's head seemed to sink into his shoulders. "I do hope you've tried to put an end to the bullying."

No, he hadn't tried to end it. Nathan studied his lap. To be honest, he'd enjoyed it.

"You realize"—Dad balled up a napkin and threw it on the table—"that makes you as guilty as those calling her names. I expect this behavior to end. Now!"

"Yes, sir." Nathan kept his head and voice low.

"Listen, sweetheart." No surprise, Mom played the good cop. "We know this isn't going to be easy for you, but we also know you're mature enough to handle the change, and we know you will do whatever you need to make Lauren feel comfortable. You can't change what's happened in the past, but you can change your mindset now."

"I hear ya." Nathan refused to make eye contact. Yeah, he probably wasn't any better than his friends, but what would they say when he started sticking up for that girl? He supposed he should at least try. "I'll do my best," he mumbled.

"We know." His parents spoke together.

"Still time?" Mom asked.

"Time for what?" Nathan looked up.

"I think so." A grimace clung to Dad's face.

Now what? Hadn't his parents dumped enough on him already?

Dad reached into his jeans pocket, pulled out a wad of keys, and tossed them at Nathan. Nathan grabbed them out of the air and stared down at his hand. He usually had to beg to drive. What was up now?

"So, what do you say we go spend that money you've been saving up?"

*My money?* Hope overtook his dread. There was only one thing he was saving up for, and his dad kept putting it off. Kept saying he was too busy. A smile threatened to break out, but Nathan didn't dare set it free. "You mean ...?"

"Let's go do some car shopping."

Yes! A full-fledged grin wanted to escape. Things had to be bad when his parents started using a car as bribery, instead of sweets. But, with his own wheels he'd be able to escape this place once in a while, which almost made rooming with his brother tolerable. Almost. Nathan closed his fingers around the keys, keeping a straight face, and nodded toward the garage door. "Let's go."

HER DAD WAS DEAD.

Lauren stared out her kitchen window at the line of pickups hitched with trailers that turned onto her gravel driveway—at least it used to be her driveway. Strange people were coming to remove her from her home, confirming the fact that her dad wouldn't be back. Ever.

She shuffled from the kitchen to her living room, now devoid of life, and ran her hand over a spot where their family portrait used to hang. That photo was now tucked away in a box, like so many of her things.

This house was to be put up for sale, along with her dad's business. Sure, it was the right thing to do. She was too young to take care of a home, and the sale of the house and business would pay her way through college and provide a decent trust fund. Still, that didn't make losing her home any easier to deal with.

Voices, many voices, sounded through the open windows. Those people—strangers—were coming to remove all remnants of her parents' memories, to empty her home of its furniture, its dishes, knick knacks, and pictures, leaving only carpet and wallpaper. Wallpaper her mother had chosen and meticulously pasted on every wall. Wallpaper that would hold no meaning to anyone else, that would probably be stripped to give the home an updated look for a quick sale. The final remnant of her mother would then be dead too.

Lauren ran her hand down the yellowed, curling wallpaper. Of course the Brooks family, her new temporary family, would have no clue of the wallpaper's sentimental value. It was silly, really. Wallpaper was meant to be put up and look pretty and generally be ignored, to blend in to the background and not be noticed, to have no real value.

Just like herself. Always merging into the background, with no one noticing her, except for those jerks who occasionally teased her. But, like good wallpaper, she ignored the hurtful comments, letting them slide off her. Over time, though, even the hurt left its smudged fingerprints. She was expendable, like the final remnants of her mother's hard work.

The voices were louder. Closer. She trudged to the kitchen window and watched them approach. Smiling. Laughing. Hugging.

Maybe with this new family she would finally be noticed. Nathan's family had certainly never slipped anonymously through a room as she and her dad always had. They all seemed so confident and bold. Others seemed to be drawn to them. Their faith was real, of that there was no doubt, and they were always very nice.

Nathan's laughter came through the window.

Well, most of them were nice.

A knock interrupted her reminiscing and her stomach roiled. Didn't they realize that emptying her home of its furniture and pictures and memories would be the final admission that her dad was dead?

Holding back tears, she leaned against the refrigerator. Maybe if she ignored them, they'd go away and she could live among her memories.

A knock sounded again and Lauren thumbed the tears from her cheeks. Unfortunately, reality didn't allow for living in dreams. Forcing a smile, she walked from the kitchen to the porch and answered the door.

"Sweetheart." Janet embraced her. A mother's hug. Lauren had forgotten what that felt like. Janet pulled back, placed her hands on Lauren's shoulders and looked in her eyes, probably searching for confidence. She wouldn't find any. "Are you ready to meet the family?"

Lauren stared at the floor, shaking her head, giving her most honest response.

"Really, they're not so bad." Janet wrapped an arm around her shoulders and led her from the enclosed porch into a kitchen lined with labeled boxes. A few of the boxes would end up in a storage warehouse until she was on her own again. But most were filled with memories of her dad and labeled for donation.

Within seconds she heard the door open again, followed by shoes clomping on the porch's linoleum. Voices echoed in its emptiness. Marcus, Nathan, Joshua, and five strangers walked into her kitchen. An older man and woman, two men about her dad's age, and a woman who probably was the same age as Lauren's mom. Had her mom lived. Lauren retreated into Janet's arm.

"Lauren." Janet kept her arm braced around Lauren's shoulders. "Let me introduce you." The five unknowns stood silent, wearing smiles that showed pity. "This is Bern—"

"Bernie and Marlene." The older man held out his hand. "We're Marcus' folks."

She accepted his thick, farmer-sized hand, and he clasped his other one over the top. Wrinkled, calloused, and strong. Yet, warm and comforting.

She forced a shy smile. "Nice to meet you."

A younger, yet balding man next to Bernie extended his hand. "Jerry Verhoeven. I'm married to Debbie, Marcus' little sister. She's at home watching our kids. She's looking forward to meeting you."

"I look forward to meeting her." Typical, pat response, but it was all she could think of.

"Richar"—The next man, a slightly taller, more slender version of Marcus, exchanged a glance with the pretty woman standing next to him. He held out his hand. "Ricky Brooks."

The woman winked at him, and he smiled back. Obviously two people in love. She nodded in Ricky's direction. "He's Marcus' older brother. Consider yourself special. That's the first time I've ever heard him introduce himself as Ricky." The couple shared another glance before the woman reached out. "And I'm Sheila, Ricky's wife. Unfortunately, I'm only allowed to provide moral support today. I'm pregnant, and they won't let me lift anything."

"Nice to meet you." Same old worn out phrase, but what else was there to say? "Thank you all for helping today. I appreciate it."

"We're more than glad to help." Marlene offered a warm smile and a hug then stepped back, keeping her hands on Lauren's shoulders. "I know this is hard for you, dear. My heart breaks for you, but we'll do our best to make you feel welcome. Whatever you need, you let us know, okay?"

Lauren nodded and tried to shake her stiffness. It was difficult to take kindness and physical affection from strangers when all she wanted to do was hide herself, to fade back into the wallpaper. But maybe with this family, she'd finally be seen.

## CHAPTER *five*

Sheila strangled Friday's newspaper between her hands and paced her living room. How dare they take her words out of context? Richard had warned her against doing the point/counterpoint piece, but had she listened? No. This was what she got for being stubborn. Tonight, this paper would feed the fire pit.

The distorted news, on top of that memory box still sitting by the front door, made her sick to her stomach, and not from morning sickness. That box seemed to glare at her, challenging her to open it. Rarely did she back down from a challenge, but this one was different. If only she could keep avoiding it.

"Theophilus." The familiar bass voice interrupted Sheila's thoughts.

With narrowed eyes she looked at Richard standing in the archway between the kitchen and living room, hands braced behind his back.

What mischief was he up to? Again. "Theo-fo-what?"

"Theophilus Marcus Brooks." Smiling his adorably lopsided smile, he walked to her and placed a hand on her belly. "Has an air of intelligence about it, don't you think? We could call him Theo or Phil for short."

Ah, yes. Now she understood. They didn't want to settle for an ordinary, popular name, but Theophilus? "No way."

His smile widened. "It's Biblical. Means friend of God, lover of God. Theophilus was a friend to Luke, the physician. Probably a man of great importance in Rome."

"Good for him. He can keep his name."

"Can't blame a guy for trying." Richard's grin widened.

She shoved away from him and shook the paper. "Did you read this propaganda?"

"I—"

"Don't you dare say I told you so!"

He raised both hands in surrender. One hand held an orange rose. "That's why I brought you this. Thought you could use a little cheering up."

Huffing out a breath, she dropped onto the sofa and flung the paper into the air. It floated down, landing at her feet. "I've talked with them before, and they've always been fair."

"That's when you agreed with their perspective." Richard sat next to Sheila and offered the rose. "Regardless, you got your point across. People will see through the newspaper's bias."

She breathed in the fresh scent of the rose and her frustration eased.

"You won't like this, but I have more news." Richard kicked at the paper on the hardwood floor.

"That good, huh?" Not what they needed today.

He heaved out a breath. "ACM upped their offer."

She started to laugh then studied her too-quiet husband. Head down, hands cupped on knees.

He wanted this job? Richard had loved New York City and had thrived in the fast-paced business world. His longing to return couldn't be disguised.

But there was no chance they'd upset their lives and move to New York. She rubbed her forehead, massaging a threatening headache. One more worry added to her plate today. "I didn't think their offer could get any higher."

"They're playing to my excuses, realizing family's number one for me now."

"I can't wait to hear this." Would it be enough to tempt him? She kneaded her temples, trying to soothe her budding headache. She couldn't bear to leave his family—her family—behind, not when she was beginning to create good memories.

"I've been offered use of the CEO's Cessna to fly home on weekends." He quirked a smile.

She held back a relieved sigh and swatted his back for teasing her. "They don't get it, do they?"

"Entenza is very pro-marriage. He's been married four times." Richard laughed, but it was quick and forced.

"I hope you told them what they can do with their offer." Of course he'd told them no. Hadn't he? Or had he encouraged them to do better?

"I'm afraid I laughed. They took the hint."

Whew. "Let's hope they leave you alone now." Please God, make them leave Richard alone.

"Tell me about it. But I do have a fantastic offer I'd like to make to you." Richard leaned in for a kiss, but she backed away. Apparently the discussion was over. Hopefully for good. Now, they could move on to a happier topic.

She touched a finger to his lips. "Hold that thought." She reached across him and picked up a card from the end table. This letter had softened the newspaper article's blow for her, and would most certainly bring out Richard's tender side. "Got a letter from Meghan today."

"Meghan? Really?" He grabbed the card and struggled to open it. Richard and college-aged Meghan had a complicated relationship. Over two years ago, Richard had killed Meghan's older brother in an auto accident, and she'd hated him for it. But then in a twist only God could have orchestrated, Richard had talked Meghan out of getting an abortion. It was that very talk that changed Sheila's perspective forever.

He finally dragged the card from the envelope and read it aloud. "Dear Richard and Sheila, I appreciate your kindness in sending me a gift card for maternity clothes. I'd pretty much been wearing large T-shirts and knit pants. It's nice to have something that actually fits and looks nice. I'm showing really good now, and I'm even feeling her move some.

"I also want to thank you again for being there for me and Mom and Dad at the hospital. After the way I treated you, you didn't have to be there. Thanks for accepting my apologies and, Richard (so you have it in writing, sometimes for me it makes the words more concrete), I do forgive you." His voice choked and he muttered the last words. "Sincerely, Meghan."

Richard cradled the thank you card as if it were a delicate flower. "I need to get this to Mom so she can scrapbook it."

"Better her than me." Sheila's gaze settled on Richard's memory box. It had been two weeks since she'd received it, and it still pleaded to be opened. As much as she dreaded going through it, she could not longer avoid the task. "Speaking of scrapbooks ..." Her gaze met his. "I want to go through your memory box."

"Are you sure?"

"No, but I can't put it off any more."

He squeezed her hand and kissed her cheek, then retrieved the trunk and placed it in front of the couch. After another glance her way, he raised the lid, letting loose cedar scent, and grinned.

But she felt like crying. Why did this bother her so much? These were happy memories for Richard, memories their child would appreciate someday.

He pulled out a crocheted blue blanket—what was left of it anyway. "My blankie. I never went anywhere without it. It mysteriously disappeared when I was probably six."

*I used to have a blankie ...*

Richard picked up a framed photograph. The dark-haired boy in the picture wore cuffed jeans, a long-sleeved flannel shirt, and a red cap. He had a well-stocked tool belt—real adult sized tools—buckled around his waist. The tattered blanket lay on a bench. His tongue crooking out of the side of his mouth, he stood beside the bench, hammering a nail into the blanket.

"Dad always said that if something's worth fixing, it can be fixed with a hammer and nail. Guess I took that to heart."

"So you were already fixing things when you were little?"

"I've always been a fixer. Didn't always do it right at first, but I learned."

He set the picture on an end table then took out a cassette. She ripped it from his hands and chuckled. "Air Supply? Seriously?"

"Must be Mom's." He snatched it back.

She smirked. "I thought we promised to always tell the truth."

"Fine." He dropped the cassette on the end table. "I liked them in grade school. At least my musical tastes have evolved since then."

"Thank goodness." Although, personally, her tastes hadn't changed much. She still liked the sounds of REO Speedwagon and Journey, but those cassettes and CDs had remained at her parents' home. Journey's "Open Arms" had once been a favorite, perhaps because she so badly wanted her parents to open their arms to her.

It had never happened.

She curved a hand over her stomach. This baby would have an endless supply of open arms waiting to hold her. The thought brought a smile, convincing her that she could handle the remainder of Richard's memories. She chose a book from the box. Appeared to be part of a teen series. "*Three Investigators*?"

His eyes lit up as he pulled out more books, all dog-eared from use. "I thought I'd lost these!" He paged through one, releasing the musty scent of old books into the air. "All the other boys my age were reading *Hardy Boys*. But these were more clever—the kids less perfect, more real."

"Like *Nancy Drew*. I read them but preferred *Trixie Belden*." At one time she'd had the entire *Trixie Belden* series, but she'd left those behind when she went off to college. What she'd give to have them now so she could share them with a daughter someday.

Could that be one of the items her parents had left behind when they'd moved? Would Estelle Barrows still have that box of Sheila's belongings?

"You okay?" Richard brushed hair from her face. "We can do this another time."

She shook her head. "Let's keep going. There's not much left." His baptism outfit, a white suit which included a vest and tie. Richard's baby book. Had her mom even made a baby book for Sheila? She couldn't recall ever seeing one.

"Almost done." Richard dug out a school years memory book, clearly his mother's handiwork. He paged through schoolwork, artwork, awards, report cards, pictures from each year. He flipped quickly past a picture, so all she saw was a blur. What was he hiding?

"Whoa there. Turn that back."

"You really don't want to see this." His hand guarded the page.

She removed his hand, turned back to the previous page, and giggled. "A mullet?"

"It was in style then."

She ran her fingers up the back of his head. His hair was thick but not long enough to weave between her fingers. "I think you should grow it out again."

"You think so? Maybe I could revive the trend."

Picturing forty-year-old Richard in a mullet made her laugh out loud. Only Richard could get her to smile when her heart was breaking.

"Look at this." Richard opened a hand-sized photo album, one that displayed non-professional pictures from their wedding. Her first dance with Richard as a married couple. Guests taking goofy selfies. Meghan Keene and her parents talking with

Richard's folks. The unposed memories were even more precious than the posed ones. Paging through the book warmed Sheila's heart, but sadness crept back in as Richard repacked all the memories into the box.

She closed the lid, hoping the action would shut down her feelings. But tears leaked out anyway.

"Are you going to tell me what this is about?" Richard kissed tears from her cheeks.

"It's silly."

"It's not silly if it hurts you this bad." He combed hair away from her face. "Tell me. Please."

She turned toward the living room picture window. An outdoor panorama green with life, proof of roots digging deep into the earth's soil. She needed to move forward in life, but it was difficult when her roots were nonexistent. "I don't have anything."

She looked toward the ceiling and closed her eyes. Darkness stared back. "No memories from my childhood. No baby book. No high school memories, yearbooks, nothing. Nothing to show our child who I was when I was growing up. All my tangible memories begin in college. I *did* have a life before then, but I have nothing to show for it. I want something of myself to share with our baby. I want her to snuggle with my old blanket and read my worn-out books. I want to laugh together at my old pictures."

Tears flowed unhindered, accompanied with deep, painful sobs. Richard drew her in, wrapping his strong arms around her back. His shirt absorbed her pain.

"Maybe it's time." His calm voice whispered when her crying slowed. He handed her a tissue.

"Time?" She patted her eyes.

"To see if we can find what your parents left behind."

"I doubt it's there anymore." She sat up straight and shrugged out of his arms. "That was eighteen years ago. I'm certain Mrs.

Barrows has moved by now or passed on or gotten rid of whatever Mother and Father left."

"We won't know if we don't look."

She had thought about retrieving her belongings. Frequently. And it always made her queasy. But with Richard beside her, giving her strength? Yes, she could return to her old neighborhood, see if her neighbor was still there. She owed it to herself, to Richard, to their baby.

"You're right, Richard. We should go."

## CHAPTER *six*

### *White Plains, New York*

Meghan Keene walked up the concrete steps to her parents' home, Shane's hand resting protectively in the small of her back. Who would have ever thought the two of them could have such a good time? Who'd have thought she could laugh again without feeling guilty for being happy? Who'd have thought anyone would look twice at her now?

Shane opened the door for her and let her pass through before following her in. Shane was different, had always been different. She was finally seeing that difference as a positive attribute, so unlike Doran.

Why did all her thoughts go back to him? No, she wasn't going to ruin her evening by thinking about that jerk.

Taking Shane's arm in hers, she walked into the living room.

Her dad sat cuddled with her mom on the couch, even though it was past eleven o'clock at night. Ever protective of her. She'd proven to them, she needed their protection. Her dad stood and offered his hand to her date. "Good evening, Shane. Nice to see you around here again. It's been a long time."

"Too long, sir." Shane shook her dad's hand. "I hope to be seeing you a bit more often, now." Shane looked at her and grinned.

Her heart did a little patter.

"You're always welcome." Her mother joined the small huddle and gave Shane a hug.

"Thanks, Mrs. K. I appreciate it."

Shane brushed Meghan's arm. "Give you a call?"

Her cheeks heated. When was the last time she'd actually blushed? "I'd like that."

He squeezed her hand, said goodbye, then left. A true gentleman.

From the living room window Meghan watched him get into his little Honda and drive off. She placed her hand on her very pregnant belly and shook her head. Only eight weeks till her due date and the pregnancy didn't bother him.

Why couldn't the baby's father have been more like Shane?

"Is she moving?" Her mother pressed her hand to Meghan's stomach.

"No. She's quiet." But earlier in the evening, she'd been kicking like David Beckham. Although Shane wasn't the father, he'd beamed when feeling the baby's kicks.

"Tell us about your evening." Her father took her arm and guided her to the recliner.

"We had fun." Meghan sat and brought up the footrest, easing the pressure on her swollen ankles and calves. "It's funny. When Shane and Justin used to do everything together, I never gave him a second glance. Why didn't I notice him before?"

"You're growing up. You've been through a lot these past few years." Mom returned to the couch. "And you're gaining a new perspective on people." Dad sat next to Mom and put an arm around her. They finally looked happy again, two years after burying their son. Meghan eyed the empty space next to her mother. Their entire family fit on that couch now. Would that ever stop making her sad?

Meghan's gaze flitted to her brother's high school graduation picture, with him in his cap and gown, giving a two-handed thumbs-up to the camera. One of her last memories of him. Her parents had weathered these past two stormy years well. Losing Justin had only been the beginning of the storm. Then she'd stirred it up more. It took this pregnancy to realize it. She was blessed to have two loving, very forgiving parents. She caressed her stomach. Every child deserved two loving parents.

"I wish I'd noticed him before." Nineteen years old and very pregnant. Why would Shane want to go out with her, knowing what kind of girl she'd become?

"The fact is, you're noticing him now, and Shane likes you. Always has."

"Oh, yeah." She laughed. "He always liked to tease me."

"And you always liked it." Dad smirked.

"I guess." Meghan shrugged. "But more in a brother-sister type way, not a boy-girl way. It's odd thinking of him as anything but Justin's best friend." But she was willing to try. He wasn't the kind to take advantage of her, unlike ... No! She clenched her fists. She would not think of Doran, not when she had someone like Shane interested in her. She didn't deserve him. "You know, it doesn't even bother him that I'm pregnant."

"He's not the kind of man to hold this mistake over your head." Her dad drew her mom even closer.

No, he wasn't. Shane was a man like her father. A man who would never abandon their child, no matter what happened. "I'm realizing that." With a sigh, Meghan relaxed into the chair cushions. "I'm sure Justin would be happy to know I said 'yes' to Shane." He probably would have been ecstatic.

"We are too. That reminds me." Dad slapped his thighs and stood. "You received a call when you were out." Her father's voice took on a somber tone that scared her. He retrieved a slip of paper from next to their phone and handed it to her. "Doran called."

*Doran?* Her entire body tensed. *He calls now?* For nearly two months she'd hobbled around the University of Wisconsin-Madison campus on crutches. One would think a pregnant woman on crutches would attract sympathy. Huh! Even worse, Doran had gone out of his way to avoid her for the remainder of the school year. Five long months of being disregarded by the person she once considered spending a lifetime with. Maybe he felt guilty for her predicament. Well, he should. This whole mess was his fault, yet it hadn't cost him one thing.

How dare he intrude on her life now?

She read the note. Only Doran's name and phone number. No message. "What did he want?" He better not be asking for his Kindle back. That's all she had from him.

That and the baby.

"He's coming to New York with his family next week for the Fourth of July, on vacation." Mom glanced at Dad then back to Meghan. "He wants to see you,"

Meghan snorted. "Like I want to see him."

"He said he was sorry." Mom dug into her yarn basket, pulled out the nearly-completed, knitted baby blanket, and began working the needles.

"Oh, isn't that sweet?" Meghan pushed down the foot rest and sat straight up. "Doesn't matter. I don't want to see him."

"He is your baby's father." Her dad sat beside her mom. "He has a right to—"

"He gave up that right when he told me to have an abortion, to kill my baby." Meghan crossed her hands over her stomach, feeling her baby wake up with a long stretch. "When he said he wanted nothing to do with me anymore."

"We told him you'd see him." Mom's needles clacked as they worked together. "Call him. Tell him yourself how you feel."

Meghan slumped back into the recliner and pouted. Oh, she'd tell him all right. She didn't even have to practice a speech. She'd been running that speech over in her mind every night for weeks, months even. Maybe it was good that she'd finally be able to deliver it. "Fine." Then he'd be gone from her life for good.

SHEILA STARED OUT THE car's window and sighed. Going to find her box of belongings was likely a wasted effort, one that would bring on more heartache. How had she let Richard talk her into this?

Ah, who was she kidding? She'd talked herself into this.

But there was always the chance they'd find her things, and that slight possibility made this drive worth it.

Closing her eyes, she imagined the top was down on the Audi, the steamy air whipping her hair behind her, and scents from international food merchants making her stomach growl. But with the top down, Sheila's hair would have required attention again, and she couldn't travel down the street of memories without being perfect. For that, she blamed her mother.

Richard sat silent in the driver's seat. For the first hour of their drive she'd ignored his efforts to make conversation. Her dear husband was learning to respect her need for solitude when facing a difficult dilemma or decision. She should let him in on her thought process, but eighteen-plus years of being independent had trained her otherwise. She needed to work on this, but not today.

Instead, she focused on the scenery outside the window. The neighborhoods siding Fiftieth Street South had changed very little in eighteen years. Most homes were built in the early twentieth century and were adorned with stucco exteriors and varying roof lines, gables, turrets, and covered porches. Much more character than homes built today.

The streets were shaded with trees as old or older than the homes. Tiny garages opened into alleys Richard's pickup would have difficulty squeezing through. Franchise-free shopping areas were home to an eclectic collection of shops and cafés with curbside seating, most of which were occupied with lunch hour guests. Here and there she spied a jogger, presumably making their way to the asphalt paths surrounding the chain of lakes beginning just north of here.

Those lakes had once been her refuge, but she'd run from those as well.

Every cell in her body tensed as she spotted the sign for France Avenue. "Take the next right." She pointed out the street.

"I know." His curt response knifed, but she'd earned it with having shut him out for the past hour. More than likely he knew the area better than she, having spent many of his college days studying by the lakes. At that time he'd probably been accompanied by a pretty co-ed and a case of Old Milwaukee. Today she almost wished for that twelve-pack to help her through this experience. Almost. Instead she lowered her head to pray.

"I'm sorry," he said as the blinker began its rhythmic tick. "That was uncalled for. I think I'm as nervous as you."

"Forgiven," she whispered as the car turned. She peeked out her window and her heart sped up. She closed her eyes and counted as she breathed in and blew out. It didn't help. Fortieth Street and the house she'd grown up in were mere blocks, minutes, seconds away.

The blinker flipped on again. The last ten blocks had sailed past too quickly. She opened her eyes and a familiar street appeared around the corner. The street where she'd ridden her tricycle. The street on which she'd pushed her scooter and pulled her wagon carrying her bat and balls. The street where she'd learned to ride her bike—with no help from her parents.

The street with *his* house, that so-called boyfriend who'd stolen her innocence and her virginity, gifting her with a devastating choice. The street she'd vowed never to return to. How had she let Richard talk her into coming back?

Richard steered the car into an open parking spot beneath the same oak tree where her '76 Toyota once sat. "Is this it?"

Her gaze landed on the house behind the tree and she nodded. He turned off the car. The house looked smaller than she remembered, but otherwise appeared to be very much the same. Stucco and evergreen trim decorated the outer walls of the story and a half structure. The front steps were concrete with thick cement banisters sloping beside them and curving down at the end. Her childhood slide. The small front lawn was neatly manicured and a colorful garden skirted the house. A newly-poured concrete sidewalk led to its front steps. Perennials framed the sidewalk.

"It's been kept up well." She spoke through pinched lips. "Father would be pleased."

For all she knew, her father and mother still lived here. It wouldn't surprise her if her mother had lied about their move in order to keep her away. The front door began to open. Sheila held her breath as the screen door was pushed outward. A young couple dressed entirely in black spandex came out and took off jogging. Sheila expelled her breath. What was she so afraid of?

"You ready?" Richard's hand rested on her forearm.

*No.* She shook her head. As much as she wanted her keepsakes, she feared the pain they'd conjure up.

"Hon, I know how hard this is for you, and I understand that whatever we might find could awaken more painful memories, but you also might find some treasures. Think on that. No matter what we find, I'm right beside you."

"But what if Mrs. Barrows doesn't live there anymore?" She had retired by the time Sheila went to college. Why hadn't she listened to Richard and done her research first? It wouldn't have been that difficult to find out if Mrs. Barrows still lived here or where she might be found. Assuming she was alive. Researching would have been the practical thing to do. If Mrs. Barrows was gone, Sheila could have avoided this return.

But Sheila's gut had told her no. Perhaps she needed this opportunity to finally say goodbye and good riddance.

"Come on, hon." Richard's hand stroked her arm down to her fingers, and then locked them with his.

Her heart still racing, she looked down at his comforting

hand then at his serious face.

He gave a gentle squeeze but didn't let go. "It's time."

She breathed deep then forced it out. Her gaze met Richard's and she nodded.

"I'll get your door." He got out and jogged around the car, opened her door, and offered his hand.

She kept hers pinned to her lap. "I'm sure nobody's home. I'm sure she doesn't even live here anymore, if she's alive at all."

His hand remained extended. "There's one way to find out."

*Okay.* She sucked in her breath as she accepted his hand then stepped outside. They walked down the sidewalk to the home next door to the one she'd grown up in. Estelle's place. Her grip tightened as they climbed the steps leading to the door. She rang the circular doorbell, and held her breath.

The tap of light footsteps came from inside the house, and the inner door opened. Richard smiled at the young woman, probably in her twenties, who opened the door. She moved the screen door lock into place.

"We're look—"

"I'm looking for Estelle Barrows." Sheila spoke over Richard. "I used to live next door.

The young woman frowned. "I'm very sorry. Aunt Estelle passed away a few years ago."

Sheila's hand flew to her heart. "I'm so sorry."

Richard caressed Sheila's back.

"Thank you." The woman nodded and her eyes darted between them. "Is there something I could help you with?"

"Maybe." Sheila drew in a breath then pointed toward her childhood home. "My parents moved when I was in college, and they left some items with Estelle. I never had an opportunity to retrieve them. Is there any chance they would be here yet?"

"I'm afraid not." The woman laid a hand on her chest. "We moved Aunt Estelle from here into a nursing home about five years ago. The family had an estate sale, and the home was completely empty when I moved in. I really am sorry."

Richard curved his arm around Sheila's waist, keeping her from collapsing. "Thank you for your time."

So, that was it. The end of her search. Her past was gone. Erased. And she had nothing to share with her child.

With Richard's arm still supporting her, they walked back to the car. He kissed her forehead and whispered, "We'll make our own memories."

She shook her head. "You don't understand. Losing my belongings ... it's like being abandoned all over again."

A deep sigh seemed to deflate his body. "Babe, I'm sorry. You're right, I can never understand. My family can't replace yours, but they love you like a daughter, sister, aunt, and we will never abandon you."

She fingered tears from her eyes. Richard was right. Fussing over a past she couldn't change made no sense, but she could learn from this. The same mistakes would not be repeated with her and Richard's child. She splayed her hands over her belly. This child would be mightily loved.

RICHARD KISSED SHEILA'S FOREHEAD as they walked back to the car. She wasn't crying but he could he feel her body tremble from the force of holding it in. For days he'd prayed they would find something, anything with a positive remembrance attached.

But this was one minor setback. He wasn't about to give up on those prayers. Not yet. There were other means of uncovering one's past, especially in this information-driven age. He opened her car door and assisted her in then closed it softly behind her.

Sheila was leaving her old neighborhood, troubled by her failure. He was leaving with a mission in mind: uncovering Sheila's past. He opened his door and slid behind the steering wheel. He had to find something for her, some memento of her childhood to pass on to their child, even if it meant finding her parents.

# CHAPTER *seven*

*July*
*White Plains, New York*

H ey Meggie." Doran's voice was the same but the young man standing behind the screen door was barely recognizable. Doran's once shoulder-length hair had been cut above his ears, and its original color had been allowed to grow through, giving him a mature and even professional appearance. That layer of self-reliance he'd always worn had been wiped away. Had she played a role in erasing that conceit? She could only hope.

Meghan stared at him, her thoughts and feelings suddenly a mess. In that once arrogant boy's place stood a young man who was still disturbingly cute and surprisingly unsure. All the nasty things she had formed in her mind to tell him fell away. He looked like he needed a friend. But he'd excelled at letting appearances deceive, and she refused to be fooled now.

"Come on in." She opened the door, and he stepped inside. His gaze flitted to her stomach and his mouth pinched as he took in its truth, but he said nothing.

"Mom and Dad left for the day." She said flatly. "They wanted to give us privacy."

She led him through the living room, into the kitchen, and then out the patio door onto a small wood deck. She sat in one of the woven chairs and propped her ankles on top of a round plastic beverage table. He took a chair, placed it a yard away, facing her, but his gaze lowered to his hands massaging each other.

"You're looking good, Meggie." His eyes met hers.

She huffed. "For someone seven months pregnant, right?"

"No!" He brushed a hand over his hair and sighed. "I mean it. You look good. How are you feeling?"

She laughed with her lips shut. "Fat. Uncomfortable. Hot. Hungry." She gulped then breathed her last word. "Scared."

His gaze found his hands again. "Me too." His cheeks flexed. "I'm not going to duck out on you anymore, Meggie. I realize I can't let you go this alone."

"Oh really?" Cynicism pitched her voice. Doran wasn't the type to hold any responsibility. At least he never used to be.

"I can take a semester off school. Be here when the baby comes. There's a college nearby where I could complete my graduate degree. I don't know what you want, but I want you to know I won't abandon you and the baby anymore."

He looked sincere, but then again, he was a good liar. There was no reason to believe him now. Besides, she didn't want him in her life. With what she'd decided to do, he wouldn't have to be. "Why the change of heart?"

He dragged his fingers through his hair again. "I kept thinking back to the hospital—after you'd been hit by the car. Maybe I realized then that I'd forced you into something you didn't want, that I was being selfish."

"And you couldn't have told me this before I left school? You ignored me for months!"

"I'm sorry. I was confused. I didn't want to take responsibility."

"Tell me about it." She rolled her eyes.

"That was then, Meggie."

She shook her head, not believing him. What was he up to?

"I'm serious, Meggie. My parents always said I should

64

experience what life had to offer, especially while I'm young. But if that were true, then you wouldn't be pregnant. I wouldn't have to be a dad." He laughed wryly and shook his head. "Knowing there are consequences is totally different from living through those consequences. I guess I never thought it would happen to me—to us—to you."

She shifted in her chair. These words were coming from Doran? Maybe he had grown up since she'd seen him.

"But what got me thinking the most was what that one guy said, you know, the one who stayed at the hospital with me and your parents after you'd been hit."

"Richard Brooks?" Her stomach turned over. Yes, she'd forgiven the man responsible for her brother's death and had even credited him with convincing her not to go through with an abortion. Her parents had become friendly with him. But his name still conjured up bad memories.

"Yeah. Him. He and his girlfriend stayed at the hospital all afternoon and they knew how much you hated them. Before they left, he told me that making a baby isn't what makes a boy a man. He said it was what that boy chose to do about the baby that determined what kind of man he would be."

His gaze flitted to her stomach then back to her face. "I had to think about it. Did I want to be the kind of man who looked for the easy way out, or would I be the kind to step up and be accountable? I'm sorry it took me five months to come up with the right answer. He gave me his business card. Told me to call anytime. I haven't yet, but I'm thinking about it."

Doran got up from his chair and squatted next to Meghan. He covered her hand with his and his other hand reached for her stomach. He paused inches above. "Can I?"

Touching her like that would almost be too intimate and could open doors to him again. But it was his baby, and he was making an effort. No, she wouldn't deny him the opportunity to feel his child. She nodded, and he tentatively lowered his hand.

"There's a baby in there." His eyes grew wide. "Do you feel it move?"

"Quite a bit. It's odd. At first it felt like I swallowed a butterfly. Now I actually feel limbs moving, and she hiccups like crazy."

"She?"

"Yeah, it's a girl."

"Cool." He smiled. She'd forgotten about that great smile. "Would I be able feel her?"

"Oh yeah. When she's moving, I can even watch her. It's pretty cool, but I think she's sleeping right now."

He removed his hand from her stomach and kept her other hand clutched in his but remained squatting. "I'm ready to take responsibility."

"Doran ..."

"Seriously. I mean it. I want to be part of our child's life."

"But there's something else I need to tell you."

Worry creased his forehead.

"I'm putting the baby up for adoption."

He dropped her hand and fell back on his behind. "You can't," he whispered.

"It's the best thing." Yes, it was the best choice. She'd prayed and prayed about it, hoping to hear another answer, but it always came back to this impossible decision. Doran's sudden interest was going to make giving her up all the more difficult. "I'm too young. I want to finish school. I screwed up at school last year. I need to make it right. This is the right choice."

"But I said I'd be around for you."

"Being *around* for a weekend here or there isn't what a baby needs from a father. Our baby needs someone there full time, not a dad who visits on weekends."

"Maybe I could be there full-time."

"I'm not living with you."

"That's not what I'm talking about." He kept her hand in his.

Brenda S. Anderson

His thumb massaged her ring finger.

"Marriage?" She stared at him. Had he been drinking too much Kool-Aid or what?

He nodded.

Obviously, he wasn't thinking things through. No way would she marry him. "It wouldn't work. You know that. We're too different."

He released her hand. She placed her hands on her abdomen and caressed it. This child deserved the best.

"Do I have a choice in what happens?" He nodded toward the baby. His arms circled his knees, and his eyes were misty. She'd never seen him cry before.

"Yes," she breathed out. As much as she didn't want him around, involving Doran was only fair, as her dad had suggested. "You have a choice. But this is more than feelings, it's more than what I or you want. It's about what's best for her."

He shook his head slowly. "I'd gotten used to the idea of being a father."

"You still can be someday—at the right time, with the right girl." Meghan patted her stomach. "I believe this is the right thing to do."

His jaw shifted back and forth. "If I agree. What do we do next?"

*We?* He said we? Maybe he had matured over the last few months.

"I've already contacted an agency. I'd like to pick out the parents, maybe someone I know, so I know she'll be raised the right way. Mom and Dad told me there's a couple at church who've been looking into adopting."

"Would you want them to be that close? I mean, wouldn't it be more difficult letting go if you saw your baby all the time, knowing she wasn't yours anymore?"

"I'm not sure. That's the hard part. But I don't know anyone out of state, anyone I'd trust, anyway."

"What about that couple from the hospital?"

"The Brookses?"

"They're married?"

"Yeah. This spring." She hadn't even considered them.

"They seem nice enough. I got the impression that money wasn't an issue with them. And in those few minutes I talked with him, he gave me more fatherly wisdom than my dad ever had."

Meghan circled a hand over her stomach. Doran was right. Richard and his wife probably would make good parents, and they'd raise her daughter in a Christian home. That was the ultimate litmus test for choosing a couple. One more item for her prayer list.

"If I agree with the adoption, will you let me be involved in choosing the parents?"

As much as she hated the thought of spending any more time with Doran, how could she deny him? If he wanted to be involved, she had to let him. She nodded. "I want you to help me."

Then they could say goodbye for good.


A BOTTLE ROCKET SQUEALED from a nearby home, a family getting an early start on their Independence Day celebration, as Richard shoved the lawnmower across his backyard, its steady drone calming his chaotic thoughts. Sheila seemed resigned to the fact that any tangible remnants of her past had been discarded, and she had no desire to begin a search for her parents. He wished she'd at least consider it. It would be the best way to free herself of the bad memories ... and her disdain.

But was he any better? He circled the mower around a silver maple, bumping over the shallow roots. He'd forgiven Marissa, the woman who'd deliberately robbed him of fatherhood. He had to forgive her daily, it seemed, as memories of their relationship butted into his bucolic life. If not for Marissa, he never would have driven that night, and Justin Keene would still be alive. If not for Marissa, Richard would never have fled New York City in the first place.

But then, he wouldn't have met Sheila. Thanks to Marissa.

So why did Manhattan's summons tempt him so? The longing went against everything he preached about in his business. To return there would be all about him, rather than living out his company motto Faith and Family First. Moving back to New York would mean abandoning his family when Sheila needed them the most, and God knew, Richard still needed his family.

He pushed the lawnmower faster, wanting to drive the thoughts from his head, wanting to fall to his knees and beg for forgiveness for his clear lack of contentment with his perfect life.

He brought his gaze to the deck as he approached it. Sheila was stretched out on a lounge chair wearing what he called the "swimsuit for his eyes only" and he grinned. Yeah, this truly was the perfect life, and he should be perfectly content.

Sheila flashed a smile as he pushed by. *Oh, yeah, I've got it good.* Thoughts of New York floated away, his gaze locked on his wife. The mower coughed, pffft, pffft, pffft, and he released the handle, shutting off the engine. Terrific. Now he'd have to waste the afternoon repairing—

"Richard!" Sheila screamed. She jumped up and wiped furiously at her belly.

Blood!

In seconds he was on the deck, fear tensing his muscles.

That fear turned to choked laughter, and he covered his mouth. The mangled remains of a garter snake and grass trimmings lay on the deck beside Sheila's chair.

So that's what happened to the lawn mower.

"This is not funny!"

He reached for her hand. "Oh, but I think it is." One should always be honest with their wife, shouldn't they? He pulled her close and kissed her.

She pushed him away and glared. "I'd almost swear you did that on purpose."

"Sweetheart, would I do that?"

Her raised eyebrows spoke her answer. "You clean up the deck. I need to shower."

The right side of his mouth tipped up. "Need any help?"

She threw him a flirting glare. "I think you've helped enough already." She nodded to the bloody snake. "Clean the deck ... first."

Grinning, he watched her enter the house and pass through the kitchen. The phone rang before she was out of sight and he spied her through the patio doors. She picked up the handset and her smile evaporated. Her face grew taut and she wiped at her eyes before slamming the receiver down.

Now what? He hurried into the house and stopped just inside the door.

"That was Stephen Peterson." She nodded to the phone.

He shook his head. There was only one Stephen Peterson he knew of, but a call from him made no sense. "Your father?"

Sheila picked at her manicured fingernails. "Yes, my father."

# CHAPTER *eight*

Nathan Brooks and his best friend entered the workshop on Lauren's property looking for his newly acquired "sister."

He mentally rolled his eyes. There was a concept he'd never get used to. He and Jon had a busy night planned, so Lauren better be ready to go. The machines were quiet and music played lightly in the background. He found her seated on a metal stool, her back to them. Safety glasses rested on her head and her unruly hair was busting out from behind her ears.

"Lauren." Nathan called to her.

She didn't even flinch. He gestured to Jon to follow him as he moved closer. "Lauren," he said again. No response. Was she deaf or what?

He placed his hand on her shoulder, and she tumbled off her stool, landing with a thump on the concrete floor. She looked up at him, mouth open and eyes wide and glassy, as if she were about to cry. Again. "We've been calling for you." He crinkled his mouth to show his irritation and crossed his arms at his chest, not bothering to help her up. Jon pushed him aside and offered a hand.

"One second." She accepted Jon's hand and stood, wiping dust from her backside. Keeping her gaze downward, as if she were afraid of him, she removed plugs from her ears. "Sorry, I couldn't hear you."

*Stupid!* He palmed the side of his head and studied the floor.

"Nah, I'm sorry. I didn't realize you had ear plugs in. The machines must get rather loud, huh?"

She nodded.

Didn't this girl have a voice? She'd been in their home three weeks already, but she'd barely said two words to anyone, except maybe to Jaclyn and his mom. Most of the time she spent hiding out in her bedroom, doing who knows what. Sure she was polite enough and helped his mom out, but she could at least talk once in a while. "Dad's been trying to call you, see how things are going. He was getting worried when you didn't answer, so he sent us over."

"I'm sorry, Nate. I couldn't hear the phone. I'll go call him." The girl appeared ready to cry again. Sheesh, it wasn't that big of a deal.

He touched her arm as she headed past him for the office. "I'll take care of it."

"Thanks, and I am really sorry."

*Talk to my face, not my feet.* "No prob. So, you almost finished here? Dad wants to know when to expect you."

"Half hour at the most. I have a few more parts to make then I'll be done." She picked up a metal cylinder from a table next to the machine and stared at it. "I'm glad your dad let me finish this final order. The guy was a good customer of Dad's, and Dad always wanted to treat him well."

Man, what was wrong with him? Her whole life had been turned upside down this last month, and all he could think of was what this was doing to him. If he weren't so grouchy all the time, maybe she'd loosen up a bit. "Does it feel good to be back out here?"

"I guess. Dad always let me do the simple parts." She put the part on the table, next to a set of blueprints.

"This is simple?" Jon examined the blueprint.

"Basically, yeah. I have to program the CNC and it does the rest."

72

"Is this the CNC?" Jon pointed to the grey machine in front of Lauren.

"Yeah."

"Okay, you two have lost me." Nathan crossed his arms. Lauren must be speaking Jon's language. They both wanted to go into engineering.

"Computerized Numerical Control." Jon glanced at the machine, then back at the blueprint, eyeing them as if they were a Lamborghini. "Can you show me how it works?"

"Sure." Lauren even smiled as she explained the process.

Had she smiled once since she moved in? Not that Nathan had seen. Figures Jon would be the one to break through. He seemed to have that effect on people.

"Cool." Jon picked up a metal part and rolled it around in his hand.

Eyes narrowing, Nathan studied his friend. The dude actually seemed to be impressed with Lauren. It had to be their mutual interest in engineering. Nothing more.

"Is this what you want to do?" Jon scanned the shop area.

"Make parts?" Lauren laughed.

She laughed! Nathan didn't realize she knew how.

"No way, although I'd like to design them. Actually, what I'd like to learn is drafting, to design molds."

"Molds?" Nathan wrinkled his nose. What did drafting have to do with mold?

"Yeah. One second." She hurried to her dad's office and returned with a plastic, multi-cylindered pencil holder. She rotated the piece as she talked. "I'd like to design the mold to make something like this or things like it. It's more of a challenge than putting numbers into a machine and watching the machine do the work."

"Cool." Jon took the pencil holder from Lauren. "Where are you going to school?"

"The technical college in Minneapolis, off I-94 and 394, by

the Sculpture Garden. They have one of the best programs in the state and a good placement rate."

Unbelievable. Nathan resisted rolling his eyes. In a few minutes, Jon had accomplished what Nathan's family had been trying to do since Lauren moved in. She was talking, the subject even seemed to energize her. Problem was, it seemed to energize Jon too.

"Studying design has given me a greater appreciation for everything God's made." Lauren held up the small metal part the machine ground out. It was a simple part, in the shape of a cylinder with a notch circled in the end. She pointed to the blueprint that explained how to create it. "See how complex the design is for this small, ordinary part, then think about the blueprint God used for creating the universe. Earth. Us—a constantly changing blueprint. No two trees are alike, no two snowflakes, no two people. It's all unique. All I want to do is learn to design a simple part that can be duplicated over and over again."

"Wow." Jon took the part from Lauren and turned it over in his hand. "I never thought of it that way."

Oh brother. These two were making Nathan nauseated. It was time to get out of here, and bring Jon back to reality. "Is there any way we could help you out so you can get done faster?"

"Sure. It's not very exciting, but it'll help." She pointed to the two dozen or so parts on the table. "These need to be deburred. That's what I was doing when you came in. Take a cotton swab and wipe out the metal shavings. Then I can deliver the parts." She turned her back to them and dragged her arm over her face. "After that I'll be done. Your dad can sell it all."

Sell it all ... Her dad's business. His machines. Her home.

And he'd complained about losing his bedroom. Talk about being a jerk! Well, he'd have the rest of the year to make it up to her.

RICHARD SIGHED WITH CONTENTMENT. The crescent moon seemed to be smiling at him and Sheila tonight. A breeze waltzed through the air, enough to chase some of July's humidity. The crackle of fire was always calming, and he needed that calm to get her to open up about her father.

Sheila sat in the lawn chair next to him, her eyes closed and her mouth curved slightly, but not really smiling. A week since her father had called, and she still refused to talk about it. All too often he'd caught her crying and trying to hide it. He didn't even get an eye roll when he brought up the names Hezekiah and Hephzibah. Hopefully soon he'd see her deep dimpled smile again, the one she gave freely, with no pain behind it. But that wouldn't happen if she continued to repress the anger toward her parents.

With a cricket chorus serenading them, he skewered two marshmallows on the end of a branch and held the marshmallows over the red embers. No phones ringing. No beepers buzzing. Only God's whispers in the breathy wind.

"Remember the first time we did this?" Richard rotated the stick and peeked over at his wife. Ah, there was a smile. Not the one he longed to see, but a smile nonetheless.

"I thought you were crazy, dragging me out into the middle of the woods at midnight—"

"It wasn't quite midnight."

"—through knee-deep snow. Not to mention it was only twenty degrees."

"It was beautiful wasn't it?" He pulled his stick back and studied the marshmallows. *Perfect.* He sandwiched the marshmallows in between two fudge-frosted shortbread cookies. Marshmallow and chocolate dripped over the side as he handed Sheila the finished s'more. She groaned her appreciation as he stuck two more marshmallows on the end of his whittled stick and then lowered it to the fire.

"I was actually enjoying that evening until you started

preaching at me. If we hadn't been in the middle of nowhere, I would have been gone."

"I planned it that way."

"I don't doubt that."

"Was I that bad?"

"No, just my first impression, but you taught and didn't push." She cupped her hand over his. "You explained what happened that brought about your change. I appreciated that."

His change. His return to his faith after twenty years of running from it. The change that had helped Sheila know Christ. The change that allowed them to be together today.

"You made me want to learn more. I still do."

"I like learning with you." He raised the stick. The marshmallows weren't ready yet. And this was not the right time to bring up her dad's phone call. That would probably make her smile disappear for another week. He returned the stick back to the flames.

To be honest, there probably was no good time, and putting it off was only making both of them miserable. "Are you ready to talk about your father's phone call?" There. The words were finally out and he couldn't take them back.

"I don't know." She gripped his hand tighter. "I'm sorry. I know I've been grouchy. Talking to my father again, it's something I thought I'd never have to deal with. They were out of my life. They've been out of it for eighteen years without a single bit of correspondence. I've gone on without them and have been happy. Now, out of the blue I get a call? It's a complication I don't need."

"It won't go away by not talking about it." He rotated his stick and frowned at the brown bubbles on the marshmallow. Too close to the fire.

"He wants to see me again." She wiped her cheek. "He saw the article in the Minneapolis paper. It caught his eye because, for a brief second, he thought it was an old picture of Mother. My hyphenated name under the picture convinced him it was me. You were right. I should have dumped 'Peterson' altogether. I still don't know why I kept it."

"Could have something to do with that independent streak of yours." A slight smile emerged on her face. Good. He could go on. "Do they live around here?"

"Arizona. One of those retirement villages. He said they still subscribed to the Minneapolis paper to keep tabs on what's going on up here. I'm surprised it matters."

"I see." A lot could have changed in those eighteen years of absence. "What do you want to do?" He knew what he wanted her to do. Maybe her parents were sorry for what they'd done to her. Maybe they'd want to be a part of their grandchild's life. He couldn't imagine grandparents not being drawn to their own grandchild. Sheila should give them the chance.

She shook her head. "One moment I want to see them, to ask why they abandoned me. Then I think I'd be better off if I ignored his phone call and pretended it never happened. Then, part of me wants to see them and hug them and show you off."

"Show me off, huh?"

"To show them how well I've done without them."

"To be loved."

She covered her face with her hands.

He dropped the roasting stick and knelt in front of her, taking her hands in his. "Hon, you don't need their acceptance. You've got me, my family. You've got a heavenly Father who loves you more than we can imagine."

"Heavenly Father." She yanked her hands from his. "I was to address my dad as Father. Not Dad, especially not Daddy. Father and Mother. Somehow it made them more impersonal. Maybe that's the way they were, the way they wanted it to be. When you say 'heavenly Father' it doesn't conjure up a positive image. How do I imagine a loving 'heavenly Father' when the father I knew didn't love me at all?"

"My dad loves you."

"I know." She shook her head. "Let's drop the subject."

"But you need to talk about it, don't you see? Your father's call was an answer to prayer. We didn't find that box of memories your parents left, but God gave you something better: a chance for reconciliation."

"Hah! That's just it. I don't think I want reconciliation." Her voice rose in pitch. "I don't want them in my life. All I wanted were some mementos, maybe my high school report cards, maybe some of the music I grew up with, a baby picture. The good memories, those things my parents weren't involved in."

He grasped her hands again and focused on her eyes. "Honey, you've got to forgive them. I hate what this whole thing has done to you lately. I almost wish Mom would've kept that memory box. It's given me too much grief."

"Oh, you poor thing." Sarcasm laced her voice as she yanked her hands from his grip. "I'm so sorry I've been such a pain to you lately."

"That's not what I meant."

"Yes it is. You want to fix me, make everything in here nice and tidy." She pounded her heart with a clenched fist. "It's not neat and tidy, and seeing my parents won't change a thing. You want me to forgive them? Fine." She stood and raised her chin so her eyes were focused on the sky. "Mother. Father." She yelled into the wind. "I forgive you for not loving me, for deserting me, for leaving me broken." She brought her head down and glared in his direction. "Happy now?"

"Sheila."

"No." She held up two clenched fists. "This discussion is over. I've made up my mind. I'm not going to see them. I don't want to talk about them again. Can you understand that?"

He stared at the dying fire. This was what he got for pushing. He should know better.

"I'm going to bed." She strode toward the house.

"Sheila!" He hurried after her and grabbed her arm. "Please, don't run away from this."

She looked down at his hand then glared up at him. "Let it be, Richard."

He let go of her and she disappeared into the house. The last time he'd seen that anger was right before they broke up—nearly a year ago. The three months without her, following the break up, had been the loneliest months of his life. That would not happen again.

He scanned the stars. "Father, she's yours."

SHEILA LOOKED IN HER full-length mirror and a wild woman with red eyes and smeared mascara stared back. Not the confident and composed, elegant and accomplished woman she had groomed herself into, the façade she'd created for others to see, the veneer her husband easily saw through. It was frightening how transparent she'd become to him, bringing out the worst in her.

Why did her parents still retain the power to reduce her to the level of an insecure adolescent still yearning for love? It was as if she was still holding out her report card with straight As for the sixth time in a row, hoping for praise and hearing "Just keep it up" instead. No pats on the back. No "Great job!" No "I'm proud of you." If their approval didn't truly matter, she wouldn't have become upset. Richard obviously knew that. How could she convince him to stay away from that issue without resorting to the lunacy she'd so intensely displayed moments ago?

"I'm sorry." His unexpected voice startled her. He stood in the doorway, propped against the doorframe with his hands placed securely in his front pockets. His head was bowed, but his eyes peered upward. "I shouldn't have pushed."

Great. Now she felt guilty. Insecure and guilty. She could blame her parents for that as well. Her arms hung heavy at her sides, pulling down her shoulders. "I'm sorry too. I overreacted."

His head rose a bit, as did his lips. "Just a tad." He raised his hand, holding his thumb and forefinger an inch apart.

"But that doesn't mean I've changed my mind." She needed to ensure that her scene would not be reenacted. The only way to do that was to evade the topic altogether. "I'm abiding by their wishes and staying out of their lives."

He nodded, setting his mouth in a straight line, acquiescing almost too quickly. Clearly, it wasn't over for him. He approached her and circled his arms around her, and then he crooked his finger beneath her chin and tipped it up. "I want you to be happy." His other hand caressed her stomach. "I want us to be happy."

"I promise." She covered his hand with hers and followed the caress. "We will be." She would keep that promise without the support of her parents.

NATHAN STRETCHED HIS ARMS behind him on the beach blanket and leaned back on them. Sitting in the mid-July sun with Jon, watching bikini-clad girls play beach volleyball, was everything he'd imagined it to be. And as a bonus, he didn't have to watch Jaclyn today either. He'd always been responsible for his little sister, putting a serious crimp on his fun.

He might even tell Lauren thanks for the afternoon.

The ball screamed over the net, angling toward the sand, but was dug up by a player unafraid to get dirty. Lexi. Man, what a catch she'd be. Authentic. Played to win.

Experienced.

Exactly the type of girl his dad preached against.

The type every teenage boy dreamed of dating.

What Nathan would give to go on one date with her, but with his goody-two-shoes reputation, he didn't stand a chance.

He frowned at his hair-free, tan-resistant chest. He'd bulked up a little bit over the summer, though. Helping his dad in his construction business had toned his muscles somewhat. Not too bad, for a high school kid that is. Now if only Lexi would notice.

She jumped up, her arms straight above her head and blocked an attempted spike, scoring a point for her team.

"Yeah Lex!"

She glanced his way, drew her red-streaked blonde hair into a ponytail, and threw a sideways smile.

She'd noticed him! That was a miracle in itself.

"Hey, doofus." Jon's elbow jabbed his side.

"What do you think you're doing?" Nathan growled.

"Don't even think of her."

"What? Who?" He hadn't been that obvious, had he?

"Dude, she's trouble. You know it too."

Nate felt his mouth slant. "Yeah? So?" Maybe a little trouble, now and then, was what he needed. Maybe he was tired of being the good kid all the time. "You don't have to worry. She's way out of my league."

"So why does she keep staring your way?"

"She is? Really?" Nate almost gave himself whiplash spinning his attention back to the game. To Lexi. She *was* looking at him. His lips curled up, and he knew his pale face wouldn't hide his blush. She winked and turned away. She was playing him. Had to be. Bad girls like Lexi never went for guys like him.

He reached into a cooler, dug out a bottled water and a handful of ice cubes. Anything to help him cool down. He rubbed the ice cubes over face and chest as Lexi leaped and spiked the ball out of reach from her opponent. Game and match.

Man, she was something.

He jumped up and whooped. Jon got up too, but was silent. So what? If Jon preferred the Borin' Lauren type, he could have her.

The players ran up the beach toward the Food Hut.

All but Lexi.

She walked toward Nathan, hips swaying. Her string bikini left little to the imagination, exposing a rose tattoo on her breast and a diamond in her naval.

His throat constricted and any intelligent thoughts fled.

She tucked hair behind an ear revealing several piercings. Not that her tattoos and piercings were any different from other girls he'd gone out with. It was commonplace in his school—just not with him. Never with him.

"Hey, Nate."

She knew his name!

"Hey there." That's all he could think of saying? Man, he was as bad as Lauren.

"Got some room on that towel?" She threw him that sideways grin again.

"Sure." His voice squeaked as if he were going through puberty again. He scooted to the edge of the towel and his heart raced like NASCAR when he saw how little room was left.

She took a seat beside him, leaving no space between them. Rumor had it she was fast, but this? Sweet!

He felt a tap on his shoulder and looked back. Jon stood there, arms crossed, frowning like he was Nate's dad. Nate jerked his head slightly, trying to give Jon the hint.

"Whatever." Jon rolled his eyes. "I'm gonna help Lauren."

"You do that." Relief washed over Nate as Jon walked away. Maybe it was time to reevaluate some of his parents' expectations. Maybe it was time to shed some of that good boy image. Lexi might be just the one to help.

## CHAPTER *nine*

Richard paged through the client's folder then stared at his computer screen. Jumbled numbers glared back. Nothing was making sense. He threw the folder onto his desk, scattering the pages. Terrific. One more mess to clean up. Last night's argument was mess enough. Their first disagreement since they'd been married, and it was making him miserable. There couldn't be a worse way to begin the work week. It could only get better from here. Right?

The beep of the intercom intruded on his misery. "Yes, Emma."

"Dalton Andrews from ACM Technologies is on line one."

Dalton? His stomach churned. The week just got worse. This wasn't a mess. No, catastrophe described it better. What he didn't need right now was a phone call from the man who'd long coveted Richard's position at ACM then led the charge to get Richard fired two years ago. Fifteen years of superior service to the company, fifteen years of praise and accolades, and they dump him to protect their reputation. And Dalton got a promotion.

Yet, hindsight told Richard ACM had made the right decision. Someone who kills a teenager, even if it was an accident, didn't deserve a Vice Presidency. He'd shown no mercy to Justin. ACM showed no mercy to him. Fitting.

The intercom buzzed again. "Shall I tell Mr. Andrews you'll

return his call?"

"No. I'll take it," he said between gritted teeth. But, he'd make Dalton wait a bit longer. He leaned back in his chair and watched the second hand of his wall clock make a full rotation. Then he gathered the papers strewn on his desktop and made certain all the edges lined up perfectly before tucking them into the folder.

No more delaying. Clearing his throat, he punched the button for line one. "Dalton, what do you want?" Not exactly professional, but hopefully it got Richard's point across: Leave him alone.

"I get the impression that you're not too happy to hear from me."

"You figured that out all on your own. Brilliant man." Richard sat straight up and planted both feet on the carpet. "I'm busy. Get to the point so I can return to work."

He heard Dalton clear his throat. "The point is, ACM wants you back and would make it very worth your while to return."

Richard laughed out loud. It had to pain Dalton to come begging for his services. "They've already offered the world and I've turned it down."

"Don't be so quick to shrug this off, Brooks. The opportunity won't present itself again. At least agree to meet with us, listen to our proposal."

The word "no" stuck to his tongue as an inner nudging urged him to go hear what they had to say. The nudge couldn't be from God. He wouldn't want Richard to return to New York. Wasn't that the life God had urged him over and over again to flee? "Give me a moment." A one-on-one with God couldn't wait.

"It's all I've got."

Right. Richard pushed the *hold* button, brought the receiver to his chest, and stared at his ceiling. "What do I do?" No audible voice answered, but the prompt remained in his heart. "Are you sure?" *Please say no.* But *Go* whispered through his thoughts. Richard pinched his eyes shut and slumped in his chair. If that's what God wanted, then so be it.

Richard brought the receiver to his ear and pressed Dalton's line. "Let me check my schedule." He pulled up his calendar on the computer and rubbed his chin. "So, you've got a sinking ship and you need someone to stop the leaking?"

"Listen, Brooks, I don't have to take any crap from you. It's bad enough they made me call."

Richard sighed. Dalton was right. Placing this phone call was probably one of the most difficult tasks the man had been assigned. Besides that, Richard's attitude toward the man was anything but Christlike. "Sorry. That was uncalled for." He studied his agenda for the week. "Thursday's the first day I can free up, but I need to talk it over with my wife first." No, he didn't always clear his business travel with Sheila first, but this was different.

Dalton coughed and Richard couldn't hold back a smile. No one from ACM would believe he was married, that he'd settled down. Watching their reaction to his news would be worth the flight alone.

"Fine. Clear it with the little woman then be here Thursday. Noon. You won't regret it."

Richard hung up and a fist-sized lump filled his throat. Why had he said yes? Did God really want him to go back to New York, the place where, for Richard, God had disappeared? He'd loved his employer, his position, and the fringe benefits that had swallowed his integrity. What if he hadn't changed?

He picked up the framed photo from his desk, the one taken at the local amusement park, of him making bunny ears behind Sheila's head. The day he admitted he'd fallen in love. The line of women he'd dated before Sheila had convinced him unselfish love didn't exist. Marissa had been the queen of selfishness.

Thinking of her gave him the shivers. He'd forgiven her for what she'd done to him, for aborting his child, but that didn't mean he wanted to see her again. Yet going to New York almost guaranteed he would. His latest research of his old employer showed that she was back at the Manhattan office tower. Yes, it was a large building, but he couldn't imagine Marissa missing an opportunity to gloat over his dismissal over a year ago. Could he see her and not dredge up the hate he once felt toward her? Was the hate really expunged from his heart or was it lying dormant waiting to erupt?

Was meeting with ACM a date with the devil? Logically, it sure looked like it. So why couldn't he shake the feeling that the call to return had come from God?

He placed the portrait back on his desk. Maybe he was called to show people the miracle God could work in someone's heart. No one could deny he'd changed. Or maybe he was to set the example for Sheila. If he wanted Sheila to meet her past and stop burying it, perhaps it was time for him to do the same.

RICHARD CIRCLED HIS ARM around Sheila's shoulders as they silently walked the asphalt path winding along the Mississippi River. It had been a mere fifteen months since they'd gone on their first date, then returned to Sheila's condo—now their second home—taking the same walkway they used now. On that date, they had each donned figurative masks to cover the darkness in their respective pasts. Today those pasts were no longer cloaked in darkness, but they were pasts still begging, pleading to be dealt with. Richard had thought they'd already done that long ago, but Sheila's withdrawal, coupled with his undesired yearnings to return to New York, proved that their pasts still retained an unnatural grip on their lives.

And now he had to tell her, he was going back to New York.

"What are you thinking?" she asked as they walked past the modern Guthrie Theater.

He shrugged. "About you, your father, New York."

"Hmm. I'm not the only one struggling with their past."

"No. No, you're not."

"Want to talk about it?"

He sighed. "No, but I will anyway, once I get my thoughts straightened out." He focused on the renovated Stone Arch Bridge which curved gracefully over the Mississippi. Decades ago this bridge carried trains, now it was repurposed as a walking, biking path.

Had his purpose changed over the years? At one time his mission had been to conquer Manhattan, and he'd achieved that goal only to remain unfulfilled. And then that city, combined with his prodigal lifestyle, took its revenge. He was no longer the bright-eyed farm boy who'd escaped to New York, or the defeated man who fled the city. Was God calling him back to Manhattan to carry out his true purpose, this time doing it God's way? That answer didn't sit well, either.

Keeping his arm around Sheila's waist, he rested against the bridge's wall then embraced her tight against his side and looked out at the cityscape. "Don't you love how this area merges past and present together?"

"What do you mean?"

He shrugged. "Look at the Guthrie, such a modern structure positioned among all these century-old buildings. But somehow it works. Then you've got the Washburn A Mill. Over a hundred years ago, it was the most modern and technologically advanced mill in the country. As times changed it fell into ruin, then was mostly destroyed by a fire. Now it's repurposed as a hands-on, learning museum for all ages."

A remainder of a crumbling wall still faced the Mississippi.

The broken past had been restored.

Was that possible for him and Sheila too?

He kissed her temple, and she sighed. One of contentment.

It was time to break his news.

"ACM called me." He stared outward, trying to speak without emotion. Sheila's grip grew stronger, but she remained silent. "I'm going on Thursday."

She pulled from his embrace and stepped aside. "Why?"

"I'm not sure." He kept his tone flat. "I just know I'm supposed to go."

"Supposed to? According to whom?" He wasn't sure what he heard in her voice. Anger? No. Frustration. Maybe.

"I think God wants me to go."

"Oh." Definitely sadness. "We're not moving."

"No. No way." At least he hoped that wasn't why he was being called to return.

"Then why? Is it strictly business?"

"It's business, yes, but I'd be lying if I said that's all it was. Financially speaking, working with ACM would be a prudent business venture."

"But ...?"

"But, I don't know, maybe I've been too resentful of the way I was treated. Maybe I need to go back and say I'm sorry. Maybe I'm supposed to forgive them." Or perhaps it was nothing that altruistic, it could be he simply longed for the life he left behind. He prayed that wasn't it. "Part of me is energized to return. It was a good job. A great life, until ..." Until Marissa. Until the accident. "But then, part of me gets sick to my stomach thinking about it."

Facing him, Sheila took both of his hands and spoke softly. "You're thinking about Marissa."

A mere four months married, and Sheila could already read his thoughts.

He nodded.

"Tell me about her." No jealousy tinged her voice. Maybe sympathy. But talk to his wife about his former lover?

"Was she pretty?"

Pretty? No. He pinched the bridge of his nose. Stunning was more accurate, with her long, shiny, blue-black hair and the high cheek bones she claimed were courtesy of her Cherokee heritage. "Yeah, she was pretty." Although her demanding personality had dulled much of the beauty. How sad that her personality hadn't mattered to him.

"Did you love her?" Sheila's thumb caressed the back of his hand.

Hardly. He hadn't known what love was. "Why let love get in the way of good sex?" He looked down and squeezed his eyes shut. How could he be so crass to the woman he loved? "I'm sorry." He raised his head.

And her eyes met his.

Her finger traced the outline of his jaw. "I think you did love her."

"No—"

She held her finger at his lips. "Let me finish."

He sighed and nodded.

"I know how strongly you feel about her."

"It's not love." Far from it.

"No. But there's a very fine line separating love and hate. Apathy doesn't make the division."

That was certainly true. When he thought of Marissa, apathy was no where around.

"When she hurt you, you crossed that line."

He kicked at the stone bridge with his heel. This was not a conversation he wanted to have. Marissa was a topic best avoided. Whatever his feelings had once been were now obliterated. He grasped Sheila's other hand and squeezed. "I love you."

Sheila stepped closer. "I know, I have no doubts, but don't you think it's important to acknowledge the truth? Maybe those hurt feelings will fade."

"Like yours have?"

She dropped his hands. "We're not talking about me."

He raised his palms signaling a truce.

With a sigh, she leaned against him and whispered. "I think she's why you need to go."

He rested his chin on her shoulder, trying to be honest with himself. "Maybe. I'm not sure. I don't want to see her or face all the other memories, to see my mistakes with my new eyes. I don't know how I'll react, but I know I need to go."

"Then go."

"Will you come with me? We could stay in New York till Sunday, catch a show, maybe a concert, visit the Keenes?"

"Broadway, huh?" Dimples appeared on her cheeks.

His heart flipped seeing her smile. He prayed he'd always feel this way, that he'd never take their love for granted. "On or off. Your choice."

"Maybe take me to that little Italian place we went to on our honeymoon?"

"Wherever you want to go."

"I guess I could come."

A breath escaped his throat. Hopefully history would release its hold once he stared it down and, in following his example, Sheila would find confidence to confront her past too.

MEGHAN HELD THE EARRINGS up against her cheeks and studied herself in the mirror, ignoring the home phone's ring. Perfect. The ideal complement to the maternity dress she'd purchased specifically for tonight. That she was getting this dressed up for Shane, and feeling excited about doing so, was a testament to how much she had changed over the last months.

She attacked a stray curl with her flat iron, straightening it. A few years back, Shane had been little more than her brother's annoying friend who'd constantly teased her about her red hair and freckles. *Strawberry-blonde*, she'd always reminded him. There was a world of difference between strawberry-blonde and "red."

Her stomach fluttered at the thought of seeing Shane again. Like her, he had matured since Justin died. He still had a great sense of humor, but he was no longer the clown who had complemented her far-too-serious brother. Shane never used to care about his appearance. Garish Hawaiian shirts and scraggly, uncombed hair had defined his look. What others thought about him never mattered, and he probably dressed that way to make his point. She couldn't wait to see him dressed up in a suit.

He wouldn't win any "beauty" contests either. Skinny, a nose that was too long for his face, and thin receding hair. None of that mattered to her anymore. Shane was mature, caring, fun, supportive.

Forgiving.

Exactly what she needed.

Barefooted, she hurried down the hall and peeked through the living room blinds. Not here yet.

"Meghan." Her mom's voice had an upward lilt to it.

Meghan looked over her shoulder at her mom.

"No Shane yet?"

"Nope. Should be here anytime."

Her mom peeked through the blinds. "That was Richard Brooks on the phone."

Meghan's stomach did a little dive. No matter how hard she tried to think positively about the man, her first reaction was always negative. How could she even consider him adopting her baby?

Because like her, he'd changed. And now he was exactly the type of father she wanted for her daughter. Why was it so hard to let go of the past? "What did he want?"

"He and his wife are going to be in town this weekend. They want to stop in on Sunday. It would be a good time for you to talk to them. Doran will be here by then, won't he?"

"Yes." Her joy from seconds ago fell to the floor and splattered. The two people who'd wounded her heart beyond healing would be here. Together.

"Doran should be in town on Friday." Meghan dropped into the recliner. He would be in town, staying with her mom's friend, interning with a congressman. That liar of a boyfriend working for a professional liar. Doran would make a good politician someday.

"Why don't you call him? Invite him over for lunch on Sunday? The Brookses will be here then."

The doorbell rang.

"Can it wait for tomorrow?" Meghan waddled toward the door and slipped on her sandals. She had to get out of the house now. "Doran's probably on the road. Another day shouldn't hurt."

"Tomorrow's fine." Her mother opened the door. "Please come in, Shane."

Meghan bit her lip trying to keep her smile down. Shane looked sweet in a suit coat and tie. An evening with him, and she'd forget all about the dreaded lunch on Sunday.

## CHAPTER *ten*

Richard pushed open the oversized doors to ACM Technologies' lobby and immediately felt the stares, heard the whispers, saw the raised eyebrows. Part of him had hoped that, in his absence, he'd been forgotten. Clearly, that hadn't happened.

He clutched Sheila's hand as they passed between marble pillars that stretched up to coved ceilings, and through an open lobby paved with marble. A far cry from the aging concrete and brick, former warehouse-building where Sheila now worked, and where he'd met her.

He'd hurt a lot of these people gawking at him. But it was the attention of the women that made him most uncomfortable, especially with Sheila at his side. He couldn't count how many of these women he'd dated, not caring about the hurt he left behind.

Including the woman strutting toward him. She was still striking with copper hair that waved down to the small of her back, and a face covered in freckles she'd chosen not to hide. But she was no longer appealing.

"I heard rumors that you were returning." Rayna touched his arm.

Tensing up, he pushed her hand away and wrapped his other arm tightly around Sheila's waist. "I'm married."

"So the rumors are true." Rayna stepped back, crossed her hands over her chest, and laughed. "When did that ever stop you?"

"I never ..." He clamped his mouth shut and practically dragged Sheila to the elevator. He'd drawn the line at dating married women, but he owed no excuses or explanations. Let them think what they wanted. He knew the truth. God knew the truth.

The elevator became his refuge. Perspiring, he sagged against the wall and focused on the low-napped carpet. Was Sheila uncomfortable? Jealous? Angry? "I'm sorry, Sheila." He swallowed the Jurassic-sized knot in his throat and peered up.

Sheila's smirk grew into a wide grin.

"You're enjoying this, aren't you?" And he loved seeing her smile. Perhaps it had been the right choice to bring her along today.

"Immensely." Sheila tugged on his jacket lapels. "You weren't kidding about being a playboy, were you?"

"You would think I've been away long enough for them to forget."

"Sweetheart, you're unforgettable. Remember, I tried once, and it didn't work."

"We'll take another way out." He stood straight and curved his hands on Sheila's hips. "It's a miracle in itself that you've made me a one-woman man." He kissed her, relishing the minty flavor of her love as the elevator rose to the sixtieth floor.

The doors slid open and Richard glanced at his watch. Thirty minutes to spare, as he had planned. Keeping Sheila's hand in his, he led her down a carpeted hallway to a reception area. A plump woman with silver-gray hair and black-framed glasses sat at the reception desk, fingers dancing over her keyboard.

"Verna?"

The woman looked away from her work. Her eyes grew wide and she grinned, but didn't stop typing. "Richard Brooks. Land's sakes, it is you."

He returned her grin. How he'd missed this lady.

"I heard you were coming today." Her southern drawl still sounded heavenly in the sea of New Yorkers. "I was hoping I'd get to see you, then that old sourpuss of a boss of mine gave me this project today that was due yesterday." She struck one final key on the computer and stood. He walked around her desk and drew her into a hug.

She leaned back and braced her hands on his shoulders. "My word, don't you look good."

"So do you, Verna." He waved to Sheila to come around the desk. "There's someone I want you to meet."

Verna's eyebrows arched.

He grasped Sheila's hand and pulled her to his side, keeping her hand in his. "Sheila, this is Verna, my assistant for the duration of my time at ACM. She's the one who actually runs this place. Without her I'd have been an average Joe. She made me look good."

"Oh, pshaw. You know that's not true. This man here was the backbone of this company. When he left, well, I'm sure you've seen how this company's fared. Finally our dear CEO decided to grovel a bit and bring you back."

"I'm not coming back."

"You're not?" Verna pouted and braced her hands on her ample hips.

"Nope." He felt Sheila's eyes boring into him. His pronouncement would be a discussion for later. The decision had become reality when he passed through the lobby. He had no desire to return to New York. His yearnings of late had most likely been nothing more than nostalgic longing. Maybe that's why God had nudged him to come, to remove any hint of desire for his old life. If that had been God's purpose, it worked.

"I wouldn't be so quick to decide if I were you." Verna tapped a stack of paper on her desk. "You haven't even heard our offer yet. I know what's in it. I typed it up. I don't know how you could turn it down."

"Let's say that I have other priorities now. Getting booted out of here was the best thing that ever happened to me. Got me to straighten up my act, find God again, meet my wife."

"Your wife?" Verna pressed her chin to her chest and adjusted her glasses.

He nodded and grinned. "Verna, this is my amazing wife, Sheila Brooks."

Sheila offered her hand.

"I don't do handshakes, young lady." Verna wrapped Sheila in a hug then stepped back and shook her head. "You're married?"

He nodded.

"Over four months." Sheila held out her ring hand.

"My word, isn't that a beauty?" The ring wasn't ostentatious. Neither of them had wanted that. Instead they'd nestled small diamonds among a weave of three narrow bands, two yellow gold and one white gold. "You must be something else, young lady, if you got this boy to settle down."

He kissed Sheila's cheek. "She is."

"I didn't think I'd ever see the day."

"Me neither, but God had other plans."

"He most certainly does. Well, I'll be." Verna's smile became a frown and she propped fists on her hips. "So you went and got yourself married, and didn't even let me know."

"I'd severed all my ties to this place, unfortunately that included you."

"You just knot those ties back together, young man. I need to know what's all going on in your life."

"In that case, I have more news."

"More than you getting married?" Verna crossed her hands over her chest. "That's about all my heart will take for one day."

"I won't tell you we're expecting a baby then."

"A baby? My Richard's gonna be a papa? It's about time, young man. You make sure y'all send me pictures won't you now?"

"I'll make sure of it." Sheila took Verna's hand. "He's always spoken very highly of you. I can see why."

"This boy was like my son. My heart broke when he had that accident and then left without as much as a goodbye. It blesses me to see things have turned out well for you."

"I've been blessed too." He kissed Sheila's cheek then nodded toward his old office door. "Who's taken over?"

"That would be Dalton. Dalton Andrews. Remember him?"

He huffed. "Of course."

"That man, he's an arrogant one. Makes me miss you all the more. Are you certain you're not coming back?"

"Positive." He pointed to the closed door. "Is Dalton in?"

"He's down at the conference room, putting final touches on our presentation to woo you back."

"Mind if I take a peek into my old office? Show Sheila the view?"

"You go right on ahead. Take your time."

"Thanks, Verna." He squeezed Verna's hand then led Sheila into his former office. He watched peripherally for her reaction. It was as expected.

"Wow." She gaped at the two walls of windows framing the Statue of Liberty in one and downtown Manhattan in another. "You gave this up," she said softly, as if in awe.

The view was spectacular, but that wasn't close to reason enough to come back. "You should see it at night. At home the stars are in the sky. Here, the lights surround us. It's unbelievable."

"You'd described this before, but I never grasped all that you achieved."

"And threw away."

"Think of what you've gained."

"You." He patted her stomach. "Slugger." He breathed in deeply as he encompassed Sheila in his arms and stared in her eyes. "This is nostalgia. I've got everything I want—everything I need—back in Minnesota."

"Remember that." She poked his chest.

"With you, I could never forget."

RICHARD SAID HIS GOODBYES to Verna then escorted Sheila to the elevator. All he had to do now was go to the business meeting and tell ACM "no," then he could treat Sheila to an evening she'd never forget. One he'd never forget either.

As he'd hoped, the elevator was empty when they stepped in. "I'm feeling a little nostalgic." He took Sheila's hand and pulled her tight against him.

"What could—"

He pressed his lips to hers. He'd done his share of making out in these elevators, but this was much more fun. God was reminding him what was truly important in life. Even Sheila was loosening up. For the first time in weeks, she seemed to forget about her lost belongings. The forgetting wouldn't be permanent, but he'd enjoy it while it lasted.

The elevator door opened and someone snickered. Dalton Andrews waited outside the door, smirking. "You haven't changed, Brooks."

"Yes, I have." Richard grinned. "This is my wife."

"Why don't you have your lovely wife join us?" Another voice spoke. Richard and Sheila stepped out of the elevator and came face to face with Mr. Entenza, the company CEO. He gestured to the conference room.

"Wouldn't you rather wait out here?" Richard whispered to Sheila and nodded toward cushioned leather chairs outside the conference room.

"I would love to join you." Sheila led the way into the room.

Richard shook his head. She was enjoying herself far too much.

They sat at a mahogany table surrounded by ACM executives, including Richard's former intern, Connor August. Now there was someone who could make a difference for ACM. If Dalton Andrews got out of the way.

Entenza sat at the head, a manila folder in front of him. "Welcome back, Richard, and I'd like to welcome your lovely wife, Ms. Sheila Peterson-Brooks, an executive for Wharton Sports based out of Minneapolis."

Richard's stomach curdled. What was Entenza doing with information on Sheila?

The CEO folded his hands on the table, a counterfeit smile secured on his face, and directed his gaze at Sheila,

To think Richard had once been duped by that smile.

"We are delighted that you have joined us today, Mrs. Brooks."

*I'll bet you are.* Richard clenched his fists in his lap.

"We have a very enticing offer to make to your husband, one I'm presuming he cannot refuse, and with you here I'd personally like to sweeten the proposal. We are prepared to offer you an executive sales position at ACM Technologies for a substantial increase over your current salary, along with the more than generous offer we are about to present to your husband. I'm certain you won't refuse us."

"She's not interested." Richard's cheek muscles flexed.

"Let your lady speak."

"His *lady* says we're not interested." Sheila folded her hands on the table and returned Entenza's stare.

*That's my girl.* Richard held in a grin. Entenza had no chance.

"You are aware—" Entenza leaned in closer "—that Mr. Brooks' work here was beyond superlative."

Richard's eyes narrowed. "I'll remind you that you were the ones who suggested I resign."

"A tactical error on our part." The CEO sat back and stole a glance at a scowling Dalton Andrews.

Richard held back a smile. So, he'd never really been

replaced. "That notwithstanding, we came today to discuss what ACM needs to do to affect a change in the company's bottom line, and I'm willing to offer my expertise as a subcontractor only. If you aren't satisfied with my offer, we'll excuse ourselves." Richard took Sheila's hand and prepared to stand.

"That ... will not be necessary." Entenza retreated into his chair back and handed Richard and Sheila a copy of their proposal.

Richard didn't bother scrutinizing the documents. "My company, Integrity Business Solutions, is prepared to work one-on-one with Connor August, to conclude his training." Training that had been suspended along with Richard's job termination. "He's got the skills and savvy you need to affect a positive turnaround for the company." Richard's gaze met Connor's. The younger man's eyes were wide as quarters. Richard nodded his assurance. Dalton's face was turning red, witnessing the underling's apparent crowning.

"You haven't even looked at our offer." Entenza's voice held a hint of a whine.

"I don't need to." Richard pushed the contract away. "I've found my home in Minnesota, and I'm not leaving. Money isn't an issue."

The CEO drummed his fingers on the table. "You'll work with Connor?"

"I will. That's the best I can offer you, and that's pretty darned good. Give him the same leeway you gave me. Listen to him. If you don't, I'm confident I could make him an offer equally tempting." He might make the offer anyway, if Connor were interested.

Entenza shook his head. "We were foolish to let you go."

Richard raised an eyebrow. "I know." He stood and held out his hand for Sheila. "Time to leave."

"Gladly." Sheila squeezed his hand then let go and led him out the door. It took all his strength to keep from doing a little dance and shouting out "Thank you, God." He could fly home content that he'd faced down the past and won. It no longer called to him. It no longer chained him to regret. He could move on—

"Richard?"

The woman's silky voice froze his thoughts and his pulse quickened. He'd lied to himself. He hadn't confronted the past. Far from it.

He grasped Sheila's hand, looked to his left and saw her, that piece of his history that still held a vise-like grip on his heart. "Marissa."

## CHAPTER *eleven*

M arissa hadn't changed. She was still as stunning as she had been two years ago. Right before she shattered his dreams of being a father and sent him running.

Justin Keene hadn't seen him coming and paid for that with his life.

Richard grasped Sheila's hand tighter, and words jumbled in his head. If only Marissa had never told him about the baby. If only he'd been able to convince her to keep it. Justin might still be alive.

"Hi, I'm Sheila, Richard's wife." Sheila extended her hand, helping him through the awkward silence. The woman he loved shook the hand of the woman he despised. Months ago he'd gotten on his knees and told God he forgave her. Had he forgiven her, or had those words been empty?

Brows raised, Marissa's focus darted between Richard and Sheila, settling on Sheila. "I'm Marissa. I'm ..."

*Richard's ex-lover. Should have been mother to his child.* He blocked out Marissa's voice, not wanting to hear how she described their once-tumultuous relationship.

"You're still looking fine." Her voice came through his murky thoughts.

So was she, even better than he recalled. Far too attractive. Droplets of perspiration tickled the back of his neck. Maybe he'd changed less than he'd led himself to believe. Maybe Sheila was right about his feelings for Marissa. Two years of antipathy toward her had skewed his recollection of them being together.

Seeing her now, he remembered why he had been drawn to her in the first place, why the gossip chain had declared them to be the perfect couple. Like Barbie and Ken. It was true. They had been the perfect superficial couple.

Had been.

Today he refused to give her the satisfaction of a returned compliment. He smiled politely, pushing back the unwanted feelings. "How can I help you, Marissa?" Good. Keep it businesslike. Withhold emotion.

"Do you have a few minutes to talk?"

Sure he had the time, but it was time meant for Sheila. He made a show of glancing at his watch.

"I promise I won't be long."

He combed his fingers through his hair.

Sheila squeezed his hand and let go. "It's okay," she said softly.

That's not what he wanted to hear. Sheila should be offering reasons to escape.

And then he'd bury his feelings for Marissa again until they festered. Sheila was right.

He turned to her and wrapped his arms around her, placing his hands on the back of her waist. Leaning in, he rested his forehead against hers. "Are you sure?" He searched her eyes for jealousy or fear.

What he found was warmth and trust.

She trusted him. How had he been so blessed to find her?

"It's all right, Richard." She smoothed her hands up and down his arms. "I'll head back by myself."

That was unacceptable. He pulled from Sheila and glanced around. Connor was coming out of the conference room. "Connor." He waved his former intern over.

"Richard." Connor shook Richard's hand. "Thanks for the

recommendation, for your vote of confidence. I appreciate it."

"It wasn't given lightly. I trusted you when I worked with you before. You've got good instincts. I doubt you've lost the edge."

"I don't believe I have."

Richard nodded. "Can you do me a favor?"

"Anything"

"Escort Sheila back to the hotel."

"Richard." Sheila frowned and propped her hands on her hips. "I do *not* need an escort."

"Please." He stared at her with eyes that said he wouldn't take "no" for an answer. "For my sanity."

"You mean what's left of it?" She kissed him softly. "I love you, Richard."

"I love you, too, hon." He whispered and pulled her toward him. Marissa needed to see his deep love for Sheila. He ran his thumbs down Sheila's cheeks then kissed her as if he hadn't seen her for days. Sheila didn't seem to mind.

Conner cleared his throat, and Richard crooked a smile toward his former colleague.

Smirking, Conner crossed his arms over his chest. "Are you ready or are you catching your breath?"

Richard kept Sheila close. "Take good care of her. I'll be at our room shortly." He watched Connor and Sheila until the elevator door slid shut. Was this why God called Richard back? To truly forgive Marissa? It all made sense now. But why did God ask the impossible?

Pressing his arms at his side, Richard turned back to Marissa. "You want privacy?" He gestured toward a vacant conference room, and she entered. He followed her in, leaving the door wide open. With the door closed it would be too easy to say things he'd regret. He sat across from her, leaned as far back in the chair as possible, crossed his arms, and waited.

Marissa looked down at the table and drew imaginary shapes with her finger. "I heard rumors you'd gotten married. I couldn't believe it. I had to come see if it was true."

Because back then he was enjoying the bachelor life too much to think of settling down. Common knowledge for the people who knew him. When Marissa told him she was pregnant, he'd made a hasty proposal in an effort to convince her to keep the baby. She had been right to say "no". Regardless of his feelings for her, whatever those feelings had been, their marriage never would have lasted.

"The two of you look happy." She peered up, but barely made eye contact.

"We are, and we're expecting our first baby." He kept his tone dry. This might be his and Sheila's first child together, but he should have another.

Her eyes widened and her mouth opened slightly, then she clamped it shut.

"I'm sure you didn't come here to discuss my marriage." It was time to get this unwanted reunion over with, forgive her, and escape from this building.

"You're right," she said quietly, fiddling with her necklace. A cross hung from the end of a gold chain. A cross? When did Marissa start wearing a cross? "I want to tell you that I'm sorry about the accident. I feel responsible."

She was admitting her guilt? The Marissa he remembered never looked back, never showed remorse. But the woman sitting in front of him was sincerely contrite.

And he was being a jerk. Not exactly the Godly man he claimed to be. This visit to ACM was about more than him facing his past. It was about God pruning him, shearing off pride and judgment so Richard could become a stronger, healthier man of God. Why did pruning have to hurt so much?

Richard uncrossed his arms, sat up straight, and folded his hands on the table. His actions from that night were his responsibility and his alone. No one else should carry the blame. "It wasn't your fault, Marissa. I made the decision to drive."

"But there wasn't a person at the party that night who didn't feel somewhat responsible. We all watched you leave."

Richard ran his hand over his mouth, preventing a snide remark. Yeah, they all watched him leave. They did nothing to stop him and probably cheered as he drove off.

Whew. How quickly he resorted back to blaming. God apparently had much more pruning work. He blew out his breath, purging the unforgiving feelings one more time, but still felt as if God had more trimming to do.

Marissa's eyes glossed over. "If I'd have known what would happen that night, I never would have confronted you. I shouldn't have told you about the pregnancy. I had no clue you would react like that—that you actually wanted to be a father."

"You needed to tell me and then I made bad choices." Horrible, life altering choices. But they hadn't all been made that night. "Actually, I made bad choices from the beginning. I used you and that was wrong. If not for me, you wouldn't have been in the position to make the choice you did, and I'm sure it wasn't an easy choice." Sheila had proven that to him. "Regardless, if I'd treated you the way you deserved, it wouldn't have been an issue in the first place. I'm very sorry. Can you forgive me?"

Marissa stared at him, her eyes narrowed. "But I pursued you."

"It doesn't matter. What I did was wrong. So much of what I did here at ACM was wrong, and I paid dearly. But what's worse is so many others paid for my selfish decisions. Especially you. That's why I need to ask for your forgiveness."

"Of course I forgive you." Her eyes remained narrowed, as if confused. "You've changed."

A smile tugged on Richard's lips. Pruning complete. For now. And God had gifted him with an amazing opportunity. He leaned toward Marissa and rested his forearms on the table. "Yes, I have. Can I tell you why?"

Marissa nodded.

Richard told his faith story—how a little child had led him. It had been his and Marissa's unborn child that led the way. After the night of their fight and his accident, it had taken him over a year to finally realize he needed God back in his life.

Marissa listened without scoffing, without arguing. So unlike the Marissa he remembered. Apparently he wasn't the only one God had been working on. Perhaps this was another reason why God had called him back to New York. To plant a new seed.

He finished his story and Marissa bowed her head. He allowed her introspection, and prayed silently for her heart.

Sniffling, she put her purse on top of the table and pulled out her wallet and a tissue. Wiping her eyes, she opened the wallet and stared down at it.

Did she still keep their portrait there? The same one he'd once insisted on carrying to show off to his family. He'd burned his copy long ago.

"Richard?" Her gaze remained downward.

"Yes?"

She looked up with a pale face and puffy, red eyes. "I ..."

Had she hoped for reconciliation? That opportunity had been burned long ago, too.

She wiped tears from her cheeks. The Marissa he remembered never cried. Obviously, something else was going on here.

"Is something wrong?"

She shook her head and whimpered. "No. I'm happy for you. That's all. I'm glad you're finally going to be a father. I'm so sorry I took that away from you." She wiped her eyes, folded her wallet, and tucked it back inside her purse.

Regret.

That's what this was about. A word he was intimate with. He'd take the first step in helping her deal with it. Blinking back a tear, he reached across the table.

She took his hand and her watery eyes met his.

"I've forgiven you." His gaze remained locked with hers.

She stared at him, unblinking, then tugged back her hand. Her face returned to the emotion-free facade he was so familiar with. "You'll be a good father." Marissa pushed back from the table, stood up, and strode away.

"Marissa?" She didn't even hesitate, but kept going. He sat, his mouth agape, staring out the open door. What was that all about?

He'd done what he could. He'd planted the seed, perhaps it was someone else's turn to water and fertilize it.

But there was something else he could do. He folded his hands on the table and closed his eyes. "God, go with her."

# CHAPTER *twelve*

Lauren's fingers ran smoothly over the piano keys her mother's fingers had once touched, and her voice harmonized beautifully with each note. Well, maybe, it wasn't that flawless and the only one who ever complimented her on her singing voice had been her father, but her heart was in the song, and she was sure that was how God heard her praise. God didn't care if her voice was soft and wobbly. He didn't care that she could never play a piece without striking wrong notes. He loved her as she was and for him she would sing. With music lightening her spirit, she might even make it through the day without crying.

She turned the page on the music book, relishing this time alone. How long had it been since she'd had time all to herself? This Brooks family insisted on hovering every second, not giving her space to breathe. Maybe they were afraid of what she'd do if she were left completely alone. Who knew what they were thinking? She was glad they finally listened to her and went to Nathan's baseball game as a family without her, giving her freedom to play her mom's piano and sing. She finished the song hitting A above middle C with flute-like quality. *Yes!* She thrust her fists downward in silent victory.

"I didn't know you could sing."

Her hands trembled and she stuck them between her legs. How long had Jon been listening?

"That was beautiful. I love that song."

She slid her legs around the end of the piano bench, keeping her eyes closed and her fists tense. He had to be joking. No one complimented her singing or playing. Not ever. Slowly she opened her eyes and peered up. Jon grinned at her.

She couldn't help but smile back.

Then she saw Nathan standing silent in the doorway between the living room and kitchen, the usual frown on his face, and hands stuck in his back pockets. His agitation with her was understandable. She'd invaded his life, his last year at home, and he clearly wasn't happy about it. But what was she supposed to do?

As soon as school started next year, she'd be off on her own, and he'd never have to put up with her again. He could have his family all to himself without her getting in the way. Then they'd all be happy again. The Brookses would be happy anyway.

"Sing something else." Jon walked to the piano, picked up her music book, and paged through it. "You know this song?" He spread the book open on the music stand.

Lauren nodded. The song was one of her favorites, but ... She glanced back at Nathan, and his frown deepened.

"Maybe some other time." She cleared her throat. "My voice is a little raw."

"Gotcha." Jon nodded toward Nathan. "Without old sour puss here."

Nathan rolled his eyes and shuffled into the kitchen. She heard him rummaging through the refrigerator.

She shrugged. "Maybe." *Probably not.*

Jon slid onto the bench beside her, and she scooted to the edge. "Why don't I see you at the Bible study on Saturday morning?"

She shrugged. "I've never been asked."

"You don't have to be asked." Nathan was back in the doorway, an apple in his hand, that frown ever present. "You just come."

"I'm sorry." She curved her fingers into her palms, trying to fight back tears. "I didn't know." Why were tears always so close to the surface when Nathan was around?

He bit into his apple then spoke with his mouth full. "Sheesh, would you stop saying you're sorry for every little thing?"

"I'm sorry." She pinched her eyes shut. "I need to go to bed." She hurried past him to the stairs.

"Lauren," Jon called after her, "you don't have to go."

She ignored him and bounded up the steps. Hopefully the tears would wait until she could soundlessly close her bedroom door. Then she'd be able to thrust her face in her pillow and let the tears come so no one could hear her.

WHAT WAS THE MATTER with him? Nathan stomped into the kitchen and brought the cookie jar to the table. Mom always kept it full. He liked to empty it. For once, couldn't he learn to leave Lauren alone so she didn't feel like emptying her tear ducts all the time?

Jon joined him at the table and reached in for a cookie. "Gingersnap." Jon took a bite and rolled his eyes. "I love your mom's gingersnaps."

Yeah, so did Nathan. Usually. He bit off a chunk. Not even that tasted good. Lauren's hasty departure left him with a bitter taste that didn't want to be covered. "Need some milk?" Maybe dunking the cookie would help.

"Sure." Jon finished off his cookie and reached for a second.

Nathan brought a gallon jug of milk and glasses to the table.

"Why do you do that?" Jon poured himself a glass of milk.

"Get milk?" Nathan heard the door to the garage open. His parents. This was not a conversation he wanted to have around them. They were upset enough with his behavior lately.

"No, stupid. Why do you treat Lauren like that?"

And this was not a discussion he wanted to have with his best friend. Nathan frowned as the door to the garage slammed shut, and family voices echoed from the porch.

"Jon." For once his dad had perfect timing. "Imagine finding you here. Eating my cookies." His dad sauntered to the table and grabbed a handful of gingersnaps as Janet, Jaclyn, and Joshua walked into the kitchen.

"Hey, Mr. Brooks. Thought I should do some taste-testing, you know, in case they weren't any good."

"Glad you're looking out for us." Dad and Joshua pulled out chairs and sat. "We rather like having you around."

Yeah, right now they'd probably trade Nathan for Jon.

"Hey, not a problem. Besides, I have to come and see my little Jack-o-Lantern, don't I?" Jon stretched his arm out and grabbed Jaclyn as she walked past. He pulled the giggling four-year-old onto his lap.

"It's Jaclyn."

"Okay. Let me try it again. Jack – o – Lynn."

"No, siwwy. It's Jack – Lynn!"

"Jack – Lynn. I think I got it now, Jack – o – Lantern."

Jaclyn tried wriggling from his lap.

Mom set glasses on the table. "It's time for little Jack-o to go to bed." She took Jaclyn's hand and the preschooler bounced from Jon's lap. "It's been a long night and it's way past her bedtime."

"Good night, Jack – Lynn."

"Night-night, Jon-Jon."

If four-year-olds could have crushes, Nathan was sure Jaclyn had one on Jon. There could be worse things.

"Great game tonight." Dad grabbed another handful of cookies and set them on a napkin in front of him.

"Thanks." Nathan relaxed, that touchy subject of Lauren apparently avoided. "Wasn't so bad. Would've been better if I didn't have to cover left field, too."

"Maybe you should've been covering center like you were

supposed to." Jon cuffed the side of Nathan's head. "Then that ball wouldn't have scooted under your glove. Should've been an easy pick up. Could've thrown the guy out at third."

"It was more fun throwing him out at home."

"Make sure you've got the guy played right next time." Jon got up and put his glass in the sink as Nathan's mom returned to the kitchen. "Thanks for the cookies, Mrs. Brooks, but I gotta get going. Told my folks I'd be home by eleven." He tapped Nathan's shoulder. "I'll pick you up tomorrow morning, so make sure Lauren knows she's invited to the Bible study. There's no reason she can't ride with us."

Nathan's mouth pinched. "Yeah. Whatever." Why did she have to be included in everything he did? He should have a life without her.

"And Mr. Brooks, make sure bonehead here doesn't discourage Lauren from coming."

"Quiet, Jon." Nathan grumbled in the tone usually reserved for his mom and dad, catching himself too late to stop. Great. Now he'd done it. Nathan slumped as the porch door slammed shut. Without looking, he knew his folks were staring at him, the ingrate son.

"Josh, would you excuse us a moment, please?" Dad asked in his "I'm doing my best not to yell" tone.

Without question or backtalk, Joshua hurried to the basement. The little suck-up.

Dad glared at Nathan, his arms crossed over his chest. "What's going on?"

"About what?" Stupid! Like that was going to keep his folks from hassling him.

"Lauren." Mom handed him two cookies. Bribery by sweets again. "We know it's been tough on you. I guess we expected things to improve by now."

"You said treat her like a member of the family, right? That's exactly what I'm doing." Why couldn't he stop his mouth from

115

saying stupid things?

"We said, welcome her." Even his mom's voice had an edge to it tonight.

Man, he'd really messed up now. "I know, but it'd be a lot easier to welcome her if she'd at least smile once in a while or talk or stop hiding out in her room."

"Sweetheart, she's working on it." Mom picked up the jug. "More milk?"

"Nah." He waved his hand. Milk hadn't covered the bitter taste either.

His mom returned the milk to the refrigerator then sat back down. "Think of what she's been through."

"I have." Good thing his mom was doing the talking, not his dad. Although his dad's furrowed eyebrows screamed disappointment.

"Think how scary it's got to be for her to leave her life behind and come live with our crazy family. She's terribly shy, and we won't draw her out if we're not friendly. It's going to take time and a lot of patience on our part. She needs friends."

Yeah, but why did it have to be him? "Does that mean she's included in everything I do?"

"If it's a family event, Lauren's included."

"I know, but the Bible study? That was for my friends."

"Excuse me?" His dad's face flushed. "Your friends?"

Nathan puffed out a breath. Oh boy, he'd totally messed up now.

"Since when are Bible studies for 'friends only'? I've been wondering why you haven't included her before this."

"It was never by invitation, Dad. People just come. If they come, they're welcome. We don't invite anyone. We don't exclude anyone. It's open to everyone." But he loved it that Lauren always stayed home.

"Maybe you should start inviting." His dad slammed down a cookie and crumbles bounced across the table. "I find it hard to believe that you've intentionally excluded her."

"We didn't—"

"No, but she was never welcomed either."

Nathan searched his brain for a retort, one that would silence his dad, and inspiration hit. "Maybe I learned from the best, Dad. Until that last month, I never saw Lauren's dad at your men's Bible study either. How come you didn't invite him before that?"

Nathan had never seen that expression on his dad's face before, with the mouth open in silence and eyes that seemed to look inward. For some reason, Nathan didn't feel any better.

The kitchen clock ticked behind him as he waited for his dad's comeback, for his parents to dish out their punishment. His heart pounded louder and faster than the clock's tick. Oh man, oh man. He'd done it now. He'd probably be grounded for a month. That meant no seeing Lexi. She'd dump him faster than an Olympic sprinter.

Without a word, his dad pushed his chair back, got up and trudged to the living room. Nathan glanced at his mom. Her neck was craned toward the living room, and worry tented her brows. Man, oh man, what had he done now?

Nathan crept to the doorway separating the kitchen from the living room and braked. His dad stood staring at the picture wall. Lauren's piano now occupied the space below the portraits. Where Mom's linen buffet used to sit. More evidence of Lauren's intrusion on his family.

Dad picked up a framed photograph centered on top of the piano, the one of Lauren and her dad. His dad's chest and shoulders rose and fell before he put the picture down. Then he reached above the instrument and took the Brooks' generation portrait off the wall, the one taken nearly four years ago before his grandparents' fortieth Anniversary celebration. His dad and Uncle Ricky had fought the day the photo was taken. Before and after the photo. It was amazing anyone had smiled.

But back then they always fought. Maybe after Uncle Ricky's

baby was born it would be time for a new portrait, one that would show the complete family. A picture that wouldn't be remembered for its quarrel.

One without Lauren.

Mom joined Nathan in the doorway. He opened his mouth to say something, but she shook her head.

His dad rehung the family portrait. Once again his chest and shoulders heaved as he settled on the piano bench, facing away from the kitchen. He clasped his hands behind his head and pulled down, resting his elbows on his thighs. "I'm sorry, Ricky." His dad's normally strong voice trembled. "Oh God, I'm so sorry."

"Dad?"

"Marcus?"

He and his mom spoke together.

His dad sat up and turned to look at them. The whites of his eyes were streaked with red and they were glassy. His gaze stopped on Nathan.

And Nathan's Adam's apple stuck in his throat.

"Son," his dad's voice quivered. "You were right." His words were slow and solemn. "I'm so sorry. This is all my fault."

## CHAPTER *thirteen*

### *White Plains, New York*

Meghan laid her final card in the discard pile and grinned while the others seated around her parents' dining room table sat in shock.

"Is that any way to treat guests?" Richard Brooks slapped his cards down on the table in obvious mock anger. "You realize I had two, count 'em, two wild cards in my hand. That's sixty points for me."

"Sorry?" Meghan giggled. Boy it felt good to laugh again. It hadn't happened very often lately. And it certainly wouldn't be happening once Doran arrived, which would be soon.

"I don't know about guests"—her dad crossed his arms and shot her an angry stare—"but I'd think she'd have more respect for her father. Forty-seven points for me."

Meghan covered her mouth and tried to give her dad a penitent look, but failed.

"Thirty-two." Sheila told Meghan's mom who was tallying up the scores. "I suppose that puts me in second place now."

"Sure does." Meghan's mom said as the door buzzer rang.

*There goes the fun.* Meghan took her time heading to the door. What she'd give to not have this upcoming conversation. It would be one more step in the right, but very painful direction of letting go of her daughter.

She opened the door, and Doran smiled at her. She waved him in. "We're playing cards."

All the players stood as Doran approached.

Richard held out his hand. "Good to see you again. Remember my wife Sheila?"

"Of course." He shook both their hands as well as her dad's. Her mom drew him into a hug as if he were family. That would not happen. Once this baby was born, Doran would be gone.

He joined them at the table, right next to Meghan, then her mom offered him lemonade and M&M cookies. "What are you playing?" He grabbed a cookie.

"We call it 'thirteen.'" Meghan started dealing out the cards. "It's an old family favorite." She explained the rules as she dealt seven cards to each player. They'd chosen this game because it would be easy to add a fifth player, but more importantly, it didn't require a lot of concentration, so she and Doran could easily relay their news. And the sooner they shared it, the sooner Doran could leave.

Richard picked up his cards and moaned. "Nothing goes together."

"Poor baby." Sheila patted his hand and grinned.

"That reminds me." Richard laid his cards face down on the table. "Sheila and I have some news."

Sheila took her husband's hand and they shared the glowing smile of people in love. Just the type of couple Meghan wanted to raise her child. "We're expecting a baby."

"Congratulations." Meghan said as her mom got up to give the couple a hug, but Meghan's heart sank. If they were already pregnant, they probably wouldn't even consider adopting her little girl.

"I'm sure you guys'll make great parents." Doran shook Richard's hand across the table, but then shared a worried glance with Meghan.

She shrugged and whispered. "Let's tell them anyway." The

worst they could say was "no."

"You sure?"

She nodded. "You do it."

He wiped his hands on his jeans and she heard his deep intake of breath. "Meghan and I have a little announcement of our own."

Her mom gasped, her hand flying to her chest, and her dad clenched his jaw. Oh boy, they probably thought Doran was announcing an engagement. That was not ever happening.

"Um," Doran wiped his hands on his shorts as he glanced from Richard to Sheila. "Meghan and I have decided that the best thing for our baby is to give her up for adoption."

Her parents relaxed, and Meghan did too. Having the information out in the open seemed to remove a weight from her shoulders.

But Sheila's and Richard's eyes were misty.

Sheila dabbed a napkin at her eyes. "I am so proud of you two." Her voice quivered and Richard tucked his arm around her shoulders. "I can't think of a more loving, brave thing to do. I wish I would've had the courage to do the same." Several months ago, Sheila had confided in Meghan that she'd had two abortions, both of which she deeply regretted. Thank God, Meghan would never have to live with that same regret.

Richard offered his hand to Doran and shook it firmly. "We greatly respect your decision."

Wow. Not the reaction she expected at all and it made Meghan's eyes fog up. Most people chastised her for making this already difficult decision. "Thanks, but it's not easy."

"Doing the right thing seldom is." Richard kissed his wife's moist cheek.

Yeah, they were the perfect couple to raise her child. Worlds above her and Doran. They were right to make this adoption choice.

But chances were, Richard and Sheila wouldn't even consider

adopting, what with them being pregnant and all. Regardless, she and Doran would give the couple the option to say "no." She whispered in Doran's ear. "Go ahead."

Doran circled his shoulders and sighed. "I guess that's why I'm here today. Meghan and I, we're looking for a couple who would be interested in adopting our baby. We initially thought of you, but with you already ..." Would they even consider it?

Richard leaned forward, his gaze darting between Doran and Meghan. "You thought of us?" His voice wobbled.

Meghan thought she saw moisture in Richard's eyes before he bowed his head.

"We're talking to a few different couples." Meghan caressed her stomach. "We want to know our baby will be well taken care of, and we want to have an open relationship with the adoptive parents. We didn't realize you were already expecting. I'm sure you don't want ..."

Sheila placed an arm around her husband's back, his head still bowed. "We're honored that you'd even consider us. Please don't rule us out simply because we're pregnant. Maybe this is God's plan. Would you mind if we took a day or two to pray about it, or do you need our answer now?"

"You'll think about it?" Doran's eyes grew wide.

"Absolutely." Sheila's eyes glistened. "For you to consider us, it's very humbling."

"Thank you." Meghan blinked rapidly, fending off her own tears, and picked up her cards again. "How about we get back to the game." With this couple saying "yes" that brought the adoption one more step closer to reality. One step closer to saying goodbye to her precious daughter forever.

NATHAN GOT OUT OF Jon's car, grabbed his sport bag then quietly shut the door, although he wanted to slam it. How could Jon do that to him? They were supposed to be best friends.

He trudged to the house, digging a trench through the gravel driveway and up the concrete steps to his house. The screen door banged shut behind him as he stomped through the porch.

Once in the kitchen, he dropped his sport bag on the floor.

"Bad day?" His dad sat at the kitchen table, nursing a cup of coffee.

Fresh chocolate chip cookies awaited on a plate in the middle of the table, sending their mouth-watering aroma into the air.

"Unbelievable." A heckuva way to begin a week. Nathan sat and grabbed two cookies without looking up at his dad.

"Want to talk about it?"

No. Nathan cocked his head to the side and shook it. How could this be happening?

Dad got up, went to the fridge, and returned to the table with a jug of milk. He filled two glasses without saying a word. Actually, his dad had said very little since his breakdown the other day, just that he had unfinished business with Uncle Ricky. Whatever had happened, it had mellowed his dad out. Nathan hadn't decided if he liked the change or not.

Didn't matter though. Not with this new problem.

Nathan dunked his cookie and took a bite. "He's gonna ask her out." He mumbled while chewing. Nathan stuffed the rest of the cookie into his mouth.

"Who's asking who out?"

Nathan rolled his eyes. Who did his dad think he was talking about? "Jon. He's gonna ask Lauren out."

"Really?" His dad shifted in his chair. "And, this is a bad thing?"

"Well, yeah!" What could be good about his best friend dating Borin' Lauren. Jon had more sense than that.

"Forgive me for being a little dense. I realize I am just your father."

Nathan rolled his eyes again and slumped.

"You'll have to enlighten me on why it's a bad thing."

Nathan stuffed the second cookie into his mouth.

"You're jealous!" His dad laughed.

The cookie came back out in spray form and Nathan choked. "What?" No way was he jealous of Jon. Lauren was continents away from Nathan's babe-radar. "You've got to be kidding."

"Not at all." His dad picked up a napkin and wiped his mouth.

He was serious! "Sorry, Dad, but Lauren is so not my type. I don't care who she dates."

"As long as it isn't Jon, right?"

"Huh?"

"It all makes sense now. Your cranky attitude, your droopy face."

Nathan scrunched his lips and grabbed a fresh cookie. This was a stupid conversation.

"You're not jealous of Jon for asking Lauren out, you're jealous of Lauren for the time she's spending with Jon."

Nathan slumped further, wanting to sink under the table. No way.

"Jon's allowed to date too, you know. You can probably understand how he's felt all those times you've turned down doing something with him because you're going on some date. Didn't you cancel something the other night so you could go out with this new girl? What's her name?"

"Lexi."

"Yeah, Lexi."

True. He had cancelled out on going to a movie with Jon just the other night so he could take Lexi instead. He hadn't given a thought to how Jon would feel. "You think he felt like this?"

"Probably. He doesn't keep it in like you do though. Doesn't let it bother him."

"Nothin' bothers Jon." Problems slid off his friend like cars on ice.

"It's life. You're both growing up and you're both developing broader interests. Girls being one of them. It doesn't mean he won't still be your best friend and that you won't do a lot together, just not as much as you're both used to. There's always double dating, too."

Nathan blew his breath upwards, and his hair fluttered.

His dad got up and walked to the window overlooking the driveway.

Dad was spying on his friend. Un-freaking-believable.

The door to the basement stairs opened and his mom walked into the kitchen with a laundry basket of folded clothes. "What are you looking at?" She placed the basket on the table and joined his dad at the window.

"Jon's asking Lauren out." His Dad grinned.

"No." Mom's eyes grew wide. "Seriously?"

Nathan groaned. Logical or not, he didn't like Jon asking Lauren out.

"This is so exciting!" Obviously, his mom felt differently. "I need to take Lauren shopping. Get her some fun new clothes."

"You?" Right. Like his mom was some kind of fashion diva. Not. "Sorry, Mom, but in case you haven't noticed, your wardrobe isn't anything to brag about either. If you ask me, the person you need to talk to is Aunt Sheila. Lauren won't come out looking like Sheila, but it couldn't hurt either."

His parents exchanged a glance and nodded to each other.

"You know, Nate." His mom walked to the table and removed the cookies. "I'm even going to overlook your insult and call Sheila, see if she's available this Saturday. We three girls could have a day out together. Maybe you could drive us to Ricky's and work on your car while we women shop."

Now there was an excellent idea. Uncle Ricky hadn't seen his new car yet, and Nathan was dying to show it off. Jon could come too and the guys could work on the car together. "Let's do it."

## CHAPTER *fourteen*

Nathan patted the dashboard on his new car. Getting Uncle Ricky's approval of the car today would be the highlight of the week. With Lexi seated next to him snapping her gum, Nathan steered his Honda Civic onto his uncle's gravel driveway then glanced in his rearview mirror. His dad, Lauren, and Jon pulled in right behind in a Ford Super Duty pickup. No Mom today, with Jaclyn sick. All the better for Lauren to have only Aunt Sheila's fashion influence.

This was going to be some kind of weekend. Work on his car with Jon and Uncle Ricky today and watch the Minneapolis Aquatennial's milk carton boat races tomorrow. He and Lexi would have to ditch Lauren and Jon, as much as his dad frowned on the two of them spending time alone.

It sure would be nice if his dad trusted him.

He pulled to a stop in front of the open garage and got out. Lexi came around his car and put her arm around his back. Her hand traveled downward. He jerked away and glared at her. "Not here," he said through closed teeth.

"Later." She grabbed his hand and threw him a sideways grin that sealed the promise he wasn't sure he wanted her to keep, but would be disappointed if she didn't.

He perspired thinking about it.

A door on the house slammed as Dad parked his pickup next to Nathan's car. Uncle Ricky walked out through his garage, his arms crossed and his gaze on the Civic. Nathan sweated even more. Nothing, not even Lexi, was more important than having Uncle Ricky's approval of his new set of wheels.

Nathan nodded toward the vehicle he and Jon had labored over for two days, detailing every inch, inside and out. "What do you think?"

Uncle Ricky ran his hand across the car's newly waxed hood. No expression at all.

Still clinging to Lexi, Nathan placed a hand on the roof on the driver's side and tapped his fingers.

Jon stood on the opposite side of the car from Nathan, crossing and uncrossing his arms. Dad perched on the home's front steps, a stupid grin on his face, and Lauren sat next to him, her head down as usual. Good thing she was going to be shopping with Aunt Sheila all day. He wouldn't have to worry about saying or doing the wrong thing.

Ricky walked around the car, his gaze combing every inch, including the new tires: white walls with hubcaps even. He walked around to Nathan's side, running his finger along the red racing stripes, and said nothing.

Nathan wiped his forehead. Uncle Ricky hated his car.

Why did his opinion matter so much?

Ricky stopped next to Nathan then leaned his backside against the vehicle. Still no comment. So what if it wasn't a two-door convertible with a V8 engine. It was a decent car for a high school senior.

"Well?" Nathan drummed his fingers faster on the roof. Waiting was going to give him an ulcer.

Ricky turned to Nathan. "What's this?" He tugged on Nathan's ear.

Wincing, Nathan swatted his uncle's hand away. If only he could melt into the gravel. "What's it look like?" How he'd let Lexi talk him into getting his ear pierced, he'd never know. And right before seeing Uncle Ricky. Stupid. Plain stupid.

Lexi tugged at his pierced ear, and whispered. "I like it." She better like it. He'd done it for her.

"Your dad approve?" Uncle Ricky shot a quizzical glance toward Dad.

"Mom did." Nathan blurted out and imagined his dad rolling his eyes. No, his dad hadn't approved. Nathan knew he wouldn't, so he'd asked his mom so she could convince his dad. Of course, asking for a tattoo first softened her so an earring wouldn't sound nearly so bad. "She likes it." Maybe not totally, but she did tell him there were worse things he could do.

"Very nice ride, Nathan." Aunt Sheila's voice sounded sweeter than cookie dough ice cream. Nathan released the breath he hadn't realized he was holding as Aunt Sheila walked from the garage toward his car.

"Thanks." Glad someone liked it.

She peeked in a passenger side window. "Leather interior even."

"Yep." That was an added bonus he hadn't expected to get.

"Enjoy it, Nathan. That first car is something special."

"I'll treat her like a baby."

"I'm certain you will." Sheila walked around the car and offered her hand to Lexi. "You must be the young lady Nathan's talked so much about."

Lexi spat her gum out on the ground. "I hope none of it's good."

Why did she have to say crap like that? Now no one would approve of her. Nathan dropped Lexi's hand and stuffed his hands in his back pockets. She kept grinning.

"If you want the truth, the answer's no, it wasn't good." Sheila crossed her arms over her chest, smiling back at Lexi, but with cold, determined eyes, a stare Nathan would hate to be on the receiving end of. "But I intend to see something different this weekend. And you can start by picking up your gum."

Lexi obeyed. Without talking back. Unreal.

"Now, you can get your luggage, and I'll show you and Lauren to your room."

Man oh man. Nathan squeezed his head between his hands. No one talked to Lexi like that. This was it. They were done.

Sheila waved to Lauren, the edge in her voice gone. "Come on, sweetie. I'll get you two settled."

Lexi pecked Nathan's cheek and whispered. "You owe me."

He gulped. Why did that petrify and excite him all at the same time? He watched Lexi and Lauren follow Sheila into the house and released a sigh. That was enough drama to last this century.

Now, could they please focus on his car? All he wanted was Uncle Ricky's approval.

"Honda Civic, eh?" Uncle Ricky cocked his head toward Nathan, pokerfaced.

"A top of the line EX." As if that would make any bit of difference.

"What year?"

"'97. I know it's old but it's only got 154,000 miles and seems to be a good runner so far."

"Pop the hood."

Nathan cringed as he reached through the open window, under the dashboard, and pulled the lever. This would not be good.

His uncle stared at the cylinder block, shifting his jaw. "Four cylinder, huh?"

"It's all Dad would let me get." He glared at his dad, hoping to get his uncle to take sides. "I wanted at least a six."

Uncle Ricky smiled. Did he disagree with Dad? "Your dad's smart. I've seen you drive."

Okay. Maybe not.

Ricky pulled out the oil stick then wiped it on a rag he took from his back pocket. He dipped the stick back in then pulled it out again. He studied it then peeked at Nathan, his smile a little broader. "Change the oil yet?"

"The people I got it from said they just changed it."

"Not good enough." Ricky shook his head. "Better do it again, to make sure." He replaced the dipstick. "I've got all the supplies here so we won't have to run for that."

Bummer. He'd looked forward to checking out the auto parts store with his uncle. There he could do some serious shopping. "Check out the inside." Nathan held open the driver's door. "For an old car it's in pretty good shape. No rust or anything. I think it was from New Mexico or something."

Ricky sat in the driver's seat and stretched his long legs out. "Decent leg room. Good head room." He clutched his right hand over the gear shift. "Five speed. Excellent."

Nathan's tension eased a fraction. Maybe Uncle Ricky liked the car after all.

Ricky rubbed a hand over his chin. "It's a sweet ride, Nathan, but there's one little problem."

"What?" Nathan wiped his forehead. What was wrong now?

"We'll have to do something about this." Uncle Ricky tapped the empty slot where a CD player should have been. "Guess we'll have to go to the auto parts store after all. Consider it my gift."

Yes! Nathan pumped his fist. Exactly what he was hoping for.


OH, THAT LEXI WAS trouble. Sheila steered her Lexus off of I-94 onto the Fourth Street Exit heading into Minneapolis. Trouble Sheila recognized too well from her own teen years. That girl had one thing on her mind and Nathan was the target. Marcus was right to be concerned.

She drove past Target Field then glanced at her silent passenger. *Lord, help me reach Lauren.* Her shoulder was tucked against the door, and her head tilted toward the window, as if attempting to be invisible. What a contrast between two teenagers. One willing to say or do anything to be seen, the other afraid to speak for fear of being noticed

Sheila took another glimpse at Lauren, as she drove across

Nicollet Mall. Thus far, Janet had little success in getting Lauren to open up. Not that Lauren's quiet was unusual given her circumstances. The teen clearly had little female influence in her life. Her fingernails were short and uneven, but not bitten. Her brown hair, with a hint of red, was thick and wavy and belled out at her shoulders. An unflattering cut that made Lauren's face appear rounder than it was. The right hair style could do wonders for the girl's self-esteem.

The right clothes, too. Lauren's jeans were high-waisted, a style that had been out of vogue for years. Could they have been hand-me-downs from the girl's mother? And the orange T-shirt she wore advertised her church's vacation Bible school. Sheila had seen her in little else besides T-shirts. Maybe she didn't own anything else. Today, Sheila would rectify that. Lauren would learn fashion from the master.

Now, if only Sheila could get her to open up. "Are you excited for the day?"

Lauren shrugged but didn't look away from the window. "I guess."

*Lord, help.* "I figure we'll get a couple hours of clothes shopping in first, then do lunch. After that I've got hair appointments later for both of us. You know ..." Sheila briefly turned toward Lauren as they waited at a stop light. She reached over to feel Lauren's hair. "You have gorgeous hair. Most people would kill to have hair that thick, and the color, with the hint of red, is striking."

"Thank you," Lauren said softly with a slight smile that disappeared as quickly as it came.

"We need the right style for your face. Pauly—he's been my stylist for years—he can do wonders with any type of hair, find the right style for any face, any personality. I'm sure you'll love what he can do for you."

Lauren sniffled and wiped her eyes.

What had she said wrong? "Sweetie, are you all right?" Sheila

132

flicked her signal.

"I appreciate you taking me shopping, I just ..." Lauren shrugged, keeping her head turned away.

"You what, hon?" Sheila pulled into the parking ramp and took the ticket that popped from the metal box. The yellow arm rose in front of them and she accelerated into the ramp. "I've been told I'm a good listener."

Lauren sat soundless as Sheila drove up into the claustrophobic garage. The question hung in the air until she parked, then she turned toward Lauren and placed a hand on her shoulder. The poor girl didn't move.

"Sweetie, I know what it's like not to have someone to talk to when things are bad. I understand not wanting to complain. But if anyone has a right to grumble, you do."

A tear rolled over Lauren's cheek and Sheila handed her a tissue.

Lauren wiped her eyes. "I'm not good enough for Marcus' family—for anyone." Lauren crumpled the tissue and dabbed at her cheeks. She turned her head from the window only to look at the car floor. "Why does everyone want to change me? I'm too shy. I'm not athletic enough. I'm not pretty enough. Why can't someone like me for me?"

Sheila squeezed her eyes shut. No wonder Lauren was being so quiet. "Oh, honey, is that what you think today is about?"

Lauren sucked in trembling lips. "This was Janet's idea. I'm not good enough for Jon the way I am."

*Dear God, what can I say?* Sheila placed her hand on Lauren's arm. "Hon, I'm so sorry. It never occurred to me—or to Janet—that you would think this way. We thought you'd like to have a girls' day out, like she used to have with her mom. Like I used to have with my mother."

*Like I used to have with my mother.* Sheila's stomach fluttered uneasily with the thought. Was that what today was about? Reliving the one affirming connection, the one positive memory she had of her mother?

She'd make sure Lauren never knew of those feelings. Today was to be a day of optimism, a day of breakthroughs, and she wouldn't allow old wounds to be sliced open again.

Lauren pulled a tissue from her pocket and wiped her eyes. "Did you go out with her often?"

One lousy day per year her mother treated her like a daughter. "Once a year." Sheila feigned enthusiasm. Suppressing honest emotions was a skill she had thoroughly mastered over the years. It's what had made her a financial success—and almost buried her. She smiled, praying happiness would show through. "Mother would plan the day out, like I have today. We'd shop for clothes. She taught me how to find outfits that matched my body shape."

Her body shape ... Sheila brought a hand to her stomach, circling her now-changing body. At least style had discovered maternity clothes. She shouldn't have to search too hard to find a designer motherhood wardrobe, a wardrobe she'd be wearing all too soon, a fact she realized only this morning when she'd pulled on her jeans and then struggled to zip and button them. The baby was making itself known through her expanding belly. Richard loved it—told her it was sexy. The man had to be nuts.

She could imagine what her mother would say—nothing complimentary, of that she was certain—but Lauren didn't need to be burdened with those thoughts. *Keep it positive.* "We'd experiment with makeup at the makeup counters. We'd get our hair done, and then dress up and go eat at the most expensive restaurant in town. That day I always felt like the most special person in my mother's life."

"What a beautiful memory."

"Yeah. A memory." Sheila couldn't drum up a smile for Lauren. One lousy day she felt special. But then she'd spend the remaining 364 days anticipating that one day. She should have realized then that her mother's motives were entirely selfish. The

134

day wasn't intended to be a day of mother-daughter bonding. No, it was a classroom, so Sheila could learn how to look and act and become a clone of her mother. Unfortunately, for most of her life, that's exactly who she'd become.

Sheila gave Lauren another tissue. "Are you ready?"

Lauren nodded and a hint of a smile appeared. That's all Sheila needed. Lauren deserved more than spending a day in life's classroom. She deserved to be pampered and spoiled. Most of all, she needed to be loved for who she was, something Sheila had never experienced.

"Today, sweetie, you're going to feel like a princess because that's exactly who you are."

RICHARD HELPED MARCUS SPREAD blueprints out on his kitchen table, Marcus' plans for remodeling Richard's home, a home that would soon be too small for his growing family.

He studied the layout out of the main floor then the second floor addition. Exactly—no—Marcus' design was better than what Richard had envisioned. "You've nailed it." His brother was more talented than he realized. "This is just what we had in mind. I can't wait to show Sheila. You know, with all the time I've worked on building projects with you, I never realized what a gift you have, how much you take after Mom. You have her same eye for design and the ear to listen. I'm impressed."

"Thanks, I appreciate it." Marcus rolled the blueprints back up, fit them into a canister, and handed them to Richard. "I've got copies back home. We should be able to start in a week or two, if everything's a go. I've prioritized your job."

"That fast, huh? Guess I better start packing. Glad we kept Sheila's condo. At least we'll have a place to live during construction." Richard placed the blueprint canister on the kitchen counter. "Tomorrow, I'll go over these with Sheila and let you know what we decide, but I can't see anything major we'd have to change." Richard walked around the counter to the fridge. "Need something to drink?"

"Got a Pepsi?"

"Pop? What's that?" Richard stared inside the refrigerator. "Water, grape juice, skim milk—"

"Skim? Don't tell me you've gone to the dark side."

Richard huffed. "I can't drink the stuff, but Sheila won't buy anything else. This pregnancy has turned my health-conscious wife into a health czar."

"Janet was the same way with Nathan. With Josh, she didn't care. I'll take a water."

Richard grabbed two water bottles and a container of carrots. He returned to the table and sat across from his brother. A round table with room for four. It was all this dining area would hold. Soon he'd have a place to fit his entire extended family. "You said a week or two before you start?"

"Probably a week. I'll let you know in a few days."

"Good."

"Just think, pretty soon you're gonna have an extra little voice to fill up all that new space."

The thought alone made him grin. "I'm going to be a daddy. There's nothing—except for Sheila—that could be as important to me. Nothing."

"Remember, you're talking cute little babies that don't talk back. Those babies grow into messy toddlers, then there's puberty, then there's the inevitable teenage know-it-all."

"Are we talking about Nathan?"

"Could be."

"He's a good kid."

"Usually, but having Lauren in our house bothers him. I think he feels like he's been left out or is maybe less important, and he's trying to tell us he's still here."

"Is he getting into trouble?"

"No trouble, really. Not yet, anyway. But the attitude is driving Janet and me crazy. He treats Lauren worse than he treats Josh. He's moody. He's been talking back, and now his choice of girlfriends."

"That's the big issue isn't it?"

"You could say that." Marcus grabbed a peeled carrot and bit into it. "Ummm, grow these yourself?"

"You bet." Richard took one too and held it up. "Not too bad, if I do say so myself. The miracle is, I've even enjoyed working the soil. When I left home, I thought I'd left field work behind me for forever. Now I look forward to it." Richard bit into his carrot.

"Funny how that happens when we grow up, isn't it?" Marcus took another bite then leaned back in his chair. "What do you think of Lexi?"

Richard crossed his arms and frowned. "She's every teenage boy's dream."

"And a dad's nightmare. He's only been seeing her for a few weeks, and he already follows her around like a lovesick puppy."

"The earring her idea?"

"What do you think?"

He didn't have to think too hard. It had been a girl like Lexi who had prompted his own fall. Not that he'd fought it too hard. "Sheila warned me to keep an eye on her. The boys'll be busy all day. I don't know how there could be a problem. I'll keep a close eye on them."

"Janet says I worry too much."

"You've taught Nathan well. He'll make the right choices."

"It doesn't always work that way, though, does it?"

It sure doesn't. Richard was proof of that himself.

"Hey, I'm sorry. I didn't mean ..."

Richard shrugged it off. "Don't apologize for speaking the truth. It's good that you recognize even good kids can get into trouble. My behavior was a slap in Mom and Dad's faces. They didn't expect it from me. But I might have an opportunity to make up for some of that."

"Oh?"

"Meghan Keene's ex, Doran Jans."

"The baby's father?" Marcus took a sip of water.

"Yep. I've offered him a paid internship, starting after his baby comes. He plans on staying in New York till then."

"That's quite the step."

"I see something in him. Something familiar, like I'm watching an image of myself some twenty years ago." Richard thought back to his college days when he believed he was invincible. What a lie that had been. "What the kid needs is an adult male mentor who isn't a 'yes' man. With the proper support I think the kid's got a promising future. Hopefully I can give it to him. He's been calling a lot to talk. Asking for advice, that type of thing."

"Interesting." Marcus stared at his water bottle, as if deep in thought, then he focused on Richard. "Would you consider talking to Nathan?"

"Me? You're joking right?"

"No, not at all. He looks up to you. Maybe if he could hear what you've gone through, it might teach him a lesson."

"Or maybe it'll teach him that a playboy lifestyle sounds pretty good. I don't think that's such a good idea." His nephew idolized him too much already. The last thing Richard wanted was to encourage Nathan to follow his footsteps.

"If it comes up, I give you permission."

Richard nodded, although he disagreed that he could help. He hoped to keep Nathan miles away from his past.

"Speaking of angels." Marcus shifted his eyes to the left. Nathan and Jon lumbered into the kitchen, wearing grease-stained clothes, and headed straight for the fridge.

Nathan stared at near-empty shelves, moved a few things around, then grabbed two bottles of water. He handed one to Jon then began opening Richard's cupboards.

"Hey, hey, there, Nate," Marcus knocked on the table to get his son's attention. "What do you think you're doing? You're a guest."

"Sorry." Nate shut the cabinet door and grimaced at his uncle. "Got any munchies? We're starved."

"Munchies?" Richard laughed. Munchies were disallowed too. "We've got apples, grapes, bananas."

"No, I mean munchies, you know, cookies, chips, pies, stuff like that."

"Oh, you mean the stuff Sheila doesn't allow in the house. Just because she's on this health kick doesn't mean I should suffer, does it?"

"That's part of the marriage vows, remember?" Marcus grinned.

"I don't remember saying 'I promise to have nothing unhealthy in the house.'"

"Oh, it was there. You had to read between the lines a bit. So where's your secret stash?"

"It's not terribly secret, but I'm forbidden to touch it." Richard nodded toward his basement door. "Downstairs freezer. Girl Scout Thin Mints are especially good when they're frozen."

Nate and Jon hurried down to the basement sounding like elephants on a warpath and returned with two boxes of Girl Scout cookies. "Kaitlynn sure hit you up, didn't she?" Nate opened a box of Thin Mints and pulled out a sleeve of cookies.

"Blame it on your Aunt Debbie. Katydid called me at work. I ordered enough boxes to last two years. I didn't realize Sheila did the same thing. Don't know why since she won't eat any of them. I asked Debbie if there was a patch for most gullible cookie buyers. She laughed at me. You'd think a little sister would show her older, wiser brother some respect."

"You'd think, wouldn't you?" Nate laughed back.

"Oil's changed?" Marcus reached for a Thin Mint.

"All done." Nathan sat on the edge of his chair, craning his neck toward the living room, then the outside door. Looking for trouble by the name of Lexi. Richard planned to keep him too busy for that.

"I suppose you want to find a stereo system now." Richard was as geared up to go as Nathan. Since he didn't have his own son—yet—to share these moments with, he was ecstatic that Marcus' boys eagerly included him in their projects.

"Give it a minute, okay Rick?" Marcus scooted closer to the table, his tone suddenly much too serious.

"Sure." Richard sat back in his chair. "What's up?"

"Jon, would you mind keeping Lexi occupied for a bit?"

Nathan's face contorted.

"Not a problem." Jon took an unopened box of cookies and stepped out the patio doors onto a wooden deck. Marcus got up to slide the glass door shut.

Nathan flopped into a chair. "What'd I do now?"

Richard pushed his chair back, preparing to stand. He didn't need to witness whatever Marcus had planned for Nathan. "I'll go keep Jon company."

"No. Sit." Marcus pointed to a chair. "I need you here."

Richard sat next to Nathan.

"I need to apologize to both of you." Marcus gaze flitted between the two of them.

Nathan sat up a little straighter.

"Apologize?" Richard couldn't think of anything his brother needed to apologize for.

"Got a deck of cards?" Marcus asked.

"Sure. One sec." Richard retrieved a worn deck and handed them to Marcus.

Marcus set the deck in the center of the table, took the top card, and held it upright on the table.

"Your turn." Marcus nodded to Richard.

Richard narrowed his eyes as he took a card. It had been years since he'd built a house of cards with his brother. He wanted to ask what was going on, but knew Marcus wouldn't say anything until he was ready, so he balanced his card against

Marcus's jack. They let go and the two cards remained standing.

"Your turn." Marcus nodded at Nathan

Nathan stood an ace perpendicular to his father's.

Marcus completed the square with a king of diamonds. "As a contractor, as a builder, one thing I've learned is that to be successful I need to pay attention to detail."

Richard added a new wall to the card house, while focusing on Marcus.

"Perhaps the most important component of that detail is people. All employees want to be noticed. Everyone wants praise for a job well done."

True. That was something Richard stressed in his consulting business.

Nathan balanced another card.

And Marcus added a side. "I learned early on that there are two types of workers I struggle with. There's the guy who I know is a good worker, but makes stupid mistakes every so often. I'd get on his case, tell him I expected more out him, and it would get worse. Then there's the quiet worker who always shows up on time, always does a good job. A guy who does what he's supposed to do without begging for attention." Marcus placed a queen, sealing off another room.

"I lost one of my best subcontractors because I never let him know how much I appreciated his work. He needed that pat on the back, the attention I never gave him. I've learned to give the silent worker their due. I've learned to treat the guy who made mistakes with respect. I learned to teach rather than yell and berate."

Richard suspended a card in the air. "Are you going somewhere with this?"

Marcus scratched an eyebrow. "I never applied that to life—to us."

Richard laid his card flat and blew the breath from his mouth. The house of cards tumbled down. He winced. "Sorry."

"No." Marcus held up his hands. "That makes my point. When we ignore key elements of the foundation—when I ignored those working under me—it compromised the foundation of my business. All it would have taken was a little wind, a little storm, to upend the company. I learned from my mistakes and built a better business because of it."

All true. But where was Marcus heading with this? "I frequently look to you as an example of how to run a tight business."

"I appreciate that, but I guess I'm not talking about the company."

"Then what?"

"Lauren's dad." Marcus shook his head. "He was the silent worker. Shy. Humble. Uncomplaining. He was the guy who always showed up at church and did whatever anyone asked of him. Did I notice him? Did I ever take the time out to be a friend? Did anyone ever really see him?" Marcus wiped below his eye. "The guy died alone, Rick, just like he lived. I should have been there for him."

Richard combed his fingers through his hair. "I'm sure it's not as bad ..."

Marcus held up his hand. "Nathan had to point it out to me. My son had to teach me how to be a friend."

Nathan slumped. "'Cuz I've been rotten to Lauren."

"I taught you that, Nathan, and I'm sorry." Marcus took a sip of his water. "Let's hope I set a better example in the future."

"We all make mistakes." God knew, Richard had made more than his share of them.

Marcus drew in a breath. "The biggest ones I've made have been with you." He nodded at Richard.

"That goes both ways. Neither of us treated the other with respect."

"Don't you see, Rick?" Marcus shook his head, then turned his attention to his son. "I need you to listen, Nathan. I don't want you to make the same mistakes with your brother."

Nathan shifted in his chair, remaining silent.

Marcus focused on Richard. "Rick, you're that other worker. The one who would get sidetracked and make mistakes. What do I do? Do I talk to you? Listen to you? Encourage you? No. I criticize you. Call you names. Here I've been raising my self-righteous voice for twenty some years, ragging on you every chance I could get."

"Marc, you don't have to—"

"Oh, yes I do. I need you to hear this. It's been a long time coming." Marcus gulped down his water. "After all that, after all the years of being sanctimonious, preachy and condescending, of putting you down and chasing you away, you apologize to me. You, the one who'd turned away from God, took the first step in bridging the gap between us. I was the so-called Christian. I should have been the one to apologize."

"Are you sure you want me here, Dad?" Nathan fidgeted with the cards on the table.

"Yes," Marcus said. "There's a lot you can learn from our mistakes, and hopefully not repeat them."

Richard nodded. "Your dad's right. We can all learn from this." Then he steered the conversation back to the apology. "I only apologized to you because Sheila guilted me into it."

"Maybe. But the fact is you did it. You took the step I should have taken years ago. If I had, if I'd have been Jesus to you the way he commands us to be, you might have come home sooner. Maybe the accident—"

"You think what happened in New York is your fault?"

Marcus rested his elbows on the table and laid his forehead on folded hands. "I played a part in it."

Richard stared up at the ceiling. He'd always said he stayed away from home because of Marcus. It had been an easy place to direct the blame, but the tragic events of that one night were, in no way, his brother's fault. Richard had made his own choices,

choices no one could have talked him out of. "I kept myself away. If you'd have apologized, I'd have stuffed it back your face, like I did everything else. I wasn't ready to hear it. The difference between us is that you were always ready. Yeah, I would have liked a little less preaching."

Marcus snorted. "A little?"

Richard half smiled. "Okay, a lot less preaching, but you wanted to show me the light."

Marcus raised his head and stared into Richard's eyes. "Oh, and I did, didn't I? I took that light"—Marcus made a fist and pushed it toward Richard—"and shoved it in your face. You had no choice but to turn away."

He blinked, from the fist and from Marcus' confession. It made sense, but Richard wouldn't let Marcus accept the blame for Richard's mistakes. "Listen. The only thing that was going to change me was for me to hit rock bottom, to need God again. You loved me when I despised you. You prayed for me when I didn't believe in prayer. I couldn't ask for a better brother." He turned to Nathan who was shuffling the cards, clearly uncomfortable with the conversation. Richard put a hand on his shoulder. "Nathan, you couldn't ask for a better father, and I thank God for him daily."

Nathan stopped mid-shuffle. Cards slid across the table, and several drifted onto the floor. His gaze shifted from Marcus to Richard then back again, and he nodded. "Yeah, I know."

Marcus got up and circled the table. Richard and Nathan followed suit, and met Marcus halfway around the table. Richard offered his hand, but Marcus drew him and Nathan into a hug slapping their backs. "And I thank God for both of you."

# CHAPTER *fifteen*

Lauren studied herself in the dressing room mirror. Who was that girl with the in-style haircut and professionally done makeup and earrings? She fingered the emerald beginner studs and giggled with happiness. And this amazing dress? She did a little whirl and the A-line dress danced with her. She never would have chosen it on her own, had even balked when Sheila recommended it, but she was so glad she tried it on. She couldn't wait to show Sheila.

Stocking footed, she stepped out of the dressing room into a waiting area filled with tufted chairs and wall-length mirrors. Nothing like she was used to at all. What had she done to deserve such kindness from Sheila?

Sheila walked into the waiting area, carrying another couple of dresses, and came to a dead stop. "Wow." She hung the dresses on a nearby rack. "I think we've found your dress. You look beautiful, sweetie."

A blush rose to Lauren's cheeks. "I do?"

"You're going to leave your young man speechless."

Her cheeks heated even more, and she covered them with her hands.

"But we have one little problem." Sheila tapped a finger against her lips.

Lauren looked down at her dress, then into a three-way mirror, and frowned. She couldn't see anything wrong. Sheila came up behind her, put an arm around her shoulders, then pointed down.

"Those are darling socks, my dear, but they don't quite go with your dress."

Lauren laughed. "I guess not. But let me buy my shoes. I don't feel right—"

"Absolutely not." Sheila shooed her toward the dressing room. "This is my treat."

No sense in arguing. Lauren practically floated into the dressing room where she changed into the skinny jeans and peasant top she'd picked out earlier in the day, one of the many outfits Sheila had helped her find. She shook her head. She'd never before believed she could pull off the look of skinny jeans. Wait till Jon saw her!

What had she ever done to deserve this star treatment? She thanked God for this amazing day, for Sheila, her husband, the entire Brooks family. Even Nathan. He had his good moments here and there.

She pulled on her new heeled booties and draped her dress over her arm. It was easy to see how Sheila's annual shopping date with her mother had become a cherished memory. Lauren would always treasure this day and prayed it would be an annual event.

Walking on these heels would take a bit of getting used to, but Lauren was up for the challenge. She met Sheila in the waiting area and handed her the dress. "I don't know how to say 'thank you.'"

"By just being you." Sheila hugged Lauren, then carried the dress to the checkout counter. She paid for it and asked them to add it to the bundles she'd already purchased. "Now let's find you some dress shoes." She aimed for the shoe department with Lauren keeping pace at her side. "Our limo is scheduled to—"

"A limo?" A giggle escaped Lauren's mouth. She'd never been in a limousine before.

"Of course. To take us to supper, after we've gone home and changed into our dazzling new dresses. This is a special day. We need to end it in style."

Wow. This was Christmas in July! Would today's surprises never end? "It's not necessary." They stepped onto the down escalator crowded with other shoppers.

"Of course it is. It's how Mother and I did it, and I plan on doing it just like her."

"You must have had a special relationship with your mom."

A frown stole Sheila's dimples. "That, my dear, is a conversation for another day."

So Sheila and her mom didn't get along? Or was it something else? Regardless, Lauren knew better than to force the topic. Besides, she didn't want to spoil the day for her or for Sheila.

They found the shoe department where Lauren tried on several pairs of dress shoes. Their choice ended up being black open-toed pumps with a two-and-a-half inch heel. A classic and flexible style that Lauren could wear for any special occasion.

Then they gathered their purchases and brought them back to Sheila's condo where they prepared for the evening out. After dressing, Lauren stared at herself in the guestroom mirror and tears threatened. Very happy tears. She felt like a princess.

As Lauren glided down the stairs, Sheila was primping herself in the mirror on her front door. She must have seen or heard Lauren come down, because she spun around, her hand over her mouth. "Sweetie, you look divine!"

Lauren blushed. "I actually feel rather divine"

"Well you should, and tonight I get to show you off. The limo should be here in about fifteen minutes. If you're ready, have a seat. Those shoes will take some breaking in." She gestured to the couch, and Sheila joined her there. "I hope you've had a fun day."

"Fun?" That didn't even begin to describe her day. "It's been amazing. I just wish Mom or Dad were here to see me now."

"Oh, sweetie." Sheila gave her a side hug. "They would be so proud of you. On any day. You're a special young lady."

"They were special." Rats. Her eyes burned with threatening tears and she waved fingers in front of her eyes."

Sheila gave her another hug. "I'd like to know about your mom and dad."

"You would?"

"Of course."

Lauren stared down at her newly manicured fingers and bit into her lower lip tasting cherry lip gloss. No one ever asked about her parents. Maybe people thought if they didn't mention her dad or mom, it would be easier for her to move on, and life would somehow be less painful. But she wanted, no, she needed to remember them. She'd been so close to her dad and he understood her. She'd always wanted to talk with someone about how she missed having a mother. Finally someone cared enough to ask.

She sniffled and Sheila handed her a tissue.

"If it's too hard ..."

"No, no, I'm just happy you asked." She wiped her nose and dabbed at her eyes. "Mom was always singing, and we constantly had music in our home." Lauren closed her eyes and envisioned her family portrait, with the three of them standing by her mom's piano. Lauren's last picture of her mother. The perfect way to remember her. "She'd sing to me every night and trace my face with her finger. She played piano and Dad would sing duets with her."

Lauren looked down at her own hands that played piano, at fingernails shaped and glossed with a clear polish. She didn't need to hide her fingers anymore.

She didn't need to hide from her mother's memory either. "When Mom died, the music stopped. I took piano lessons for a few years and always hoped Dad would sing again."

Sheila rested a hand on Lauren's arm. "I'm so sorry, sweetie."

"But he did start singing, This past year. He sang with me, like he had with Mom. I thought things were going so well. And then ... and then ..." She balled her fingernails into her palms and squished her eyes closed. She couldn't cry. Not now. Not when the day had been so perfect, when she actually had on makeup that would record her emotions.

But tears seeped out anyway and then gushed like a waterfall down her cheeks.

Sheila enveloped arms around her and their tears mingled. But they weren't all tears of sadness. Lauren finally found a friend: someone who listened to her, someone who laughed with her, and now someone who shed tears with her.

SO FAR, SO GOOD. Lexi hadn't had a moment to try anything with his nephew, but better yet, when Sheila called earlier in the night, she actually sounded happy. Richard didn't want to get his hopes up, but he prayed this was a permanent change.

He heard the garage door go up, then moments later, laughter came from Richard's kitchen, just as aliens streamed a deadly ray down on San Francisco. On the television. He paused the movie, and Nathan, Jon, and Lexi groaned, but he hadn't heard Sheila's genuine laughter for weeks and needed to know what Lauren did to bring it back.

Sheila flicked on the living room lights and the kids whined again.

Blinking, Richard eyed Sheila and Lauren standing near the kitchen entrance. Lauren was certainly not the mousy creature who'd left with Sheila earlier in the day. The jeans and blouse Lauren wore were a definite step up from the tired outfit she'd begun the day in.

"Hey there." Jon sat up, his eyes wide. "Wow."

"Lauren?" Surprise even rang in Nathan's voice. "You look awesome."

"Thanks, Nate." Lauren smiled without looking down and her

eyes connected with Nate's as quiet acceptance seemed to pass between the two.

Richard stifled a grin. His wife had performed a miracle in transforming this shy, insecure girl into a pretty, young woman with confidence, and clearly the boys took notice.

Apparently, so did Lexi. She somehow velcroed herself tighter against Nathan and would have been on his nephew's lap if Richard allowed it. Sheila had been prophetic when she said to keep an eye on the girl.

Jon got up from the couch where the three teens sat and pointed toward his seat. "Join us?"

"Sure." Blushing, Lauren took the space vacated by Jon. He sat on the floor in front of her with his shoulders grazing the girl's legs.

Sheila touched Richard's shoulder and whispered, "That's our cue to leave."

"I'll be right in." Although he'd like to be a mouse in the corner. He filled a bowl of buttered popcorn for Lauren and brought her a bottle of Pepsi. He stepped toward the bedroom but turned back to the kids. "It's bedtime right after the movie's done."

Oh brother, he'd become his father.

There couldn't be a better man to emulate.

And Richard couldn't wait to apply his father's teaching to his own child.

They dressed for bed quickly, with TV explosions and teen laughter providing sweet accompaniment. Once in bed, Richard pulled the silk sheets over his shoulders and Sheila cuddled up next to him, her breath restful and her touch lacking the tension he'd become used to. If they didn't have a roomful of teens only ten feet away, he'd definitely take advantage of the moment.

Perhaps Lauren had performed some magic of her own today.

He circled his arm around Sheila's shoulder, breathing in his favorite scent, Dior's Midnight Poison, and kissed her forehead.

Kissing her lips would be far too dangerous tonight. "I take it you two had a good day."

"Um-hmm." She snuggled even closer, circling her hand over his chest. "She's an amazing girl."

And he was married to an amazing woman, one who was tying his body into knots. "Tell me about it?"

She rested her head on his shoulder and relayed the highlights of their afternoon. He heard enough to know that she had bonded with this girl in a way that transcended friendship.

"There's something more important I need to talk about now." She rose to her side and leaned on her elbow.

"Something good, I presume."

She ran a hand over his chest, twisting his insides into a pretzel, and whispered in his ear. "I want to see my parents."

## CHAPTER *sixteen*

Richard still grinned at the revelation Sheila had made nearly four hours ago, one that took away his desire for sleep.

She wanted to see her parents.

Not that he minded lying in bed, his wife's legs tangled with his. He couldn't get over the change he saw in Sheila and in Lauren. God was definitely busy working miracles today.

A scraping sound came from outside his open window, drawing Richard's thoughts away from Sheila. He closed his eyes and listened.

Crickets chirping. Breeze rustling leaves.

Wood creaking, soft footfalls, and muted giggles.

Nathan!

And Richard thought he could trust his nephew. He untangled his leg from Sheila's, gently wrested her arm away from his chest, and then slid out of bed praying for one more miracle.

"Richard?" Sleep filled Sheila's voice as she reached across the mattress.

"Be right back," he whispered and leaned down to kiss her cheek. She stretched then lay motionless.

He slipped on a pair of jeans and a T-shirt and then tiptoed out of his bedroom, down the short hall, through the kitchen, to the patio doors.

The deck light was off, but he could see them in the

moonlight, already too engaged to be aware of him as he noiselessly slid open the door and remained in its opening.

"Lexi," he said then cleared his throat to awaken his vocal cords. "It's bed time." The two teenagers tumbling off the lounge chair would have been comical on video, but this situation was far from humorous.

Marcus was going to kill him.

The two of them lay still, staring wide-eyed back at him, like he was some specter hiding in the shadows. "Lexi." He kept his tone low, but his intent was clear and unyielding. "It's. Bed. Time."

He had become his dad.

The kids leapt up. Lexi tugged on the hem of her shirt, straightening it. She led the way to the house, arrogantly eyeing Richard all the way. She brushed past him and gave her hair a pompous flip. A challenge, asserting that this wouldn't be the last time.

Not on his watch.

Nathan followed Lexi, shuffling his feet, his neck bent toward the deck. Richard stretched out his arm, blocking Nathan's entrance. "Not you."

"Oh, man." Nathan mumbled and dragged his feet back along the decking before flopping onto a patio chair.

Richard closed the door then walked to the deck's railing. He peered out into the darkness of the woods, its gloom pressing in on him. Was this how his dad had felt every time Richard had gone on a date, knowing his son had already strayed way beyond his pre-set boundaries, wondering how much leeway could be given without driving his son away?

What could Richard say now that would have an effect on his nephew?

"We weren't doing anything." Nathan's voice came out in a whimper.

Richard kept his chuckle to himself. No, not yet. Not until

they'd gone so far there was no turning back. *God, help me know what to tell him.* Silence lingered in the air as he debated how to proceed.

Hopefully that silence was invoking a soundless agony in Nate, forcing the teen to contemplate what he'd been doing.

"You didn't wait for Sheila." Nathan offered as a statement of fact rather than accusation, perhaps a hope of finding approval in a kindred spirit.

Approval was the last thing Richard would offer. "No. I didn't." Richard's confession, months ago, to his family that Marissa had aborted his child was also a confession of sorts to his nephews that he hadn't led a wholesome life. It was something they hadn't deserved to be burdened with, yet it proved how even seemingly solitary actions, ones he once believed affected only himself, had rippling consequences.

How could he encourage his nephews to be different from him when they looked up to him so much, when they thought he could do no wrong, when he'd done so many things in the wrong order? How could he convince Nate, now, that he wished he could take it all back?

Nate came to stand by him at the railing. Richard turned his eyes enough to see that Nathan's gaze had become lost in the woods' darkness.

"How old were you?" Nathan picked at the oak railing.

Richard kept his sigh to himself. *God, can I lie? Please?* Again God's response was quiet but Richard knew the answer. Marcus was going to have his head. He stared out at the shadowed trees. "About your age."

"Oh," the word escaped Nathan's mouth in a breathy whisper. "We really weren't going to do anything."

"Right." Richard chortled through his nose. "That's exactly what I told myself the first time too, and then things ... well, they got out of hand. The first times I never planned on it, had even told myself I could stop anytime, that I'd hear and obey God's whispers. Oh, I heard them, all right, but when you're in the moment, there's nothing else that matters. Pretty soon, I stopped hearing him altogether, in every aspect of my life."

"I don't understand what's so wrong about it. I mean if we're careful and all. I hear the talk at school, guys joking, questioning my orientation. I tell them I'm waiting for marriage, and they think that's the funniest thing on earth. Everyone does it. Guys at school. Guys in my church youth group. Everyone but me."

"Nate, you know better than that."

"If I weren't a Christian, it wouldn't matter. No one would care. They'd toss me a condom and tell me to be safe."

"Oh, I'm sure they would, but they'd be tossing a lie. There's only one thing that's one hundred percent safe. Believe me, I know." Richard turned to face his nephew whose gaze remained outwards. "Besides, it does matter. Purity is a gift that, once it's opened, can never be rewrapped." Never. There's no turning back. Richard nodded toward a lawn chair. "Sit."

Nathan silently obeyed as Richard pulled another chair close, facing his nephew. "I used to think the same way. I was always careful, always safe. I wasn't hurting anyone. The girls—the women—they wanted it as much as I did. Most pursued me. But that doesn't matter. I was still taking something that wasn't mine to take, and it was slowly killing my spirit. Why do you think I'd go so long in between visits home? Why I'd miss out on Christmas, Thanksgiving, Easter, birthdays? More than anything I wanted to be here with the family, but I couldn't face everyone knowing my behavior was wrong, knowing I hurt them badly. Knowing how badly I hurt you."

Nathan remained still, his head down. Richard hoped something he said was sinking in, but knowing teenagers, how they look at everything with the eyes of immortality, he doubted it. It was time to make this lesson personal. He leaned in close to Nathan and lowered his voice.

"Think of Jaclyn, ten, twelve years from now, when she

begins to date. What do you want for her? What kind of boy do you want her going out with? Someone like me who can't even remember the names of the women I've slept with, or someone like your dad who treated your mother with the respect and honor she deserved."

Nathan fidgeted with the chain around his neck. "I'd wanna kill the guy who touched her."

"Exactly. Do *you* want to be *that* guy?"

"No." Nathan kicked his heel on the wood deck.

"*I* was that guy. I was that guy who went out with little sisters ... daughters. I was that guy who showed no respect for women, who thought only of myself." In the end, that me-centric view had only produced seclusion and loneliness. "Let me tell you, once I realized what I was doing, it's a pretty rotten feeling.

"My behavior ended up costing lives, Nathan. The life of my baby." Richard pointed out to the corner of the yard where four small lilac bushes had been planted this past spring in an arc around the fire pit. "Each of those bushes are planted in memory of a life taken by us—me and Sheila. That's the cost, Nathan." He steadied the quiver creeping up in his throat. "Justin Keene died because I was so distraught over losing my child that I didn't pay attention when I was driving. That's the cost." Those memories still cost him sleep and most likely always would.

"God forgives, Nathan. He knows we make mistakes, yet he graces us with forgiveness, but that doesn't undo what I've done.

"Then I met Sheila. Fell in love with her, and for some inexplicable reason she loves me back. Didn't think it could happen to me. Didn't think I deserved that kind of love. But before we could even think of marriage, I had to get myself tested—AIDS, all the STDs. How sad is that? If you do things in the right order, that's not a concern. I got tested because I love Sheila. If I found out I was sick, she would know what she was getting herself into. I wanted her to know she didn't have to be stuck with me."

"You okay?"

Richard nodded. "Lucky, when you consider …" He personally knew of too many other people who weren't so fortunate. He often wondered why he'd been spared. "Sheila and I waited for marriage, you know. I couldn't offer her my purity, but we'll never regret waiting. I discovered there's a huge difference between having sex and making love. One is selfish—all about that momentary high, then the guilty lows, and then wanting more to fill the void created by the behavior in the first place. The other is about giving, about sharing, and truly loving, becoming one flesh. But, best of all, it's blessed by God and, believe me, that makes a difference."

Richard allowed the night to absorb their thoughts. The decision was Nathan's. Hopefully, in the future, he'd make the right one.

"You dated my mom." Nathan's eyes rose to meet Richard's. Worry lined his forehead and tensed his shoulders. Perhaps making this personal had been the right path to take.

"I did." Richard allowed a smile. "After a slap on the face and her calling me a few choice names, she showed me the door. Of *my* car. I had to walk five miles to get home. Should have learned my lesson then."

Relief relaxed his nephew's shoulders, but they tensed again. Nathan stood and stuffed his hands into his pockets while staring at the deck floor.

Richard waited for Nathan to make the next move. Make his nephew think some more.

Nathan pulled a hand from his pocket and held it out as if to offer a handshake. Richard grasped his nephew's hand and stilled.

Thank God he'd been awake earlier. Another minor miracle.

The square, nearly flat package Nathan pressed into his palm said the boy wasn't as innocent as he claimed. Richard stared at Nathan, but his nephew refused to look up.

"It was Lexi's," Nathan said timidly. "I hadn't planned on using it."

Richard ran his thumb over the sealed package he'd once been so familiar with. "I know." But plans have a way of changing. This proved his nephew was anticipating the change.

"You gonna tell Dad?"

"No."

Nathan sighed happily.

"I expect you to."

Nathan grunted something unintelligible.

"Go to bed." Richard nodded to the house. "And stay there."

Nathan jogged to the house.

Richard stopped at the patio door and watched Nathan disappear into the basement where his bed was set up.

So this was what fatherhood was going to be like. How could a heart take it?

How could God's heart take it? Here, Richard was worrying about one child. God bore that burden for everyone.

He walked to the railing, rested his forearms on the top, and subconsciously wove the condom between his fingers. Marcus was going to draw and quarter him.

Richard looked up at the sky, at the flickering stars, the nearly full moon with a hazy rainbow circling it. *God, how do you do it? Am I ready for this?* It was the first time he'd asked that question, the first time he wondered if he was cut out to be a father. He chuckled. It was a bit too late to worry about that, wasn't it?

The scent of Midnight Poison drifted toward him, preparing Richard for the arms that circled his waist and the sleepy, yet silky voice that breathed in his ear. "What's so funny?"

"I'm going to be a father." He had to admit, that was rather funny. Was this how Abraham felt when God told him he was going to be a father at such an old age?

Maybe Isaac would be a good name for a boy.

"So I hear. And that brought you out here at three o'clock in the morning?"

He turned around without letting her arms withdraw, rested his hands on her hips, and leaned his backside into the railing. Fatigue darkened her eyes, but the corners of her mouth lifted. Apparently she was still content with the decision she'd announced at bedtime.

"I was getting in some father practice."

Her eyebrows tented inward. "Nate?"

He nodded and rubbed his nose against hers. "You were right to be concerned about Lexi, but then Nate's not exactly putting up stop signs either." Richard showed her the condom.

"Oh, no." Breath rushed past her lips.

"We had a talk."

"Did he listen?"

Richard rested his forehead against hers and spoke softly. "I think so, but how do I know? How do I know I said the right things? What if I only encouraged him to follow in my footsteps? It'd kill me if Nathan did that."

"You can't control him."

He sighed. "I wish I could. To think this is what I put my parents through. Talk about feeling helpless."

"And if he does make that choice?"

He shrugged. "What more can I do? I guess it helps me understand God better. If Nathan makes that decision, we'll be disappointed, but we'll still love him. Nothing could change that. I finally understand how my family could love me with what I put them through, why they didn't write me off."

Sheila's hands climbed to his shoulders and her fingers kneaded his knotted muscles. "Maybe I have to think of my parents in another way. Maybe they did love me, but didn't know how to show it." She shrugged. "At least I have parents yet. Lauren's all alone. Today she helped me see how selfish I've been, how fortunate I am. I need to give them another chance.

Maybe God wants me to introduce them to him."

Richard pulled Sheila tight against him and gave her a soft, lingering kiss. If they didn't have a house full of guests ... He pulled from the embrace. "You'll call tomorrow?"

"Tomorrow." She nodded.

He kissed her again and led her back to bed. Tomorrow, once all the guests left, then he and Sheila would share their love the way God intended.

LAUREN LAY IN THE grass by Sheila's condo, and Jon sat beside her gazing up at the stars. Nathan and Lexi were supposed to meet them here nearly an hour ago, and their late arrival was marring an otherwise perfect day. Jon was becoming frustrated, and rightly so because he'd promised to have Lauren home by midnight. That was no longer possible. How could Nate be so selfish? She expected it from Lexi, but Nate? Although he had been testing his parents of late.

There was nothing Lauren could do about Nathan, but she could try to distract Jon, get him to think of other things. She pointed off to her right, above Sheila's condo. "Is that the big dipper?"

"Hmm, I think so." He didn't even look. He just sat, plucking the grass. "I'm not too into stargazing."

Shoot. There went that idea. She stared at the sky sprinkled with far fewer stars than back home, at least stars they could see. Astronomy wasn't her thing, but she still loved the night sky, and she loved making up her own constellations.

Wait. That could be a good idea. She pointed toward the south. "That star cluster, above the bridge, it looks like a trombone."

Jon leaned back on his elbows, staring off. "Huh, you're right. I think we should give it a name."

"Oh, good idea. How about The Slide, you know for the slide on a trombone."

"Excellent." His voice regained the upbeat tone it usually held. "Now, it's my turn."

"Go ahead." She blew out a breath. Thank God, the diversion worked.

He looked all around, then stilled, his gaze just over her head. "Over there." He pointed upward and to her left. "You know what that is?"

Wrinkling her nose, she stared at a cluster of dim stars. "A cotton ball?"

He snorted. "Good one. No, it's an inverse Dalmatian."

"Say what?"

"You know, instead of white with black spots, that one's black with white spots."

She laughed out loud. "My turn again." She searched the stars until one grouping stuck out to her. "Found one." Leaning on her right hand, she pointed with her left. "Straight ahead, just above the trees by the Mississippi."

"Where?" He raised his right arm, pointing everywhere but at her find, so she grabbed his hand and pointed with it. "Right there. It's a heart. See it?"

He entwined his fingers with hers, and stared at her, not the sky.

Her heart zoomed into orbit, it beat so fast. He wasn't going to kiss her, was he? Was she ready?

He leaned closer, and a familiar laugh came through the semi-darkness, propelling Jon off the ground. Nathan and Lexi stepped around the corner of the condo, arms entwined and holding hands, laughing as if nothing was wrong.

Jon crossed his arms over his chest as Nate and Lexi walked toward them, the street lamps spotlighting their faces.

Nathan's laughter halted. "Hey, Jon, what's up?"

"Where've you been?" Jon's anger came through in his husky voice. Lauren had never heard him use that tone before.

Nathan glanced between Jon and Lauren and shrugged.

"Walking."

"Do you have any clue what time it is?"

"No." Nathan shrugged as if he didn't care.

How could he not care? Lauren wanted to shake him to his senses. The fool didn't know how good he had it with an entire family who loved and cared for him.

Lexi kept her arm wrapped with Nathan's while resting her open hand on a hip that was cocked to one side. Her mouth tilted up.

"We were supposed to meet over an hour ago." Jon's voice rose.

"No. It's not that ..." Nate drew up his arm, keeping Lexi's hand in his, and stared at his watch. His face drooped along with his arm. Lexi didn't let go. "Oh man, Jon, I'm sorry. I had no clue. I lost track of time. Honest. Why didn't you call me?"

Jon's eyes seemed to bug out of his head, so Lauren took his arm hoping to calm him. "We both tried. You didn't answer."

"What? I never felt it." Nathan shook Lexi's hand from his arm and pulled his phone from his back pocket. His face drooped some more. "I was sure I had 'vibrate' on. I swear."

"Remember you turned it off when we walked across the bridge." Lexi grinned like the Cheshire cat. "You didn't want to ruin the romantic experience."

Oh brother. Lauren was no romance expert, but anyone could see that Lexi wanted more than a romantic experience.

"But I thought ..." Nathan looked upward, pinching his lips. "I could swear I turned it back on."

Lexi shrugged, a guilty smirk on her face. "Guess not."

"You realize I promised." Jon shook off Lauren's arm and poked Nathan in the chest. Nathan tumbled back a step. "I *promised* your dad I'd have Lauren back by midnight. I don't like breaking promises."

Neither did Lauren. How would Marcus react to Jon bringing her home late, even if it wasn't Jon's fault?

Nathan looked from Lauren, then to Jon. "Guys, I'm sorry."

"What's the big deal? So, you're a little late?" Lexi again circled her arm around Nathan's.

"You don't get it, do you?" Nathan's voice raised a notch, and he glared at Lexi. "Dad trusted me."

*Yeah, Nathan. You're finally waking up!* Lauren wanted to applaud him.

"So?" Lexi smirked. "What can he do to you?"

"Take away my car." Nathan kicked at the grass. "Ground me for forever."

Lauren gnawed on her lip. Would she be grounded for the first time in her life?

"And you'll let him?" Lexi jerked her arm away from Nathan.

"Well, yeah." He crossed his arms and got in Lexi's face. "It's not a matter of letting him. It's the way it is." He turned toward Lauren and Jon. "Guys, I really blew it. This whole weekend, I blew it big time."

"Yeah, you did." Jon shifted his jaw.

Yes, he had, and he'd spoiled the day for Lauren and Jon too. Not that she hadn't had fun, but this put a damper on an otherwise awesome day.

Nathan shook his head while glancing between her and Jon. "I'm sorry guys. Really I am." He shoved away Lexi's arm again.

Lauren wasn't one to judge others, but Lexi was trouble for Nathan, and before tonight he'd seemed to welcome that trouble. Maybe Nathan was finally getting wise to that girl.

Lexi's smug expression began to fade. She crossed her arms and tossed her hair over her shoulder. "I don't think it's such a big deal. I'm always late. My folks don't care."

How sad was that? Lauren actually felt bad for Lexi.

"Mine do"—Nathan stabbed a finger to his chest—"and it is a big deal. Dad said I could get a car 'cuz he thought I was mature enough. Trustworthy. So what do I do with that trust? I cram it in his face." He kicked at the grass and stuffed his hands into his front pockets.

"It's not getting any earlier." The angry edge in Jon's voice had dulled to disappointment. "Let's go."

"Here." Nathan held his keys out to Jon. "I gotta call Dad. I have a feeling I won't be fit to drive."

Jon quietly accepted the keys then nodded to Lauren. "Join me up front?"

Gladly. She sat beside Jon and anxiety crept up her spine as he headed for home. Was she in trouble too? Marcus and Janet had been so good to her, she hated causing them worry.

But at least she had someone to worry over her, unlike Lexi, and for that she was very grateful.


TODAY, A DECISION HAD to be made, the toughest decision Meghan would ever have to make. She sat at the dining room table with Doran too close in the chair beside her. Being in the same house was too close. The same town. Even the same state.

"Ready?" Doran tapped the notebook in front of him.

*No.* She circled her hand over her stomach. Four weeks left till the due date. At least four more weeks with Doran, then it was adios for good.

The baby shifted beneath her hand and Meghan blinked back tears. Four more weeks until this baby belonged to someone else. Could she really do this?

"Hey, it's okay." Doran wiped the tear off her cheek and she jerked back.

"Don't." Her chin quivered. This was tough enough without him being kind and caring. "Let's get it over with." She shifted her chair further away and blotted her eyes.

With a sigh, Doran flipped open his notebook to a chart checkmarking the pros and cons of the three couples they'd narrowed their decision down to. The checkmarks were added up beneath each couple's names, bringing Doran's decision down to a question of mere numbers. Two couples were virtually equal with checks in the pro column. But making a choice wasn't that simple. He'd forgotten to list the one point that carried the most weight: gut feeling.

"Tell me what you're thinking." Doran pointed to his chart. He was asking her opinion first? When had he started caring for someone other than himself?

"I'm uncomfortable with this last couple we interviewed." She pointed to the third column, the one with the fewest marks under pro. The young couple from her parents' church was nice enough, but they were too young, too idealistic. Although Meghan was younger than they were, she felt more mature.

"I agree." He drew an X over the column. "They were a bit too bubbly, you know. Maybe trying too hard to impress. I'm sure they'll have plenty of other options."

One down. But now came the hard part. Both of the remaining couples would make excellent parents.

"What about these other two?" Doran pointed to the names. "Is there someone you're comfortable with? I like them both and I don't think either would be a bad decision. They all seem to have good jobs, they're well-grounded, and they go to church. I know that's important to you."

He was being way too thoughtful, too concerned with her opinion. What was his angle? He pointed to a column. "This couple's older. They live further from you—closer to me, if I go back home. How do you feel about that?"

"I'm not sure." She studied the chart. She liked the idea of the couple living far away, where she wouldn't see them regularly, although the other couple lived fifty miles away and chances of running into them would be slim as well. One couple was in their late twenties. That was a definite pro, but the other had lots of nieces and nephews. With them, her baby would grow up surrounded with loving family, and a sibling a few months younger. They'd practically be twins.

"What are you thinking, Meggie?"

That she didn't want to make this decision. That she wanted to be her baby girl's mom.

That her daughter would have a much better life with two parents.

Why was this so hard? She looked down at folded hands. *God, what do we do?*

Doran pushed away from the table and returned with a box of Kleenex and a plate of freshly baked M&M cookies.

He handed her a cookie saturated with M&M's, and she wiped her eyes. Who was this man seated next to her who anticipated her needs and placed them before his own? He certainly wasn't the arrogant fool she'd dated in college.

She bit into her cookie and sighed. Warm, soft, and totally delicious. Exactly what she needed.

"Better now?"

She nodded and took another bite. No more putting off the painful. The couple they chose deserved to have some time to prepare.

Swallowing the cookie along with a heart-sized knot, she pointed at the middle column, the one her gut told her to go with. "I'm leaning toward this couple."

He smiled.

Now, why did he have to go and do that? His smile always turned her brain into mush.

"I agree." He tapped the column with his pencil.

"You do?" No way did she expect that. She was certain he'd choose the other couple.

"Call it gut instinct, I don't know. Like I said, either couple would be great, but this one"—he pointed to the name again— "they just seem like the right one, somehow."

Without thinking she turned toward him and threw her arms around his neck. He startled, then wrapped his around her back.

And she kissed him.

He returned the kiss, resurrecting feelings she thought long buried. He pulled away and scratched the back of his head. "I'm sorry. I shouldn't have ..."

"No. It was my fault." She wiped her lips, trying to rid them of the sweet sensation his kiss left behind. She couldn't care for him. Not now. That would ruin everything.

He got up, evading her eyes as he spoke. "I should go."

Yes. He needed to leave now. His presence was far too confusing.

"I'll come back later when your parents are around. We can make the phone calls together."

She nodded as he hurried out the front door.

Then she went to her bedroom and cried.

# CHAPTER *seventeen*

Richard steered the rented BMW into the clubhouse parking lot and looked over at Sheila. For the umpteenth time today she was primping herself in the mirror. He'd never seen her this on edge, this insecure. Even this morning, after they arrived at their Arizona hotel, she had pleaded with him to let her cancel the lunch with her parents. But if they flew home without seeing her parents, she would eventually regret it. He wasn't about to let her squander this opportunity, even though he was getting the silent treatment because of it.

After today he would drop the subject of her parents. He prayed she wouldn't want to.

The car's clock read exactly noon as he parked next to a Mercedes. Right on time.

"Are you ready?"

Ignoring him, she smoothed her hands over her pale green, cotton maternity sundress that stretched over a tiny bump where his child lay. Sexy beyond words.

She pulled down the visor and adjusted single strands of hair, as if one hair out of place would somehow alter her parents' opinion of her. Why their opinion even mattered, after all these years, he had no clue. Why wasn't she content to be herself and let them accept—or not accept—her for the person she was?

That logic clearly didn't work on her today. She reapplied lipstick and mascara to a face that was already perfect. Her hands fell to her lap and she frowned.

"Done avoiding yet?" He made a show of looking at his watch. He hated being late.

"I'm not avoiding."

"I can see that." His lips curled into a smile. "You're beautiful, perfect even."

"You don't know my mother."

"True. But she's had eighteen years to change. Give her a chance."

"They get one chance."

"That's all I'm asking."

"Then I'm ready."

SHEILA TOOK ONE FINAL glance in the mirror as Richard walked around the car, his grey Hugo Boss suit emphasizing strong shoulders and a svelte waist. The stained-glass tie accented his plum dress shirt and brought out his indigo eyes. Simply gorgeous. Mother would approve.

He opened her door and held out his hand.

He was right about avoiding. Ever since she'd made the call to her father, a mere two nights ago, and they'd arranged a time and place to meet, she'd literally felt sick to her stomach, and those feelings weren't due to morning sickness.

"I don't bite." He waggled his fingers.

No. But her mother might. She drew in a breath and grasped his hand. A hand firm with love and protection. He helped her stand and she straightened her dress, one she'd spent all the previous day searching for, one her mother would approve of. Why that even mattered, she didn't know.

Richard was right. It shouldn't matter. But all the shoulds and shouldn'ts didn't have to face reality and didn't erase her emotions.

Side by side they walked toward the clubhouse, her heart accelerating with each step. Today she was being asked to ignore the last eighteen years she'd spent forgetting her parents. Hopefully, she'd be able to call upon the diplomacy skills she'd carefully nurtured since her abandonment.

Richard's hand squeezed hers. At least she was no longer going it alone.

He escorted her into the restaurant. No crystal chandeliers hung from the ceiling, and the waitstaff wasn't dressed in tuxedos. Not the atmosphere she expected. Perhaps her parents had changed.

Richard asked for the Stephen Peterson table as she looked around, studying faces. Would she recognize them anymore? Eighteen years could age a person greatly. Maybe not her mother. Wrinkles wouldn't dare set in on the impenetrable Lois Peterson's face.

So far, no one familiar sat in the crowded clubhouse. Richard pressed her back, directing her to follow the maître d' to their table.

Ah, yes, this was more of what she expected from her mother. The table—empty yet, thank goodness—was located in a semi-private alcove that had large windows overlooking the eighteenth hole. Pale blue skies blanketed lush greens and deep blue water hazards. Gray mountains hemmed in lifeless brown deserts. Vibrant life and lonesome death all in one picture.

It was amazing how God could breathe life into such a desolate place.

She laughed silently. She'd just described herself.

Richard pulled out a chair for her, the one closest to the window. "For a better view."

But now her escape route had an obstacle. "You think you're clever."

He grinned. "Yes, I do."

She was trapped. By her own husband. Reluctantly, she sat on the cushioned leather seat and he gently pressed her chair toward the table. Now she could get comfortable before her parents arrived.

If they arrived. She wouldn't put it past her mother to not show up. Her father had said over the phone that her mother was not keen on the reunion. Maybe though, she'd embrace the grandmother role. It was the least Sheila could ask for.

A waiter strode to the table and Richard ordered two ice waters with lemon slices. The waiter walked away and Richard grasped her hand beneath the table. "Are you okay?"

"No."

He grinned and patted her arm. The nerve of him.

Sheila shivered yet felt herself perspiring. This must be what cold sweat felt like.

She glanced at Richard's watch. Ten minutes late—fashionably late, according to her mother. Fashion had seemed to play a part in all her mother's decisions.

With her fingernails digging into Richard's hand, she forced her gaze toward the entrance. Somehow he remained silent although he must have puncture wounds. An elderly couple walked toward their table. Her heart galloped faster. Was that them?

A chrome walker supported the man's slightly slouched posture and the woman led him along, her arm wrapped around his. The man's silver-gray hair circled the perimeter of his head, and his face was mapped with wrinkles.

Her father.

No gray dared stay in her mother's neatly styled hair, although its dark blonde hue was definitely courtesy of a stylist. She did have wrinkles, downward slants by her mouth and eyes, a permanent record of a frown from a lifetime of dissatisfaction. Her sleeveless, grass-green linen sheath showed off a still slender figure. But Sheila was drawn to her mother's hollow gray eyes and prayed she wouldn't look that hard, that distant, when she grew older.

Neither of her parents had dimples. Interesting. Sheila hadn't remembered that detail.

Her mother walked with her chin forward and her back straight. Lips straight too. Still strikingly beautiful and still intimidating. It was obvious the woman didn't want to be here.

"That's them?" Richard whispered.

Sheila nodded, one slow nod. Her carefully fashioned speech had deserted her memory. She had nothing to tell these two, nothing God would approve of anyway.

Richard kissed her cheek. "You'll be fine."

Yes she would be. In about one hour, when she finally had the chance to say goodbye, the opportunity they'd stolen from her eighteen years ago.

Richard stood and Sheila glanced at his hand she'd skewered with her fingernails. He was subconsciously rubbing out the indentations. Thankfully, no blood.

Her parents neared the table, and she debated standing. They didn't deserve that act of courtesy, but she stood anyway.

Richard smiled and offered his hand. "Mrs. Peterson." Her mother's hand limply accepted.

"Mr. Peterson." Her father gripped Richard's hand. He even smiled.

"It's a pleasure to meet you. Richard, is it?" His voice was lower than she remembered and had a slight vibration, but it was confident. Apparently his faculties had aged less than his appearance.

"Yes sir."

"Sheila." Her father's gaze sought hers and her eyes stung. "You've blossomed into a beautiful young woman."

Sheila caught herself smiling until her gaze fixed on her mother. The woman's cheeks were drawn in, pinching her lips forward. More wrinkles appeared above and below the lips. She still hadn't said a word, at least not out loud. She moved past her husband's walker to her seat.

"Let me help you." Richard glided to the woman's chair,

directly across the table from Sheila, and Sheila's gaze met her mother's.

Sheila shivered beneath the icy glare she remembered from childhood. She also recognized a familiar scent. Not a favorite perfume, although she detected a faint citrus fragrance. Rather, it was what the perfume covered. Apparently cigarettes still held some power over her mother. It gave Sheila little satisfaction knowing the only thing her mother bowed to was tobacco.

Richard pulled out a chair for her father and supported him as the man sat. Her husband was being too kind.

"Thank you. Thank you." Her father wiggled his chair closer to the table. "I had hip surgery recently, and the recovery hasn't been too kind to me. I'm fortunate to have Lois here to help me." He patted her arm and smiled. She even smiled back. A genuine smile. Huh.

Her parents still loved each other. Amazing. Too bad they couldn't have spread that love around a little bit.

Richard seated himself and the waiter glided to the table.

"A Chateau Margaux." Her father raised an open hand toward Richard. "For you?"

"None, thank you."

The waiter nodded then left.

"Teetotaler?"

Richard politely nodded.

"He's sympathizing with me," Sheila heard her voice say. "Since I can't drink, he won't either." She felt Richard's knee jut into hers. Why did she feel the need to justify the fact that her husband abstained from liquor? Why was it so difficult to be herself?

"That's right." Mother spread the cloth napkin over her lap. "You're pregnant."

Sheila smiled in spite of her mother's condescending tone, but didn't dare say anything. A meal never tasted good coated with regret.

"You're a little old for that, aren't you?" Her mother took a sip of water then eyed Sheila over the top of her glass.

*One ... two ... three ...* Sheila drew in deep breaths. "I'm only thirty-six."

"And you'll be thirty-seven by the time the baby's born. Then what? Give up your life like I had to? Delay your retirement? You clearly weren't averse to abortion in the past. At least that newspaper article put your choices in the proper perspective."

Sheila squeezed her palms below the table. *Four ... five ... six ... seven ...*

The corners of her mother's mouth lifted with her supposed victory as the waiter returned with wine. Mother sat momentarily silent as the man poured the reddish-caramel-colored liquid into goblets.

"Are you ready to order?" The server held the wine carafe at his side.

Order? "Not yet, thank you." First of all, they hadn't even looked at the menu. Second, her appetite had fled. And third, it was clear her mother wasn't done with her rant.

The waiter nodded. "I'll give you a few more minutes."

Her mother picked up her menu, but peered above it, her gaze firing lasers toward Sheila. "To think you'd allow yourself to be pregnant at this age. What were you thinking?"

Sheila pinched her eyes shut. *Eight ... nine ... ten ...* Richard's hand reached beneath the table and gripped hers tightly and muscles twitched in his cheeks. It seemed he finally understood what Sheila had told him about this woman she called Mother.

He held his tongue, but she couldn't any longer. "I was thinking that I love children and, you know what? They love me." She leaned forward. "I was thinking, I have this wonderful husband, and the two of us together have plenty of love to share. I was thinking I don't want to retire if I have to do it alone. I'd lived my whole life alone until I met Richard. I'm not giving anything up, anything that matters."

Richard's hand loosened, and then he gave her hand a single squeeze. She'd done well. She'd exploded, but not accused. Better yet, she'd silenced her mother. Sweet victory.

"We weren't thinking ..." Her father's eyes misted. He glanced at her mother, as if seeking approval. She frowned but he didn't let that quiet him. "We shouldn't have left you as we did. But you were already so independent, so spirited, and we ... we wanted to retire and were finally able to."

"You didn't even tell me where you were going!" She kept her voice low but couldn't conceal her aggravation. "I'd just turned eighteen!"

Her father's eyes averted her accusing glare, but her mother almost seemed energized by Sheila's outburst as their gazes locked. "Did it matter? You couldn't wait to get out of the house. How do you think that made your father and I feel, after all the years we'd sacrificed raising you, training you to be an independent woman, you couldn't show the least little bit of gratitude. You've clearly done well for yourself. I would think you'd be grateful."

Grateful? For not loving her? "Right."

Richard's hand squeezed tighter in a gentle warning.

She inhaled a calming breath then rested back in her chair. "There's more to being a success than having a good job and making money. It took Richard to show me that." She raised her menu and hid behind it. Her mother hadn't changed one bit. She had hoped, even prayed that her mother would love to be a grandmother. But no, Sheila's pregnancy was one more inconvenience for the woman.

But her father?

He actually seemed excited. She studied the listing of salads on the menu. Richard had told her to keep an open mind regarding her father. Perhaps he was right.

Silence consumed the four as they all read their menus. When the waiter returned, they were ready. A salad of mixed greens was all she could think of eating.

After placing the order, her father whispered in her mother's ear, and then he attempted to stand.

"Now wait, Stephen." How could her mother sound so loving when talking to her father, then loathing when talking to her daughter? What had Sheila done to merit such hate? Her mother stood and prepared to shoulder her husband as he attempted to stand. His physical load was clearly difficult for her mother to handle, but she did it without protest.

Richard quickly got up and rounded the table. "Mrs. Peterson, please, let me help."

She nodded and returned to her seat, fatigue slumping her shoulders. Helping her father must be taxing, but her mother hadn't complained. Was that love?

Sheila wished she still had her menu to hide behind as Richard escorted his father-in-law to the restroom. Maybe her parents loved each other, but it was clear her mother had no intention of loving their daughter.

"He seems to be a very nice young man."

Sheila startled and squinted at her mother. Wow. No criticism. "He is. The best."

"You treat him well." It was an admonishment, not a compliment.

"I do."

"Don't let anyone else ruin that for you."

Sheila eyes narrowed. "I don't intend to." Where was her mother going with this?

Her mother folded spindly-fingered hands on top of the table. Her eyes changed from firing lasers to gazing off in the direction her father had taken. Maybe her father wasn't well. That could account for his eagerness to see her again. Besides, her parents had been married for over fifty years, undoubtedly no small accomplishment in the world today. To lose your life partner would be devastating. As hard as it would be, perhaps she should give her mother the benefit of doubt.

"I may as well get this over with." Her mother's laser eyes recharged. "We had a very good reason for raising you as we did. You should consider yourself fortunate."

Sheila bit the insides of her cheek and her stomach fluttered again. This conversation wasn't going in the direction she anticipated and this new path felt rockier than the first.

The frown left her mother's face, even though the frown creases remained. Her lips drew into a flat line. "Your father is sterile."

Sheila stared back. Why did she need to know that personal information? Why ...?

Oh no. Her eyes blinked rapidly and a golf ball-sized mass clogged her throat. "You mean ...?"

"Precisely." It was amazing how her mother could utter such harmful words and yet maintain a cool composure, showing no emotion. "You are the product of an affair."

# CHAPTER *eighteen*

Sheila gulped down her water but found it difficult to swallow her mother's confession. Why hadn't she connected the dots sooner?

The prim, perfect, and proper Lois Peterson had had an affair.

Stephen Peterson, the man who'd always hovered in the background, wasn't Sheila's biological father.

"Then who—"

Her mother waved her hand. "That doesn't matter. It was a one-time dalliance that cost a lifetime of hurt. I won't inflict my pain on someone else."

Except her own daughter.

"And if it weren't for Stephen, you wouldn't be here at all."

"What do you mean?"

"He wouldn't allow me to get an abortion."

Nausea coated Sheila's throat and her eyes lost their focus. Burning eyes distorted her vision even more. She didn't want to cry, to make a scene in front of this hardened woman seated across from her.

The reality she had lived with all these years was a lie.

But, did it even matter? Should a question of paternity affect the woman she'd grown into? Perhaps it shouldn't matter, but at this moment it mattered. Very much.

"So, you can see, I couldn't love you."

*Oh, God, please make her be quiet.*

"Whenever I looked at you and saw those dimples, all I could see was my mistake. You were an ever-present reminder that I'd hurt the man I loved, and I did love Stephen. I still do. I've always loved him. I was just ..." A tremble infiltrated her mother's voice. So the woman was human after all. "I made a bad choice, a very bad choice. Until now, it was Stephen's and my secret."

A secret she'd lifted off her shoulders and heaped onto her daughter's.

Sheila's insides convulsed and she covered her mouth. She rushed to the bathroom, making it just in time.

WOULD THEY STILL BE out there?

Sheila's watch showed she'd hidden for fifteen minutes. Long enough to freshen her makeup and to bury her hurt, confusion. Anger. Tonight she would unleash those feelings, but not before. She needed to demonstrate that she was unaffected by her mother's news.

She practiced a smile in front of the mirror then strode out of her sanctuary. A server stood at the table, placing their meals. She felt bad leaving Richard to fend for himself, but he could handle it. They'd eat, pay the bill, and then go, leaving her past right where it belonged.

Richard rushed toward her, weaving around tables and dodging waitstaff. Stopping by a table that had recently been vacated, judging by the dirty dishes covering it, he took her hands and studied her face. "You okay?"

*No.* She shook her head.

He pressed the back of his hand to her forehead. His mouth scrunched to one side, and then he kissed her forehead. "You're clammy."

*That, and a few other things.*

"Do you want to go?" He nodded at their table. "I'll offer an excuse."

It was the question she'd been waiting—longing—to hear, but she couldn't bring herself to say "yes." She wasn't going to leave things like this. Too much needed to be said, things she didn't want to say, but she'd traveled this far to speak her mind, and she wasn't going to be denied.

"Are you sure? You don't look well."

A busser squeezed past them and started cleaning off the table.

Mustering strength, Sheila put her hand over his and whispered. "While you were with Father, Mother surprised me with some information. I'll tell you about it later. She's not going to chase me away that easily. Right now, I'm going to sit and eat."

He raised his eyebrows. "You're sure?"

"Positive." Maybe not one hundred percent certain, but it was the right thing to do.

Richard took her arm and escorted her back to the table.

"Are you all right?" Her father cut off a bite-sized portion of steak. Genuine concern filled his voice.

"I'm fine." She smiled. Her parents would not have the satisfaction of seeing her in tears again.

"Is the baby giving you trouble?" Was that a worried grandfather's question? Did he honestly care about her child?

"No." Sheila frowned at her mother's dispassionate expression. "He's fine."

"He?" Her father's eyes brightened.

"We don't know. We want to be surprised."

"Foolishness." Her mother muttered.

Eat, say her piece, then return to her life, her future with Richard, and leave this bitter past behind for good.

She cut a portion of her spinach then glanced at her father. His eyes were downturned and, as usual, he was silent, but the sag in his jowls indicated he didn't agree with his wife's feelings. Maybe her mother hadn't changed, but her father?

Her father.

Had that really been a lie? Would her life have been so different if she'd known she wasn't Stephen Peterson's biological child? What good would it have done to burden a child with that information?

None whatsoever. She forked another piece of spinach. They'd made the right decision not to tell her. Maybe she didn't feel loved, but he hadn't hated her. No, he'd stood mute in the background, indifferent.

Maybe that hurt more.

She sat silently, listening to the conversation between the two men, talking about trains. A hobby that had filled her childhood basement. A hobby she was only allowed to observe, never touch.

As a preteen she'd been happy with that.

As she'd grown older, though, she tired of being a spectator in her father's games. Perhaps that was why she'd forgotten about his beloved hobby.

Regardless, the man seated across from her was the man she called father. *He* had earned the designation, not some anonymous sperm donor.

And Stephen Peterson had paved the path toward reconciliation. Perhaps "father" was a role he still wanted to play. She couldn't deny him that. Nor would she deny her child a grandfather, even if the grandmother didn't care.

# CHAPTER *nineteen*

Sheila mulled over the words she still needed to say, words she'd stuffed away, as they walked toward the tan Cadillac.

Once those words were delivered, then the relationship would be over. If that's what her parents desired.

They arrived at the sedan and her mother reached for the passenger side door.

It was now or not at all. "Mother, Father, I—"

"One more thing." Her mother released the car handle.

Sheila's shoulders sagged and she politely listened, waiting for her moment again.

"You didn't pick up your belongings from Estelle Barrows. The woman was kind enough to store it for you, and you never showed up."

Sheila clutched her fists and sucked on the insides of her cheeks. She would not part with regretful words. Now was the time for diplomacy. Besides, her curiosity was piqued. Was there a chance her keepsakes had survived? "I apologize for that. I should have taken Mrs. Barrows into consideration."

"What's done is done." Her mother shrugged. "Estelle shipped them to us a few years back. If you want them, we have the boxes in our trunk. If not, I'm certain there's a dumpster around here somewhere. You may dispose of them however you wish."

Boxes? Even with her mother's snide comment, hope stirred

within Sheila. "We'd be pleased to take them off your hands."

Her mother clicked the key remote and the trunk popped open.

Inside, two copy paper boxes labeled Sheila Peterson held the remnants of her childhood. She bent to lift one, but Richard gently patted her stomach. "Let me get them."

He carried both boxes to their car only a few rows away, then returned and curled his arm around her waist. "Go ahead," he whispered. "I'm right here." She may not have had loving parents, but she'd been abundantly blessed with a caring, supportive husband.

"Mother, Father."

Her mother made a show of looking at her watch, and then heaved a sigh.

*Lord, help me.* These words were going to be so hard to say, but they were necessary. "I realize we never had the kind of relationship I wanted." Her gaze bore her mother's. "And now I understand why."

Richard's grip tightened around her waist.

She leaned against him for support. "I used to hold my upbringing against you, but I've moved past that. I've found an incredible peace with my newfound faith, a faith that's built around forgiveness."

Sheila walked from the safety of her husband's embrace and placed her hand on her father's arm. He didn't pull away. One small victory. "I apologize for my selfish attitude growing up. I realize I'm not the easiest person to live with." She looked first at her father, then her mother. "With the baby coming now, I want you to know that you are welcome to be part of his life."

Her father's hand trembled. Again, his eyes were misty. "Sheila—"

"We're not interested." Her mother talked over her father, her tone coldly calm, a tone that sent shivers down Sheila's spine, even with the Arizona heat. A feeling all too familiar from her childhood.

But, she wouldn't let her mother speak for her father. Not this time. Sheila studied the man she'd always called Father. He'd made first contact. Surely, he wanted to be a grandfather, her heart told her so. Even so, his gaze was focused on the asphalt. The man was submissive to the end. Which was probably how he'd stayed married to that woman for fifty-plus years.

Sheila clasped his hand tighter. "Daddy?" She felt like that little girl again, the one who'd stood back and watched model trains roll around an infinite track, the little girl who desperately sought her daddy's approval. Her heart knew he wanted to give it. Maybe, just once, she'd win over her mother.

Her mother tugged opened the car door. "Stephen?"

He pulled away and got into the car.

And Sheila's heart splintered.

This was it. Goodbye forever. She resisted sniffling or tearing up, anything that would exhibit what they'd done to her heart.

She rubbed a hand over her baby. At least this child would have one set of loving grandparents. That was more than many had. Though she had hoped.

Richard came up beside her, securing an arm over her shoulders. She dug her fingernails into her palms, but that didn't ease the knot in her throat as her mother walked around the front of the car.

"I forgive you," Sheila blurted out.

Her mother stopped and her father stared through the windshield. "I forgive you," she said quieter this time, keeping eye contact with her father, praying he read her lips

But he looked away.

"We do not require your forgiveness." Her mother flung the car door open. "We did nothing wrong."

No. Nothing at all. "Then maybe it's time you forgave yourself."

Her mother blinked a couple of times then her eyes returned

to that hardened glare.

Sheila knocked on her dad's window, but his gaze remained forward. The motor roared to life. She refused to back away.

His window rolled down and her mother leaned across. "What do you want?"

Sheila looked at her mother, then her father, two people who couldn't wait to be permanently expunged from Sheila's life, but she had to say her final words. True words regardless of what her head told her. It wouldn't hurt so much if it weren't true.

She laid her hand on her father's arm and he finally glanced her way.

"Daddy, Mother, I love you."

She didn't watch their expressions as Richard whisked her away from the car. She couldn't bear to see them deny her love once again. But her ears were still open, hoping for words from her father.

Hope was smothered in silence.

# CHAPTER *twenty*

Meghan lifted the lid on the Crock-Pot, poked at the roast, and breathed in. The aroma filling the kitchen was as tempting as expensive chocolate. She replaced the lid. Come dinnertime, the meat would be falling-apart good. "String meat," Justin used to call it. Did it taste better in heaven? That was hard to imagine.

She hoped she was hungry at dinnertime. Making the calls today with Doran would seal her baby's future.

A future that didn't include her. Maybe someday that thought wouldn't break her heart.

The doorbell rang and Meghan circled her hand over her stomach, over the tiny girl who'd decided to play volleyball inside her. A baby she dearly loved. Giving her to a loving couple was the right thing to do, but knowing that didn't make today's task any easier.

She ignored the chime and her mother's voice calling from the back room urging her to get the door. Answering the door would mean she was one more step closer to saying goodbye to her child.

A minute later, the bell rang again. Meghan's mom hustled into the kitchen carrying a handful of folded towels and washcloths as her dad yelled, "Coming."

"You couldn't get the door?" Her mom tucked towels into a drawer.

"I was checking the meat."

"It could have waited."

Meghan opened the Crock-Pot and forked the beef while wiping her eyes with her arm. No sense blending tears in with supper.

Her mom rested a hand on her shoulder. "It's not too late to change your mind."

Meghan stilled and wiped her nose. Her mom wasn't making this any easier. "Yes, Mom. It is."

"Your father and I, we'll help you out. Doran, he's grown up this summer. I know he cares for you, honey. He said he'd support you, whatever you decide, but I know he wants to keep the baby."

Meghan turned around, her stomach pushing her mother back. "Don't you think I do too? Do you think I don't cry myself to sleep at night thinking how my baby girl's going to grow up hating me, wondering how someone could give her up, how someone couldn't love her enough to keep her?"

"Then don't do it." A tremble haunted her mother's normally steady voice. "She's our granddaughter. Our first grandchild ..."

"Mo-om." Meghan backhanded more tears. She'd never once considered how her parents would feel. They'd been nothing but supportive the entire time and she'd thought they agreed with her.

One more burden to add to this already impossible decision.

"Doran cares for you, honey. We've spent a lot of time together lately."

"I know." Time she had intentionally spent with Shane.

"Richard has been mentoring him. He's even offered him an internship."

Now that was news. The two people who'd forever changed her life had become friends. How ironic. The two people in whom she'd witnessed dramatic change, who'd taught her the meaning of forgiveness, were confidants.

Good for them, but what did that have to do with her? "I don't want to get married. He's not right for me."

"He loves you."

*Yeah, right.* "He does—"

"No. Let me finish. He didn't have to come here, leave his family, suspend his college studies, get a new job, but he did. For you. And I've seen how he looks at you—how you look at him when you don't think anyone's watching."

*How I kiss him when no one's around.* She did not love Doran. No way. She turned back to the Crock-Pot and tried pulling the meat apart.

"Think about it again, please? Before you make the calls. That's all I'm asking." Her mom rested her arm around Meghan's shoulders giving her a light hug. "Think about it?"

"I'm sorry, Mom, but I already have." She threw the meat fork into the sink, grabbed the cordless phone off its cradle, and waddled out of the kitchen. If she didn't get this over with right now, it might never happen. She hurried as fast as her body allowed her, to the patio. Doran already sat there, his notebook displaying their decision.

She made certain the drapes were wide open insuring there'd be no more kissing. With Shane, that wasn't a concern. What did that say about her feelings for Shane? For Doran?

It didn't matter. Feelings had nothing to do with this decision.

She walked out onto the deck and Doran pulled a chair out for her. Right next to him. She glanced at the chair on the opposite side of the table, but sat next to Doran anyway. Then they could talk without her parents hearing.

"Are you sure you want to do this?" He nodded to the phone clutched in her hand.

"Positive." Why were they all questioning her? Why couldn't they understand that adoption was the right thing to do? Why did everyone have to make this so difficult?

He rubbed his hands over his thighs. "About the other night."

"That was a mistake."

"Was it?" He leaned in dangerously close, and she backed away to avoid kissing him again. "The more I think about it, Meggie, the more I don't believe that." His eyes brightened as he whispered, "I don't think you do either."

*Apparently, Mom doesn't either.* But it was a mistake, as good as it felt, as much as she wanted to kiss him again. That's what got her into this mess in the first place.

He kept his voice low as he inched closer. "If you want to get married, if that's what it takes, then I'm ready. I know you care for me."

His Axe cologne was too enticing. She tried pushing her chair back, but it wouldn't budge. "Okay, so I care for you." She pushed on her chair again, dropping the phone, and the chair toppled backwards. Doran caught her before she fell, and she shook from his grasp. So what if she cared for him? That didn't justify getting married and starting a family, a family begun on a fragile premise. One she feared would be destined to break.

She hurried inside the house with Doran right behind her.

"Meggie." He grabbed her arm, and she whirled toward him. Tears stained his cheeks. "Why can't we work this out?"

She wiped her nose. "Please let me go."

"No. Not till you answer me. You said you cared—"

"That doesn't matter." She swatted away his hand.

"Why not?" His chin quivered.

She clenched her palms and held them in front of her face. "Because I can't make a commitment to you right now, and marriage is a lifetime commitment. I can't make that kind of promise."

His shoulders slouched. "It's Shane, isn't it?"

Shane? Was that her problem? She hurried to the kitchen and peeked in on the beef. Sure, she liked Shane and had enjoyed their time together, but he didn't stir up the feelings Doran did.

Shane was still very much Justin's best friend, and only that. Truthfully, she had too much growing up to do before she committed to anyone, and that meant hurting some feelings, especially her own.

"You love him, don't you?" Doran said behind her.

If she said "yes," would Doran back off? Probably.

But he deserved the truth. It was time to put an end to any speculation Doran might have. She turned toward him. "Yeah, I like Shane. I've known him for forever, but he's not the issue."

She led him to the living room where they sat together on the couch. She grasped his hands and looked him directly in the eye. "You and I, we've both changed since school. I'm amazed at how different you are. I find myself liking you again, against my better judgment. Mom even likes you. And I'm thankful for your support. I never dreamed you'd be here. But that doesn't mean we have any kind of foundation for a marriage. A baby isn't a good enough reason. What good would it do if we got married now, only to break up later? Then we'd hurt our baby even more. When I look to the future, that's what I see. I'm sorry, Doran, so sorry."

He sat back and stared up at the popcorn ceiling. He swallowed a breath and sighed. His eyes were damp, and it hurt her to see that, but the truth was in the open.

"You ready?" She sure wasn't, but she probably never would be.

He nodded one slow nod. "I'll get the phone." He retrieved the phone from the patio and returned to the living room. Clutching the handset, he gazed at her through lidded eyes. "One more question."

She bit her bottom lip. What now?

"Is there a future for us?"

*Us?* Her eyes widened. He still wanted a future with her? Even after this? Her heart danced at the idea, but pregnant emotions couldn't be trusted. "I don't know. Maybe we should finish school first. Sort things out. Take it real slow. I don't want to make any more mistakes."

He looked away failing to hide tear-rimmed eyes.

Why did making the right choices always feel so lousy?

"I'll break the bad news," he said quietly and handed her the phone. "You can tell the good."

She took the phone, and with trembling fingers, dialed the number of her baby girl's parents-to-be.


RICHARD'S CELL PHONE BUZZED as he set the golf ball on the tee. He didn't want to interrupt his time with Sheila, but being a business owner didn't give him the luxury of ignoring phone calls. He looked at the caller I.D. and was glad he'd checked. It was the Keene's home number. "This is Richard."

A voice cleared on the other end. "Uh, hi, this Doran."

"Doran. How's it going?"

"Um, well, Meghan and I have been talking and we, um, we decided to go with a different couple. We're sorry."

Richard's shoulders sagged with the disappointment. He looked at Sheila and shook his head. "No need to be sorry. You're doing what's best for your child." Unlike Sheila's so-called parents. "And Sheila and I are immensely proud of you for that."

"Um, thanks, and I was wondering if you still wanted me for the internship."

"I'm counting on you, Doran."

They exchanged a few more pleasantries, then hung up.

Sheila laid her hand on Richard's arm. "They chose another couple?"

He nodded, feeling sadness and relief all in one. The thought of raising two infants had scared him far more than any business meeting he'd attended, still he'd have taken on that father role gladly.

"Okay then." She picked up Richard's club and handed it to him, apparently cramming her disappointment inside right next to the emotional wounds from her parents.

He puffed out a breath and accepted the club. She might want to swallow her feelings, but he planned to let his out. He stood by the tee, and swung the club behind him while focusing on the ball, imagining it was Lois Peterson's head. No, that wasn't Christian of him, but that woman ... How could a mother behave so cruelly to her daughter? Decent words couldn't describe how he felt toward her.

He brought the club forward and whacked the ball. He groaned as it sailed into the air and hooked left, landing yards away from the green, and trailing away even further. Ugh!

"Golf much?" Moving up to the ladies' tee, Sheila teed off and her ball landed softly on the green, just a few feet from the hole. "That's how it's done."

"Show-off."

"If you got it, flaunt it." Her hips swayed as she led the way to their cart

Yeah, she had it all right, and that was fine with him.

What he wasn't fine with was how she was stuffing everything inside, pretending nothing was wrong. That could only result in a massive explosion of which he'd likely be on the receiving end.

She drove the cart down to the hole, and they chatted all the way. About golf and baseball and about how cute Lauren and Jon were, how worried they were about Nathan and Lexi. They even talked about their disappointment in not being chosen by Meghan and Doran, but not a peep was said about her parents. By the end of the day, he was going to drag it out of her. It would hurt like heck, but they'd survive.

She got out of the cart, putter in hand, and with a light tap, she tucked her ball neatly into the hole. "That's how you do it."

Then she stood hands on hips, smirking, as he tried twice to land his ball on the green. It took two more putts to put it in. On a par three hole. Man, this was going to be a brutal day. But it was far better to take their frustrations out on the ball than to sulk in their hotel room.

Fifteen holes later, his score was well above 100, and he didn't want to talk about her measly seven over par. But it was time to talk about that figurative rhino eating up the course. With the next closest golfers two holes behind them, now was as good a time as any.

He set his ball on the tee, but instead of swinging at it, he leaned on his club and focused on Sheila. "I wish you'd talk about it."

"Your lousy golf score?"

He cocked his head to the side.

And she returned a frown. "Hit your ball."

"No." He threw his club on the ground. "Not until we hash this out."

"If you're not going to play, I will." She grabbed her club and a ball.

He blocked her way to the tee. "This is going to eat you up inside. Get it out. Whack at the ball. Yell at me. Something."

"Yell at you?" She threw her club to the ground. "About how you don't let up? How you practically forced me to come down here only to get skewered by Mother and learn that Father isn't really my father?" She snatched up her club and tried circling around him, but he moved, blocking her again.

Her words stung, but she needed to release them, so he pushed harder. "We got what you really wanted." He pointed toward the parking lot. "Two boxes of yours are in that car."

"Seriously?" She got in his face. "You think that's what I wanted? A bunch of old stuff?"

"Yeah. Yeah I do." Not really, but he wanted her to get at the truth.

She shoved him aside. "You don't know anything."

"Oh yeah?" He blocked her way again.

She pushed his chest. "Out of my way."

"Not happening." He tore the club from her hands and tossed

it toward the cart.

The glare she fired at him could melt the North Pole.

He refused to back away. "Here's what I know." He softened his voice. "That I love you and it kills me to see you hurting. That my parents love you like a daughter, my siblings love you like a sister. And you've completely stolen the hearts of my nieces and nephews."

Her glare cooled to a gentle flame.

Good. Just the reaction he was going for. "And look at Lauren. I've never seen such an amazing transformation in someone. You've become a second mom to her, and I've never been so proud of you."

Sheila's eyes grew cloudy and she sniffled.

He handed her a tissue. His pocket was stuffed with them, for this particular occasion.

"Hon, I always knew you didn't really want a box of keepsakes." He rubbed his hands up and down her arms. "That what you really want is to heal that little girl inside, and I'm"—he shook his head, stifling a curse and accusations he wanted to fling out—"I'm going crazy because I can't fix it, and as your husband, I should be able to fix it."

He looked toward the horizon where the sun was making its descent. Then he drew her into his arms, tucking her head against his shoulder. "But that fact is, I can't fix it, and there's only One who can heal you."

"It hurts." Her sniffles became heaving sobs. "It. Hurts. So. Badly."

He rubbed her back. "I know. Let it out, just let it out."

They remained there, broken together, her tears soaking his shirt, until the group behind them caught up and cast angry glares.

Richard whispered in Sheila's ear. "Are you ready to whack the ball?"

She pulled out of his arms, wiped away the remainder of her

tears, and with determination written all over her face, she retrieved her club from off the ground. "You better pray no one gets in my way."

"That's my girl." He grinned as he watched her ball sail far beyond the green. Yes, she was broken and hurting, but now that wound would stop festering and start healing. He planned to do whatever he could to speed up the process, and he knew exactly what she needed. As soon as he got home, he'd begin.

## CHAPTER *twenty-one*

Nathan stepped out of his dad's workshop to a waning sun, and stretched out the kinks in his neck and shoulders. Three days of pounding nails for his dad made him painfully aware of muscles he didn't know he had. What he'd give for a whirlpool tub.

Maybe his dad could teach him how to install one. Yeah, that'd be an excellent project for the remainder of his home imprisonment. His mom would probably agree.

He walked across the blacktop driveway toward his house as Jon came outside.

Holding Lauren's hand.

Nathan shook his head. That was a sight he'd never get used to. He walked toward them and waved at his friend. Thankfully, Jon still called Nathan *friend*. Taking full responsibility for arriving home late last weekend had helped. "Hey dude, where you taking Lauren?"

"What?" Jon grinned. "Do you think you're your dad now?"

"Just protecting the family against lowlifes."

Jon draped his arm around Lauren's shoulders and she blushed. "Who's going to protect them from you?"

"Funny boy." Nathan faked a jab to Jon's stomach. "We'll catch ya later. I gotta go sweet talk mom into a new project, something to keep me busy these next six days."

"Six more, huh?"

"Glad all I got was two weeks." He nodded toward his car that had been sitting idle for eight long days. "I've learned my lesson." Not to get caught.

"Let's do something next Monday then. Celebrate your freedom. Maybe drive to the cities for a Twins game. Just the two of us."

"You two should do that." Lauren glanced between the two friends.

Lexi might have something to say about that. "Let's do it." Nathan's phone played Skillet's "Monster," Lexi's ring. "Hey, I gotta take this. Have fun and be back by eleven."

"Yes, Dad." Jon saluted.

"Funny boy." Nathan turned and grabbed his phone. He strode away from Jon and Lauren, away from his house and his dad's workshop, toward his mom's garden. Wide open and well out of his snooping brother's earshot range. "Hey Lex, what's up?"

"Coming to the party tonight?"

He rolled his eyes. "Come on, you know I can't."

"It starts at eleven. Your parents'll never know you're gone."

Maybe not, but he'd know. "I'm grounded, or don't you remember that?" He reached the garden and sat on a tree stump skirting the dirt.

"Please, do not tell me you've never snuck out at night."

He kicked at the dirt and a dust cloud floated upward. No, he wouldn't tell her, although it was the truth. "I don't want to get grounded again."

"You're chicken."

"I am not." He leaned over, picked up a stone and hurled it across the garden.

"I guess you'll have to prove it then, won't you?"

"Fine." Just this once. "What do you want me to do?"

"I'll be waiting down the road by Ellingson's driveway at eleven-thirty. If you're not there, we're done."

What an easy way to end it. Maybe he should stand her up.

And totally kill his reputation at school. He wasn't about to ruin his senior year.

"I'll be there, Lex."

"And come prepared."

"Prepared?" His voice squeaked, and he swallowed the baseball-sized lump in his throat.

In the silence that answered, Nathan pictured Lexi's smirk. "Prepared. Yeah. No problem." Right. No problem at all, except where to find a condom. It's not like he had them lying around the house.

But maybe his dad did.

"See you tonight, Nate. I can't wait."

"Yeah, me neither." He ended the call and stared down at the phone. What had he done? Was he totally stupid? Bile climbed up his throat. A party. That meant beer, probably pot, and who knew what else.

And Lexi eager to claim his virginity. Was it worth it? He ran both hands over the top of his head and stifled the urge to yell. He should be thrilled. The sexiest girl in town wanted him, and he could finally join the majority ranks at school and church who'd shed their innocence. No one would question him anymore. No one could call him a goody-two-shoes.

Just kissing Lexi gave him an unbelievable buzz. That Saturday night at Uncle Ricky's, he'd been eager to go all the way and probably would have if his uncle hadn't intervened. The thought of being with her, the highs she'd send him on, overruled all commonsense.

So why did he feel like throwing up?

He concentrated on breathing. Three and a half hours to decide his future. He needed to keep busy until then or the time would drag. He ran back to the house, to the kitchen. Jaclyn sat at the table coloring a picture of the minions from *Despicable Me*. Despicable me? Why did that phrase seem so relatable? He ran his hand over his chin as if to wipe away the filth he felt inside. "Hey Jac-o-lantern, where's Mom and Dad."

Her bottom lip stuck out. "It's Jaclyn, silly."

"Okay, Jaclyn silly, where's Mom and Dad?"

She giggled. "Outside."

Both of them outside? This could be his opportunity to snoop through his father's things. "Where outside?"

"I don't know."

Big help she was. "I gotta go find something upstairs. Yell if you see them come in, okay?"

"Okay."

Nathan looked out the kitchen window toward his dad's shop. Lights were on and shadows moved about. Should be plenty of time. He ran upstairs to his parents' room. Now where would his dad keep his stuff? He hurried into the master bath and yanked open drawers. Nothing but cosmetics and bath junk.

Where else? He scratched the back of his head and surveyed the master bedroom. Dresser. Closet. Bedside table. Duh!

He crossed the room and pulled open the small drawer on his dad's table. Jackpot.

A whole stash of them. Sweet. Nathan grabbed three. His dad would never know any were missing.

He tucked them into his front pocket and ran back downstairs. Tonight, it was really going to happen!

Tonight it was really going to happen … Oh boy. He blew out a breath as nausea coated his throat and excitement stirred in his stomach.

Jaclyn remained at the table. He kissed her cheek. "Thanks for watching out for me."

"Jon-Jon kiss my cheek."

"Oh yeah?"

"I marry Jon-Jon."

"Better ask Dad first." Nathan sat next to his sister and grabbed a coloring page. "But if you ask me, Jon's a pretty good dude. I want the best for you."

Was Nathan giving his best to Lexi?

Perspiration beaded on his forehead and he wiped it off with the back of his arm. What kind of guy did he want Jaclyn to date? One like his dad?

Or Uncle Ricky?

One like Jon or ...

Did he want to be that kind of guy? Was that the reputation he wanted?

The green clock numbers on the microwave told him he had just three hours now to make a decision that could forever change his life. His heart sped up as he patted his pocket and he stifled a grin.

Reputation or not, he wanted to be with Lexi, and nothing would stop him tonight.

LYING IN BED AT the Arizona hotel, Richard tucked his arm beneath Sheila's head and rested his head on her shoulder. "What are you thinking?"

She grasped his hand and sighed. "About Meghan and Doran. How can I not be happy that a childless couple is finally getting the baby they've always prayed for?"

"I feel the same way." Doran's call had been bittersweet, but Richard was thrilled for the other couple.

"To be honest, the thought of raising this baby scares me to death." She caressed her stomach bump. "And raising two infants? I honestly wasn't sure I could handle it. I think this is the best decision for all involved. What Meghan and Doran are doing is such a beautiful sacrifice."

He couldn't have said it better. He joined his hand with hers, covering their child, and his cell phone rang a generic tone.

With a grunt he yanked the phone off the nightstand. Connor August from ACM. At this late hour, he could wait. Sheila was his number one priority. Richard turned over to lay the phone on the side table.

"Go ahead and a take it." Sheila patted Richard's back and got up from the bed.

"I don't want to interrupt our time with work."

"Nature's calling, dear. You're not interrupting anything."

His phone was now silent, so he called Connor back.

"Hey Richard. Thanks for returning my call."

"Sure thing. I looked over the financials you sent me. Guess I trained you well."

"It makes a difference that I don't have to go through Dalton any more. The man's not pleased with my promotion, but I've got the eyes of the company on me now."

"Too bad. If they didn't wise up, I'd have brought you out here."

Connor laughed. Richard supposed that statement was quite funny. Who in his right mind would trade a career in the world's financial hub for one in the Midwest? "Keep doing what you're doing. You know how to reach me if you have any questions."

"Sure thing, but that isn't the reason I called."

"Oh?"

"Have you heard from Marissa King?"

*Marissa?* "No. Why?" It seemed the woman would never go away.

"Just wondering. She mentioned you the other day, tried to get your phone number."

"You didn't give it to her?"

"No. Thought you should know she's looking for you."

Richard rolled his eyes. "I appreciate the warning. I'll probably fly out in a week or two for a face to face. Keep up the good work, Connor."

"Sure thing."

Richard jabbed the end call button. Couldn't the woman take the hint that he was a married man? That they had no future together?

Sheila walked from the restroom, running a brush through her hair. "Is ACM having problems?"

"If they were, it would be a lot easier to digest than this." He silenced the phone and set it on the side table. "Marissa's on the hunt."

"Excuse me?" Her brows shot up, and her mouth hung open.

He leaned against the headboard and rubbed his forehead. "I have the feeling she wants to get back together."

"You're kidding." Sheila snuggled next to him.

"I wish I were." He kissed Sheila's cheek. "So do I call her and tell her to lay off, or do I ignore her?"

"I think she'd take any call from you as a sign that you were interested. Ignore her and hopefully she'll take the hint."

"That I'm hopelessly in love with my wife?"

"Exactly." She kissed him, igniting fire crackers in his brain. "But, right now I'm incredibly hungry."

"So am I." He feathered kisses down her neck.

She giggled.

Giggled!

"You sure know how to give a man a complex."

"Sweetheart, you're talking to a pregnant woman. That means, don't stand in between her and food."

Argh. She drove him nuts.

He sat up and pounded a valley into his pillow then rested against it. No use arguing. She'd win. "What are you craving today?"

"Pizza."

"You're kidding." Pizza hadn't been on her health-czar menu for months.

"After what Mother and Father put me through today, I think I deserve pizza."

"Then pizza it is. Loaded?"

"Everything."

Yes! He ordered the pizza then flicked on the television. "Hey, it's *Seven Brides for Seven Brothers*."

"That's a horrid story. Women—girls taken right from beneath their fathers' noses. At least those fathers cared." She sniffled as "Sobbin' Women" sang from the TV.

Back to that again. He muted the television and patted the mattress beside him. "Come here."

She sidled up next to him.

"Your father cares for you."

"He has a funny way of showing it."

"I agree, but I can see it. His eyes say what his actions can't."

She huffed. "It doesn't matter, though, does it? I can't go through life worrying if he's going to love me or not. That's his choice."

"Attagirl."

She leaned into him, relaxing, and he unmuted the volume. Sheila was right, the *Seven Brides* story was hokey, but in the end it showed a father's sincere love for his daughter.

A scene came on with the kidnapped girls singing and dancing, and inspiration hit him. He nudged Sheila in the side. "Hey, how about Dorcas?"

"Excuse me?"

"For a girl. It's Biblical, you know. I looked it up a while back. She was known for doing good, and for helping the poor. The name means gazelle."

Sheila frowned. "You're joking right?"

He grinned, and she whacked him with a pillow.

"You sure know how to hurt a guy."

"Keep coming up with those ridiculous names, and we'll see how hurtful I can be."

"I'll try harder next time."

"Sure you will." She slid away from him and got out of bed. "I can't wait any longer."

"For what?"

Sheila walked over to the copy paper boxes that sat in their room like a sleeping elephant, and knelt down. "It's time I move on, and I can't do it with these two boxes glaring at me."

He shut off the movie and joined her on the floor. "You ready?"

"As I'll ever be. If what's in here is important, we'll bring it home. If not, we'll find a dumpster like Mother recommended."

She seemed more confident than he felt as she began to lift the lid. He prayed she wouldn't be disappointed, that it wouldn't set her back again. She put the cover on the floor and they both stared, bewildered, into the box.

She pulled off the other cover, then propped herself against the bed and began to laugh.

The boxes held nothing but Estelle Barrows' quilts.

## CHAPTER *twenty-two*

Nathan lay still in bed, listening. His brother Joshua had been deep breathing for a good hour and the kid slept through anything. He wasn't a problem. But sneaking past his folks' room? That was another story. His clock read eleven pm. Plenty of time to meet Lexi if he left now.

Already dressed completely in black, he slipped out of bed, grabbed his shoes, socks, and a flashlight. He clipped the flashlight to his belt and tiptoed past his brother's bed. The kid didn't move. No surprise there. Holding his breath, Nathan opened his bedroom door. No squeak thanks to the WD-40 he'd sprayed on it earlier. He stepped into the hall and pulled his door shut, holding the knob until the door was in place, then he slowly turned the knob until it rested.

Two doors down, his parents' bedroom door was closed and their television on. Sweet. If only they knew how easy they were making this for him.

But then, they did trust him.

He shook the thought away and tiptoed down the hallway, testing each step for creaks as he set his foot down. There wouldn't be any squeaking though. Not with a perfectionist contractor for a father.

His folks were talking as he passed their room, and there were no silent gaps that showed they were listening.

Other kids would die to have it this effortless.

He eased down the stairs; the only sound was the thumping of his heart. He crossed the kitchen's hardwood floor to the mudroom. There, he finally put on his socks and tennis shoes. He double checked his pockets for his keys. His fingers touched the condom package and his body over-heated.

There was still time to return to bed.

And kiss his relationship with Lexi goodbye.

*Man up, Nathan.* Clenching his jaw, he opened the door to the garage and it squealed. Dang it. Why hadn't he thought of greasing it too? He stood still and listened. Nothing but his own breathing.

Without opening the door further, he squeezed out the narrow opening then slowly closed it, but it still protested. There was nothing he could do about it now, and he certainly wasn't going to give up.

He walked around the front of the garage past his mom's Saturn and his dad's Ford to the side door. He slid open the deadbolt and stepped outside, then relocked the door with his key.

Almost home free.

He checked the windows at the back of the house. His parents' overhead light was off, but a flickering light told him the television was still on. Walking around the front would be safer. His and Jaclyn's rooms faced the front, and she slept sounder than Joshua.

Time to make a run for it.

He stole a glance at Jaclyn's and Joshua's windows and ran across the grass. July's humidity added to his already perspiring body. He should have thought to bring deodorant. Too late now. He reached the ditch and leaped across it to the gravel road. Another hundred yards and he'd be beyond the pines bordering his home.

Staying on the grass, he jogged alongside the road until he was well past the trees. Finally he stopped, braced his hands on his knees, and breathed.

He looked back. All was quiet.

He'd made it! So why didn't his heart slow to normal?

Just a football field's length away was the Ellingson's half-mile long driveway. He flipped on his flashlight and shone it ahead. Lexi's Kia Soul sat there, as she'd promised.

He still had time to turn back, be the son his dad expected, the big brother his little sister respected. But the thought of Lexi's kisses and the euphoria they'd lead to spurred him on. He jogged toward her car. As he approached, the car purred to life and the lights flickered on. She pulled out onto the road and stopped beside him.

One last chance to turn back.

He grabbed the handle and tugged the door open. The floral scent of her perfume sifted from the car. He peeked inside and stilled, his mouth hanging open. Her too small knit top was unbuttoned past her chest and it was very evident she wasn't wearing a bra.

"What ya waiting for? Hop in."

He nodded and sat down. Before he had the door closed, she cruised off down the gravel road, right past his home. It was still quiet. He backhanded the sweat from his forehead. Whew.

A mile up the road, Lexi paused at a fork, then hung a left.

"Hey, isn't the party at Krueger's?"

"Yep." She kept driving, the crunch of gravel echoed through the car.

"Then why—"

"Nate, you are way too innocent."

His stomach knotted as she turned onto a driveway of a home deserted long before Nathan was even born. She was nuts if she expected him to go in there. It wasn't happening.

She parked her car on dense grass and weeds in the back of the house. An overgrowth of trees shaded even the moon. No one would ever know they were here. "Why are we stopping here?"

He knew her answer, but asking helped prolong the wait.

"Nate, I'm about to give you an education." She leaned toward him, pressing her lips to his, chasing away his guilt-ridden thoughts. She let up and motioned to the tiny backseat. *The backseat?* Didn't matter. Right now he'd follow her anywhere. She squeezed between the seats and he started trailing after her.

He waited as she pulled down a seat back, reached into the trunk, and grabbed a small cooler. After she readjusted the seat, Nathan squished in beside her, perspiration trailing down his spine.

"Have a drink." She pressed a beer can into his hand. "You need to loosen up."

Beer? In a car? That's where he drew the line. He put the can back into the cooler. "Babe, I want to remember this night."

"Oh, I'll give you something to remember all right." She removed the can from the cooler and stuck it in a cup holder. Then she pinned Nathan to the side door.

He kissed her first. It was time to man up and take the lead. His fingers fumbled with her shirt buttons and Jaclyn's innocent face flashed through his brain.

Whoa. What was he doing? He pushed Lexi away and shook his head.

"First time jitters?" She grinned and drew her finger down his chest stopping at his naval.

"It's not my—" His voice came out falsetto.

She stopped him with a "yeah, right" look.

"Maybe I'll take that beer after all." Anything to chase his baby sister from his thoughts.

Lexi popped open the can, took the first swallow then handed it to Nathan. He stared at it for a second. Tonight was truly a night of firsts, but he couldn't tell Lexi he'd never even had a sip of beer. He chugged down a couple of gulps and nearly spewed it back out. Nasty stuff.

"You are a rookie, aren't you?" She leaned back and started to unbutton her shirt.

"No." He took her hand away and picked at the top button.

She reached for the zipper on his jeans, and he saw Jaclyn's face instead of Lexi's.

With a curse, he pushed Lexi away. He swore again and pounded the seat. Did he want to be the kind of guy who slept with someone's little sister?

"Nate, you'll be fine. Have another drink." She shoved the beer can toward him and he swatted it away. The beer sprayed over the two of them and across the back seat. Lexi let loose a string of profanity.

He squeezed his head between his hands. "I can't do it, Lexi. I just can't do it."

She called him a crude name, reached across his stomach, and pushed open the door. He tumbled out of the car, landing his backside in the damp grass.

"You can walk home." She slammed the door shut and by the time he managed to stand, she had the car started.

"Wait!" He reached for the door handle as the car's tires spun and churned up mud. A second later, the wheels gained traction and she was off down the driveway. Leaving him alone.

He cursed again and plopped down in the grass. Now what? How could he go home smelling like a brewery? He felt for his flashlight.

It was still in the car. Wonderful. This night couldn't get any better.

Blinking away tears, he lay back in the grass and stared up at a sky sprinkled with stars.

Who'd he been kidding to think he could hide? Even if his parents never found out, God knew.

He wiped his eyes and stood. It was time to man up, head home, and face the consequences. He'd walk home with his innocence marred, but still intact. Just like his mom had done years ago with Uncle Ricky. She'd kept her honor, and so had he.

Yeah, God was here all right.

He walked down the lonely driveway and out onto the gravel road. Thirty minutes later he was at his driveway, the house still quiet. He'd go in and sleep off this night, and tomorrow he'd make a full confession. If that meant losing car privileges for the rest of the month, so be it.

He walked to the garage door and inserted his key.

"Have a nice walk?"

A curse word flitted through his thoughts but he didn't say it out loud. "Dad." So much for waiting till the morning. Shoulders stooped, Nathan looked over at his dad sitting on the deck in the dark.

"Come join me."

Nathan sighed and forced his feet to carry him forward.

His dad pulled a chair next to him and patted it. "Have a seat."

Nathan plopped down on the chair, keeping his head down, his body reeking of sweat, Lexi's perfume, and beer.

His dad said nothing and Nathan perspired more. Why didn't he get the lecture over with and dole out the punishment?

Well, if his dad wasn't going to do it, Nathan would do it for him.

He reached into his pocket, pulled out his dad's condoms, and handed them over. "I didn't do it. I wanted to real bad, but I didn't."

Still nothing from his dad.

Nathan kicked at the decking, his breathing labored. "I couldn't treat her that way, Dad. I know I messed up again and I'm sorry. I know I'm grounded for life." But with his virtue intact.

"Can I ask what changed your mind?" Finally, his dad spoke.

Nathan breathed easier. "You can thank Uncle Ricky."

His dad nodded. "I will." He slapped Nathan on the back. "Let's head on in."

Great. Now he'd have to sleep on it. His parents would have all night to come up with the worst punishment ever.

His dad stood and Nathan followed suit. Dad spread an arm over Nathan's shoulder. He coughed and he waved a hand in front of his nose. "Whoa. Guess we better throw those clothes in the wash."

"I guess." Nathan kept step with his dad up to the patio door, then his dad stopped and turned to face Nathan.

Now the punishment was coming. Nathan tensed his shoulders but held his head high. He'd take it like a man.

His dad laid a hand on Nathan's shoulder. "Tonight, son, you grew up. Someday Lexi will appreciate you for this."

"Yeah, right."

"Not now, but someday she'll remember the young man who put her integrity before his own desires, and she'll whisper thank you. You won't hear it, but know it's there."

"So how come I feel so lousy? I feel like such a loser."

"Those are Satan's words. Tonight, heaven's cheering your victory." His dad reached into his jeans pocket and pulled out a set of keys. Nathan's car keys. He handed them to his son. "Tonight, Nathan, you've learned what it really means to be a man, and I'm very proud of you."

# CHAPTER *twenty-three*

Richard carried the two copy paper boxes marked with Sheila's name up the steps to Estelle Barrows' former home.

For nearly three weeks they'd sat in his garage. It was time to get rid of them and erase more disappointment. Balancing the boxes on his hip, he rang the home's doorbell at the same time his phone signaled a text. It would wait till he got back into the car.

Sheila's old neighborhood was such a quaint area with no two houses alike, and Lake Calhoun only blocks away. It should have been the perfect place to grow up. Should have been the birthplace of fond memories for his wife, not the source of nightmares. He was glad he'd talked Sheila into a Saturday of shopping with Lauren instead of returning here with him.

The home's inside door opened and Estelle's niece waved him inside. "Please, bring them in."

He stepped into the foyer and set the boxes on the hardwood floor.

"We all wondered what Aunt Estelle did with her wedding quilt and all her quilting supplies. Our family can't thank you enough for returning them. They're family heirlooms."

"Glad I could help." Wish he had help locating more of Sheila's past. What he'd discovered already might not be her family heirloom, but it was a treasure, and he couldn't wait to give it to her. But, that wouldn't happen until he had all the right pieces together, and he was still looking. She may not end up with the memory box she imagined. No, this might even be better.

"Can I offer you a drink? Coffee maybe? Cookies?"

"No thank you. But I appreciate the offer." Although the cookies almost sounded too good to pass up. He might have to stop at a bakery on the way home to get a taste of sugar.

"Thank you again for bringing these over. Our family's extremely grateful."

"It was my pleasure." He walked out the door and down the sidewalk taking periodic glances at Sheila's house. He'd do what he could to erase those bad memories and replace them with the good. When he got home, it would be time for more research.

He stopped by his Audi and leaned against the door as he pulled his phone from his belt. Probably Sheila telling him she transferred more funds to their checking account during her shopping excursion today. His wife excelled at spending money.

Or maybe the text was from Doran. Meghan's due date passed yesterday. He brought up the message and groaned. Not Sheila, not Doran, but Marissa. How had she gotten his number?

He shouldn't be surprised. The woman had always been resourceful.

Grimacing, he read her message. "Call me." Not in this lifetime.

Or maybe he should send off a quick text to leave him alone, that he was ecstatically in love. But heeding Sheila's advice, he deleted the note then shoved the phone into its holster. Hopefully, his non-answer would give Marissa the hint to stay away.

The same hint Sheila's parents had sent to her eighteen years ago when they attempted to extricate her from their lives.

He prayed he'd be just as successful at removing Marissa.

SHEILA FOLLOWED LAUREN OUT of the baby store, her

checking account a few thousand dollars lighter. Who knew choosing baby furniture and bedding would be so much fun? And the afternoon wasn't done yet. With Lauren along to help her decide, it made this humid July afternoon bearable.

More than bearable even. What a blessing this young woman had been for Sheila. The austere Lois Peterson had no clue the joy she missed out on by abandoning her daughter.

They walked side by side on the sidewalk in the new lifestyle center mall that had been created to look like a turn-of-the-century downtown area. "Ice cream?" Sheila pointed to a shop advertising an old fashioned ice cream experience. Ice cream sounded very good right now. Chocolate with pecans. Maybe even caramel and whipped cream with a cherry on top.

Lauren shaded her eyes and peeked in the store window, then patted her stomach. "I don't think so. I'm still full from lunch."

"Maybe later." Before they went home. If Richard knew she craved ice cream after all her talk of healthy eating, he'd never let her live it down. "Before we head home?"

Lauren smiled. "I'd like that."

Good. Richard would never know. "Where else would you like to shop? Need anything for school?"

"Nope, I'm set. I just like being with you."

"Sweetie ..." Sheila stretched an arm around Lauren's shoulders and gave her a quick squeeze. "You are wonderful for my ego."

"Hey, can we check out that store?" Lauren pointed up ahead.

Sheila read the signage on the store front and stopped, her body tense. "Music Emporium?"

"Can we? I love looking at pianos."

Sheila's heart rate quickened. Once upon a childhood, she loved looking at pianos too, but her mother had stolen that dream along with all her others.

"Of course we can take a look." As long as it was quick.

It took them only a few steps to reach the store. Lauren

pointed at the window, her face lighting up. "They've got a baby grand."

Sheila swallowed hard and forced a smile. "I'd love to hear you play it." In spite of her queasy stomach, she wasn't about to spoil this afternoon for Lauren. The girl didn't need to know this upset Sheila.

Besides, maybe it was time to allow music back into her life.

She opened the door for Lauren and followed her in. Lauren hurried to an ebony Kawai staged in the center of the store. "Mom always wanted one of these." Lauren floated her fingers over its glossy top. "Are you sure I can try it?"

Sheila touched a key and high C rang out. What beautiful clarity. "That's what it's here for." Maybe she'd have to give it a try too.

Grinning, Lauren sat on the padded bench.

Sheila hesitated then sat beside her. How many years had it been since she'd sat at a piano? Probably eighteen. Far too long. It would be a miracle if she remembered anything.

Lauren's fingers floated over the keys and Pachelbel's "Canon in D" resonated from the piano's chamber, not flawless, but heartfelt.

Sheila closed her eyes and listened to the emotion streaming through Lauren's touch.

That same emotion once flowed from Sheila's fingers, and was the only thing that had ever made her mother smile.

So when her parents abandoned her, she'd abandoned music. How foolish! To think she let them steal the joy of music from her too.

Well, that was about to change.

Lauren hit the final note then sat back on the bench, biting her lower lip, but smiling.

"That was beautiful, sweetie."

"Thanks." Lauren kept her fingers splayed over the keys. "That was the bridesmaid processional at Mom and Dad's wedding. Dad loved to hear me play it. I know I'm not perfect—apparently Mom was—but Dad loved it anyway." She jerked her hands away from the keyboard and stuck them between her legs. "Omigosh. I can't believe I played that in public. I never played for anyone but Dad." Lauren's cheeks pinked. "And now Jon."

Thank God for the change of topic. "Things are going well with him?" The young man treated Lauren with the care and respect she deserved.

Lauren lowered her head but couldn't hide the flame in her cheeks. "Yeah. He's real nice."

Mother-daughter talk. Sheila had missed out on it, she wasn't about to let Lauren miss out too. "Has he kissed you yet?"

"Yeah." The girl's cheeks grew even more crimson as she pressed her chin into her chest. "Last date. When he brought me home after a movie," she said quietly but with a smile. "I like him."

"I like him, too. Richard, too, and he's a very harsh judge."

"May I help you ladies?" A male voice interrupted.

Sheila had enjoyed the conversation so much she nearly forgot they were in a public setting. The young man dressed in ratty jeans and a T-shirt advertising Green Day looked like he could tell the difference between a Les Paul guitar and an Ovation, but pianos? "Yes, please. Could you find me a copy of Beethoven's works? Moderate difficulty?"

"Ah, someone who appreciates the classics. I'll be right back." The man hustled to the corner of the store that housed music books.

"You play too?" Lauren ran a scale up, then down.

"I used to." Sheila studied the ivories and her fingers itched to play. "I want to see if I still can."

The man returned with a piano book and handed it to Sheila. He gave the lid a tap. "Feel free to give this baby a test drive. It's a sweet ride."

"I'll do that. Thank you."

He gave her a thumbs up and walked away whistling "Ode to Joy." She should know better than to judge someone by their appearance.

She opened the book to the table of contents, found what she was looking for and turned to it. Lauren got up and Sheila scooted to the center. She stared at the music. "Fur Elise." Her favorite. And her mother's. Playing "Fur Elise" was the one thing Sheila had done that had made her mother happy.

Sheila stared down at the keyboard, stretched out her fingers, then spread them over the keys. She hit the first two notes and grimaced. It would help to start off on the correct keys. It would probably take her years of daily practice to regain what she'd lost.

She inhaled and looked down at the keyboard again. This time she placed her fingers correctly. She studied the music, held her breath, and played. Two excruciatingly slow bars without an error. She exhaled and continued on. So, her talent wasn't completely lost, thank God. She finished the page, closed the book, and waved down the sales clerk.

"I'll take this." She handed him the book then placed her fingers back on the keyboard. Telling Richard about the purchase wouldn't be difficult, but sharing the talent she'd long buried? That would be the tricky part.

# CHAPTER *twenty-four*

## *Mid-August*

The craft store was bright and cheery, just like this mid-August morning sun. It was also crammed with customers.

Sheila tugged on Richard's hand, leading him down aisles stuffed with shoppers and colored papers and Disney stickers and multi-colored pens. For experienced crafters like Marcus' wife Janet, this mega store would be an enchanting wonderland in which they could easily spend a whole day perusing the neatly sorted aisles, but for Richard and her, the mere idea of locating a basic baby album among the extensive assortment was daunting.

"Is there anything I can help you find?" A female store employee walked toward them from the end of an aisle brimming with albums of differing shapes, colors, and textures. The girl's cheery outlook matched the brightness of the store's interior. The woman must actually enjoy working here.

"Please. We'd love your assistance." Sheila patted her stomach. "We're expecting our first child and wish to begin the baby book."

"Girl or boy?"

"We're waiting to find out." Sheila smiled.

"Oh, cool. That's so neat."

"Keep in mind"—Sheila clung to Richard's hand—"we do not scrapbook. We are not artistic, and I will not be spending all day creating a page of stickers or cutting pictures into cute shapes." How people like Janet could find relaxation in such an activity, Sheila would never understand. Attempting to be artistic only induced stress. It would almost be worth it to pay someone else to create the baby album. Almost. "All we want is a book where we can attach the pictures and then record a line or two of thoughts. Nothing more."

Even with that simple approach, it would be much more than what she had left from her childhood.

"Then I know exactly what you're looking for." The employee led them to a different aisle near the front of the store.

A little over an hour later Sheila and Richard sat side by side at their condo's dining room table, having moved completely out of their rural home. A twelve by twelve leather-bound book lay open on the table awaiting its first page. Sheila pulled an ultrasound picture from an envelope and stared at it for what seemed like the hundredth time this afternoon. Even at nineteen weeks, their child was wondrously formed. The doctor said the baby looked healthy and normal.

And to think, she once believed the fetus was little more than tissue. Two of her babies had paid with their lives for that belief.

Earlier today in the doctor's office they'd watched their precious miracle on a monitor. A slightly enlarged head with unmistakable features and identifiable fingers and toes. Its little legs were curled up enough to conceal Slugger's gender. Then there was the sound of a quickened heartbeat declaring life— glorious and heartbreaking all at the same time.

She'd cried then and now the tears returned. "I wish I would have known."

Richard circled his arm around her shoulders and held her until the tears drained away. He'd obviously learned that silent hugs were the best way to deal with her wavering moods. Hopefully these out-of-control emotions would return to normal after the baby came. Another twenty-one weeks.

With the tissue Richard handed her, she dried her moist cheeks and then reached for the photo-safe tape. She scrolled it onto the back of the picture and then held the picture above the page angling it toward the corner, visualizing the page before making it permanent. "What do you think?"

He shrugged. "You're asking me? I'd slap it in the middle and declare the page finished."

Laughing, she placed the picture in the corner and then chose a purple pen for her journal entry. She wanted this child to know her thoughts and feelings, to know infinite love.

From both of them. "I need you to write too." Sheila handed a clean page and colored pen to Richard.

"I'll take this with me. I don't want to rush my words." He put the items in his briefcase and pulled out his laptop.

Sheila wrote a few lines and heard Richard mumble. "You know. I should have noticed the popularity of this crafting industry, what with how Mom and Janet are into it."

She glanced at his laptop screen displaying up-to-the-moment DOW readings. "Seriously? I thought you were getting ready to go." His flight to New York was leaving in less than four hours. Considering the rush hour traffic he'd have to drive in to get through the city, that wasn't a lot of time.

"I needed to check this out while I was thinking of it, see if that business was traded publicly." He drummed his fingers on the table and continued to stare at the computer as he clicked through websites. "We should invest."

"So, I'm sitting here contemplating our child's future and you're working." She raised her pen off the page.

"Considering Slugger's financial future, of course." He focused back on the computer.

"Of course. We must have our priorities straight now, mustn't we? As in getting ready to go." She gave him a playful shove.

"Yes, ma'am."

Ma'am? She threw him an icy stare as he rose from his chair

but his lopsided smile quickly melted that ice. He took the stairs two at a time and disappeared.

Thinking of the coming nights without him already made her lonely. It wasn't like they hadn't been apart before. Both of their jobs frequently sent them flying across country, but New York was a special place. They'd spent the first leg of their honeymoon there, and she'd thoroughly enjoyed their weekend in New York a few months ago. She was eager to return, take in another show, eat at an exquisite restaurant, take a carriage ride through Central Park, visit with Meghan and her family.

*Meghan.* The girl had been due a week ago, yet they hadn't heard anything. Doran promised to call when the baby came. Richard seemed to have found a new niche in guiding the young man. She heartily encouraged the relationship.

Richard came down the stairs carrying a garment bag and a small carry-on. "I'm packed. Now I need to spend time with you." He placed the luggage by the door then stood behind her, resting his hands on her shoulders. He leaned over and kissed her cheek then handed her a piece of paper with his meeting and flight schedule written out. "I've got meetings all day tomorrow and Saturday morning, supper with Doran tomorrow night. I'm surprised I haven't heard from him. I know he's anxious to leave. And poor Meghan."

"I understand it's common to be one to two weeks late." She curved her hand over her stomach. As long as this baby was healthy, that was all that mattered.

"Not me. I came right on my due date."

"Naturally." Precise right from the beginning. "Did you get the apartment for Doran?"

He sat in the chair next to Sheila again. "All done. Small, clean, efficiency in a safe area, with a minimum six-month lease, just off the U's campus. Not too far from my office. Should be able to take the bus. The place reminded me of my college days. Of course, I had two other guys living with me in that studio apartment. Those were quite the days." He rolled his eyes and shook his head. "I think this young man has already outgrown that behavior. At least I hope so. I hope I can influence him to avoid making my same mistakes."

"He's done a lot of growing since we first met him. I know he's appreciated being able to call you, and I'm very proud of you for being there for him." His becoming a mentor to the young man had enriched all of their lives, as Lauren had enriched hers. There was so much they could learn from the younger generation.

Richard leaned over, reading the first sentences she'd written in the baby book, and smiled. "My thoughts exactly." He kissed her. "You're going to be a terrific mom."

She hoped so.

"Two nights away is an awfully long time." He took her hand and massaged her fingers. "You sure you won't come with me?"

"I'd love to, but Lauren and I have plans for tomorrow." Plans Richard knew nothing about. A surprise—a secret revealed—she hoped wouldn't anger him. It shouldn't. He'd most likely be thrilled. "Lauren would be so disappointed if I cancelled. *I'd* be disappointed if I cancelled." Saturday couldn't come fast enough.

He cupped her chin and turned her face toward him. His mouth curled to one side. He planted his kiss on her lips and then rested his forehead against hers. "So Lauren's more important than me."

"No, but I keep my commitments."

"And that's exactly what I love about you. At least one of the things." He kissed her again then checked his watch. "You know, I do have a little extra time."

She raised her eyebrows. "Really? For what?"

"I need some insurance that you're going to miss me." His lips caressed hers then his kiss explored deeper.

Oh yeah, she was going to miss him.

MEGHAN WALKED DOWN THE paved path, trees shading her overheated body from the searing sun. These walks were supposed to help induce labor. Sure they were. That's why her baby was already a week late. She'd give anything to deliver this baby today, so she could get on with her life.

And not become even more attached to her precious baby girl.

Was that a curse, prolonging the agony of giving up her child, or was it a blessing of having more time with her unborn baby? Both fit. Neither made her feel better.

She sat down on a park bench and leaned back, giving her baby and her lungs room.

Both Shane and Doran had given her space. Just as she'd requested. Why had she insisted on doing this alone? She hadn't realized how much she longed for Doran's support.

A twinge pinched her stomach. Shutting out the bird calls and children's laughter singing through the park, she focused on her baby. Please, let it be time.

Nothing.

With her arms, she pushed off the bench and stood up. Oh, to be able to stand without effort again. She waddled past a playground brimming with toddlers and mothers and fathers and massaged her belly. This little one would have great parents.

And maybe someday Meghan would have a child she'd push on the swing and help down the slide.

Her stomach cramped again. She curved both hands over her baby. "Are you ready little one?" *Please God, let it be time.*

Home was a mere three blocks away. She dug into her back pocket and touched her cell phone, making sure it was there. Just in case.

She walked toward home, one hand supporting her back, her breathing strained. What would it feel like to actually take a deep breath again?

A contraction squeezed as she walked in her front door. Tension radiated in her lower back. It wasn't painful, but the sensation was new.

Her mom stepped out of the kitchen, a dishtowel draped over her shoulders. She did a double take when she saw Meghan and a smile slowly stretched over her face. "Is this it?"

Meghan shrugged. "I think so, but I don't know. It doesn't hurt."

"That will come." Her mother hugged her. "Why don't you go sit, pick a movie, take your mind off things. When the contractions start coming seven—"

"Seven minutes apart. I know the drill."

"Right. Well, let me know when that happens. I'll put your bag in the car so we'll be ready when it's time."

Meghan nodded as her mom hurried off. She found the television remote and flipped through the channels. Nothing interesting. She lumbered to the DVD shelf. No love stories today. Kid movies, either. That narrowed the selection to nearly nothing. She pulled out *Auntie Mame*. Laughter would probably be healthy.

She settled into the recliner, bringing her legs up, and her mother brought her water. As opening credits played, her eyelids grew heavy and she closed her eyes. Rest could be a rare thing over the next twenty-four hours.

A burning contraction forced her eyes open and her hands to her stomach. Meghan blinked and stared at the TV playing the final scene of her movie. The contraction evaporated as quickly as it had come.

"Feeling something?" said her mother, seated on the edge of the couch.

"I think it was a contraction." But it was gone so quickly and it hardly hurt. It couldn't be a contraction, could it? "How will I know?"

"Sweetheart, you'll know. For now, watch the clock." Her mother got up and put in Danny Kaye's *The Inspector General*. Halfway through the movie, Meghan timed the contractions at eight minutes apart. With each one the pain grew, but it was far from intolerable. Maybe giving birth wouldn't be so bad after all.

"Mom," she hollered toward the kitchen, her mother's sanctuary.

Her mom hurried out and offered Meghan a freshly-baked chocolate chip cookie. "How is it going?"

Meghan bit into the cookie then wiped her mouth. "They're eight minutes apart now and pretty consistent. What do you think?"

Her mom wiped her hands on her apron. "I suppose that's close enough. Go ahead. Get in the car. I'll be right there."

Meghan accepted her mother's help to stand then she slowly walked from the living room, through the kitchen, to the garage. A contraction swelled as she touched the car handle and Meghan gasped. Okay, that one she felt.

And, if what other mothers claimed was true, the pain was only going to get worse.

She grasped the car door and tears burned her eyes, the reality of the situation hitting her. This was it. In a few hours she would be experiencing excruciating physical pain.

After that would come the emotional pain.

*God, I don't want to do this.* She lowered herself into the front seat and strapped the seatbelt beneath her belly.

There was still time to change her mind. She could call the adoptive parents and tell them she was sorry. They'd be hurt, but another baby would come their way. Meghan's parents would be ecstatic. And Doran …

Maybe marriage wasn't such a bad idea after all.

RICHARD'S PHONE VIBRATED AS ACM's CEO Entenza summarized Connor's reports. He grabbed the phone. Doran! This call was far more important than any board meeting. He nodded to the conferees and quietly slipped out of the conference room before tapping the answer button. "Doran?"

"Yeah. It's me." His voice shook. "It's time. Meghan's going into the hospital—"

*Finally.*

"— and I need to be there. I won't be able to make our dinner tonight."

"Go. Be with Meghan. Give me a call when you know anything."

"I will."

"How are you holding up?"

A sigh whistled through the phone. "I'm doing."

The poor kid. Richard could easily imagine the pain of losing a child. "If you need to talk, don't hesitate to call. Anytime. Understand?"

"Yeah, I hear ya. I'm gonna go help Meghan through this."

"I'll see you in Minnesota soon." Richard hit *end* and slumped onto a waiting room chair. Some couple was about to receive the greatest joy of their lives.

At Meghan's and Doran's expense.

What an amazing thing those two were doing. Richard couldn't imagine a greater love.

The doors to the conference room opened and Connor stepped out followed by the rest of ACM's executive board.

"Lunch time?" Richard doubted he could eat anything.

"Yep." Connor nodded. They walked in step to the elevator. Other attendees lagged behind leaving Richard alone with Connor when the elevator doors closed.

Time to focus back on business. He'd connect with Doran later. "You've done a good job, Connor. The board's as impressed with you as I am."

"I had a darn good teacher."

Richard nodded.

"By the way, have you heard anything from Marissa?" Connor asked.

*Marissa?* It was bad enough that she was bugging him, but to put Connor in the middle was way out of line. "Yes, and I'm doing my best to ignore her."

The elevator stopped on the ground floor. The two men stepped out and walked toward the company lunch room.

"You should give her a call."

"Why would I want to do that?" Richard unbuttoned his suit coat and loosened his tie. Although he might give her a call, telling her to bug off, and to leave Connor out of this.

"She's been ill. Pneumonia, I think. Missed a few weeks of work."

*And I need to know this because?* He took a deep breath. "So?"

"So, she wants you to call her."

Richard set his jaw as other ACM employees hustled past them. Just because he'd forgiven her did not mean that she had any place in his life. Was her illness his concern? "It's not happening, Connor. All she wants is to worm her way back into my life."

They walked into a cafeteria which buzzed with laughter, and Connor nodded toward the far corner. They sat at a table far from employees who would love to listen in so they could spread spicy gossip. He'd once been the main food source of that hungry rumor mill and he had no desire to feed it again.

Connor leaned back in his chair, his hands in his lap. "What happened between you two is none of my business, but the woman's changed—"

"And I'm married."

"I get that."

"But does she?"

Connor looked down, his mouth wrinkling. "I think so." He looked back up, his gaze meeting Richard's. "She wants to see you."

Richard pushed away from the table. "This conversation is over."

"You should go talk to her."

"Give me one good reason why."

"I can't."

"Can't or won't?"

"Both."

Richard groaned and stared up at the ceiling.

*Call her.* His inner voice spoke.

Uh-uh. No way.

*Call.*

Richard brushed both hands through his hair. Arguing with God never worked. "Is she really that sick?"

"From what I hear. I guess mortality makes you think things over."

Richard frowned and pulled out his cell phone. "I'll get her off your back." Maybe he needed to tell her to her face not to bother him, that they had no future.

"Catch ya later." Connor left Richard alone at the table.

Feeling sick, Richard punched in the number he hoped he'd never have to call again.

## CHAPTER *twenty-five*

Richard wiped his palms on his jeans before ringing the doorbell to Marissa's house in Staten Island. He heard footfalls right before the door swung open. The woman who answered could have come straight from a photo shoot for AARP. Her shoulder length black hair was sugared with enough gray to be stylish, yet not make her appear too young. The herringbone pantsuit accented her still-slender shape perfectly. Marissa had clearly inherited her fashion sense from this distinguished-looking woman. Her mother.

Richard offered his hand. "Good evening Mrs. King."

She smiled, and he did a double take. That woman had never offered him a smile, only a parental glare that told him she didn't like what was going on with her only child. He hadn't cared at the time. They were consenting adults behaving as the world expected.

"Richard, please come in." She reached for his arm and gently pulled him inside the tiny coat closet of a foyer. "Marissa appreciates you making the time to see her."

As if God had given him any choice. He removed his light leather jacket and she hung it from a pewter hook attached to the wall. He'd give Marissa five, ten minutes tops, then he'd make the drive back to his hotel and spend the evening Skyping with Sheila.

Mrs. King led him into the living room and gestured toward a brown leather couch. "I'll let Marissa know you're here."

With a nod, he sat down on the couch and did a survey of the room to allay his nerves. Not much had changed. The home was quaint with original dark-stained woodwork framing the windows and doorways. Textured walls were painted light beige. An oval ceiling arch was all that separated the living room from the dining room. There were two other doorways: one showcasing a galley kitchen, and the other opening to a small hallway that led to a bathroom and two bedrooms. No second floor. A laundry and storage area was housed in a basement that was otherwise unlivable.

Not exactly what he imagined for Marissa. He'd assumed she would have moved on to a high rise by now, not still be living with her mother. But then she'd always been as protective of her mother as her mother was of her. Being fatherless could do that to someone.

"Richard?" Mrs. King's voice broke his musing. "Marissa's ready to see you. Same old room."

He stood and met Mrs. King's eyes. She turned her head away, but not before he saw her tears. Man he'd been a selfish heel. Obviously, Marissa was worse off than Connor had led him to believe.

"Thank you." He softly touched her arm as he walked past into a hallway that had less wall space than door openings. If he walked straight ahead, he'd enter the bathroom. To the right was a bedroom. He took a left.

Her door was ajar a few inches. He lightly knocked pushing the door open slowly, mentally preparing himself to see a very sick woman. The bed directly in front of him was empty. His gaze traveled to the right and his jaw dropped, his mouth hanging open in silence.

Marissa was sitting up in a recliner—looking very healthy. A man sat in a folding chair next to her. In one hand he held an open book. Bouncing on his lap was a dark-haired toddler, a little boy. The boy peeked up at Richard then buried his face into the man's shirt and a scared "Daddy" whined from the boy's mouth.

"Hey, hey. It's okay, buddy." The man pulled the boy close to him and closed the book. A Bible?

Keeping the toddler in his arms, the man got up. He leaned over and kissed Marissa on the cheek then walked toward the doorway. Richard moved to let the man pass but he grabbed an arm before the stranger left the room. "Pastor?" Richard asked softly.

"No." The man grinned. "I'm Daniel, Marissa's fiancé, and I understand I owe thanks to you for that." Daniel slipped out of the room, the toddler clinging to him.

*Fiancé.* Richard breathed easier than he had since making the call to Marissa. She hadn't been attempting to pursue him.

But then why was he here when the woman sitting in front of him appeared to be perfectly healthy? She patted the folding chair next to her. "Come. Sit."

He crossed his arms and didn't move. "I heard you were sick."

She looked down at her hands folded in her lap. "I was."

"You're better now?"

"I'm tired, but yes, I'm doing much better." She patted the chair again, while avoiding his gaze. "Please sit."

"Fine." He moved the chair, adding another foot's worth of distance between them, then sat. "What do you need, Marissa?"

She kept her hands folded in her lap and lightly rocked. "I had a few days when I felt so awful, I swore I wasn't going to make it. But I couldn't die. There were too many people counting on me, too many things I'd ..." She reached for a tissue on the table next to her chair and dabbed at her eyes. "When you're faced with your own death it makes you consider some things. Things I should have done or shouldn't have done. Things I should have said." She blotted her eyes again, then her gaze met his. "Secrets I shouldn't have kept."

Bile crawled up his throat. What secrets? Whatever they were, he didn't want to know. His life didn't need any more complications. "Marissa, there's nothing else you need to say. It's over. We've both moved on. Apparently, both of us happily."

"I know, and I need to thank you for that."

"Why?" To his knowledge, he'd never done anything for Marissa that would earn her gratitude. Their relationship had been one of complete selfishness, from both of them.

"That day I saw you at ACM, you were a completely different man from what I knew before. Especially right after the accident, you had become so ... so surly. Not that I could fault you considering what you'd gone through. But you scared me."

He blew out a breath. "I scared a lot of people then. ACM was wise in asking me to resign."

"I should have realized it was temporary. I should have realized you were reacting to your situation. I don't know too many people who would have handled it any differently. But I didn't know that. My emotions told me one thing—"

*Pregnant emotions.* He knew all about those.

"—but my gut was telling me another. I didn't listen to my gut. I knew of only one thing I could do."

*Abort his baby.* He clenched his jaw. Why did she have to go over this again? Hadn't he relived it enough?

"I had to tell you—" Her voice quivered and she reached for another tissue. She blew her nose lightly.

He forced his eyelids shut and waited. Every muscle in his back tensed. How he missed Sheila.

"When I called to tell you I had the abortion." She sobbed and lightly blew her nose. "It was—"

She blew her nose again.

"It was a lie."

*A lie? What?* His eyes flew open, and he stared at Marissa. But she looked down. His body began shaking. *No. This couldn't be happening.* He balled his fists but it didn't stop the quiver.

She nodded toward the doorway Daniel had just exited through.

"Richard, you have a son."

## CHAPTER *twenty-six*

"It's a girl." The doctor announced as Meghan fell back on her pillow.

*It's over. It's finally over.* She closed her eyes and relaxed into the mattress. No more cramping pain.

The emotional ache wouldn't disappear so easily.

She opened her eyes as the nurse handed Meghan her daughter. A round, reddish face peeped through the snugglywrapped blanket. Meghan touched the flattened nose then traced perfectly formed pink lips. Strands of blonde hair peeked from the blanket's cover. She was perfect.

"She's beautiful, Meggie." Doran caressed her arm and his chin trembled. "Just like you." He bent over and kissed her on the lips. She didn't even mind.

"I'll get your father." Her mother said then walked from the room.

Doran caressed their daughter's cheek. It was hard for Meghan to believe he could be so gentle. "She deserves the best, Meggie."

"I know." But the best hurt too bad. She kissed her daughter's nose just as her mom walked into the room with her dad.

Her dad grinned and kissed her forehead. "You do nice work, honey."

"She is perfect, isn't she?"

Her dad stretched his arm behind her mother's back. "Exactly like you were."

Meghan smiled through tears at her still-in-love parents. They were the best. Two people joined for life, loving and sacrificing for their children. But they'd begun their family the right way. What kind of future did this precious child have with two parents who weren't even together? With two parents who couldn't afford to live on their own, much less care for a baby?

She wasn't ready to commit to a lifetime with Doran, and she shivered thinking what that would do to their child. Doran was right, this child deserved the best and the best was seated out in the waiting room wondering if they'd become parents tonight, or if Meghan and Doran would shatter their dreams.

A hand touched her arm drawing Meghan's gaze away from her parents. "May I?" Doran reached for their daughter with his arms already curved in cradle form.

"Here, let me help." Her mother rushed over to secure the crook of his arm beneath the baby's head. A tear fell from his eyes onto their child's cheek.

"I need a picture." Her mom retrieved her purse from under a chair.

"Here Meggie." Doran handed their daughter back then stepped away from the bed.

"No. No, Doran." Her mom held the camera in one hand, and waved him toward Meghan with the other. "Please, I need you in this, too."

Meghan nodded at him. He moved next to the bedside and leaned in slightly. She couldn't force a smile as the flash went off twice. Those were pictures she didn't think she'd ever want to see. It would hurt too much.

She snuggled her baby against her chest and with eyes glazed over, she took Doran's hand. "It's the right thing to do, isn't it?"

"It is, Meggie." He dragged an arm over his eyes. "I'll go give the couple their good news."

RICHARD'S CHIN DROPPED. *A son?* He stared at Marissa and choked out, "I have a son?"

She nodded then looked away.

His arms barricaded his stomach, and he began to rock. Acid rose in his throat, and he rushed to the bathroom, grateful for this home's close quarters. *No. No, God, no.* His prayer repeated as he kneeled at humanity's throne until dry heaves took over. He sagged against the wall, propped his head in his hands, and wept.

He had a child? He was a father? No. That couldn't be right. That baby had died two and half years ago. He had mourned that child and hated the mother.

The little boy Daniel had carried ... *Is that my son?* A quick calculation figured his child would have been around 21 months old. It fit.

He had no doubt that had been *his* child he'd seen on Daniel's lap.

His child ...

He had a child! A little boy. That little boy hadn't died. *Praise God.*

But why hadn't Marissa told him? How could she have lied? Kept his child a secret?

A child who should know him and love him, who should rush to his arms when he comes in the door, not cower in another man's shirt. Another man who was called Daddy.

Marissa had intentionally robbed him of that. How dare she!

And Justin ... he had died for a lie!

Emotional pain possessed every cell of his body. If he could hate, he would. At the moment, maybe he did.

More than anything he needed Sheila's arms around him, holding him, telling him everything was going to work out fine.

But how could it? How could he tell Sheila that their lives were about to be upended? Now that he knew the truth, there was no way he would abandon his child.

But would he be abandoning Sheila in the process? The child she carried deserved a fulltime father, not someone whose life was split between home and the East coast. Sheila didn't ask for this. She didn't deserve this.

How would he tell her?

*God, what do I do?*

He sat rocking and praying until the pain ebbed into a dull ache. Then he got up off the floor and saw a scruffy madman with red, puffy eyes staring back at him from the mirror. Splashing cold water on his face helped, as did wetting his comb and straightening his hair. He didn't want to scare his son any more than he'd already done.

Breathing in deeply, he tucked the comb into his back pocket.

It was time to get to know his boy.

His cell phone vibrated as he reached for the bathroom door. *Please, don't let it be Sheila.* He couldn't talk to her now. She'd know something was up, and what he had to tell her needed to be delivered in person. He sighed when he read the caller I.D.

Doran.

Leaning against the bathroom wall, he answered, hoping his voice wouldn't reveal his emotional turbulence. "This is Richard." His calm voice sounded much better than he felt.

"We had a girl," Doran said weakly. There'd obviously been tears on his end too.

"Healthy?"

"Perfect." Doran sniffled. "I'm leaving tomorrow. Meghan gets to carry the baby out of the hospital. Then we'll hand her over to her adoptive parents at the celebration at Meghan's church. Some celebration, huh?"

Richard didn't answer. How could a man possibly celebrate handing over his child?

"I should be in Minneapolis in a couple of days." Doran sniffled again.

"Take your time. I'll be there for you." As well as he could anyway. "You doing okay?"

"I guess. It's the right thing to do, but I feel like crap."

*Join the club.* "Call me anytime." *We'll commiserate.*

"Thanks. I will."

Richard put away his phone and took a breath before opening the bathroom door. It was time to get some answers.

## CHAPTER *twenty-seven*

Richard strode from the bathroom. They didn't need to see his uncertainty. Marissa, Mrs. King, and Daniel sat at the dining table speaking in hushed tones as the boy, *his son*, played alone on the floor. He pushed a blue train engine across the hardwood saying "Chugga chugga choo choo."

Even with his churning emotions, Richard couldn't help but smile.

No one said anything as he walked toward the table. He squatted next to his son, hopefully maintaining a non-threatening distance. "I like your train."

The boy looked up, startled. He jerked his head around apparently searching for familiar faces.

"It's okay, Matthew." Marissa pushed away from the table and knelt next to her son.

*Matthew*. "Child of God," Richard murmured.

"Excuse me?" Marissa asked.

"Matthew." Richard couldn't stop looking at the boy. "It means child of Yahweh, child of God."

"How did you ...?"

He waved his hand. Marissa didn't need to know it was a name he and Sheila were considering. Actually, Matthias, a variation of Matthew, was a name they'd agreed to add to their list. This would make telling Sheila about his son all the more difficult. His son. This couldn't be real.

"Matthew, honey."

The boy's long dark eyelashes flashed as he turned to his mother.

"I need to introduce you to someone. Someone special."

So special, Matthew was kept a secret from Richard. A 24-hour fitness center was close by. He was going to need it tonight.

"This is ..." Marissa looked over at Richard.

She mouthed "I'm sorry" and pulled Matthew onto her lap. "This is Mr. Brooks, the man we told you about, who was coming just to see you."

*Mr. Brooks*. It sounded so cold, so distant.

Matthew gripped his train and sank against his mother as if trying to hide. "I scared, Mommy, Daddy."

*I'm the one he should be calling Daddy*. That gym better have a punching bag.

"Come sit with us." Marissa returned to the table, keeping Matthew tight in her arms.

Afraid he'd lash out, Richard said nothing as he took the chair across from Marissa. Matthew's hair was dark, but then so was Marissa's. That told Richard nothing. He longed to study Matthew's face, his eyes, mouth, nose, see if there was anything familiar, if there was any piece of him in the boy, but Matthew hid his face in his mother's blouse. Afraid of his own flesh and blood.

"I'm sorry." She rubbed Matthew's back. "He's terribly shy. It takes him a while to warm up to people."

*He shouldn't have to be warming up to me.*

"Can I get you something to drink? I've got a beer in the fridge."

*Nothing would taste better*. "Have you got a Pepsi?"

"Yes."

Daniel got up. "I'll get it, hon."

"Thanks, dear."

Daniel returned with the bottled cola for Richard and three

bottles of water. Richard took a long swallow. The carbonated caffeine jolt was precisely what he needed. He placed the bottle on the table and wrapped both hands around it, wanting to strangle it. "I need some answers."

"I know," she said softly.

Daniel put his arm around her shoulders.

"Why?" Richard began with the broad question, not knowing how to narrow it down.

She whispered something in Matthew's ear then set him on the floor. "Mom, could you take him to his room, please?"

"Certainly. Matthew, come play with Gamma."

Clutching the train in one hand, Matthew bounded around the table. He grasped his grandmother's hand with his other hand and the two disappeared into what Richard believed to be Mrs. King's bedroom.

"Mom moved out a couple years ago."

So, that explained why he hadn't seen a crib or toddler bed in Marissa's room.

"She got a place at a senior housing center not too far away. I decided to stay here. I knew this was the best place to raise my, er, our son." Marissa looked in his eyes, but quickly pulled away.

"Why did you lie?" There. That narrowed his questions down a little bit.

Daniel gave Marissa's shoulders a gentle squeeze. It was obvious the man cared deeply for Marissa. Good thing someone did because, right now, Richard despised her.

She took a drink of water. "After our argument that night when I told you about the pregnancy, I thought about what you'd said about keeping the baby, about being there for me. I could tell you meant it. I didn't expect that from you. I expected you to tell me to get an abortion, so that's what I'd planned for. It would have been the easiest thing to do. But I saw something in you that night, a side of you that really cared, maybe not for me, but for the baby. By the time I got home that night, I'd changed my mind. I was going to call you the next morning and see what we could work out. I don't know what I was expecting, but I believed you wouldn't desert me. You'd convinced me of that."

His jaw tightened. *I would have been there.*

"Then I got the call from someone at work about your accident, that you were all right, but in jail. The person who called laughed about it, but all I wanted to do was cry. It was my fault, and I knew I was the last person you'd want to hear from."

*She's right about that.* He drained several ounces of the cola.

"When you came back to work the next week, you were so angry, I was terrified of you."

"I never would have hurt you." Not physically, anyway. Although, he'd hurt her in plenty of other ways, though. Maybe that pain was worse than physical abuse.

"I didn't know that. I thought you'd take your anger out on me. Maybe I felt I deserved it. By then I'd already become attached to the baby, and I knew I wasn't going to abort him, but I also knew I didn't want you around him. The only way to assure that was to tell you I had the abortion. I switched to the White Plains office so I wouldn't run into you. Ironically, you skipped town right about when Matthew was born."

Richard combed his fingers through his hair. "Why didn't anyone tell me? Even people at the White Plains office knew our history."

"I realized that. That's why I had to lie again."

Richard slumped.

"I told everyone the baby wasn't yours, and that's what we argued about that night. I told people you were jealous."

Richard pinched the bridge of his nose. Any time her name had come up in conversation, he'd snuffed out the talk, or stalked away. Maybe God hadn't wanted him to know.

"Mom was the only one I told the truth to."

"And she was probably more than glad to have me gone from your life." He laughed wryly.

Marissa bowed her head.

And his gut seethed. "Why now? At this point wouldn't it have been easier to keep the secret?"

"Because I want to get married."

"You couldn't get married without telling me about Matthew?"

"Legally, we could have, but Daniel ..." She shared a glance with her fiancé, and Daniel winked.

"Daniel insisted I tell you. He didn't want that cloud hanging over our marriage. Avoiding telling you seemed more important than getting married, I guess. But when I saw you the last time you were in town, I saw how you'd changed and how your faith had played a role in that change. Daniel and I weren't engaged yet then. He'd asked me, but I wasn't ready yet to accept his beliefs."

"She told me"—Daniel took Marissa's hand—"about your testimony, that she'd seen firsthand how God could work in someone's life. That finally convinced her to give God a try. As I told you earlier, I have you to thank for the engagement. Your coming today now allows us to set a date. I'm very grateful to you for that."

*Are you grateful that my son calls you Daddy?* Richard's hands squeezed tighter around the bottle. He wished he'd accepted the offer of beer.

Like that would have been smart. That's what got him into this mess in the first place.

"I almost told you when we were in the conference room alone."

Richard recalled her staring down at her wallet. In his arrogance he'd been convinced it was the portrait of the two of them. More than likely, she'd been staring at Matthew's picture.

"I saw how in love you were and how excited you were about becoming a daddy. It made me sick knowing I'd kept Matthew a secret from you. That was the first time I realized what a horrible mistake I'd made. But I couldn't tell you then. If you were still single, maybe I'd have said something, but I figured my confession would ruin your life so I kept quiet."

Richard shook his head. So it messed up his life now instead. "Where do we go from here? I can't stay away. I need to know my son. He needs to know me."

She got up and walked to the antique hutch that hugged the wall adjoining the kitchen. From the middle drawer she pulled out a manila file folder. Her eyes blinking rapidly, she placed it on the table directly in front of him. "That's why ..." Her voice shook and she cleared her throat. "That's why we had this prepared."

Richard opened the folder. On top was a copy of Matthew's birth certificate. Matthew Albin ... Albin? That was Richard's middle name, his great-grandfather's name. Only Marissa would have known that. "You named him after me?"

She blinked. "Keep reading."

*Matthew* Albin *King*. A smile tugged at his lips. He liked the name, even without Brooks at the end. *Mother: Marissa Louise King. Father* ... He peered over at Marissa. She nodded and he kept reading. *Father: Richard Albin Brooks*. He pinched his eyes closed, forcing the tears inside. Proof.

Perhaps Sheila would demand a DNA test. That would be fine, but Richard knew what the test would reveal. He felt it in his very soul.

"There's more." Marissa pointed to the folder.

Richard flipped the birth certificate over. Underneath was a legal briefing. He stared at it for a moment, trying to read it, but his thoughts were too scrambled to comprehend the legalese. "What is this?"

"It's offering joint physical custody of Matthew. It's only fair that you have equal rights where Matthew's concerned."

*Oh, God*. The tears threatened to come again.

Across the table, Marissa sobbed and Daniel whispered

comfort.

This olive branch she was offering was a tremendous sacrifice for her. For her and Matthew. But what would it do to Matthew? To Sheila? Part of him wanted to snatch up the forms and sign them immediately. He had a son and that son was being offered to him. All he had to do was sign the papers.

If only it were that easy.

"Thank you." He kept his tone low, respectful. "What if I don't agree with this?"

Marissa's face flamed red. "You can't take him away. We won't let—"

"That's not what I meant." He wouldn't think of trying to get full custody. That would be far too cruel to Matthew. But was joint physical custody, custody by a complete stranger, any better? Yet, not being a vital part of his child's life was unthinkable.

He would make it work, but he needed to know the contingencies just in case ... just in case it didn't work out. "*If* we decide it's best for Matthew not to be split up, what would my role be? I will have a role, regardless of how small that role might be."

"We'd tell him the truth," Daniel said without missing a beat. He must have anticipated the question. "We'd tell him that his biological father loved him enough to let him go."

"We'd expect visits." Marissa wiped her eyes.

*Visiting* his child. That wasn't a palatable idea.

"Letters ..." Marissa wiped her nose with a napkin. "Pictures, phone calls, Skyping. We want him to know you. *I* want him to know you. It's my fault in the first place he doesn't, and I'm deeply sorry for that."

*Sorry doesn't give me back what I've lost.*

"Perhaps, down the road, he could spend more time with you, like on summer vacation."

"So, I'd have the title of Daddy, with the privileges of an

uncle?" Unacceptable.

"If that's what you choose to do." Marissa bit into a trembling lip.

If only he'd had a choice in the beginning, this wouldn't be necessary. "I can't make a decision right now." But in his mind, there was only one option. He closed the folder and picked it up with both hands, clutching it tightly as if Matthew could somehow slip through his hands again. *I just found him. There's no way I'm letting him go.* "I want to sign it, you understand, and I plan on being a part of Matthew's life, but there are other people I need to consider first." He swallowed hard at the thought of telling Sheila. "Besides he doesn't know me. He's scared to death of me, and he calls someone else Daddy."

Marissa's eyes narrowed. "No he doesn't."

Richard pointed at Daniel. "I've heard him, twice, call you Daddy."

"Dan-ny." Daniel emphasized the N. "He calls me Danny."

"Oh." For some reason that made Richard feel better, as if someone else hadn't usurped his proper spot. He laid the folder back down. "Can I see him again? See his room?"

"Of course."

Richard followed Marissa to the nursery. The room was painted a pale blue with a Thomas the Tank Engine border lining the lower third of the wall. A toddler bed tucked against the wall was covered with a Thomas comforter and pillow. A wooden track meandered over the bedroom floor. Trains with magnetic ends stuck together as Matthew pulled them along while saying "Chugga chugga choo choo."

*Matthew likes trains.*

Richard could show him the model train museum at Bandana Square or take him to the Jackson Street Roundhouse in St. Paul. Better yet, take him to the Lake Superior Train Museum in Duluth. They could walk through real engines, pretend to be passengers or the conductor. They could even go on the North

Shore Scenic Railroad. Richard shook his head. He was getting way ahead of himself.

Marissa sat on the floor next to her son then scooped him onto her lap. She tickled his tummy, coaxing a giggle, and whispered in his ear. Matthew looked up. Richard squatted then sat on the floor, hoping to make himself appear smaller, less threatening. He picked up one of the wooden trains that had fallen from the track and set it back on. He mimicked Matthew's "chugga chugga choo choo" as he pushed the train along.

Matthew smiled.

Lopsided. The Brooks smile. There was no doubt now. Matthew was definitely his son.

SHEILA GRINNED AT LAUREN and caressed the lid of her baby grand. It fit perfectly in the corner of her condo's living room, as if made for this location. The corner had always remained empty and looked incredibly bare, but she'd refused to place just anything there. It needed the right piece and she finally had it. Hopefully, she could still play.

She sat down on the cushioned bench and ran her fingers up and down the keys. "Shall we give it a try?"

"Go for it." Lauren sat on the chaise lounge and curled her legs beneath her.

"Here goes nothing." Sheila opened the Beethoven book and felt a sudden pressure in her belly. Her hand automatically flew down to see if she could feel the action, although she knew her hand wouldn't sense movement yet. She couldn't wait for that moment. Richard would be ecstatic.

"Are you okay?" Lauren uncurled her legs and sat up straight.

"I'm fine. This is a true Brooks baby. Heavy and active. She's been moving a lot today." There wasn't a more exhilarating sensation than her baby's little butterfly kicks. One more affirmation of the miracle growing inside of her. And though her baby weighed less than a pound, Sheila sensed the child's weight today. Amazing.

She removed her hand from her stomach and opened up the piano book. Studying the notes in front of her, she curved her fingers over the keys and began to play. And to think her child could hear the music.

Imperfect music. At one time, she'd played the familiar notes to "Fur Elise" without hesitation or misses. Not anymore. But she forced herself to play on. With practice, the gift would return. How could she have let this talent slide so far away?

This was what bitterness produced. Bitterness over her parents' abandonment forced her to give up something she loved.

It was time for a victory over bitterness. It was time to thoroughly let it go and be grateful for this gift. Grateful that her mother had forced her to practice every day, bringing rare happiness to her parents.

Richard would be shocked to learn that she could play. He might even be angry that she'd hidden the gift, but hopefully, once he'd gotten over his initial surprise, he'd be thrilled.

She neared the end of the piece, her mistakes becoming less frequent. Beethoven would still be horrified with her butchered attempt, but she was pleased. She would begin practicing again, everyday. Unlike the rest of the Brooks family, their child would carry a tune. Their child would sense the music's pulse. She'd make sure of that, just as she made sure that she precisely hit the last chord of the song.

Lauren clapped. "You haven't played for years?"

"Not since I was seventeen or eighteen."

"Wow. You must have been good."

"I was told I was. I only hope I can get some of it back. Maybe I'll take lessons again."

"You should. Definitely. Play something else."

Sheila took out another book. Bach. She ran her finger along the table of contents. "Here's one. Why don't you sing along? I'll try the alto line."

Lauren joined Sheila on the piano bench and harmonized to "Joyful, Joyful We Adore Thee," Sheila's praise offering to God for giving her back her music.

RICHARD RAISED THE ORANGE rose to his nose as he stood outside the door of their condo. He inhaled a deep breath, hoping its bouquet would ease his anxiety. He'd gone over and over what he was going to tell Sheila, writing it down, revising it, throwing it out. No words would be able to take away the sting of what he had to tell her. That he loved her deeply, and he cherished the baby they'd created together.

That he was about to upset their perfect little family.

He rolled his head and his shoulders attempting to loosen the knots. It wasn't much help. With a sigh he inserted his key into the lock then stopped. Piano music and vocals sounded through the door, and not a professional recording either. Far from it. Interesting. Sheila would never listen to anything less than perfection.

Shaking his head, he turned the key and opened the door. And remained in the doorway, his mouth wide open. Had he entered a new dimension? He knew Sheila sang, but she also played piano? And where had that piano come from?

Noiselessly, he set down his luggage and closed the door, hoping the singing duo wouldn't hear the latch. He walked toward the piano, clutching the rose, feeling perplexed and amused. Any other day, he might have been angry that Sheila had hidden this talent, but today it was a gift that temporarily chased his problems away. God knew he needed this tonight.

They finished the verse and started giggling like two elementary school girls. What a beautiful sound.

He clapped slow and firm and their heads bobbed up, surprise stopping their laughter and widening their eyes.

Sheila frowned and her forehead wrinkled. "Are you angry?"

He grinned. "Angry that I have an incredibly talented wife?"

"Who spent a fortune without talking to her husband?"

Any other day, he may have been hurt, but God had perfect timing.

He walked around the piano and opened his arms. "I guess you'll have to make it up to me, won't you?"

She got up and melted into his embrace. How he needed this right now. He breathed in her hair's light floral scent and caressed her back. Their lips met, and he glimpsed Lauren's blushing face turn downward. As much as he wanted—needed—to continue the kiss, he pulled away.

"Welcome home." Sheila returned a quick peck on his cheek. Even that felt wonderful. "I'm going to have to surprise you more often."

"Not a good idea." He handed her the rose. "That would mean I'd have to go away more often, and I'd prefer not to." He mentally cuffed his head. What a stupid thing to say. With Matthew out in New York, Richard would be traveling more. Going to the home of his former lover, to whom he'd forever be connected.

The dread of telling Sheila returned. He'd tell her tonight after the romantic meal he'd planned: takeout Chinese, complete with soft candlelight, followed by slow dancing, followed by ... He smiled thinking of what that led to. *Slow down, boy. Save it for tonight.*

Then he'd break it to her. *Sheila, I have a son.* Would that be the best way to relay the news? To come right out and say it? That seemed far too cruel, but then the situation itself was cruel. There was no way around it.

"I'm gonna gather my stuff." Lauren broke through his reverie. "Nate and Jon should be here soon."

Lauren began to walk past him.

He stopped her with a touch on her arm. "They're coming here?"

"After the Gopher football game." Her gaze remained

downward.

Even after months of knowing her, she still avoided looking him in the eye. At least Sheila had been able to break through the girl's shyness. He hoped Lauren would soon become comfortable around him too. He liked having her visit.

"The guys won't be in a good mood when they get here. I had the game on in the car. The Gophers got kicked."

"Jon's always in a good mood." Color rose in Lauren's cheeks.

"He is huh?" That got a smile from her. "So I take it you're still seeing him?"

She shrugged, bit into her lower lip, and then nodded.

"He's treating you right, isn't he?"

Her blush deepened as she circled her foot on the floor. "Real good."

"We want to know if that changes."

Lauren giggled. "Yeah, you and Nate and Marcus. The other day Marcus greeted Jon with a rifle in his hand and asked Jon's intentions. Jon somehow turned the subject to deer hunting, and then we were late for the movie. I don't think Jon's too intimidated." She grinned and then hurried up the stairs.

Good for Marcus. There had been a time when Richard had been grateful that his girlfriends' parents seemed more interested in getting their daughters out of their hair for the evening, rather than making sure he was treating them well. Perhaps if one father or uncle or brother had shown concern, if he'd been knocked down a peg or three when he was a teen, he wouldn't be faced with this situation now. Jon seemed like a good enough young man. Richard wanted him to stay that way.

"Hey you." Sheila waved a hand in front of his face. "Tired?"

"Yeah, zoning out a bit I guess." He focused on his amazing wife, and the dread returned.

"This should bring you back to the present." Sheila set the rose on top of the piano then circled her arms under his, squeezing his shoulders as she kissed him. Her fingers kneaded his back, and his tension began fading away.

He curved his hands over her stomach and rested his forehead against hers. With this baby, he'd been able to enjoy every minute of the pregnancy—from seeing the early pregnancy test to hearing that amazing heartbeat. All those moments he'd missed out on with Matthew. "So how is little Gabriel?"

"Gabrielle has been very active today."

"Sounds like my son."

"I think she's going to be a soccer player."

"Or maybe he'll play football."

"Or maybe she'll be a professional musician."

He laughed. "With no help from me, I'm afraid." He pulled Sheila into a tight hug again, and clasped his fingers against her back. Her head felt so natural resting on his shoulder.

"So, where's my husband?" she whispered as her lips lingered by his ear.

He kept his hands locked and leaned back. "Excuse me?"

"My husband. You know, the one who would normally have felt hurt that I hadn't told him I could play piano. The one who would have a fit that I made a major purchase without consulting him first. The one whose muscles aren't tensed as hard as rocks?"

With a groan, he let go of her, walked to the couch, and plopped down. He folded his hands, rested his elbows on his thighs, and his chin on his hands. He couldn't tell her yet, not with Lauren here, not with the boys coming. It would have to wait. "I got some unsettling news last night." Unsettling for far too many people.

She sat beside him and wrapped her hands around his. "What is it? The company's not doing as well as you thought? Is Connor not doing the job?"

"No. Connor's doing a great job. Everyone's pleased with the results."

"Something happen with Meghan? Doran? The baby?"

"No. As far as I know, it's as I told you last night. Everyone's sad, but they're doing fine. Doran's driving out. He'll be here in a day or two."

"Then what?"

His gaze traveled up the stairs. "I can't tell you yet."

Sheila nodded. "I understand. It can wait." But impatience quickened her voice.

"I'll go put my luggage away and change. After supper we'll talk."

SHEILA WATCHED RICHARD CLIMB the stairs. She hadn't seen him this wound up since they'd first begun dating. His positive response to her surprise had been too glowing, his muscles too tight. He was covering up something.

What had happened in New York? If she'd gone with him, would that have changed anything?

The baby pushed against her abdomen, and she pressed her hands to her stomach. This was stronger than the light fluttering she'd become used to. Even concern over Richard's news, whatever it was, couldn't steal the joy from this moment.

Lauren walked halfway down the stairs, her arms full of bedding. "Where can I put this?"

This girl was such a blessing. "Sweetheart, you didn't have to worry about that."

Lauren shrugged.

"Laundry's right next to the guest room. Toss it in there. I'll take care of it."

"Are you sure?"

"Sweetie, you're my guest, not my hired help." Sheila returned to the piano bench. "Besides, I'd love to have a few more minutes with you before the boys arrive."

Sheila sat on the piano bench as Lauren walked back upstairs. Music always helped relieve worry. She pulled out the sheet music for "Canon in D." The piece would be soothing, meditative, cheerful. Precisely what she needed. A minute later Lauren joined her on the bench.

"Will you play this for me?" Sheila pointed to the music.

"Sure."

Sheila slid over. She sighed and closed her eyes as Lauren's fingers began their light glide over the keys. Yes, this was exactly what she needed. Her worries subsided as she lost herself in the music.

Pressure tightened her stomach. Harder than before. Sheila brought her hand down. This was more than baby movement.

Dampness seeped between her legs and Sheila stiffened. *God. No. Please. Not now.* It was too early. Way too early.

Lauren stopped playing. "Sheila? Are you okay?"

"No." Her throat constricted as she forced out the words. "I need Richard. Now." Sheila closed her eyes. She heard Lauren run up the stairs then pound on the bedroom door, telling Richard it was an emergency.

An emergency? If this meant what she thought it did, it was already too late.

Maybe if she stayed motionless, it would stop. Babies born at nineteen weeks didn't survive. She sat still as a statue, begging God to save her child.

"Sheila?"

She opened burning eyes and raised her gaze to her husband. He jogged toward her putting an arm through a shirt sleeve. "I think my water broke." Her voice was broken as well.

His eyes blinked several times. "But it's too—"

"The baby's coming."

He raised a hand palm outward. "Stay put." He turned to Lauren who leaned against the wall behind him, her arms crossed over her chest. "We're going to Hennepin County Medical Center." Calm came through his voice, although Sheila knew he was terrified. Years of functioning under pressure in his business accounted for that calm. "Can you call everyone? Ask them to pray?"

"I will." Lauren nodded too quickly.

He turned back to Sheila. She started to stand. "No. Sit." She obeyed. His tightened jaw betrayed his fear even if his voice didn't. He bent over and picked her up, cradling her in his arms like an oversized baby.

She wrapped her arms around his neck and rested her tear-streaked face against his, meshing tears as they rushed to the hospital, praying for a miracle.

# CHAPTER *twenty-eight*

I t's a boy." The doctor's quiet pronouncement echoed in Richard's mind for hours, or was it seconds, after their child was born. Not the life-giving miracle of a longer gestation that they had begged God for. Richard heaved a sigh as the nurse handed Sheila their precious boy. She snuggled him against her chest, a linen napkin his blanket.

The doctor talked through Richard's fog. Their boy was way too small to survive, his organs underdeveloped.

*Dear Jesus, how could this have happened?*

Richard kissed his son's orange-sized head as their child fought for every breath. "Can I hold him before …?" He thumbed away Sheila's tears, and she nodded.

Heaving in a deep breath, he took his son and cradled him in his hands. Their son was so tiny, smaller even than Richard's hand. His reddened, bald head was oversized and his eyes were still closed, but he had an adorable little nose, and his mouth was open as if to speak. His fingers were long, piano playing fingers, taking after Sheila.

This precious child was a person, with his own identity, his own personality.

A personality they would never get to know.

As tears fell, Richard snuggled his boy against his chest. There was a knock on the hospital door, and it opened before anyone answered. A balding man walked into the room, a Bible in his hand. The chaplain?

"You want him baptized." The man smiled in understanding assurance.

"Yes, please." Sheila answered, her voice wobbly.

With tear-fogged eyes, Richard looked to their nurse. "I'd like pictures." He nodded toward his phone on the bedside table.

"Certainly."

Richard gave Sheila their child, then showed the nurse how to use his phone. He sat beside Sheila and braced his hands beneath hers while the nurse snapped pictures. Their child wasn't going to be forgotten.

The chaplain set up a small fount. "Does he have a name?"

Richard looked at Sheila and she nodded. The name they had settled on only days ago fit perfectly. "Samuel." Richard traced his finger along his son's translucent cheek. "Samuel Richard Brooks." In the Old Testament, Samuel was the infant Hannah had given over to God, entrusting the child solely to God's care. As he and Sheila would do now.

"Samuel Richard Brooks." The pastor's voice lifted as he sprinkled water on Samuel's head. "Child of God, receive the gift of the Holy Spirit ..."

Richard's and Sheila's tears blended with the baptismal water as the pastor continued.

The baptism over, teeny Samuel Richard Brooks returned home to be with God.

SHEILA STOOD BESIDE RICHARD, yet feeling miles apart, on their condo balcony overlooking the Mississippi. A glass of orange juice and a bowl of soggy Wheaties sat untouched on the table behind them. Sheila held a cup of coffee, both hands circling it, warming her chilly fingers. Richard wouldn't like what she needed to tell him. Today. But first she needed to mount the courage.

Rain drizzled down, dripping off the awning above her. A nice soaker, cleansing the air and nourishing the ground.

If only she could let her tears fall like the rain, but her eyes remained dry five days after they lost Samuel. Two days since his memorial.

A car whooshed down the parkway, splashing up water, and swerved to avoid a large pothole that could ruin the vehicle's suspension. If only she hadn't learned that losing Samuel was her fault. Those weren't the exact words her doctor had used. Instead she'd blamed an "incompetent cervix." Sheila's research told her that was quite likely the by-product of abortion. The doctor had offered hope. Medical science could repair what was broken, but there were no guarantees of a full-term pregnancy.

If only they could repair her broken heart.

She sipped her coffee, warming her numb insides. She couldn't go through this again. No more losses, no more pain.

Was this God's judgment of her? Or was He telling her she would have been a lousy mom, taking after her own mother? She shivered, and Richard tried to slip his arm around her waist.

"Not now." She shrugged his arm off, and he stuffed his hands into his front jeans pockets.

"When?"

"I don't know." *If I deserve your compassion …*

"I want to hold you. Support you. Why won't you let me?"

*Because I killed your baby, that's why.* And with what she was about to tell him, he'd probably never want to hold her again. "I've made a decision."

His jaw shifted from side to side, and he gazed toward the river. "What kind of decision?"

*I've decided to take away your dream.* "I won't go through this again."

He turned toward her, his eyes narrowing. "What are you talking about?"

"I won't get pregnant again." And as soon as they were done

talking she was heading straight into the condo to make the appointment. No sense delaying the inevitable.

She refused to look his way. She'd see how much he loved her, even through his hurt.

"I understand." Compassion came through his trembling voice. Tears she expected, but love and understanding? "You don't want to go through this again. You want a baby to hold, not another memorial to grieve over."

"It hurts too much."

"I know." He pulled his hands from his pockets and reached up to wipe the hair from her face. Pain flickered in his eyes. "Do me one favor. Don't make a permanent decision now. Give it some time."

She nodded, allowing the concession, although her decision had been made. Once she made up her mind about something, she remained firm. He knew that too. Experience had taught him.

He checked his watch and frowned. "I need to go. Doran's coming in at noon. You going to be okay here alone?"

*Yes. Leave me alone.* Her mind yelled out. All he'd done since they'd lost the baby was hover, wait on her, and be extraordinarily kind to her, when all she wanted was to be left alone in her misery. She was finally going to get that.

He kissed her before she had a chance to object. "You know how to reach me." He passed through the patio doors, picked up his briefcase by the front door, pulled his jacket off the coat tree and left.

Surely tears would come now. But they remained as distant as she'd been to Richard.


RICHARD GOT INTO HIS Audi and slammed the door. Did she think she was the only one hurting? Did she have a monopoly on pain? And what gave her the right to make a decision about their future when Samuel had been gone less than a week? He'd wanted to grab her, pull her close, and hug her to her senses. She wouldn't even let him do that.

Maybe it was good that he was getting out today. He could focus his mind on other things. Clients awaited, albeit patiently, and they deserved his attention.

He started the car and began mentally preparing himself for the work day. His assistant, Emma, had been a godsend. She'd explained the situation to his clients who all expressed their understanding. They should. He'd stressed his Faith and Family First motto with each client. The clients who truly wanted to effect a change in their bottom line listened to him, and his recommendations paid off. Now, gratefully, his clients were returning the favor. He would make sure to communicate his appreciation to all of them today. Customer relations were the first step in building client loyalty.

His phone rang as he put the car in gear. It wouldn't be Sheila. Unless it was an emergency, she knew better than to call him when he was driving. Distracted driving had cost him dearly once. It was a lesson he would never forget, and would always have to live with. He retrieved his phone and glanced at the I.D. *Marcus.* He put the car back into park and answered. "How's it going?"

"That's exactly what I was going to ask you."

Richard sighed and wiped his cheek. "I didn't think it was possible to hurt this much."

"I can't imagine what you're going through."

"And Sheila." He sniffled. "She doesn't cry. She shows no emotion at all. With all she's lost this past month, I think she's in shock, and I have no clue what to do about it." He was failing as a husband and as a father.

"Just love her, Rick. It's what you do best."

"Lord knows I'm trying." He checked his watch. "But hey, I've gotta get to work. Was there a reason you called?"

"Thought maybe you'd like to pound a nail today."

The idea even prompted a slight smile. "You know, I think

that's exactly what I need. I'll see you after work."

"And Rick?"

"Yeah?"

"We're all praying for you."

"Thanks. I've been doing a whole lot of that myself." God knew he needed it.

SHEILA SHUFFLED BACK INTO her home and closed the screen door. She needed to hear the rain, breathe in its cleansing scent. With Richard gone, she felt like a weight had been lifted, as if his love had become a burden. But she needed this time alone to say goodbye to Samuel, in her own way

She'd tried praying, but God was quiet. Why would He allow their baby to die? Why would He tease them by blessing them with the wonderful gift, and then tear it away from them? Richard had told her long ago that there would be times when God didn't make sense. This was one of those times.

The best thing to do was try to work through her anger and her grief. Literally. She'd return to work this afternoon. Physically, she was fine and she'd had enough rest over the past four days to last her the remainder of the year. Busyness would keep her mind occupied, and there was plenty of work to do. It wouldn't be difficult at all to put in hours of overtime.

But before she could return to work, she needed to put Samuel to rest. She retrieved the receipt for the baby furniture from the office. She and Lauren had had so much fun picking it all out. It would have been perfect. She called the store and cancelled its delivery. Next she removed all her maternity clothes from her closet, folded, and boxed them up. Most items she'd never worn.

Then she went to her dresser and removed two baby outfits, the coming home from the hospital outfits: one for a boy, the other for a girl. She placed those on top of the maternity clothes then closed the box flaps and taped it up with clear tape.

Someone else would benefit from her grief.

She set that box on Richard's side of the garage so she could avoid seeing it. She'd get Richard to deliver it to Vivant Family Services as it would likely be a while before she'd resume her volunteer work there. Seeing all those young girls pregnant with healthy babies they didn't want would be too much.

Life was unfair.

She had one final task before heading for work, but it was by far the most difficult. From the bookcase in the living room she pulled out the box that held the scrapbook they'd begun for Samuel. She carried the box to the dining room table, took out the book, and clutched it in her hands, waiting for the desired tears.

Nothing. Not even a sniffle.

She laid the book on the table and opened the cover. Still no tears.

Only one page was completed. Not with skillfully-cut pieces of colored or decorated paper framing the photo. Not with stickers announcing what was on the page. No, it was done simply with one picture and one handwritten letter. A letter telling Samuel how beautiful he was, how excited she and Richard were, how blessed they were, how they were looking forward to holding him. How much they already loved him.

How things had changed. *Did Richard write his letter?* She'd forgotten all about that. When he'd returned home on Saturday there hadn't been time to talk. She'd saved an open page just in case.

From the kitchen she retrieved the envelope with the developed photographs from the hospital. Only a handful of snapshots of their son. Hugging the prints against her chest, she returned to the table, then spread out the pictures and studied them.

How someone so tiny could show such personality was truly amazing. His eyes were closed so she couldn't tell if Samuel had

Richard's eyes, but the thinner lips were definitely Richard's. Samuel was too small to determine if he had dimples, but the angular chin was clearly hers. The narrow bridge across his nose was a gift from Richard. Samuel was beautiful.

In the photos, their baby had been cradled in love, with Samuel swaddled in a blanket the size of a handkerchief, and snuggled in her hands with Richard's supporting beneath. She had shed her last tears then, comingling them with Richard's. Pure love.

She taped all the pictures in the book. Now came the hard part.

Richard's mother had created a birth announcement/ memorial card for the memorial attendees. It announced Samuel's name, his birth date, weight and length. Followed by the date God received Samuel in Heaven. Richard's entire family had been at the cemetery service, offering welcomed support and love. She wished she'd been able to return it, but her feelings had already been numb.

Even Doran had shown up for the service. That poor young man had arrived in town bearing his own grief, but the service had seemed to help him. At least something good came from this.

She centered the memorial card on the page. It alone would occupy the space, offering a singular tribute to her son. Tears stayed away as she ran her finger along the verse from 1 Samuel 1:27-28.

*"I prayed for this child, and the Lord has granted me what I asked of him.*
*So now I give him to the Lord.*
*For his whole life he will be given over to the Lord."*
*And he worshiped the Lord there.*

SHORTLY AFTER TEN, RICHARD walked into his office, two hours earlier than planned, hoping to lose himself in work, eager to welcome Doran as his intern. A positive to focus on for the day.

Emma startled when he entered, obviously surprised to see him so soon. She closed the manila folder in front of her and pushed it to the side. "How are you doing?" It was a question asked with sincerity, requesting an honest answer, not the ubiquitous and hollow, "I'm fine."

"We're doing." was the most honest response he could think of, mimicking Doran's response after his girl had been born. It described the past few days quite well. They'd get out of bed, share a silent breakfast, and then lose themselves in a book, usually forgetting about lunch. A few words might be shared at the dinner table before turning on the television. Another diversion from real life. Then they'd return to their king-sized bed that seemed a mile wide with Sheila hugging the side.

Work should do them both good. "I appreciate you covering for me. Any problems?"

"I took care of what I could, but there was nothing that couldn't wait. Everyone understood." She handed him his messages and his mail.

He thumbed through it, prioritizing the day in his head.

"You also received a couple more items addressed to S.P. I put them in the box with the rest." Emma pointed to the copy paper box behind her desk.

Finally some good news. "Terrific. I'll take the box with me when I leave today. Then maybe we'll start a new collection." As it was, the response he'd received was far greater than he ever dreamed. He fanned the mail in his hand and headed toward his office, then stopped and looked back. "By the way, Doran Jans will be in around noon today. Just send him in."

"Will do, and Richard?"

"Yes?"

"It's good to have you back."

The woman was a godsend. "I'm glad to be back."

He entered his office, shut the door, and got down to the important task of customer relations. His clients deserved a personal call thanking them for their patience with a promise of discounted service. Profit was secondary to goodwill as that goodwill would pay off in the future. By the time Doran arrived, all of his customers would have been contacted.

After making his calls, he tackled the mail. Midway through the pile he heard a knock on his door. His computer clock said it was noon already. "Yes."

The door opened slowly and quietly. Doran remained in the doorway, polished and ready for work, wearing a pinstripe suit and toting a leather briefcase. Apparently Richard had neglected to tell the young man to go casual.

Much of his consulting work was done for small machining companies and other blue collar industries who didn't necessarily appreciate a suit walking in and telling them how to run their business. To get people to accept his recommendations, first he had to demonstrate that he was one of them, or at least that he understood them. An expensive suit invariably sent the wrong message.

"Good morn ... afternoon." Barely afternoon anyway. "Come on in." He rose from his chair and offered his hand to the nervous young man. "Prompt. I like that." A smile shown through Doran's nerves. "Emma introduced herself?"

Doran nodded.

"Best assistant around. She keeps us looking good." Richard pointed to the door. "Your office is out here."

Doran stepped back into the reception area. "I get an office?"

"If you can call a converted storage closet an office. You'll have to live with no window for now." Richard opened the door to Doran's office. The "desk" was a piece of kitchen countertop he'd secured into the wall with black metal filing cabinets stored under each end. The chair was a small rolling desk chair, and a laptop and phone were the only items on the desk. Richard had

270

left the walls bare so Doran could make this space his own.

"This is mine?" Doran's ear-to-ear grin told Richard he was more than happy to have his own space regardless of the size.

"All yours." Richard remained in the doorway, leaning against the frame. "I'm waiting for one of the tenants next to us to move out so I can expand. Then you'll get your window. When I moved into this space back in October I didn't anticipate that business would grow this quickly, but companies are grasping at anything that'll help them stay open. It's our job to insure those companies survive, so needless to say, we're busy, and I'm very glad you're here to help. If we maintain our current growth, I might have to consider moving, but I'd rather not." He liked to offer a show of stability to the companies he subcontracted for. Besides that, he loved his view and didn't want to give that up.

"This'll do fine." Doran laid his briefcase on top of the desk.

"And take off your jacket and tie. Dress code is business casual unless I say otherwise." Doran didn't hesitate to rid himself of the restrictive clothing. "Come on into my office. I'll give you a quick rundown of what I do, what I need you to help me with."

Doran followed Richard back into his office. Instead of taking a seat, he walked to the large window that spanned the length of the wall. "I can see why you don't want to give this office up."

Richard joined him and looked eastward toward the Mississippi River, then northward toward his home. Was Sheila still there or had she gone in to work? He looked further north, toward Wharton Sports where Sheila worked, where they'd met over a year ago in April. He liked being able to see her building. The connection somehow gave him comfort. Skyscrapers had their definite advantages.

"You'll love winter from here," he said, trying to divert his mind away from Sheila. "The streets are all lit up with Christmas lights. There used to be a parade that headed down Nicollet Mall, between Thanksgiving and Christmas. Unfortunately, they recently discontinued it. Watching it from here was quite a sight.

"The Fourth of July's pretty good too. Sheila and I watched the fireworks from up here. Could see displays from all around." It had been a different firework-filled evening when they'd first seen the "plus" sign displayed on the pregnancy test. Although that wasn't long ago, it felt like ancient times.

"This place is way cool. Thanks again for offering me this job." He offered his hand to Richard. "You didn't have to do it. You hardly know me."

"I know enough, and generally I'm a pretty good judge of character. You've been through a lot this past year, and I like how you've held up through it. I like how you handled the whole situation. Believe me, few people would have shown the integrity you have, and integrity's one of the most important qualities I look for." Richard sat on the edge of his desk, dangling one leg with the other planted on the carpet. "Keep in mind, though, if I find that you're not suited to the job, I won't hesitate to tell you. It would do neither of us any good to keep you in a place that's a bad fit."

"Got it."

Richard doubted Doran would be a problem. "And I have high expectations: I will expect you to work hard, be on time, and above all, be courteous to our clientele."

"I won't let you down."

"I expect not."

Doran turned away from the window and leaned his backside against the glass. "By the way, I wanted to tell you again, how bad I feel for you and Sheila. I wish we hadn't chosen someone else for our baby."

Richard got up and laid a hand on Doran's shoulder. "You made the decision that was right for you and Meghan and the baby. I admire you both for making that decision. It couldn't have been an easy one to make."

"No, it wasn't, but I know it's right. I mean, those first nights it hurt so bad. I lost the baby. I lost Meghan. I had to learn to let go of something that was never mine to begin with, I guess."

Such wisdom from a young man. Richard wondered if there wasn't a lesson in Doran's words for him as well.

"A few months ago"—Doran looked down toward his hands— "I didn't even know I cared. Now, I wonder if I hadn't been so pigheaded to begin with, maybe things would have been different between us. Meghan hasn't closed the door, but, gee, with us a thousand miles apart, how can there be a future?"

"Put it in God's hands." He spoke the advice as much to himself as he did to Doran.

"That's what Meghan's family says. Me, I don't get their religious beliefs. I went to church with her parents a few times but ..." Doran shook his head.

"You're welcome to come with me and Sheila any time." He'd open the door and hope Doran would walk through. "We attend one out in the suburbs where our other home is. It seems to cater to young people." He had to be careful about proselytizing. The last thing he wanted to do was chase this boy away. Hopefully, he'd let his actions do the witnessing first.

"Sure, maybe some time."

Richard left it at that.


SHEILA STUDIED THE REMAINING work on her desk, then gathered it up and shoved it into her top drawer. Now, at least, her desk surface was neat and tidy. The mess inside that drawer would drive Richard crazy, but this wasn't his mess to worry about.

The one at home was though. It was time to go home and apologize. Maybe reconsider her assertion about not having more children, maybe listen instead of harp, and definitely let him hold her.

She grabbed her purse and headed for the door when the phone on her desk rang. She looked at the clock. After five already? Her assistant would have left for the day. It was amazing how prompt her secretary was when the end of the day arrived. Sheila hesitated a moment before answering, as few people had her direct number. It was either Richard, or her boss telling her about a new client she needed to woo. She wasn't in a wooing mood today, but that was part of her job, so she returned to her desk, picked up the phone, and pasted on the smile only Richard would know wasn't real.

"Sheila speaking."

"Hey there."

"Richard." She released a sigh and her fake smile and carried her phone to a loveseat.

"How's it going?"

*Terrible.* "Okay. I'm pretty swamped." *But all I want is to come home and see you.*

"Oh." Disappointment dampened his voice. "So you wouldn't mind if I headed out to the house? Check on Marcus, make sure construction's going okay?"

*Yes, I would.* "No. Go ahead." Why that house even mattered anymore was beyond her. That house was being built to accommodate a family. Its vacant rooms would be an ever-present reminder of what they'd lost. She didn't know if she could live there anymore. Their condo in the city would be more than adequate for the two of them. Perhaps she should convince Richard of that too.

"I won't be gone too long."

"Take whatever time you need."

No "I love yous" were exchanged before the receiver buzzed Richard's departure.

RICHARD COULDN'T WAIT TO pick up a hammer and pound out his frustrations. He steered his car onto his gravel driveway and actually smiled. He'd almost forgotten what that felt like. Marcus' construction crew had accomplished a lot in this past week during Richard's absence. A second story was already framed in—a second story holding four bedrooms: the master plus three empty rooms, rooms that would remain bare if Sheila meant what she said.

Sheila. The thought of her stole his smile.

She hadn't complained when he told her he was going to check on the house. She even sounded happy. Happy to be at work. Happy to be away from him.

White-knuckling the steering wheel, he parked his Audi behind a worker's pickup. Five forty-five and they were still here. He'd told Marcus he wanted the home done quickly, that he'd gladly pay overtime. The workers were apparently more than willing to take his money. Maybe they'd take his mind off of Sheila for now too.

He got out of his car and walked around it, surveying the muddy parking lot that was once his carefully manicured yard. If he'd been thinking, he would have driven the pickup today, but Sheila's announcement upset him too much to think straight. At the moment, he wanted to see Sheila about as much as she wanted to see him. Perhaps a date with the hammer would be good therapy.

From his trunk, he pulled out a tool belt and attached it over his hips. Then he removed a copy paper box addressed to his mother. He placed that in the cab of his brother's pickup. His mother could perform a miracle with what was in that box. What he'd give for a miracle right now.

He returned to his car and took out ten boxes of pizza: extra-large with all the fixin's. No sissy food for these guys, probably a mere snack for them.

After wiping his feet on an outdoor mat, he entered his house through the front door into what had once been his living room. It would be again someday, only larger. The fireplace he had spent so many hours constructing out of farm-picked rock and framed in with cherrywood shelves was gone. The hardwood floors were only a memory. He and Sheila had planned on building new memories together. It wasn't starting out so well.

He walked through his former kitchen and spotted the guys outside sitting on expensive lawn chairs now fused with the mud. The workers didn't care. The chairs were his, not theirs. He'd have the not-so-fun chore of cleaning them later. The deck had been torn down too. They probably struggled taking that thing apart. He'd built it solid.

But Marcus had gathered his best crew. If anyone could disassemble his work, they could. It paid to have your brother as the head honcho, especially when you were on good terms with him. Richard had worked with many of these guys last fall when he was still trying to figure out his life and had joined right in with their cussing and their male humor. At least he'd been smart and avoided the bars. Who knew where he'd be now if he'd given in to that temptation too.

So these men were a bit rough hewn, that didn't matter. They were diligent and efficient workers. They did their job quickly, and they did it right the first time. Construction was their craft, and they took pride in their workmanship. They were precisely whom he wanted working on his house. Judging by the substantial change in his home, they'd clearly earned the small break they were taking.

Richard stepped through the opening that had once been his patio door and onto his former lawn. The lawn wasn't completely gone. Tufts of grass still peeked up here and there.

If he had no child to play with, to throw the ball to, to wrestle with in the grass, to push on the swing, he'd have nothing better to do than create the perfect lawn. Maybe these guys were doing him a favor.

The perfect lawn. Some legacy that would be.

"Pizza delivery." He set the stack of boxes on his patio table which was also ensconced in mud. The workers grabbed one box each, not bothering to check out what was inside, leaving nothing for him. Didn't matter. Not even pizza appealed today.

Richard pulled the tape measure out of his tool belt and held it up. "You gals go ahead and eat. I need to check out your work."

"You finally got yourself a union card?" The small guy with the biggest mouth, a former Navy SEAL, asked, not caring that his mouth was stuffed with pizza.

"No. Just your paycheck."

"You won't find nothin' wrong."

"I'll be the judge of that," Richard said, but he didn't doubt the man. Tape measure in hand, he walked back inside the house and measured the distance between various studs. Perfect every time. He had nothing to complain about, nothing except for the fact that he didn't need this monster of a house anymore, that all but one of the bedrooms would stand vacant.

He removed a rag from his tool belt and wiped a spot on the floor before sitting down and leaning his back against an open stud. If there wasn't a group of men sitting outside, probably about to clamber back in, he'd allow himself a good cry. Since Sheila wasn't crying, he didn't feel like he should either, but oh how he wanted to.

How ironic life was. Only a few weeks ago he and Sheila were wondering how they were going to deal with two infants, born months apart. It had been a scary prospect, so when Doran told them that they hadn't been chosen to be adoptive parents, it had almost been a relief. Now he wished for the opportunity again.

Sure, he was already a father. To a child who lived over a thousand miles away, a child who didn't know who he was. A child who was afraid of him. He was father to a child for whom he could never be a proper full-time daddy. Even as a part-time father, he'd be tearing his child away from home, away from a loving mommy and Gamma and ... Danny.

Richard recoiled his tape measure. Marissa was wrong. Maybe Matthew wasn't saying the word "Daddy," but that's precisely what the child meant. To Matthew, Danny meant

Daddy. What would "Daddy" mean to Matthew? Maybe it was best if Richard left well enough alone and let Marissa and Danny raise his child. Maybe this was what God was trying to tell him, that he'd blown his opportunity. That he and Sheila deserved to be alone. Maybe things were as they were meant to be and this was God's plan after all. He prayed that wasn't so.

Regardless, he couldn't tell anyone about Matthew. Not now. Not until Sheila was doing better.

"Things looking okay?" Marcus interrupted Richard's pity-party.

"No."

"No?" Marcus took a cursory glance around. "What? Where?"

"Everything. Everywhere. Your guys are too good." Richard pulled his ball-peen hammer from his tool belt. There'd be no electric nailer for him today. He wanted to feel the full force of the hammer. "I came here to pound some nails. Your guys didn't leave me anything to fix."

"Sorry about that?" Marcus raised his brows.

Richard grunted. "I look at this place now." He spread out his arms. "Our grand mansion. It's going to be empty."

Marcus sat next to him, not worrying about the pile of dirt beneath him. "Want to talk about it?"

No. "I put a box in your truck, if you don't mind stopping at the farm on the way home. Mom's expecting it."

"I'll see that she gets it."

"Thanks."

Laughter rang from the men outdoors. Normally Richard would love to join them. But not today.

Marcus pulled out his hammer and used it to point around the skeleton-like room. "You don't think it's odd to clean out a home before remodeling right?"

"Of course not."

"Can you imagine trying to work around people's junk? Just covering it up with plastic and hoping it doesn't get wrecked. It's always best to clear everything out first, then we can fix what's broken."

Clever brother. Richard pounced the ball of his hammer in his palm. "Sheila's done trying for a baby. She told me this morning that she couldn't lose any more. I understand, but I don't. You know what I mean?"

Marcus nodded.

"I told her to give it some time, not to make a decision now. But you have to know Sheila. Once she makes up her mind about something, it's made up. I'm scared to death where that leaves us."

"Give it time, Ricky. She'll come around."

"I hope so." *And then I'll get to break the other news to her.* He wished he could tell Marcus. He was dying to tell somebody, but then Marcus would tell Janet, and then Janet would lambaste him for not telling anybody. No, better to keep it to himself.

"I believe God will give you kids. You've got a special connection with them. Always have. I always envied that about you."

"You're joking, right."

"No. Not at all. Look at Nathan. The kid is block-headed like his old man. Nothing I was saying was getting through to him. Then he spends one weekend with you and starts talking about the ministry."

"Nathan?"

"I'm not kidding. Nearly blew me away when he brought it up."

"I thought he was talking Marines."

"Chaplain. He knows that's a long ways down the road, but he's seriously looking into it."

"Wow." Richard stared at the plywood flooring.

"What I want to know is what you said to him. When he got home late that night with Jon and the girls, I was livid. But before I could say a word, he's apologizing all over himself, to me, Janet, Jon, Lauren. Then, after Jon left, and Lauren went to bed, Nate stayed up to hear his punishment. Less than a week later he's sneaking out with that girl and comes home a man."

"He didn't." Richard's shoulders and heart sank.

"Exactly. He didn't. And the kid learned what it really means to be a man. I've never been so happy in all my life. I want to know what you told him so I can pass it on."

Richards scratched his chin. "The truth."

Marcus frowned.

"I confessed my dirt and thought for sure I'd be on your Most Wanted list. But maybe a dose of reality was all Nate needed to see that what the world is offering isn't so great after all."

"Truth, huh?"

Richard nodded. "Destroyed his image of me. Guess that was okay."

"I'm glad it came from you."

"Truth." Exactly what he needed to tell Sheila. He doubted it would produce the same positive results, though.

"We're all praying for you." Marcus slapped Richard's shoulder and stood up as boisterous voices neared the house.

"Thanks. I appreciate it." Richard got up and faced the workers as they clambered inside. "You ladies ready to get back to work?" Richard raised his hammer in the air and stared at it.

The SEAL answered back in a language he must have learned in the Navy.

Richard laughed and replaced the hammer in his belt. "Good, you're doing great work. I'll leave you be."

"You're leaving?" Marcus rested a hand on Richard's shoulder.

"There are other places I need to be." And a truth that needed to be told. He'd have to trust God with the consequences, and pray that when he told Sheila about Matthew, he wouldn't lose her forever.

# CHAPTER *twenty-nine*

Sheila gripped the steering wheel as the garage door to the condo rose. No Audi. Just as she expected.

She'd done it now, hadn't she? Shut Richard out. Left him out of her decision making—a major decision that would affect both of their lives. How could she have been so selfish? Tonight she'd let him back in, let him know her feelings—or lack thereof—and let him hold her.

At least she hadn't been rash enough to make the doctor's appointment yet. Sheila wasn't saying it wasn't still going to happen, but she and Richard needed to be in agreement on this issue.

She parked her Lexus and walked into the silent home. She hung her purse and jacket in the small mudroom and then walked out into the empty living room. Living room. Without Richard, no life existed in this room at all. For several years she'd lived here alone and had loved it, but Richard had changed her entire outlook. Solitude was no longer her desire.

She needed him.

Her gaze rested on the piano. It hadn't been touched since Saturday. Perhaps music would breathe life back to the room. She sat at the keyboard. The music for "Canon in D" was still spread open, as they'd left it days before. She'd never played this piece, so it would be a good challenge for the evening.

She struggled through two measures, and the phone rang.

*Please let it be Richard.* She jogged to the phone. The caller I.D. read Unknown name. Unknown number. Just what she needed, a sales call. Well she'd get rid of them for good. That was something she could control. She answered with a firm, "Please take me off your call list."

"I'm sorry." A male voice rasped, then the man cleared his throat. "This isn't a sales call."

"Then who, may I ask, is calling." And how did they get her unlisted number?

"Is this Sheila?" The gruff voice had a hint of familiarity, but she couldn't place it.

"Yes, it is and who are you?"

He cleared his throat again.

Sheila tapped her fingernails on the table.

"This is your father."

She pulled out a dining table chair, its back to the front door, and fell into it. The man's timing was impeccable. "Father," she said flatly, trying not to care that he called.

"I'm sorry—"

*You're sorry?*

"—for how your mother and I treated you."

Sucking in her cheeks, Sheila picked up a pencil from the table and began doodling music notes on the newspaper. How does one reply to an apology overdue by eighteen years?

"I'd like another chance to be a grandfather."

She dropped the pencil and it rolled onto the carpet. "I'm sorry Father. It's too late."

A sad "Ohhh" moaned softly through the phone.

"I didn't mean that." Maybe he didn't deserve an explanation, but not explaining would allow him to believe a lie. Besides, once he knew the truth, he would have no further reason to call. "We lost the baby." Moisture fogged her vision. Tears? Now? She dabbed below her eye.

"Oh, Sheila," he said sadly as if he truly cared.

More tears flowed. Why now? Why couldn't they wait until Richard could hold her and tell her everything would be all right? She was showing vulnerability to her father, of all people.

"I'm sorry, Sheila. I didn't know."

*Because Mother told me to stay out of your lives, that you weren't interested in the grandparent role. You didn't argue.*

"But how would we know?" He laughed a quiet, dry laugh. "And you? Are you okay?"

*He's concerned about me? How sweet.* More sarcasm rankled through her. "I'm fine. Just hunky dory." Great. Now she was even talking like a child.

"Oh ... oh. That's good." He answered softly.

And now she'd offended him. What a terrific Christian witness she was. She mellowed her voice. "I am fine."

"Good. Good."

"So, you can see, now there's no reason for Mother to worry about me intruding in your life. Nature already took care of it." Was it nature, or was it God? She wasn't pleased with the alternative.

"But ... but, I'd still like to see you. Be ... be a father to you."

A father to me? *You're a tad bit late for that, aren't you?* "I don't know that that's a good idea."

"Oh. I see. Well, just so you know. If ... if you should change your mind, c-c-call me, okay?"

"Okay." She backhanded a cheekful of wayward tears. Her weakness was maddening.

"And ... and Sheila?"

Would he ever say goodbye? "Yes?" Polite, but aloof.

"I ... I want you to know that I ... I ... I love you."

Waterworks streamed full force down her cheeks and the phone buzzed the disconnection. He loved her? Why had it taken him thirty-six years to say that? She clutched her barren stomach as sobs wrenched her body. *Why, God? Why?*

Sniffling, she cradled her arms on the table and laid her face into them, no longer trying to stop the invasive tears.

A hand stroked her hair.

Sheila raised her head enough to see over her arms.

Richard sat in the chair beside her, tears trickling down his face, too. With his thumbs he dried her face then he circled his arms around her and pulled her in tight.

"I'm sorry, Richard. I am so sorry."

"Shhh, honey." He cupped her cheeks and rested his forehead against hers. "You have nothing to be sorry about."

"I've hurt you."

"You haven't hurt me. It's this whole situation that's hurtful."

"I don't know that I can go through this again."

"I know. I understand, but that decision can wait."

She nodded.

"What I know now is that I really need God." He took her hands and folded them into his own. "And I really need you."

She shifted in her chair so she could rest her face in his shirt. "I need you too."

SHEILA NEEDED HIM.

Relief was in those words, but would that change when he told her about Matthew? Richard silently sent up a prayer, asking for wisdom, praying that Sheila would accept his son, begging for more time. For the last request, he received a prompt answer. *No.* Other lives were on hold besides his.

He released his grip on Sheila and lifted her chin. "Let's go to the couch." He took her hand and led her into the living room. He sat against the couch's arm and stretched his feet onto an ottoman. Sheila snuggled in next to him, curling her legs up beneath her. He held her, caressing her, letting her cry out her pain.

Her tears went on for minutes, hours it seemed, then she heaved a sob and grew completely still and silent. Had he waited too long? Let her fall asleep? He shifted his position to prevent his leg from cramping.

She clutched at the front of his shirt and whispered, "Don't go."

Relieved, he relaxed back into the couch and kissed her forehead. "I'm not going anywhere." Not yet, anyway. Time would tell how often he would have to fly to New York. He drew her in closer. It was vital that she knew she was his first priority. "Remember when I came home Saturday night? You thought something was wrong?"

She pulled away. Redness still rimmed her eyes, but concern had replaced the sadness. "I forgot," she said quietly. She took his hand in hers and kissed it. "Tell me."

With tears still burning, preventing him from focusing on anything, he closed his eyes. He'd thought he was all cried out. Blinking his gaze into focus, he stared out the patio door. "Remember, on Friday night, I went to Marissa's."

"You said she'd been sick?"

"Had been."

Sheila dropped his hand and moved away, her forehead lined with worry. "She didn't try coming on to you, did she?"

"No. Nothing like that!" He squeezed the back of his neck. This wasn't coming out the way it was supposed to. "She and her fiancé had news for me."

"Fiancé?" Sheila smiled, then her expression fell. "Does it bother you?"

"What? No!" How could Sheila even conceive that he'd be jealous? Richard drew in a deep breath and gripped her hands. "Sheila, she has a child."

"A child?" Her gaze darted, her mind obviously trying to piece together his puzzle, probably not liking the all-too-true conclusion.

"A little boy named Matthew."

"So?" Sheila shrugged.

He looked upward. *God, help me please.* Still clutching her hands, he locked his gaze with hers and swallowed hard. "He's mine." His words rasped from a sandpaper throat.

She blinked several times without pulling away, but her hands sat limp in his. "Your boy?"

"Twenty-one months old. Dark hair. Brooks smile." He drew out his wallet, opened it, and removed a photo.

Sheila took the picture and shifted to the opposite side of the couch, her back and shoulders slumped.

"I don't understand." Sucking on her lower lip, she stared down at the photo.

"Marissa lied to me. She didn't have the abortion." How was it that such good news, something he had begged for, sounded so awful?

"Are you certain?" She handed back the photo.

He studied the picture, trying hard not to smile at the toddler's familiar grin. The same grin he'd seen on Nathan's and Joshua's faces when they were small. The same grin in his own baby pictures. "I have no doubt. We've agreed to DNA testing, if you feel it's necessary. Personally, I ..." It all made sense. Marissa hadn't been one to play the field. He knew he was the only guy she'd been with.

"What does this mean?" Sheila stared down at the photo in his hand. This picture had been his only source of happiness over the last few days.

"That's what you and I need to discuss." He tucked the photo back in his wallet. "Marissa offered me—us—joint physical custody."

He searched her eyes, hoping to see some glimmer of agreement.

But she laughed. A sad laugh as she brought a hand to her forehead, then dragged her fingers through the length of her hair. "I think I'm getting a headache."

He stood. "I'll get you some aspirin."

"No. No. I need to feel the pain. I've been numb for days, then

286

Father calls, now this."

"What?" He sat down hard. "Your father called?"

"Don't try to change the subject." She shook her head. "That's why I was crying when you came home. He called, wanting to be a grandfather. I told him he was too late."

He moaned. "Hon, I'm so sorry. I didn't know."

"And your knowing would have changed anything? How?" She got up from the couch and turned back toward him, anger now flashing in her eyes which moments ago only held sadness. "So, you get your wish. You get to be a daddy and I get … I get to be mother to your ex's child. To a Matthew, nonetheless, a name we'd chosen together. How sweet is that?" She strode to the patio doors and stared out. "Anything else you need to sucker punch me with?"

That's truly what he'd done, wasn't it? "I didn't tell her 'yes'," he said softly.

"And if you say 'no'?" She whirled around. "If you say no, what would that do to us? Would you ever be able to forgive me for taking away your chance to be a father not once, but twice within a matter of days? How can you say 'no'?" She turned back to the door and whimpered. "How can I say 'yes'? What would it mean? Would I be sharing you, too? Would you spend half your year flying to New York?"

"We could move there," he said quietly. It was another solution, by no means a perfect one. If ACM Technologies wouldn't have him anymore, he could begin a new business and Sheila would have no trouble finding a job, possibly a dream job. She was made for Manhattan.

But then what would happen to his clients who'd trusted in him, to Doran who was relying so heavily on him, his family whom he relied upon.

"I don't know." Her voice remained low.

"I won't do anything without your blessing."

"What about the boy? Have you considered his needs?"

*Constantly.*

"Have you considered what it would do to him to be whisked across the country for half a year, or however you planned on doing this, away from his mother?"

"And Gamma. And Danny." He added softly.

"Danny?"

Richard shrugged. "Marissa's fiancé. The man who's played the role of daddy." Sheila was right. How could he tear the boy away from the only people he knew?

But it wasn't Richard's fault he hadn't been there for Matthew. "If I'd known, I would have been there for him. I wouldn't be a stranger. I'd be the one he called Daddy."

"And you wouldn't have met me."

He covered his face with his hands and moaned. Why did everything have to be so complicated? Cuffing his hands in his lap, he pleaded. "You're the best thing that's ever happened to me."

"Until now."

He blinked a few times. His shoulders felt as if they had sandbags weighing them down. "No. I can't live without you." But could he live without playing a vital role in his son's life?

Moisture budded in her eyes. She bowed her head toward the floor and crossed her arms. "If you don't agree to joint physical custody? Then what?"

"I guess I become Matthew's favorite uncle." Just saying those words agitated his stomach.

"One who pays child support."

He sighed. "That wasn't her intent in telling me. And no, she didn't ask for child support."

"But you'd give it anyway."

"Of course. How can I not? I won't run away from my responsibilities."

"No. I don't suppose so." Her voice remained low, beaten.

He crossed the room and circled his arms around her waist,

resting his hands on her stomach. Thank goodness she didn't fight him. "I love you," he whispered, "and regardless of the circumstances it took to meet you, I'm so grateful that happened. I can't lose you."

Sniffles answered.

He sighed, keeping his arms wrapped around her. "We don't have to make a decision now. We can discuss it. Pray about it. It's a shared decision and—" He tried to cover the sorrow he felt thinking of the following option "—if we decide no, then I'll be content with that." He'd have to rely on God heavily for that contentment because he sure couldn't summon it on his own. "All I know is that I have to be involved. Somehow. I'm listed on his birth certificate. Matthew will know I'm his birth father. I need him to know I didn't abandon him."

With a nod, she pulled free from his embrace. "I'm going to bed."

He watched her go, a fist-sized lump stuck in his throat. Too much had been dumped on her and at such a vulnerable time. Maybe he'd made a mistake in telling her so soon. Truth was, he had no clue what was best.

He slid the patio door open and stepped onto the deck. A chill hung in the air, the kind warning that winter was peeking around the corner, a season he usually anticipated. He loved the cold, the snow, and all the activities that came with it. Now he had a son he'd hopefully be able to share those activities with.

Closing his eyes, he breathed in deeply. The rain earlier in the day had cleansed the air. Even the city smelled good tonight.

But the freshness couldn't match their country home. There he could go out under the stars' canopy and talk out loud to God. It was easier to see God there, to hear God, to sense God's presence. Here there were too many noises, too many distractions, too many bright lights impeding the view. It wasn't as bad as New York, but it was bad enough.

Excuses. He'd made the same excuses in New York and look

where that got him. It was time to put them aside and seek some fatherly advice.

He folded his hands on the balcony's iron railing and craned his neck upwards, away from manmade interference. "I'm here, Father. I'm listening."

SHEILA PULLED ON HER flannel pajamas. She was cold and was certain there'd be no cuddling tonight. That would be her decision, of course. But how could she cuddle when she was so angry? Angry with whom, she wasn't sure. Her father for trying to initiate a relationship? Isn't that what she had wanted? Isn't that why they'd flown down to Arizona?

How could she be mad at Richard? This situation wasn't his fault, but she wanted to blame him anyway. Or maybe she was jealous. Jealous of the beautiful woman who would forever be a part of Richard's life. A beautiful woman who had given Richard what Sheila had failed to provide. Richard's child would be an ever-present reminder of her own failure.

She lay down in bed and pulled the covers up to her chin. Moving to New York definitely wasn't the answer. There was no way she was going to move away from Richard's family and closer to that woman.

Would she be asked to be a mother to that woman's child? Richard's child? What did joint physical custody mean anyway? How often would they be dragged apart?

She grabbed Richard's pillow, screamed into it, beat it with her fists. None of that made her feel better.

How could she deny Richard this opportunity? He would be a great father, even if it wasn't to a child they raised together. On top of that, it would kill him to play the role of absentee father. Could she be responsible for such an emotional death?

She turned on the lamp on the bed stand. Her Bible lay there, a thin layer of dust indicated she hadn't picked it up for days, since before they lost Samuel. She blew the dust off then opened it to Matthew chapter six where she and Richard had left off before he flew to New York. Matthew, gift of Yahweh, was the first book of the Bible she had ever read. It wasn't coincidence that she turned to the book now.

Verse six jumped out at her: *"But when you pray, go into your room, close the door and pray to your Father, who is unseen."* It was more than a hint. The bedroom door was closed and silence shouted from the living room. Was Richard planning to sleep on the couch? She wouldn't blame him if he did. Once she prayed, she'd go to him, bring him in to their shared room, and stress that she wasn't angry at him.

She kneeled on the floor beside the bed, laid her Bible in front of her and read aloud: "Our Father in heaven ..."

"HOW IS THE HOUSE coming?"

The voice behind him sounded heavenly to Richard. He easily tore his gaze from the quiet river scene and turned around.

Sheila stood in the patio doorway, her arms wrapped around her upper body. Wanting her to make the first move toward any physical contact, he slipped off his sweatshirt and handed it over. She accepted the shirt and pulled it on without comment. In the evening's shadows he couldn't tell if she'd been crying or not. It would surprise him if she hadn't.

"The house is looking good." He leaned his back against the railing. "It's nice to have an in with the contractor. I'm finding out how talented my brother is. We'll be moving back in before we realize—hopefully by Thanksgiving."

"That soon?" She sounded disappointed.

"Probably."

"Oh." She stepped out of the doorway, shut the patio door, and stood next to him, staring out at the city lights across the river.

"We can keep the condo." He did like the option of having a place to crash on those days when work went far into the night.

Besides, it would be unfair to ask her to relinquish one more piece of her past. She'd been asked to give up too much recently.

"I'd like that."

"Tell me about the call from your father."

She sighed and shrugged. "There's not much to tell. He decided he wanted to be a grandfather after all. He apologized for how he and Mother treated me." She clutched the wrought iron railing. "He said he loved me."

"Isn't that good news?"

"I'm thirty-six and this is the first time he says he loves me? Am I supposed to forget all those empty years?"

"To be honest, my dad rarely says those words." He knew his dad loved him, though. There wasn't any doubt.

"Then maybe that's the problem. His words are meaningless unless there's action behind them. Your dad doesn't say it, but he shows it."

"You're going to let the issue with your father drop then."

"If you'll let me." There was an edge in her voice.

"It's up to you." But perhaps a door had opened again. He wasn't ready to completely shut her father out.

"What are you going to do?" She turned to face him, her body remaining rigid.

"About?"

"Your son."

His son.

Already he longed to see Matthew again. The only time Richard saw him, he hadn't had the opportunity to hold him, and his body ached from the longing to do so.

"We"—It was imperative to emphasize this wasn't his solitary choice—"have to discuss it. I'd like you to meet him before we make any kind of decision." She liked children as much as he did. Once she saw Matthew, she wouldn't be able to tell Richard "no."

He reached over and covered her hand. It was ice cold. "What do you say we see about flying to New York this weekend? I'll ask if we could spend some time alone with Matthew."

She ran a finger back and forth along the railing then finally nodded. "Okay."

His lips curled into a smile although he tried to prevent it. He didn't want to look too eager.

"And your family? We should tell them."

Yes, they would, but later. Getting Sheila to acclimate to their new reality first was more important. "Let's wait until after we see him."

"I agree." She turned her hand over and clasped his. "Come to bed? I need you to hold me."

Nothing sounded better.

RICHARD YAWNED AS HE inserted the key into his office door lock. Sleep hadn't come easily during the night, for him or Sheila, although they had spent the night holding each other. Too much had been dumped on her during the past week, and now he was asking her to make one more sacrifice.

But at least she'd agreed to fly to New York. One step ahead. Now, he needed to get approval from Marissa.

He pushed open his office door and was surprised to see lights on. Seven thirty in the morning and someone had beaten him to work? Most likely Emma.

But her chair was empty, and her desktop was clear of paperwork.

A pounding sound came from Doran's office and Richard peeked inside as Doran lay a hammer down on the desktop. Doran had beaten him to work. Impressive. If this continued, Richard would know he'd made the right decision in hiring Doran.

A mountain landscape picture hung above the desk giving the impression of a spectacular window view. To Doran's right was a bulletin board and, to the left, a whiteboard. Post-it notes, pens, and note paper were neatly arranged on the desktop. He even had a framed five-by-seven photo on top of the desk. "Looks like you've made yourself comfortable."

Doran jumped, then spun around, his hand on his heart. "You snuck up on me."

Richard grinned. "Sorry about that. I didn't expect you in yet."

"Thought I should come in early if I wanted to personalize my office. Didn't want to spend work time on it."

So the kid excelled in kissing up, too. Richard had probably been the same way when he'd joined ACM Technologies fresh out of college.

"Look at this." Doran picked up a printed page from off the top of his desk.

Richard took the paper and read to himself.

*Hi Doran,*
*Hope you made it to Minneapolis okay.*

A personal e-mail from Meghan. Richard looked toward Doran. The young man was grinning. "You sure you want me to read this?"

"Yeah. Sure. Go ahead."

*I attached a picture I got from the adoptive parents. Let me know if you can't open it. They look so happy and she looks so comfortable with them. I know we did the right thing. And guess what they named her. Angela Justine, after my brother. How special is that? They promised, again, that they would keep in contact with us. I forwarded them your new address. I hope that's okay with you.*

*I also attached the picture that Mom took in the hospital. I think it turned out real good, at least of you and Angela. I'm sort of a wreck. I forwarded that picture to them as well so Angela can grow up knowing how much we love her.*

*Anyway, I'm doing fine. Feeling real sad. A bit weird. After you've been pregnant for forever it's hard to adjust. I miss all the little kicks and movements. I miss her.*

*I miss you, too.*

*I realized that I never said goodbye to you. I never said thank you for being with me and supporting me. You didn't have to. Maybe I'm now realizing how lucky I was to have you. So, thanks. I hope you want to keep in touch. If not, I understand. And, if you're ever in the area, Mom and Dad said you're welcome. Maybe we could visit Angela together. I think I'd like that.*

*Good luck on your new job. I hope it all works out for you.*

 *Love, Meghan*

Richard handed the letter back to Doran who wore a goofy smile. The kid was in love. It was hard to believe Doran was the same person Richard had met this past January, a cocky young man who shunned responsibility. Doran picked up the frame from his desk and handed it to Richard. "This is us in the hospital. She's awfully pretty, isn't she?"

"Who? Meghan or the baby?"

Doran looked down, but his blush was evident.

"Do you have a copy of the other picture?" Richard handed back the portrait. "Of the new parents?"

"Sure do." Doran reached into his briefcase and took out another framed photograph. "I'm gonna put this one up, and then I'll be ready to go to work." He started to give the picture to Richard, but stopped and pulled it back. Doran's grin disappeared and a worried frown took its spot. "Can I tell you something first?"

Richard propped himself against the door frame and nodded.

Clutching the picture against his chest, Doran rested against the desk and gazed toward the floor. "You were my first choice," he said softly. "When I added it all up, you and Sheila, well, you two were the clear choice to me."

"But not for Meghan." Richard expected that.

"That's part of it, yeah, but I guess maybe I was feeling selfish, ya know."

Richard crossed a leg over the other and planted his hands in his front pockets.

"You see, growing up I thought I had the coolest dad. He let me to do things no one else was allowed to do. His idea of father-son bonding was buying my first condom. He always wanted to be my best friend. It wasn't until Meggie ended up in the hospital that I started to wonder what was right. I was scared for her, ya know?" Doran shook his head. "I guess I found out I cared for her more than I thought. Then, there were you and Sheila, waiting to hear about a girl who hated your guts. I didn't get it. Why would you do that?"

Richard shifted his jaw and stared at the print above Doran's desk.

"And then you gave me your business card, told me to call you if I needed anyone to talk to. I'd never had that before. Not someone who would listen, not someone who was willing to tell me there are consequences for screwing up. I didn't even know I was messing up until Meggie got hurt. Maybe if I'd realized earlier ..."

Doran pulled the picture away from his chest and studied it. He blinked and cleared his throat. "So, anyway, when I chose these two to be parents it was because I guess I already thought of you as a father figure. My father figure. I didn't want to lose that."

Richard sighed and tugged his hands from his pocket. He'd been paid the highest honor he could think of, and the kid had left him speechless. He accepted the frame from Doran and studied the tiny bundle held in a smiling woman's arms, and the man standing proudly behind the two. Yes, little Angela Justine was right where God wanted her.

He handed back the frame. "I'm sure they'll be wonderful parents."

"Yeah, I think they will be." Doran angled the photograph behind the other one. "I was wondering if, maybe, the offer was still open to come to church with you and Sheila on Sunday?"

Richard stood up straight and grinned, thankful for this brief reprieve from the week's gloom. "Actually, we're hoping to be out of town on Sunday. If not, we'd be more than glad to have you."

The door to the outer office creaked open. Have to spray some WD-40 on that. Richard checked the time. Seven forty-five. Still early. He turned away from Doran while pulling out his cell phone. "Good morning, Emma."

"Good morning." She stuck her purse in a desk drawer. "Nice to see you here so early."

"It's time I get back to my regular work schedule." He scrolled through his phone listings then handed the phone to Emma. "Could you get this gentleman on the phone for me? Try after ten o'clock. They're an hour behind us."

She took down the information and handed back his phone. "I'll let you know when I reach him."

"I appreciate it." He turned back to Doran. "Give yourself time to get set up. I'll be calling you into my office soon." But first he had to make a phone call, one he was excited, yet nervous, to make. He prayed Marissa would be home this weekend so he could see—hold—his son. As much as he disliked having this permanent relationship with Marissa, it was now a fact of his life he'd have to get used to. Unfortunately, Sheila had to get used to it too.

He walked to his office, closed the door, and picked up his office phone. Marissa's phone number was permanently etched in his memory. She answered after the second ring.

"Richard." Her soft voice shook.

"Marissa." Any contact with her would remain at a detached professional courtesy level. "I have a favor to ask."

"Yes?" Apparently she felt the same way.

"I'd like to fly out Saturday morning with Sheila. Introduce her to Matthew."

He spun his chair around and faced the window, watching the stoplights below change from green to yellow then red, then they ran through another cycle. What was taking Marissa so long? What he asked wasn't unreasonable.

She finally cleared her throat. "Does this mean you've made a decision?"

"No. It means that I want to see Matthew again. That I want Sheila to meet him. Spend some time together with you, Daniel, and Matthew. Maybe have some time alone with my son once he's more comfortable with us."

He watched the lights go through another rotation and then heard Marissa sigh. "That would be fine. Actually, Daniel and I were hoping to go out Saturday evening. With you sitting, Mom won't have to watch Matthew again. She's done enough of that for me recently."

"Thank you." He'd get to babysit his son. *Babysit.* He prayed it would soon be more than that. "I have to check flights yet, but we'll try to be out early afternoon."

"I'll prepare Matthew."

Prepare Matthew.

She made it sound like the child was going to receive bad news.

Richard stuffed down his frustration. He would do whatever he could to make sure his presence in his son's life would be a positive one, even if that meant getting along with Marissa. "I appreciate that." He hung up then walked out to the reception area just as Emma put down her phone. "Can you find a flight into La Guardia or JFK Saturday morning for me and Sheila? Return Sunday afternoon?"

She nodded and immediately took to the task.

Richard didn't even try to stop his grin. Come Saturday, he would get to hold his son.

# CHAPTER *thirty*

## September
## Staten Island, New York

A grin bubbled from Richard as he and Sheila walked up the sidewalk to Marissa's home. He was going to see Matthew! And later tonight, he and Sheila would get him all to themselves. He couldn't wait.

But he wasn't fooled by the fake smile Sheila offered to Marissa when Marissa answered the door. For most of the trip Sheila had been sullen and silent. Not that he blamed her.

"Please come in." Marissa's phony smile mimicked Sheila's as they stepped into the tiny foyer.

Hopefully Marissa didn't see beyond Sheila's mask. Marissa needed to see that Matthew would be placed in the hands of two loving parents. More importantly, he prayed that Sheila would fall in love with Matthew as quickly as he had.

Clutching a shoebox-sized gift in one hand, he gripped Sheila's hand and walked beside her into the living room toward a couch.

Marissa disappeared into the kitchen, and Daniel came out. The man was five foot nine at the most. He wore glasses with thick lenses, was balding, and had a slight build. Not exactly the GQ-type Marissa once hung around. But this man had a genuine smile and caring eyes behind those plastic rims. Clearly, Marissa chose this man out of love. It pleased Richard to know that Matthew would be raised by two loving parents on this end as well.

"May I offer you a drink?" Daniel walked to the couch wiping his hands on a frilly apron tied around his waist. The man obviously wasn't vain about appearances either. More proof of Marissa's change in attitude.

"Water." Richard looked at Sheila.

"The same."

As they waited for their drinks, Richard studied the room. When he'd been there a little more than a week ago, he hadn't noticed the signs of a child, but he'd only given the room a cursory glance, wanting to make a hasty exit.

Now that he looked deeper, the evidence was all over the place. Four portraits displaying Matthew's age progression sat on top of the built-in buffet. The first was his newborn photo, the second Richard guessed to be taken at six months, the third a year, and the last photo, the one Marissa had given him, was eighteen months. She'd written that on the back of his copy.

He needed duplicates of the others too. Before he and Sheila left today, he'd ask to go through Matthew's baby book and photo albums. Pictures couldn't make up for the time Richard had lost with Matthew, but he'd take what he could get.

A large wicker basket in the corner of the room held a toy collection. The buffet revealed scores of books. Dr. Seuss and the Berenstain Bears appeared to be the favorites.

Daniel returned with two glasses of ice water and Marissa placed a tray of crackers and cheese on the ottoman between the couch and the fireplace. "Thank you." Richard accepted the drink while listening for any hints of his son's presence. Marissa better not have gone back on her promise to allow him and Sheila an opportunity to spend time alone with his son.

"Matthew's still napping." Daniel sat in one of the wingback chairs flanking the fireplace and Marissa took the other.

Richard squeezed Sheila's hand. Now that they were here, his patience had grown thin as a nail's head. He wanted to see his son now.

"Have you considered what you plan to do?" Marissa looked from Richard to Sheila.

Richard shook his head. "That's what today's about. Before we make a decision, Sheila needs to know what she's getting herself into."

"I understand," Daniel said. A peacemaker. Just the type of man Marissa needed. "I know it's a lot to dump on you, especially considering your own loss." He leaned in slightly toward them. "Of which we are very sorry to hear."

"Thank you," Richard and Sheila said together.

"I can't imagine dealing with such a loss, so we understand if you want to take your time in making a decision. And regardless of which direction you choose, we want you to know that you will always be a welcome part of Matthew's life."

"I appreciate it." Richard squeezed Sheila's hand tighter. "What have you told him about me?"

"Not much, yet, just that you were coming today." Marissa toyed with her cross necklace. "We reminded him that you were the man who sat and played trains with him last Friday. He remembered that."

Matthew remembered him. Knowing that little tidbit made Richard happy.

Marissa pointed toward Richard's lap. "You brought him a gift?"

"A small token." Nothing expensive or fancy, but he believed Matthew would like it.

Marissa stiffened. "I don't want you thinking you can buy his affections with fancy gifts."

Ah, there was the attitude Richard remembered. He squeezed Sheila's hand again. Her poor fingers were going to be black and blue before the day's end. "I don't intend to." He'd learned through experience with his nieces and nephews that the best present he could give them was time. Sure, they liked expensive gifts, but they remembered the games he played with them, the books they read together, and the times he spent listening. That's why it was so important to get as much time with Matthew as possible. The last thing he wanted was to be that part-time dad who was remembered only as a lavish gift giver.

Marissa held up her hands. "Sorry. I shouldn't make assumptions." Her assumptions were logic-based, though. When they'd dated, money had been his answer to everything, not that Marissa hadn't encouraged the mindset. Clearly, they'd both changed over the last two and a half years.

Sheila looked at Daniel. "I'd love to hear how the two of you met."

And Richard was grateful for the change of topic.

"You tell it." Daniel nodded to Marissa.

Her gaze flitted to Richard. "I met Daniel after you and I broke up. Mom talked me into attending church with her, hoping it would make me feel better." She smiled at her fiancé. "Daniel served me communion."

"When she came up, I admit I wasn't exactly thinking about God's feast. She was so beautiful, but she had the saddest eyes. I knew I had to talk with her after the service."

"And he did. He found me sitting with Mom in the fellowship hall and joined right in. Daniel was the friend I'd been looking for, someone who would listen, someone who would help me through the pregnancy. I couldn't believe I opened up to him. No one else but Mom knew I was pregnant."

"Maybe I should have cared that she was pregnant, but I didn't. We started dating shortly after that."

"The sad thing was, all these church people assumed Matthew was Daniel's child. When I denied it, they would roll their eyes. I could tell they were disappointed in him, when the truth was, we'd never even been together."

"Didn't matter to me." Daniel waved his hand. "I told her don't fret about it. People would believe what they wanted to. We knew the truth. God knew the truth. Ultimately, that's what mattered."

"But it did matter to me." Marissa looked at Daniel. "That's why it took me so long to accept your faith. Those church people were so quick to judge, when they knew nothing of the truth."

Boy, there was a scene Richard knew all too well. Unfortunately, for many years people's assumptions about him had been correct. "People expect Christians to be perfect when we're far from it. Those same people are right there pointing fingers when we fall."

Daniel leaned forward. "You also have to realize that we tend to remember the negative comments more than the positive ones. I've found that the majority of the people in our church are supportive, and they know that Matthew's paternity is none of their business."

"Mommy?" Matthew's voice broke into their conversation.

Marissa grinned as she craned her neck to see over Richard's and Sheila's shoulders. "Hey, punkin, come here."

Richard squeezed Sheila's hand one more time, then let go. He turned sideways to see his son come around the couch.

Man, the boy was beautiful with his rustled hair and a thumb stuck in his mouth. Dragging an often-used crocheted blue blanket behind him, Matthew ran to his mother and held up his arms. She raised him up into the air, then brought him down just enough to press her lips to his bare tummy sticking out beneath his shirt. She blew a raspberry, and Matthew giggled the most beautiful giggle Richard had ever heard.

Marissa lowered the child onto her lap, and he snuggled against her chest, smiling with complete contentment.

Then he spotted Richard and Sheila. Sinking tight against Marissa, his lips stuck out and his brows narrowed, as his gaze flitted from Sheila to Richard, then back and forth.

"Remember, Mr. Brooks?" Marissa pointed at Richard. "He played trains with you last week."

With no hint of a smile Matthew stared hard at Richard.

"And this is Mr. Brooks' wife, Mrs. Brooks."

*Mrs. Brooks?* Was that what Marissa wanted Matthew to call Sheila? No way would that work. They'd have to discuss that later.

"Remember I told you they're going to babysit tonight? Mommy and Danny will be going out for a bit and Gamma's busy. Mr. and Mrs. Brooks are really good babysitters."

"The best, buddy," Daniel said.

"I even brought you a present." Richard got off the couch and sat on the floor, then held out the gift for Matthew. Hopefully this would help break the ice.

"Go ahead, punkin." Marissa pulled Matthew away from her body.

He looked up at her, then over at Danny before easing off of Marissa's lap.

Sheila joined Richard on the area rug, crossing her legs beneath her. She couldn't have given Richard a sweeter gift.

Blanket in hand, Matthew toddled toward them. He grabbed the present, ran back to Marissa, and held up his arms.

"Uh-uh, little man." Marissa pressed her hands to her lap. "You stay down there with your new friends."

"Mommy." His lower lip protruded and his chin shook.

"No whining allowed. I'm not picking you up."

Matthew tucked his body in presumed safety between Marissa's legs, and she rolled her eyes.

"It's okay," Richard mouthed. Forcing himself on the child would only scare his son further.

Matthew pulled off the bow and threw it on the rug.

Sheila leaned over, picked up the bow and placed it on her head.

Matthew smiled. Lopsided. Beautiful. Matthew tugged at the

wrapping with little success.

Again Sheila leaned over and held out a hand. "Can I help you get it started? Sometimes Mr. Brooks uses way too much tape."

"Much tape." Matthew shook his head and made an angry face at Richard.

"Sorry about that, buddy." Richard covered his grin by rubbing his chin. He jotted a mental note to himself to lighten up on the tape. At least for now.

With her fingernails, Sheila eased up a corner of the paper then handed the package back to Matthew.

"Tank you." Matthew accepted the box.

*Polite, too.* As much as it pained Richard to admit it, Marissa had done a great job of parenting. He never would have imagined that from her.

Matthew tore at the paper until a hundred jagged pieces surrounded him, revealing an Allen Edmonds shoebox.

Rats. He'd over taped that, too. What had he been thinking? "How about I help you this time?"

Matthew eagerly handed the gift over.

Richard slid his fingernail between the lid and the bottom, breaking the seal on all four sides, then handed back the box.

His eyes wide, Matthew yanked off the top, and then pulled out a wad of tissue paper. A blue and white striped railroad engineer's hat fell to the ground.

"Now you're an official train engineer." Richard handed the hat to Matthew while Sheila pulled a matching hat from her purse and gave it to Richard. "Just like me." Richard put the hat on.

"Tank you." Matthew pulled the cap down tight on his head and then stood to face Marissa. "See Mommy, I ejneer. Wike him." Matthew stretched his arm out in back of him, pointing at Richard.

"The best engineer ever." Marissa tapped the brim of his hat.

"Can pway twains?"

"Go ahead punkin."

"Matthew, can I play, too? Mrs. Brooks, too?" Richard held his breath as Matthew scrunched his mouth.

"Pway too." Matthew galloped toward his bedroom.

Grinning, Richard took Sheila's hand and followed his son.

For the next hour or so, the three pushed trains and built track and crashed engines. Richard was having so much fun, time rushed past him.

They'd been accepted.

Both he and Sheila, but best of all, Sheila seemed to be enjoying herself as much as he and Matthew. Just as Richard had hoped.

Richard crashed an engine into one of Matthew's and both engines tumbled off the track taking a slew of cars with them. Matthew fell backwards and giggled, showing off a round belly. It took all of Richard's strength to hold back from zerberting that precious tummy.

A knock sounded on the door and Richard looked over his shoulder at Marissa.

"Snack time."

Matthew and Richard moaned. The phrase, "Do I have to?" sailed through Richard's head. He didn't want this time to end, but he also didn't want to undermine Marissa's authority. "Come on, buddy." Richard got up and offered his hand. He'd yet to touch his son, wanting to ease himself into Matthew's life, although all Richard wanted to do was give his son a big squishy hug and never let go.

Tears burned his eyes as Matthew took his hand without hesitation. *Thank you, Jesus.* Matthew accepted Sheila's hand too. Richard exchanged a glance and a smile with Sheila as the three walked out to the dining room.

"I good ejneer." Matthew ran to his chair with the booster seat. Richard lifted him up, set the boy down, buckled him in, and then pushed the chair in. Not a peep or hint of fear.

Then he and Sheila sat on the opposite side of the table. He wanted to watch Matthew's every second, absorb every little detail of his boy. The entire Brooks family would demand a comprehensive description.

Marissa set a plate of peanut butter cookies on the table while Daniel poured milk into a sippy cup.

"Milk?" Daniel held up the carton, offering it to Richard and Sheila.

"I'd love some." There was nothing better than milk with cookies.

"I'll have water, if that's okay," Sheila said.

"Coming right up." Daniel poured Richard's milk then returned to the kitchen for water. Marissa put two cookies on the plate in front of Matthew. Richard grabbed four cookies. Sheila took the smallest one.

Richard raised a cookie to his mouth, then stopped. "Got any chocolate frosting?"

"Why?" Marissa tilted her head to the side.

"So I can show Matthew how to properly eat peanut butter cookies."

"He doesn't need to learn your bad habits, Richard." Sheila used a scolding tone, but he heard the smile in it.

"I agree," Marissa said with no allusion of a smile.

"Come on, make it a treat for when I visit."

"What'll it hurt?" Daniel handed Sheila a glass of ice water and then sat at the table. "I think I'd like to learn the proper way to eat peanut butter cookies, too."

"Me, too. Me, too." Matthew pounded his chubby fists on the table.

"There you go. Three against two. We win." Richard grinned, feeling like a kid again.

"Okay. Fine. Just this once." Marissa pushed away from the table and strode into the kitchen. Moments later she returned with a container of store-bought chocolate frosting and a knife.

"Perfect." Richard took the frosting from Marissa and chose a cookie from his plate. "Now watch, Matthew."

Matthew stared at the cookie in Richard's hand.

"Take a dab of chocolate and spread it on the cookie, thick as peanut butter, then put another cookie on top and you've got a cookie sandwich."

"Me too cookie sammich?" Matthew bounced in his chair and reached for the frosting.

Richard passed the frosting and knife to Daniel.

"Me do." Matthew reached again.

Daniel shrugged. "I guess you're a big boy now, aren't you?"

"Big boy." Matthew nodded several times quickly.

"Daniel." Marissa narrowed her eyes at her fiancé as she sat down.

But Daniel grinned as they all watched Matthew scoop a golf ball-sized splotch of frosting that immediately fell on the table.

"See?" Marissa jerked a finger toward the mess.

Matthew laid the knife down, picked up the frosting with his hand, and flattened the frosting on the cookie. He smashed the second cookie on top and pressed the cookies together as hard as his little hands could squeeze. Frosting oozed out the sides as Matthew brought the sandwich to his mouth, and a glob fell onto his shirt.

"Daniel, we forgot a bib!" Marissa shot up from the table and hurried into kitchen.

"Ah, it'll clean up." Richard covered his mouth with his hand trying to conceal his grin, but Marissa's eyes still threw darts his way as she pulled a bib over Matthew's head. Right now he didn't care what Marissa thought. Getting dirty was what having little boys was all about. Daniel probably appreciated having a male ally.

"You're giving him a bath tonight." Marissa made it sound like a punishment, but Richard knew how to make bath time fun, too. Of course, that probably meant he'd be wearing a boatload of suds and water and he'd be kneeling in a puddle, but as long as he cleaned up afterwards, who cared? One more thing to look forward to.

It didn't take long for Matthew's cookie sandwich to disappear, although frosting remnants clung to the boy's face, hair, clothes, and table. Richard volunteered to clean it up, since he'd been the instigator. He had Matthew stand on his chair, then Richard stripped his son down to his Onesie, making it easier to give him a washcloth bath.

Richard ignored Sheila's shaking head. She had to learn that massive cleanup usually followed play and snack time.

"He needs a diaper change." Marissa snatched her son up and carried him to his room. Moments later she called out, "Richard, come here." He knew that completely-miffed tone.

"Be right back." He squeezed Sheila's shoulder then jogged to Matthew's room. Matthew lay on his bed on top of a changing pad. He squirmed to get up but Marissa held him down with her hand on his tummy. Anger was written all over her red face. "You need to know how to change a diaper."

Richard crossed his arms "I already know."

"Still the same pompous know-it-all, get everything your way."

He held up his hands in surrender. "Hey, so the kid gets a bit dirty. I said I'd clean him. No big deal."

She turned around, grabbed a diaper, a box of wipes, and baby powder off the top of the dresser and flung them on the bed. "Let's see you change him."

Okay, maybe he'd been a bit too cocky. Yes, he'd changed diapers before, but not many, and he wasn't terribly efficient at it either. And with Marissa hawking at the end of the bed, it made him nervous, but he wasn't about to show it.

Thankfully, Matthew lay still for him, probably because Richard was still a stranger. For once the strangeness helped immensely. Richard bent down over his son. He stripped the tape away from the wet diaper, pulled the soaked mess off the boy's bottom, and then rolled it up into a ball, taping it shut. He pulled out a wipe, gently cleaned, and then lightly powdered. "Now, I don't want any fountains, you hear?" Smiling, Richard wagged a finger at Matthew.

Matthew grunted like he was trying to force the spray. The little stinker.

Richard grabbed a diaper and stuck it under Matthew's bottom. He lifted the sides to tape. No! It was on backwards. He prayed for no geysers as he grabbed the boy's legs, raised his bottom, and reversed the diaper. Heaving a sigh, Richard lay the boy back down, wrapped the diaper around, and then secured the tape. Even with the little slip-up, he'd changed the diaper in record time. Good thing it had only been a *number one* and not a *number two* change.

The tummy peeking out from beneath Matthew's unsnapped Onesie called to Richard, and he couldn't resist any longer. He tickled Matthew's belly and his son giggled that glorious giggle once again.

Saying nothing, Marissa slapped clean clothes down on the bed.

Minutes later, Richard had Matthew dressed and ready to play again. He picked up his son and lowered him headfirst to the floor. More giggles.

He patted Matthew's bottom. "Go play."

Matthew ran off and Richard plunked down on the bed. He was completely in love.

"You're good with him." Marissa's voice was softer than normal and it had lost its edge. Tears crept over her cheeks.

"Did I do something wrong?"

"No." She wiped her eyes. "That's the problem. I didn't believe you'd be good with kids. I hoped you'd be uncomfortable. You're not at all. I hoped you'd come here and see how shy Matthew is. He never warms up to people this fast. Never. I was hoping ... I hoped you'd decide ..." She turned away.

Richard slipped out the door and waved Daniel over. He understood what she was going through, but comfort should come from her fiancé.

He watched the couple embrace, then walked away, leaving them to their private moment. Why couldn't there be another solution to this mess? One where no one would get hurt?

Sheila sat on the couch watching Matthew rummage through his toy basket. Richard joined her and draped his arm over her shoulders. Neither said a word as their focus moored on Matthew. He prayed Sheila was falling in love too.

Moments later Marissa and Daniel rejoined them. Daniel sat in the chair by the fireplace while Marissa walked to the built-in shelves. She pulled out what looked like a fancy shoe box and then placed it on the ottoman before sitting down. Red eyes betrayed the fact that she'd been crying. Daniel mouthed 'thank you', although Richard wasn't certain what for.

"That's for you." Marissa pointed at the box.

Richard picked it up, took off the lid, and was silenced by its contents. Pictures of Matthew, from birth to now, all organized by date, and most with a description of the event on the back of the photo. And DVDs with all the pictures and videos. A living record of Matthew's life.

"Thank you." His voice choked. He didn't even try to stop the tears. "It's amazing. I don't know what to say."

"I always get duplicates." Marissa's voice was as shaky as his.

"Thank you," he said again, flustered by the gift. He couldn't wait to get it home, study the pictures, and catch up on everything he'd missed.

"Matthew." Marissa voice still shook. "Can you come here for a second?"

Holding on to a truck he'd found in the basket, he hopped to his mother. She lifted him onto her lap, gave him a hug and whispered "I love you." She then turned him around, setting him sideways on her lap so he could see everyone in the room, and held him in a protective hug.

"Remember"—Marissa looked in Matthew's eyes—"how I've told you about your daddy who lives far, far away?"

Matthew bit his lip and nodded.

She'd told Matthew about him?

"Mr. Brooks is that man." Her teary-eyed gaze flitted toward the ceiling.

Matthew looked at Richard, his brows furrowed.

"Do you understand?" Marissa stroked her son's cheek.

Matthew shook his head.

She pointed at Richard. "Mr. Brooks is your daddy."

Whoa. He didn't expect Matthew to find out this soon. Marissa hadn't discussed it, but he was all for the honest revelation.

Matthew's head rotated from side to side with his gaze winging from Richard to Daniel. Then he squinted at Marissa, holding up his hand, spreading his fingers wide apart, as if trying to show only two fingers. "Two Danny's?"

The air seemed to flee the room. *Two Danny's.*

"No, punkin. I said Dad-dy, not Dan-ny. Do you understand the difference?"

Matthew's brows furrowed and his lips puckered. How does one explain to a toddler what a biological father is? Was that even necessary? Marissa looked to Daniel for help, then over at Richard.

The truth was beyond the child's comprehension and, therefore, pointless to explain right now. The meaning behind the word would have to be earned not taught, like Daniel had earned it. For now, another less confusing solution would have to suffice. Richard smiled at Matthew. "Papa. You can call me Papa." It didn't have the ring of Daddy, but this wasn't about Richard's feelings.

"Pa-pa." Matthew mimicked the word, apparently satisfied

with the explanation.

Eyebrows raised, Richard glanced at Marissa.

She nodded and Daniel showed him a brief and discreet thumbs-up.

Sheila took Richard's hand and squeezed it. "And you can call me Sheila." So there would be no discussion with Marissa about that.

"Thseela."

It sounded beautiful.

"So, what do you say, buddy"—Richard extended his arm in Matthew's direction—"about going outside to run off some of those cookies we ate?" Then Marissa and Daniel could sneak off without Matthew seeing.

Matthew slid off Marissa's lap and eagerly accepted Richard's hand. The pudgy little fingers wrapped in his felt like heaven. Matthew stopped, looked back at Sheila, and held out his other hand. "Thseela too?"

Nothing could have sounded sweeter.

AFTER A COUPLE HOURS of fresh air, a macaroni and cheese supper with a banana snack, a bath that probably cleaned all three of them, and enough animated readings of *Bears on Wheels* to ingrain the words forever in Richard's mind, it was time for bed.

Time for goodbye. And that completely fractured Richard's heart.

How could someone capture your heart so completely in one day? Richard prayed Sheila felt the same way. He didn't know how he'd survive if he didn't play a major role in his son's life.

Matthew took both Sheila's and Richard's hands as the little boy knelt by his bed. "Pray," Matthew said as if it was the most natural thing in the world. They kneeled next to him as Matthew talked to God. "God bless Mommy Danny Gamma. Not Joey, Joey naughty."

Richard stifled a chuckle and squeezed Matthew's hand.

"God bless Papa, Thseela. Amen."

Richard pinched his eyes shut and tried to swallow. He caressed his son's velvety soft hand, a hand he never wanted to release. He coughed and cleared his throat. "And God bless Matthew." With a lump in his throat the size of a softball, Richard pulled back the covers on Matthew's bed.

Matthew hopped onto the bed and bounced a couple of times on his bottom.

"Could I get a hug?" He'd held Matthew's hand, and tickled his tummy. He'd played "this little piggy" with his son's toes and beeped his nose, but he hadn't asked for the hug yet. At first, Richard wanted the boy to become comfortable with him, but now Richard feared he'd never be able to let the child go. Yet he longed to hold this child in his arms and would regret it if he didn't.

With a wide smile, Matthew held his arms open.

Richard drew the boy in and tried to memorize every sensation: the fresh scent of baby bath and shampoo, a sweet "mmming" sound as Matthew wrapped his arms tight, and the warmth and love shared through pudgy arms nearly strangling Richard's neck. It was the most magnificent feeling ever.

But it had to end.

"Sheila too?" She stuck out her arms and Matthew leaped into them. She burrowed her face into the child's hair and hummed "Jesus Loves Me."

Matthew finally released his arms and Sheila laid him down into bed. Both she and Richard pulled the covers up to Matthew's chin and then pecked Matthew's cheek.

"Goodnight, Matthew." Richard flicked off the light.

"Night-night Papa, Thseela."

Choking Sheila's hand, they walked out of Matthew's room and sat side by side on the couch, with her head resting on his chest. Cars passing on the busy street provided much needed background music to their silence.

Had today made their decision easier or more difficult?

Marissa was a good mother, far better than what Richard had imagined, and Daniel rounded out the family perfectly. A perfect little family.

The truth was that if Richard had been in the picture from the beginning, he had no doubt that Matthew wouldn't be as well-adjusted. His son would have grown up in a home filled with arguments and accusations. Matthew probably would have grown up hating his father.

Marissa's secret was a blessing.

Somehow God had used the brokenness of the situation and had created something beautiful. Who was Richard to disrupt the boy's life?

But wouldn't it be worse to abandon him? Again? This time on purpose?

All the answers running through his mind tasted bitter.

There was only one thing he knew for certain.

Sheila curved a hand over his cheek. "You're crying."

He puffed out a sigh.

"You're in love, aren't you?"

He nodded and the ball in his throat expanded. "Completely."

"You know what?" She stroked his moist cheek.

"What?"

"So am I."

And now he was in heaven.

CHAPTER *thirty-one*

*October*

Over a month had passed—an excruciating month for Richard—since they'd seen Matthew. Richard prayed that tonight's surprise would be a game-changer for Sheila, that it would help direct their choices.

With popcorn ping ponging in his Stir Crazy, Richard put a bowl with a stick of butter in the microwave and set the cook time for thirty-nine seconds. Real butter. No oily margarine or other butter substitute that claimed to be the real thing, but couldn't come close to the taste. Growing up on a farm had spoiled Richard, or perhaps it had taught him never to settle for substandard when the best was available.

He laughed to himself. Life lessons from butter. That meant he'd actually spent a few moments forgetting about the choices he and Sheila needed to make. Should Sheila give her father another chance? If she did, would he reject her for a third time? She doubted she could handle another rejection.

Beyond the kitchen island, and out the patio window, October's air was painting the leaves brilliant colors as the trees prepared for hibernation. But that didn't mean they were dead. New life would spring next year.

If only he could convince Sheila of that.

Maybe the surprise delivery Richard had for her would

change her mind. The small package had arrived in his office mail yesterday. He'd considered opening it before giving it to Sheila, but she wouldn't want that. Whatever it was, they'd handle it together.

As far as her mother was concerned, he saw little hope. Sheila had offered to build a bridge, but her mother had soundly vetoed the idea. Perhaps it was good to have one less thing to worry about.

The buzzer rang on the microwave and Richard pulled out the liquid butter.

Then there was Sheila's assertion that she would not get pregnant again. As of yet, she hadn't changed her mind. He'd continually asked her to give it time, stressing that now was too soon to make a permanent decision. But he wasn't young anymore, either. As it was, he'd be close to sixty before their child would enter college. Yes, that was young enough to be an active influence, but waiting too much longer would be pushing the limits of what he felt was best for a child. In the end, wasn't that the ultimate issue anyway?

The popper grew quiet. Richard pulled the plug and flipped the Stir Crazy upside down and white kernels filled the popper's plastic bowl.

What was best for Matthew? Would Richard's involvement turn Matthew's life upside down? How would the constant shift between homes affect the child whom Richard knew to be well-adjusted? If Richard agreed to joint physical custody, would Matthew have a true home anymore? Was love all that was required to make a home? Matthew would have love on both ends.

Richard removed the popper's bottom and poured the full bowl into an even bigger bowl. He and Marissa needed to talk over what joint physical custody actually meant. Six months here, six months there? That sounded downright cruel. Every other weekend and holidays? A month or two of summer vacation? That was more palatable, and probably quite common, but even that meant a lack of continuity in the boy's life.

It hadn't even been five weeks since he'd last seen Matthew, and already his heart ached from needing to hold him again. How could he possibly go months on end?

Regardless of their decision, they would be heaping problems into young Matthew's life. At his impressionable age, stability was so important.

Richard poured a third of the butter on the popped corn then generously salted it. Could Richard settle for flying to New York a few times a year to be the kind of father who had to resort to offering extravagant gifts to placate the child, to apologize for not being there for the games, concerts, academic awards? Without moving to New York, being there for the important events was a logistical impossibility, but if they did move, he'd be letting his clients down and leaving his family behind.

The only absolute was that he and Sheila loved Matthew. They both wanted the best for him and couldn't wait to see him again.

Richard was being offered a stick of butter. If he accepted it, would that mean tasteless margarine was all Matthew had left? Yikes. Corny analogies meant he'd been doing far too much thinking, and his brain was turning to mush.

This past week had been filled with discussions, arguments, quiet treatments, and earnest prayer, with no answers. How does one weigh the emotional argument against the logical? Shouldn't both have a say in the final analysis?

He poured a cup of unpopped kernels onto the Stir Crazy's nonstick bottom. It was time to turn his brain off. That's why he and Sheila had planned this evening in the first place. A night spent with friends watching movies that didn't involve a lot of thinking. The kind of movie where it was obvious who the good guys and the bad guys were, where a clear line was drawn between right and wrong. The kind of story built on absolutes with obvious, yet fulfilling, endings. All while eating butter-saturated popcorn.

Maybe, for the first time this week, he and Sheila would be able to set aside their worries and differences and have fun. Tomorrow their heads would be clear and ready to focus.

The kernels began pinging off the plastic top, and the doorbell rang. With Sheila up in their bedroom yet, Richard hurried to the door, opened it, and did a double take. "Come on in, Doran, Meghan. Wow, this is quite the surprise."

They stepped into the condo, their arms full with liters of Mountain Dew. Richard took the pop bottles from Meghan. "Doran said he was picking up a friend at the airport. I had no clue it was you."

Richard heard a squeal behind him.

"Meghan!" Sheila rushed over and wrapped the girl in a hug. "What a beautiful surprise." Sheila took Meghan's hand. "Why don't you and I catch up and let the men do the cooking?"

"Guess that's our hint to leave them alone." Richard nodded toward the kitchen.

Doran followed him in, and they squeezed the pop into the refrigerator.

The popper slowed down and Richard stayed next to it waiting for the precise moment to remove the plug. "Want to talk about her?"

His cheeks blooming with redness, Doran looked down at the ceramic tile. "Uh, we've been talking since I got her e-mail and decided if we could find a cheap airfare, she'd fly in this weekend. She tried one of those online bidding deals and it worked. Bad thing was, she left home at six this morning and had two transfers. It's the same type of deal when she goes back on Monday."

Richard pulled the plug on the popper and flipped the appliance over. "So things are going well between you?"

Doran planted his hands in his back pockets. "We don't know.

That's why she wanted to fly in, to talk in person, ya know, about things we'd avoided before."

"I hope it all works out between the two of you. I like Meghan."

"Yeah. Me too."

"Do you want to go join the women or help me pop popcorn?"

"In there, alone with two women? No way."

"I thought you'd say that." Richard poured oil and a cup of popcorn into the Stir Crazy then covered it up. As the popcorn started jumping, the doorbell rang again. Probably Nate, Lauren, and Jon. Soon they'd all be able to sit and relax and forget their worries, if only for the night.

"I've got it." Sheila hurried to the door.

Richard expected squeals of "I've missed you" but all he heard was the raucous pinging of popcorn. No voices. A chill ran up his spine. Was something wrong?

"Richard, come here." Was that alarm in Sheila's voice or surprise?

He peeked out of the kitchen. Nate stood behind Lauren and Jon.

And each held a laundry basket filled with wrapped gifts. What was that about?

"Please, come in," Sheila finally said with bewilderment written in her tented brows. His face probably mirrored hers.

He gave each of the kids the narrowed-eye look as he took the basket away from Lauren. "Bring it on in." He set his basket in the middle of the living room floor. Nate and Jon followed suit.

Richard stood next to the gifts and crossed his arms. "Okay, what gives?" He studied each guilty face, looking for an answer. All he saw was mischief.

"Uh, Richard," Doran yelled from the kitchen. "How do you turn this thing off?"

*Rats!* He'd completely forgotten about the popcorn. "Unplug it," he yelled and rushed back into the kitchen. By the time he got there, Doran had it stopped and flipped over to prevent further burning. Thankfully, it hadn't burned enough to set off the fire alarm. They should be able to pick out most of the scorched kernels.

He dumped the popcorn into the nearly full bowl and poured the remaining butter over it.

"You got a surprise out there?" Doran handed Richard the salt. The smirk on the young man's face told Richard, Doran was in on the surprise.

"Something tells me you knew about it." Richard scooped popcorn into extra-large cereal bowls.

Doran shrugged. "Could be."

"Just as I thought. Come on." Richard nodded to the living room. "We'll get popcorn after you all fess up."

Grinning, Doran led Richard to the living room. The kids had made themselves comfortable on the floor. They were all young yet. They could have the floor.

"Tragedy averted." Richard joined Sheila on the couch. "The popper is safe."

A mild cheer went up from the kids—young adults—whatever they were. His popcorn was always one of the highlights of a movie evening.

"You all introduced yourself to Meghan?" Richard circled his arm around Sheila's shoulders.

"Yep." Nate leaned back, propping himself up with his arms.

"And you remember Doran? He's interning for me while he finishes his graduate work at the U."

The group nodded as Doran said, "We all met a few weeks ago."

That's right. At Samuel's memorial.

What a blessing to have all these young people supporting him and Sheila. Young people who were now involved in some sort of mischief. He wasn't going to move until he got some answers. "You guys have some explaining to do."

"I think we should wait till after the movie." Nate held up the remote control.

Richard grabbed it from him. "No can do."

Lauren took Jon's hand. "Here's the deal. Everyone still feels awful about Samuel."

Richard and Sheila exchanged a glance. "Thank you," she said. Any additional sentiment would be inadequate.

"And, so when Grandma told people about it, they wanted to do something." Nate took a small gift out of a basket and juggled it. "You see, everyone loved Aunt Sheila's idea about donating stuff to the pregnancy center, and people thought they should still do that, in honor of Samuel."

Richard stared at the baskets of gifts.

And Sheila gripped his arm. "You mean ...?"

"Yep." Jon pulled out a shirt-sized package. "People have been dropping stuff off at your folks all week." He looked at Richard. "Then, after school today, we went around and collected from anyone else who said they wanted to give."

"Wow," Richard said through a quiet breath.

Sheila looked upward and sighed. "Should we bring it all to Vivant, have them open the gifts?"

Nate's mouth curved into the lopsided smile. "Nope. You guys get to unwrap. Besides, there's something for you too, Sheila, but it's not marked."

"But you know which one it is, I presume." Sheila lasered a stare at her nephew.

"Maybe I do. Maybe I don't."

Sheila crossed her arms, but happiness shone from her eyes. "Where did you learn such impertinence?"

"From Uncle Ricky." Nathan grinned.

And Richard laughed. "Hey, how come I'm suddenly getting blamed?" Then he glanced at Sheila who was dabbing at her eyes with a tissue. "You up for it?"

She nodded. "This has got to be the most generous and

unselfish thing I've seen people do." Her voice wobbled. "I don't know what else to say."

"Then don't say anything. Just open." Lauren stood up. "Where can I find some paper to write things down?"

Richard motioned toward the dining room table. "Next to the phone."

Meghan handed a gift to Sheila. "How about you start?"

SHEILA ACCEPTED THE PRESENT from Meghan and stared at it. How could people she barely knew care so much, be so generous? She wiped the last of her tears away, then read the tag on the gift. From Grandma Marlene. Normally, Sheila would take her time unwrapping the gifts, and save the paper for reuse, but there were too many, and that would take them till midnight.

She ripped into the paper and let its torn pieces flutter to the ground.

Nate jogged to the kitchen and returned with a paper bag to collect the scraps.

Once he sat back down, Sheila raised the box lid. A baby blanket crocheted with a myriad of bright colors. She'd seen Marlene working on it so it wasn't a surprise, but she teared up anyway. To think that her mother-in-law would go through this much work to give away.

Nathan handed her another gift, the size of a small shirt box. The card read from Elaine Lawhead. She looked at Richard. "Who?"

"One of mom and dad's neighbors."

A stranger had given this gift. Someone Sheila didn't even know. She ripped the paper and opened the box. Two infant outfits, appropriate for boy or girl, in the gender-neutral colors of green and yellow.

Other gift boxes and bags contained baby bottles, boxes of diapers, sleepers, baby toiletries, towels, toys, thermometers, gift cards. If a baby needed it, someone gave it.

Doran handed Sheila a card. "This is from me and Meghan."

Inside the card was a personal letter from Doran. "Should I read this aloud?"

Doran shrugged. "I guess. Won't bother me."

"Want me to read it?" Richard thumbed a tear off Sheila's cheek.

"I can do it." She sniffled. "'Dear Richard and Sheila, I know I'm not a particularly religious person. I guess, before I met Meghan, I'd given no real thought to the existence of God. Now it's something I think about all the time. I'm seeing, through your unselfish gift of time to help out a messed up kid, that maybe it's time I give serious thought to there being some higher power. I even found something in the Bible—Meghan pointed it out to me—that's helping me get through this adoption thing. Meghan told me about Jesus, that God, who is the perfect father, allowed his perfect son to be raised by an imperfect father. Wow! Even God gave up his son for adoption! I suppose if it's good enough for God, that it should be good enough for me. And the fact that you wanted all your baby shower gifts to go to help people like Meghan make it through their unplanned pregnancy is a way cool idea. We're glad we can give something back. Anyway, thanks again for everything—especially your parental love and advice. I love you guys! Doran.'"

With more tears threatening, Sheila glanced at Richard.

He rested his forehead on his fists. Obviously he was failing to hold back his emotions too. They'd never be able to properly thank people. A mere "thank you" seemed insufficient. Perhaps if she got pregnant again, then they'd ...

If she got pregnant again.

The thought didn't terrify her.

Could Richard be right? Perhaps time was needed to make the best decision. Her initial declaration of not wanting to try again *had* been made in haste and decided with emotion not logic. Or prayer.

They would talk later tonight. Then she would tell Richard that she was reconsidering. She couldn't wait to see his reaction to her news. But in the meantime one final package lay on the floor, too big for the baskets. With shaking fingers, she opened the card. *To Sheila from Richard (and Mom)*.

Sheila leaned away from Richard and glared at him. He grinned. That big conniver. "You knew about this!"

He rested his hand on the unopened package. "This? Yes." He gestured to the gifts spread out on the floor. "Those were a surprise."

She wouldn't be ripping this package open. This one required a deliberate touch. And her husband deserved to be antagonized for keeping this a secret. She loosened the tape with her fingernails, carefully removing the paper without a single rip, then folded it up and removed the box's lid.

"How ...?" Tears stung her eyes again. She reached into the box and pulled out her high school yearbook. From her senior year.

"I'm resourceful."

"And amazing." Her husband deserved a very special kiss, but that would wait. She paged through the book, smiling at the positive memories, grimacing at the dated haircuts. So, this didn't have the autographs she'd collected so many years ago. It was still a memory she'd lost, that she never thought she'd see again, a link to her past she thought she'd never retrieve.

She set the yearbook aside and found her sophomore and junior yearbooks. Once she and Richard were alone, she would share the pieces of the past that had created who she was today: basketball, debate, band, and all the other activities she drowned herself in to avoid going home.

"There's a lot more." Richard took the yearbooks from her and set them on top of the senior book.

Sheila took another book from the box, book one from her tomboy literary hero: *Trixie Belden and the Secret of the*

*Mansion.* Was everything going to make her cry tonight? Sniffling, she covered her mouth. This wasn't even one of the new copies that had been released recently. It was the hardcover version released in the early seventies.

"Trixie Belden?" Meghan sat up straight and craned her neck toward the cover.

"Better than Nancy Drew." Sheila handed Meghan the book.

Richard patted the book. "The rest of the series is in a box in the garage."

"All of them?" She closed her eyes. The lump in her throat prevented her from saying thank you. What had she done to deserve this beautiful man?

"There's one thing left." Richard bent over and pulled out the final item, a fat scrapbook, and handed it to Sheila.

She accepted it as if it were a fragile piece of crystal and ran her hand over its hunter green and gold cover, the official colors of her high school. She dreaded opening it, afraid she'd need a bucket for her tears. Already, she'd made a fool of herself in front of these kids.

"Come on, sweetheart." Richard squeezed her shoulder. "Open it."

Their guests sat silent. She opened the book and her baby picture stared back at her: a black and white five-by-seven with a short description beneath it giving her name, the names of her parents, the date she was born and where, and the ever-important weight and length. She turned her head toward Richard. "How? Where?"

"Newspaper. Birth announcement." He grinned.

"My parents announced my birth?" she asked out loud, yet the question was to herself.

Richard shrugged. "Keep going."

She flipped the page. Unlike the scrapbook she'd created for Samuel, this one made full use of colorful background papers cut with shaped scissors, yet was very tastefully done. All her school pictures covered one page, most in tiny one by one-and-a-half inch size, the earliest photos in black and white. Copies of report cards were attached to other pages.

"You'd be surprised what the schools hold on to." Richard fingered her senior year report card. "An A-? I'll have you know I got straight As my senior year."

"Basket weaving wasn't an option for me."

Everyone chuckled.

Sheila kept turning the pages. Pictures from grade school play dates, the earliest were square and trimmed with white edging. And then letters, recently written to her from the old friends. Friendships that had lasted through graduation. Friendships she'd disposed of after her parents disposed of her.

Friendships people were willing to restore ... like her father.

She didn't read through all the letters. That would come later when she was alone, when she could let her emotions flow, but the ones she glanced through, said that they were sorry she'd lost all her school memories and that they were more than happy to share what they had saved thanks to the advent of scanners and photo-perfect printers.

How had Richard known who to contact? "How ...?"

"It wasn't that hard," he said as if reading her mind. "I got your yearbooks first and went through them to see what you were involved in. You're in a lot of pictures so it was easy to figure out who you hung around with. Once I found those friends, they helped me find others. Most were excited to help out. I've got phone numbers and addresses so you can contact them."

Blinking back tears, she closed the scrapbook and clutched it to her chest. What had she ever done to deserve such love? Her husband would get a personal thank you later on, but a gentle kiss expressed her appreciation for now. She'd call her mother-in-law tomorrow, or better yet, go visit, thank her personally. That was the least she could do. But right now she had a room full of young people to thank.

One by one they received a hug and a kiss on the cheek, usually blended in with tears.

This wasn't what she and Richard had planned for tonight, but clearly, God knew what they needed and he'd bestowed the gifts in abundance. This was their family. Before they could start the movies, she needed to offer thanks to the one who brought healing. They stood in a circle and prayed.

"AND THANK YOU ALL, again." Sheila stood alongside Richard beneath the condo's outdoor canopy and waved at their departing guests. "We'll bring everything to Vivant tomorrow." Vivant Family Services would be thrilled to receive the baby products.

They remained on the top step until the kids disappeared down West River Parkway.

Then Sheila checked the time on her phone. After midnight? Where had the evening gone? And sleep would be a long time coming. Too many things swirled through her head. Decisions that had appeared murky a few hours earlier, now shone with bright clarity, and she couldn't wait to share them with Richard.

"Now, we can talk." She squeezed his hand and led him into their home. After Richard locked the door, she pulled him tight against her. "But first, I need to say thank you." She stood on her tippy toes and brushed her lips across his. She leaned back, but he drew her close again and pressed his lips to hers, sharing love the flavor of buttered popcorn. Visions of fireworks flamed in her head. Breathless, she pushed out of his arms and backed away.

He remained still as stone, his jaw slack and hands and shoulders raised. "What ...?"

"Not now." She put a finger to Richard's lips and he shook it off.

"Then when?

She took his hand and tugged but he didn't move. "We have a

scrapbook to go through, remember?"

"How about you go through the book and I'll clean up?"

"Perfect." She leaned in for another kiss and he backed away.

"Uh-uh. I'm still recovering from that last kiss."

She pecked his cheek anyway then stretched out on the couch with the scrapbook open on her lap. Soon she was engrossed in reading letters from friends she'd abandoned, yet they hadn't forgotten her.

As she read the final paragraph of one of the letters, she felt her legs lift.

Richard slid beneath her legs then rested them on his lap. "Keep reading." He began to massage her feet. A sigh escaped her throat as she closed her eyes and leaned back into the couch's cushions. It was amazing how a singular touch could sooth her entire body.

But now wasn't the time to relax. She sat back up and closed the scrapbook. "I'll have time for reading later. I'd like to talk now."

"Nope, not yet." He bent down, reached beneath the couch, and pulled out a book-sized postal box. "Do you think you can handle more?"

"More?" The box was addressed to S.P. and was sent to Richard's work. The return address? Stephen Peterson. Now what had Richard done?

"I called him a little while back." Richard ran his hand over the box. "After he called you this last time. I wanted to explain to him …" Richard gazed at her with worried eyes, clearly fearful that she'd be angry with him. Before tonight, she would have been.

"It's okay." And it was. Tonight's events had made that clear.

"You sure?"

She kissed him, providing the answer. Now to see what the two men had conspired on.

Richard offered his pocketknife to open the package. "Wait

one second. I have one more important little detail."

"More?" Hadn't she just asked that?

He picked up the remote on the end table, clicked it and their Bose system lit up.

She sighed, relieved. Background music she could handle. She breathed in deeply and her shoulders tightened as she broke the box's seal. A gentle piano melody surrounded the room and tears filled her eyes for the umpteenth time this evening. She closed her eyes and felt Richard's fingers beneath her chin lifting it up. He kissed her moist cheeks.

"'Open Arms'," she whispered.

"'Open Arms'," he repeated quietly.

"How did you ...?" Know that it had been her favorite song in high school. That the words of the chorus had backlit her fantasies of having a loving family, one that would welcome her with open arms.

As Richard and his family had done.

"You've got some very helpful friends."

"Talkative, too." She couldn't wait to contact them all.

"Go ahead." He pointed toward the opened box as the chorus keyed up around them.

She fingered her cheeks dry and then raised the flaps on the box. A spiral-bound notebook lay nestled among tissue paper. A picture of a steam engine barreling through fields of golden wheat graced the notebook's cover. She picked up the book and ran her fingers over the ink doodlings on its worn cover. The paper edges of the notebook were yellowed, slightly ripped, and dog-eared. She opened the cover and a loose page fell out.

A new, crisp page.

A letter addressed to her. She read, keeping her father's words to herself.

*Dear Sheila,*
*I am very sorry to hear about the loss of your son. It was*

*plain to see, when you and Richard visited, how much you both looked forward to his birth. I cannot fathom the hurt you must feel. I, too, weep for him. Believe it or not, I anticipated becoming a grandfather.*

*I realize, though, that was not the impression I gave when you visited. Unfortunately, I am not a strong man and have never been able to stand up for what's right when it comes to your mother. In spite of her failings, and mine, I still love her very much, and I feel I need to honor her wishes—in most circumstances.*

*There's a slim thread known as "the present" that separates what has been from what is to become. It's that same thread that weaves together the fabrics of our past and our future and brings color and beauty to our lives. I cannot change what has been, but in this moment I can change what is to become. It is my hope that the fabric of my life will become richer. Without you, I'm afraid my personal tapestry is quite dull.*

*Your husband is such a kind man, a strong man, and he loves you very much. He told me what you found in the storage boxes we gave you. He called to inquire if we had any other mementos to pass on. Unfortunately, Lois felt the need to purge those memories long ago. Again, in my weakness, I did not argue.*

*All I have remaining is the book you now hold in your hands. It is a journal I have kept for a number of years, one that exposes those feelings I had learned to hide. I hope you are able to see a part of me I was forbidden to show you, the part that was never able to tell you, I love you.*

*Sincerely,*
*Your Father*


Journey's "Open Arms" repeated in the background as Sheila reread the letter. The fear of reading her father's intimate thoughts cautioned her against opening the journal. Long ago she had learned to accept his indifference. How could these pages reveal anything but what he had shown her years before?

Richard's arm snaked around her shoulders, pulling her close, waiting silently. Perhaps she too had learned to react with indifference. That was about to change. She opened the cover, revealing the first page.

Her father's penmanship was shaky and angular, even back then. The first page was dated with her birth date.

*Today I became a father. It wasn't supposed to happen, but it did. I believe Lois when she says it was a terrible, one time mistake that will never happen again. I have forgiven her because I love her. I doubt she will ever forgive herself.*

*That belief became abundantly clear when Sheila was born this morning. She is a beautiful baby. A miracle, to be precise. Upon seeing her, I realized it did not matter that I was not her true father. Unfortunately, Lois has not had the same response. Perhaps that is normal for a woman who has undergone hours of labor. I do not know. I do know that I will give her time. She will love this child, and then I will be able to love Sheila too.*

Sheila wiped away a tear. *Mother never did love me.*

She flipped through the remaining pages of the journal. Another day she would read through the entire volume. But for now she read snippets about how proud he felt watching her play basketball, how he loved to hear her make music, how, when he expressed any of those feelings, he was immediately subdued by her mother's disparagement. He'd even told Lois, once, that her scorn only served to remind him of her affair, that if she learned to love Sheila, all would be forgotten. It was as if she existed to punish herself. Time had taught him to remain silent as he privately recorded the emotions Lois wouldn't allow him to display. Thus, he believed, it was for Sheila's benefit that they left her behind.

Mere glimpses of the heart of the man she called Father.

When he saw her in Arizona years later, he realized he had been wrong, that he had missed out on so much. Although he was elderly now, or perhaps because he was elderly, he had decided he didn't want to miss out on anymore. If Sheila would allow him.

Her father was approaching her with open arms.

Did she want to run to him?

"What do I do, Richard?" She didn't expect an answer and he didn't offer one. It was her decision.

She thumbed through the book again then laid it down. Tomorrow she'd read it with fresh eyes. She grasped Richard's hand. "Let's go for a walk."

"Now?"

"Now." She nodded. It was time for their talk.


RICHARD UNDERSTOOD HER NEED to escape. He too could think much better outside, walking, taking in the fresh air. They both had a lot on their minds, so much to mull over. He believed those choices would become clear tonight.

He helped Sheila with her spring jacket and smiled to himself as she stuffed her pockets with mace and sets of keys. "Sure you can protect me?" A little ribbing never hurt to loosen her tension.

"You know I can." She was serious. To be honest, she was probably right.

They looped their arms together as they descended the concrete stairs to the city sidewalk. They walked, exchanging few words for nearly an hour, eventually finding themselves back by their condo, but instead of going inside they settled on a bench overlooking the Mississippi. He draped his arm around her and tucked her head against his shoulder. She'd wanted to talk, but so far remained silent. He wouldn't press her.

Besides, the quiet walk had given him plenty of time to review the evening, to think over what he needed to do, cataloging the

pros and cons of accepting joint physical custody of Matthew.

How could he so quickly have fallen in love with the child? And Sheila too? The ache to see Matthew, to hold him, to hear that contagious giggle, was ever-present. When Richard considered everything, there was only one right thing to do. He prayed Sheila would see things the same way.

"Hon?" He squeezed her shoulder.

"Mmm, hmmm."

"I've made a decision." He waited a second for a response, but she sat still. "When I sat there tonight with those young people, I knew for certain we'd be good parents. This summer I've seen a shift in each of their personalities, their maturity level, and I think we played a hand in that. For God to use us in such a way is ..."

He shook his head, unable to think of a grand enough word to describe his feelings. "I always knew I could handle the infant years, but the teen years terrified me. I know how badly I messed up at that age, and I was afraid that would encourage our kids to do the same thing. I'm finding that God even uses my rebellion for His purposes."

He continued to divulge his thoughts and feelings, at times wiping away a drifting tear. In the end, they shared tears and agreement. Now all they had to do was deliver the legal contract back to Marissa.

Sheila nuzzled her cheek next to his. "I've made some decisions, too."

"Oh?"

"Tonight my father gave me what I think I've been looking for: acceptance, affirmation. Love."

"Open arms?"

"Open arms." She nodded. "How can I turn my back now? The Bible tells us to honor our father and mother. I intend to do that. If Mother won't accept it, then, that's her choice. Maybe what she needs is a little grace. I'll be praying for her."

"Me too," he answered quietly, at ease with her choice. In the long run, Sheila would be happier because of it.

"And there's something else."

He waited, wondering, hoping ... praying.

"You were right to tell me to give it time. When I first told you I didn't want to try to have a baby again, I was prepared to make the appointment right away. That would have been a monumental mistake, and I realize that now. My emotions were too all over the place to make a wise decision."

Hope clogged his throat. He turned to face her then took her hands, entwining his fingers with hers. "Does that mean ...?"

She nodded. "I'm thinking maybe around Halloween we can start trying again."

As much as he wanted to shout praises, there was another concern to be addressed first. "What about your incompetent cervix?"

"When we get pregnant again, I'll have a medical procedure that can prevent miscarriage."

"You're certain you want to try again?"

"After tonight, I've never been more certain."

*Praise God.* His lips tipped upward as he leaned in toward her. He wove his fingers through the back of her hair and drew her to him, letting his silent lips communicate his love. His heart pumped faster, joining in the expression. He pulled away for a moment to ask the critical question. His voice came out breathy with hopeful anticipation. "Does that mean we start practicing, again?"

"I see the doctor on Monday. Maybe then." She took his hand and stood. He remained sitting and stared at her, his mouth open in silence. Her cocky smile showed too much pleasure with his predicament.

"Monday?" He frowned, upset with the idea of taking a cold shower this late at night.

"Monday." A smile rang in her voice as she led him back to the condo.

He moaned. Monday seemed like a long way off.

# CHAPTER *thirty-two*

*Two weeks later*

L et's wait here." Richard pointed to a row of empty seats by LaGuardia Airport's baggage carousel. A two-hour layover was just enough time to take care of this necessary business before flying on to their next destination. The task there would be a difficult one as well.

Sheila rummaged through her carryon bag again after they sat. Probably the tenth time she'd checked it. She claimed she was making sure the samples of carpet, paint, wallpaper, and other décor were still there.

Obviously a nervous response to today. Although their guest ... Their guest? Was that what someone calls a family member? Perhaps when it wasn't the permanent home, "guest" most aptly defined him. He would only be with them periodically, a holiday here and there, and perhaps longer stays between the holidays. He would always be welcome and Richard agreed with Sheila that their guest should have a say in the final decision of how his room was to be decorated. It was important for him to be as comfortable as possible in their home.

His home. His room. Not merely a place to visit.

Sheila pulled out a home décor book and turned to the page she liked best. It was nice, but Richard would add one final touch to the room. A train track, circling the perimeter of the room would be suspended below the ceiling. The train would run via remote control.

Wanting to avoid a theme room, Sheila had tried talking him out of it, but he won that argument. Once she saw the train in motion, she'd like it.

She'd probably help play with it.

Richard looked away from her book and down at his hand. The briefcase tugged heavily on his arm.

Heavy with the contract that would legally change their lives.

"There they are." Sheila touched his arm.

He jumped up and turned to his left.

Matthew, proudly wearing his engineer hat, walked between Marissa and Daniel holding tight to their hands. The picture of a perfect family.

No. Not just the picture.

They were the perfect family. His gut churned and acid crawled up his throat. Who was he to rip that family apart? Who was he to undermine Matthew's stability?

Marissa and Daniel wore cautious smiles as they drew near, as if they, too, were asking those same questions.

Richard resisted the urge to run up to his son and swoop him up in the air. Instead he and Sheila held their ground and let Matthew come to them. He'd sworn off tears for now. Undoubtedly, they would come later.

"Marissa." He nodded to her then offered his hand to Daniel. "Thank you for meeting us here." He used his professional business tone. After all, this was in essence, a business transaction, even if it was one that played heavily on human sensitivities. This transaction could stand no more delays. Lives had been put on hold in anticipation of this moment. In a few minutes, those lives would be able to move on.

He squatted down, coming face to face with his son, but Matthew ran in back of Daniel, clutching to and hiding behind Daniel's legs. It didn't surprise Richard that he had already been forgotten, but it hurt nonetheless. He pinched his eyes shut and took a deep breath. Sheila's hand rested on his shoulder, helping to ward off the sting of his son's rejection.

"Come on, Matthew." Daniel took Matthew's arm and gently drew him out front and squatted next to Richard. "Remember, Matthew? This is your Papa. He plays trains with you." Matthew shyly looked at Richard again and slowly nodded. Daniel pulled the cap from Matthew's head and showed it to him. "Papa made you an official train engineer."

A slim smile flashed on his boy's face. A smile edged with fear.

Richard stood and patted his son's head. Hopefully, before they left today, that fear would be gone, and Richard would get that hug his body ached for. He wanted to tell Matthew it was okay, but he didn't feel okay. He'd daydreamed of this meeting for days, always seeing Matthew's eyes light up when he saw them, watching Matthew release Marissa's and Daniel's hands and run to meet him, fulfilling Richard's need for that embrace and unconditional love. But life wasn't lived in daydreams.

*We're doing the right thing*. It was time to get that right thing over with.

"Why don't you all have a seat?" Sheila hugged his arm as they sat.

He couldn't look at her. She'd see his disappointment in Matthew's rejection. He'd see hers. That would be more than enough to keel their emotions.

Richard opened his briefcase and pulled out the contract agreeing to joint physical custody. He handed it to Marissa. "It's as we agreed upon."

Her eyes were moist.

Tears of joy.

The moisture gathering in his eyes had no joy behind them. "I've left it unsigned." His cheeks tightened. He looked at Daniel and his throat clogged. These would be the hardest words he ever had to say, but they were the right ones. "Let me know when you have the new paperwork drawn up." Yes, they'd share joint legal custody, but because of the miles between them, Marissa would retain physical custody.

Richard focused on Matthew sitting safely in his mother's arms. He loved Matthew too much to destabilize the boy's life. No six months at one parent's home, then six months at the other. No shuttling their son back and forth. Love meant doing what was best for his child.

Sometimes love hurt like ... Like the pain would never go away. Honestly, he didn't want it to ever leave.

But this wasn't the end. Marissa and Daniel said he and Sheila were welcome to visit and Skype any time, and they would. They might even get a condo near Marissa and Daniel's home. Then when Matthew got a little older, he would come to Minnesota and stay with him and Sheila, sleeping in the room that was to be decorated for his grandfather. Already Stephen Peterson claimed the role of grandfather for himself. No one argued.

Richard tried to swallow, but the Matthew-sized lump wouldn't budge. His next sentence to Daniel would make his decision irrevocable. Not legally, of course, that would come later. But his word was as good as the paper it was soon to be written on.

"Let me know when you have the papers drawn up so you ..."

He wiped his eyes and clutched Sheila's hand.

"So you can be Matthew's full-time Daddy."

*"This is love: not that we loved God,*

*but that he loved us*

*and sent his Son*

*as an atoning sacrifice for our sins."*

**1 John 4:10**

*Dear Reader,*

*Thank you for traveling this tough journey with Richard, Sheila, and their family. It was a difficult story to write, knowing how it needed to end, but it's also probably my favorite story. Real love isn't selfish; it's about doing what's best for others. True love is about sacrifice which takes a lot of courage, but when those sacrifices are made, beauty arises.*

*I love reading stories about adoption, but all-too-often those stories don't portray the birthparents in a positive light. It was my goal to show birthparents choosing to love their child by doing what was best for the child, not the parents. Birthparents who choose to go the adoption route are some of the most loving, selfless people I know, and I applaud them for their courage.*

*I hope you will continue to follow Richard and Sheila's story in the Coming Home series finale. In* Hungry for Home, *Richard and Sheila take in a homeless teen and learn lessons about what really makes a home. If* Memory Box Secrets *was your introduction to the Coming Home series, I encourage you to read the first books,* Pieces of Granite *(prequel) and* Chain of Mercy *(book #1).*

*To make certain you don't miss a book, you can Follow my blog at www.BrendaAndersonBooks.com, sign up for my e-newsletter on my website, Like my Facebook Author Page (https://www.facebook.com/BrendaSAndersonAuthor), and Follow me on Twitter (@BrendaSAnders_n) and Pinterest (https://www.pinterest.com/brendabanderson/).*

*Also, if you enjoyed* Memory Box Secrets, *I'd be very grateful if you spread the word and posted a review.*

*In Him,*

*Brenda*

# ACKNOWLEDGMENTS

While writing a book can be a very solitary venture, fashioning that story into a publishable novel requires input from many. I'd be remiss not to mention those who've helped birth *Memory Box Secrets*.

Thank you, readers, for picking up my books! You make writing worthwhile!

To my first readers: Gayle Balster, Kelly Jo Yaksich, Lisa Laudenslager, Deb Berglund, and Sandy Pippo. Thank you for your encouragement from the very beginning. You've helped me persevere on this potholed publication road.

Thank you Lesley Ann McDaniel for your hawk-eyed edits and for helping me polish this manuscript.

To my fabulous critique partners: Lorna Seilstad and Shannon Taylor Vannatter. As always, thank you for helping me spruce up this story. I greatly value your input! And thank you, thank you for helping me see that the ending did not read as I intended it to. It's all fixed now!

Steph Prichard and Stacy Monson, I'm so glad I haven't been alone on this indie pub journey. Thank you for walking side by side with me, offering wisdom and encouragement, along with critique.

I'm very grateful to my Monday Writing Retreat group (Sharon Hinck, John Otte, Chawna Schroeder, Michelle Griep, and Carol Oyanagi) for helping me figure out how to speed up the first chapters of *Memory Box Secrets*. It's so much better now!

I'm blessed to be part of the wonderful ACFW MN NICE group. I've learned so much from all of you! Your encouragement and support of authors at all levels is a treasure!

And to the ladies at Inkspirational Messages. I cherish the

friendships I've made through this blog.

Thank you, Mom and Dad, for being my loudest cheerleaders! (Dad, I'm still looking for a hat that's big enough for us!)

Sarah, Bryan, and Brandon, it's so much fun watching the three of you embark on your own writing journeys! You're all better writers than I am! Thank you for not complaining (too much) when I don't have time to cook and for enduring mac-e-cheese and hot dog meals.

Dear Marvin, I would have quit writing long ago if not for your support and encouragement. You've always had more confidence in my writing than I've had myself. Thank you for always believing in me.

And to the Ultimate Creator who gave me this gift. It's humbling to know that I get to experience the joy of creating new worlds and lives. Thank you for working through those lives to reach people in ways I'd never imagined!

COMING SEPTEMBER 2015!

# Hungry for *home*

## The Coming Home Series Finale

*After a troubling encounter with a pregnant teen, Sheila Peterson-Brooks hurries from the crisis pregnancy center into the frigid Minnesota winter where she is mugged and left for dead. After a frantic search, Richard, her husband, finds her, and the police quickly nab the mugger ...*

*A hungry, homeless teen.*
*The brother of the pregnant girl Sheila had just counseled.*

*The girl pleads for her brother, and Sheila and Richard choose not to press charges. Instead, they open their home to the boy, a move that could cost them their possessions, and their hearts.*

*And, in the process, teach them the true meaning of home.*

# MORE FROM BRENDA S. ANDERSON

*To learn more about Brenda and her books,*
*visit www. BrendaAndersonBooks.com*

*pieces* of GRANITE

Coming Home Series
Prequel

CHAIN of *mercy*

Coming Home Series
Book 1

 **Brenda S. Anderson** writes authentic and gritty, life-affirming fiction. Her debut novel *Chain of Mercy* released in April 2014 and *Pieces of Granite* came out in November 2014. She is a member of the American Christian Fiction Writers and is currently President of the ACFW Minnesota Chapter, MN-NICE. When not reading or writing, she enjoys music, theater, roller coasters, and baseball, and she loves watching movies with her family. She resides in the Minneapolis, Minnesota area with her husband of 28 years, their three children, and one sassy cat. Learn more about Brenda at:

www.BrendaAndersonBooks.com.

55901866R00213

Made in the USA
Lexington, KY
09 October 2016